CIRCUS
OF THE
DAMNED

LAURELL K.
HAMILTON

JOVE BOOKS, NEW YORK

THE BERKLEY PUBLISHING GROUP
Published by the Penguin Group
Penguin Group (USA) Inc.
375 Hudson Street, New York, New York 10014, USA
Penguin Group (Canada), 90 Eglinton Avenue East, Suite 700, Toronto, Ontario M4P 2Y3, Canada
(a division of Pearson Penguin Canada Inc.)
Penguin Books Ltd., 80 Strand, London WC2R 0RL, England
Penguin Group Ireland, 25 St. Stephen's Green, Dublin 2, Ireland (a division of Penguin Books Ltd.)
Penguin Group (Australia), 250 Camberwell Road, Camberwell, Victoria 3124, Australia
(a division of Pearson Australia Group Pty. Ltd.)
Penguin Books India Pvt. Ltd., 11 Community Centre, Panchsheel Park, New Delhi—110 017, India
Penguin Group (NZ), 67 Apollo Drive, Rosedale, North Shore 0632, New Zealand
(a division of Pearson New Zealand Ltd.)
Penguin Books (South Africa) (Pty.) Ltd., 24 Sturdee Avenue, Rosebank, Johannesburg 2196,
South Africa

Penguin Books Ltd., Registered Offices: 80 Strand, London WC2R 0RL, England

This is a work of fiction. Names, characters, places, and incidents either are the product of the author's imagination or are used fictitiously, and any resemblance to actual persons, living or dead, business establishments, events, or locales is entirely coincidental. The publisher does not have any control over and does not assume any responsibility for author or third-party websites or their content.

To Ginjer Buchanan, our editor,
whose faith in Anita and patience with me have been most appreciated.

CIRCUS OF THE DAMNED

A Jove Book / published by arrangement with the author

PRINTING HISTORY
Ace mass-market edition / May 1995
First Jove mass-market edition / June 2002

Copyright © 1995 by Laurell K. Hamilton.
Cover illustration by Jody Ake.
Cover design by Judith Lagerman.

ISBN: 978-0-515-13448-3

JOVE®
Jove Books are published by The Berkley Publishing Group,
a division of Penguin Group (USA) Inc.,
375 Hudson Street, New York, New York 10014.
JOVE® is a registered trademark of Penguin Group (USA) Inc.
The "J" design is a trademark of Penguin Group (USA) Inc.

PRINTED IN THE UNITED STATES OF AMERICA

25   24   23   22   21   20   19   18   17   16

ACKNOWLEDGMENTS

To the usual suspects: my husband, Gary, and the alternate historians M. C. Sumner, Deborah Millitello, Marella Sands, and Robert K. Sheaff. Good luck in the new house, Bob. We'll miss you much.

There was dried chicken blood imbedded under my finger-nails. When you raise the dead for a living, you have to spill a little blood. It clung in flaking patches to my face and hands. I'd tried to clean the worst of it off before coming to this meeting, but some things only a shower would fix. I sipped coffee from a personalized mug that said, "Piss me off, pay the consequences," and stared at the two men sitting across from me.

Mr. Jeremy Ruebens was short, dark, and grumpy. I'd never seen him when he wasn't either frowning, or shout-ing. His small features were clustered in the middle of his face as if some giant hand had mashed them together before the clay had dried. His hands smoothed over the lapel of his coat, the dark blue tie, tie clip, white shirt collar. His hands folded in his lap for a second, then began their dance again, coat, tie, tie clip, collar, lap. I figured I could stand to watch him fidget maybe five more times before I screamed for mercy and promised him anything he wanted.

The second man was Karl Inger. I'd never met him before. He was a few inches over six feet. Standing, he had towered over Ruebens and me. A wavy mass of short-cut red hair graced a large face. He had honest-to-god muttonchop sideburns that grew into one of the fullest mustaches I'd ever seen. Everything was neatly trimmed except for his unruly hair. Maybe he was having a bad hair day.

Ruebens's hands were making their endless dance for the fourth time. Four was my limit.

I wanted to go around the desk, grab his hands, and yell, "Stop that!" But I figured that was a little rude, even for me. "I don't remember you being this twitchy, Ruebens," I said.

He glanced at me "Twitchy?"

I motioned at his hands, making their endless circuit. He frowned and placed his hands on top of his thighs. They remained there, motionless. Self-control at its best.

"I am not twitchy, Miss Blake."

"It's Ms. Blake. And why are you so nervous, Mr. Ruebens?" I sipped my coffee.

"I am not accustomed to asking help from people like you."

"People like me?" I made it a question.

He cleared his throat sharply. "You know what I mean."

"No, Mr. Ruebens, I don't."

"Well, a zombie queen . . ." He stopped in mid-sentence. I was getting pissed, and it must have shown on my face. "No offense," he said softly.

"If you came here to call me names, get the hell out of my office. If you have real business, state it, then get the hell out of my office."

Ruebens stood up. "I told you she wouldn't help us."

"Help you do what? You haven't told me a damn thing," I said.

"Perhaps we should just tell her why we have come," Inger said. His voice was a deep, rumbling bass, pleasant.

Ruebens drew a deep breath and let it out through his nose. "Very well." He sat back down in his chair. "The last time we met, I was a member of Humans Against Vampires."

I nodded encouragingly and sipped my coffee.

"I have since started a new group, Humans First. We have the same goals as HAV, but our methods are more direct."

I stared at him. HAV's main goal was to make vampires illegal again, so they could be hunted down like animals. It worked for me. I used to be a vampire slayer, hunter, whatever. Now I was a vampire executioner. I had to have a death warrant to kill a specific vampire, or it was murder. To get a warrant, you had to prove the vampire was a danger to society, which meant you had to wait for the vampire to kill people. The lowest kill was five humans, the highest was twenty-three. That was a lot of dead bodies. In the good ol' days you could just kill a vampire on sight.

"What exactly does 'more direct methods' mean?"

"You know what it means," Ruebens said.

"No," I said, "I don't." I thought I did, but he was going to have to say it out loud.

"HAV has failed to discredit vampires through the media or the political machine. Humans First will settle for destroying them all."

I smiled over my coffee mug. "You mean kill every last vampire in the United States?"

"That is the goal," he said.

"It's murder."

"You have slain vampires. Do you really believe it is murder?"

It was my turn to take a deep breath. A few months ago I would have said no. But now, I just didn't know. "I'm not sure anymore, Mr. Ruebens."

"If the new legislation goes through, Ms. Blake, vampires will be able to vote. Doesn't that frighten you?"

"Yes," I said.

"Then help us."

"Quit dancing around, Ruebens; just tell me what you want."

"Very well, then. We want the daytime resting place of the Master Vampire of the City."

I just looked at him for a few seconds. "Are you serious?"

"I am in deadly earnest, Ms. Blake."

I had to smile. "What makes you think I know the Master's daytime retreat?"

It was Inger who answered. "Ms. Blake, come now. If we can admit to advocating murder, then you can admit to knowing the Master." He smiled ever so gently.

"Tell me where you got the information and maybe I'll confirm it, or maybe I won't."

His smile widened just a bit. "Now who's dancing?"

He had a point. "If I say I know the Master, what then?"

"Give us his daytime resting place," Ruebens said. He was leaning forward, an eager, nearly lustful look on his face. I wasn't flattered. It wasn't me getting his rocks off. It was the thought of staking the Master.

"How do you know the Master is a he?"

"There was an article in the *Post-Dispatch*. It was careful to mention no name, but the creature was clearly male," Ruebens said.

I wondered how Jean-Claude would like being referred as a "creature." Better not to find out. "I give you an address and you go in and what, stake him through the heart?"

Ruebens nodded. Inger smiled.

I shook my head. "I don't think so."

"You refuse to help us?" Ruebens asked.

"No, I simply don't know the daytime resting place." I was relieved to be able to tell the truth.

"You are lying to protect him," Ruebens said. His face was growing darker; deep frown wrinkles showed on his forehead.

"I really don't know, Mr. Ruebens, Mr. Inger. If you want a zombie raised, we can talk; otherwise..." I let the sentence trail off and gave them my best professional smile. They didn't seem impressed.

"We consented to meeting you at this ungodly hour, and we are paying a handsome fee for the consultation. I would think the least you could do is be polite."

I wanted to say, "You started it," but that would sound childish. "I offered you coffee. You turned it down."

Ruebens's scowl deepened, little anger lines showing around his eyes. "Do you treat all your . . . customers this way?"

"The last time we met, you called me a zombie-loving bitch. I don't owe you anything."

"You took our money."

"My boss did that."

"We met you here at dawn, Ms. Blake. Surely you can meet us halfway."

I hadn't wanted to meet with Ruebens at all, but after Bert took their money, I was sort of stuck with it. I'd set the meeting at dawn, after my night's work, but before I went to bed. This way I could drive home and get eight hours uninterrupted sleep. Let Ruebens's sleep be interrupted.

"Could you find out the location of the Master's retreat?" Inger asked.

"Probably, but if I did, I wouldn't give it to you."

"Why not?" he asked.

"Because she is in league with him," Ruebens said.

"Hush, Jeremy."

Ruebens opened his mouth to protest, but Inger said, "Please, Jeremy, for the cause."

Ruebens struggled visibly to swallow his anger, but he choked it down. Control.

"Why not, Ms. Blake?" Inger's eyes were very serious, the pleasant sparkle seeping away like melting ice.

"I've killed master vampires before, none of them with a stake."

"How then?"

I smiled. "No, Mr. Inger, if you want lessons in vampire slaying, you're going to have to go elsewhere. Just by answering your questions, I could be charged as an accessory to murder."

"Would you tell us if we had a better plan?" Inger said.

I thought about that for a minute. Jean-Claude dead, really dead. It would certainly make my life easier, but...but.

"I don't know," I said.

"Why not?"

"Because I think he'll kill you. I don't give humans over to the monsters, Mr. Inger, not even people who hate me."

"We don't hate you Ms. Blake."

I motioned with the coffee mug towards Ruebens. "Maybe you don't, but he does."

Ruebens just glared at me. At least he didn't try to deny it.

"If we come up with a better plan, can we talk to you again?" Inger asked.

I stared at Ruebens's angry little eyes. "Sure, why not?"

Inger stood and offered me his hand. "Thank you, Ms. Blake. You have been most helpful."

His hand enveloped mine. He was a large man, but he didn't try using his size to make me feel small. I appreciated that.

"The next time we meet, Anita Blake, you will be more cooperative," Ruebens said.

"That sounded like a threat, Jerry."

Ruebens smiled, a most unpleasant smile. "Humans First believes the means justifies the end, Anita."

I opened my royal purple suit jacket. Inside was a shoulder holster complete with a Browning Hi-Power 9mm. The purple skirt's thin black belt was just sturdy enough to be looped through the shoulder holster. Executive terrorist chic.

"When it comes to survival, Jerry, I believe that, too."

"We have not offered you violence," Inger said.

"No, but ol' Jerry here is thinking about it. I just want him and the rest of your little group to believe I'm serious. Mess with me, and people are going to die."

"There are dozens of us," Ruebens said, "and only one of you."

"Yeah, but who's going to be first in line?" I said.

"Enough of this, Jeremy, Ms. Blake. We didn't come here to threaten you. We came for your help. We will come up with a better plan and talk to you again."

"Don't bring him," I said.

"Of course," Inger said. "Come along, Jeremy." He opened the door. The soft clack of computer keys came from the outer office. "Good-bye Ms. Blake."

"Good-bye, Mr. Inger, it's been really unpleasant."

Ruebens stopped in the doorway and hissed at me, "You are an abomination before God."

"Jesus loves you, too," I said, smiling. He slammed the door behind them. Childish.

I sat on the edge of my desk and waited to make sure they had left before going outside. I didn't think they'd try anything in the parking lot, but I really didn't want to start shooting people. Oh, I would if I had to, but it was better to avoid it. I had hoped flashing the gun would make Ruebens back off. It had just seemed to enrage him. I rotated my neck, trying to ease some of the tension away. It didn't work.

I could go home, shower, and get eight hours uninterrupted sleep. Glorious. My beeper went off. I jumped like I'd been stung. Nervous, me?

I hit the button, and the number that flashed made me groan. It was the police. To be exact, it was the Regional Preternatural Investigation Team. The Spook Squad. They were responsible for all preternatural crime in Missouri. I was their civilian expert on monsters. Bert liked the retainer I got, but better yet, the good publicity.

The beeper went off again. Same number. "Shit," I said it softly. "I heard you the first time, Dolph." I thought about pretending that I'd already gone home, turned off the beeper, and was now unavailable, but I didn't. If Detective Sergeant Rudolf Storr called me at half-past dawn, he needed my expertise. Damn.

I called the number and through a series of relays finally got Dolph's voice. He sounded tinny and faraway. His wife had gotten him a car phone for his birthday. We must have been near the limit of its range. It still beat the heck out of talking to him on the police radio. That always sounded like an alien language.

"Hi, Dolph, what's up?"

"Murder."

"What sort of murder?"

"The kind that needs your expertise," he said.

"It's too damn early in the morning to play twenty questions. Just tell me what's happened."

"You got up on the wrong side of bed this morning, didn't you?"

"I haven't been to bed yet."

"I sympathize, but get your butt out here. It looks like we have a vampire victim on our hands."

I took a deep breath and let it out slowly. "Shit."

"You could say that."

"Give me the address," I said.

He did. It was over the river and through the woods, way to hell and gone in Arnold. My office was just off Olive Boulevard. I had a forty-five-minute drive ahead of me, one way. Yippee.

"I'll be there as soon as I can."

"We'll be waiting," Dolph said, then hung up.

I didn't bother to say good-bye to the dial tone. A vampire victim. I'd never seen a lone kill. They were like potato chips; once the vamp tasted them, he couldn't stop at just one. The trick was, how many people would die before we caught this one?

I didn't want to think about it. I didn't want to drive to Arnold. I didn't want to stare at dead bodies before breakfast. I wanted to go home. But somehow I didn't think Dolph would understand. Police have very little sense of humor when they're working on a murder case. Come to think of it, neither did I.

2

The man's body lay on its back, pale and naked in the weak morning sunlight. Even limp with death his body was good, a lot of weights, maybe jogging. His longish yellow hair mixed with the still-green lawn. The smooth skin of his neck was punctured twice with neat fang marks. The right arm was pierced at the bend of the elbow, where a doctor draws blood. The skin of the left wrist was shredded, like an animal had gnawed it. White bone gleamed in the fragile light.

I had measured the bite marks with my trusty tape measure. They were different sizes. At least three different vamps, but I would have bet everything I owned that it was five different vampires. A master and his pack, or flock, or whatever the hell you call a group of vampires.

The grass was wet from early morning mist. The moisture soaked through the knees of the coveralls I had put on to protect my suit. Black Nikes and surgical gloves completed my crime-scene kit. I used to wear white Nikes, but they showed blood too easily.

I said a silent apology for what I had to do, then spread the corpse's legs apart. The legs moved easily, no rigor. I was betting that he hadn't been dead eight hours, not enough time for rigor mortis to set in. Semen had dried on his shriveled privates. One last joy before dying. The vamps hadn't cleaned him off. On the inside of his thigh, close to the groin, were more fang marks. They weren't as savage as the wrist wound, but they weren't neat either.

There was no blood on the skin around the wounds, not

even the wrist wound. Had they cleaned the blood off? Wherever he was killed, there was a lot of blood. They'd never be able to clean it all up. If we could find where he died, we'd have all sorts of clues. But in the neatly clipped lawn in the middle of a very ordinary neighborhood, there were no clues. I was betting on that. They'd dumped the body in a place as sterile and unhelpful as the dark side of the moon.

Mist floated over the small residential neighborhood like waiting ghosts. The mist was so low to the ground that it was like walking through sheets of drizzling rain. Tiny beads of moisture clung to the body where the mist had condensed. Beads collected in my hair like silver pearls.

I stood in the front yard of a small, lime-green house with white trim. A chain-link fence peeked around one side encircling a roomy backyard. It was October, and the grass was still green. The top of a sugar maple loomed over the house. Its leaves were that brilliant orangey-yellow that is peculiar to sugar maples, as if their leaves were carved from flame. The mist helped the illusion, and the colors seemed to bleed on the wet air.

All down the street were other small houses with autumn-bright trees and bright green lawns. It was still early enough that most people hadn't gone to work yet, or school, or wherever. There was quite a crowd being held back by the uniform officers. They had hammered stakes into the ground to hold the yellow Do-Not-Cross tape. The crowd pressed as close to the tape as they dared. A boy of about twelve had managed to push his way to the front. He stared at the dead man with huge brown eyes, his mouth open in a little "wow" of excitement. God, where were his parents? Probably gawking at the corpse, too.

The corpse was paper-white. Blood always pools to the lowest point of the body. In this case dark, purplish bruising should have set in at buttocks, arms, legs, the entire back of his body. There were no marks. He hadn't had enough blood in him to cause lividity marks. Whoever had murdered him had drained him completely. Good to the last drop? I fought the urge to smile and lost. If you spend a lot of time staring at corpses, you get a peculiar sense of humor. You have to, or you will go stark raving mad.

"What's so funny?" a voice asked.

I jumped and whirled. "God, Zerbrowski, don't sneak up on me like that."

"Is the heap big vampire slayer jumping at shadows?" He grinned at me. His unruly brown hair stuck up in three separate tufts like he'd forgotten to comb it. His tie was at half-mast over a pale blue shirt that looked suspiciously like a pajama top. The brown suit jacket and pants clashed with the top.

"Nice pajamas."

He shrugged. "I've got a pair with little choo-choos on them. Katie thinks they're sexy."

"Your wife got a thing for trains?" I asked.

His grin widened. "If I'm wearing 'em."

I shook my head. "I knew you were perverted, Zerbrowski, but little kids' jammies, that's truly sick."

"Thank you." He glanced down at the body, still smiling. The smile faded. "What do you think of this?" He nodded towards the dead man.

"Where's Dolph?"

"In the house with the lady who found the body." He plunged his hands into the pockets of his pants and rocked on his heels. "She's taking it pretty hard. Probably the first corpse she's seen outside of a funeral."

"That's the way most normal folks see dead people, Zerbrowski."

He rocked forward hard on the balls of his feet, coming to a standstill. "Wouldn't it be nice to be normal?"

"Sometimes," I said.

He grinned. "Yeah, I know what you mean." He got a notebook out of his jacket pocket that looked as if someone had crumbled it in their fist.

"Geez, Zerbrowski." ·

"Hey, it's still paper." He tried smoothing the notebook flat, but finally gave up. He posed, pen over the wrinkled paper. "Enlighten me, oh preternatural expert."

"Am I going to have to repeat this to Dolph? I'd like to just do this once and go home to bed."

"Hey, me too. Why do you think I'm wearing my jammies?"

"I just thought it was a daring fashion statement." He looked at me. "Mm-huh."

Dolph walked out of the house. The door looked too small to hold him. He's six-nine and built bulky like a wrestler. His black hair was buzzed close to his head, leaving his ears stranded on either side of his face. But Dolph didn't care much for fashion. His tie was tight against the collar of his white dress shirt. He had to have been pulled out of bed just like Zerbrowski, but he looked neat and tidy and businesslike. It never mattered what hour you called Dolph, he was always ready to do his job. A professional cop down to his socks.

So why was Dolph heading up the most unpopular special task force in St. Louis? Punishment for something, that much I was sure of, but I'd never asked what. I probably never would. It was his business. If he wanted me to know, he'd tell me.

The squad had originally been a pacifier for the liberals. See, we're doing something about supernatural crime. But Dolph had taken his job and his men seriously. They had solved more supernatural crime in the last two years than any other group of policemen in the country. He had been invited to give talks to other police forces. They had even been loaned out to neighboring states twice.

"Well, Anita, let's have it."

That's Dolph; no preliminaries. "Gee, Dolph, it's nice to see you too."

He just looked at me.

"Okay, okay." I knelt on the far side of the body so I could point as I talked. Nothing like a visual aid to get your point across. "Just measuring shows that at least three different vampires fed on the man."

"But?" Dolph said.

He's quick. "But I think that every wound is a different vampire."

"Vampires don't hunt in packs."

"Usually they are solitary hunters, but not always."

"What causes them to hunt in packs?" he asked.

"Only two reasons that I've ever come across: first, one is the new dead and an older vampire is teaching the ropes, but that's just two pairs of fangs, not five; second, a master vampire is controlling them, and he's gone rogue."

"Explain."

"A master vampire has nearly absolute control over his or her flock. Some masters use a group kill to solidify the pack, but they wouldn't dump the body here. They'd hide it where the police would never find it."

"But the body's here," Zerbrowski said, "out in plain sight."

"Exactly; only a master that's gone crazy would dump a body like this. Most masters even before vampires were legally alive wouldn't flaunt a kill like this. It attracts attention, usually attention with a stake in one hand and a cross in the other. Even now, if we could trace the kill to the vampires that did it, we could get a warrant and kill them." I shook my head. "Slaughter like this is bad for business, and whatever else vampires are, they're practical. You don't stay alive and hidden for centuries unless you're discreet and ruthless."

"Why ruthless?" Dolph said.

I stared up at him. "It's utterly practical. Someone discovers your secret, you kill them, or make them one of your...children. Good business practices, Dolph, nothing more."

"Like the mob," Zerbrowski said.

"Yeah."

"What if they panicked?" Zerbrowski asked. "It was almost dawn."

"When did the woman find the body?"

Dolph checked his notebook. "Five-thirty."

"It's still hours until dawn. They didn't panic."

"If we've got a crazy master vampire, what exactly does that mean?"

"It means they'll kill more people faster. They may need blood every night to support five vampires."

"A fresh body every night?" Zerbrowski made it a question.

I just nodded.

"Jesus," he said.

"Yeah."

Dolph was silent, staring down at the dead man. "What can we do?"

"I should be able to raise the corpse as a zombie."

"I thought you couldn't raise a vampire victim as a zombie," Dolph said.

"If the corpse is going to rise as a vampire, you can't." I shrugged. "The whatever that makes a vampire interferes with a raising. I can't raise a body that is already set to rise as a vamp."

"But this one won't rise," Dolph said, "so you can raise it."

I nodded.

"Why won't this vampire victim rise?"

"He was killed by more than one vampire, in a mass feeding. For a corpse to rise as a vampire, you have to have just one vampire feeding over a space of several days. Three bites ending with death, and you get a vampire. If every vampire victim could come back, we'd be up to our butts in blood-suckers."

"But this victim can come back as a zombie?" Dolph said.

I nodded.

"When can you do the animating?"

"Three nights from tonight, or really two. Tonight counts as one night."

"What time?"

"I'll have to check my schedule at work. I'll call you with a time."

"Just raise the murder victim and ask who killed him. I like it," Zerbrowski said.

"It's not that easy," I said. "You know how confused witnesses to violent crimes are. Have three people see the same crime and you get three different heights, different hair colors."

"Yeah, yeah, witness testimony is a bitch," Zerbrowski said.

"Go on, Anita," Dolph said. It was his way of saying, "Zerbrowski, shut up." Zerbrowski shut up.

"A person who died as the victim of a violent crime is more confused. Scared shitless, so that sometimes they don't remember very clearly."

"But they were there," Zerbrowski said. He looked outraged.

"Zerbrowski, let her finish."

Zerbrowski pantomimed locking his lips with a key and throwing the key away. Dolph frowned. I coughed into my hand to hide the smile. Mustn't encourage Zerbrowski.

"What I'm saying is that I can raise the victim from the dead, but we may not get as much information as you'd expect. The memories we do get will be confused, painful, but it might narrow the field down as to which master vampire led the group."

"Explain," Dolph said.

"There are only supposed to be two master vampires in St. Louis right now. Malcolm, the undead Billy Graham, and the Master of the City. There's always the possibility we've got someone new in town, but the Master of the City should be able to police that."

"We'll take the head of the Church of Eternal Life," Dolph said.

"I'll take the Master," I said.

"Take one of us with you for backup."

I shook my head. "Can't; if he knew I let the cops know who he was, he'd kill us both."

"How dangerous is it for you to do this?" Dolph asked.

What was I supposed to say? Very? Or did I tell them

the Master had the hots for me, so I'd probably be okay? Neither. "I'll be alright."

He stared at me, eyes very serious.

"Besides, what choice do we have?" I motioned at the corpse. "We'll get one of these a night until we find the vampires responsible. One of us has to talk to the Master. He won't talk to police, but he will talk to me."

Dolph took a deep breath and let it out. He nodded. He knew I was right. "When can you do it?"

"Tomorrow night, if I can talk Bert into giving my zombie appointments to someone else."

"You're that sure the Master will talk to you?"

"Yeah." The problem with Jean-Claude was not getting to see him, it was avoiding him. But Dolph didn't know that, and if he did, he might have insisted on going with me. And gotten us both killed.

"Do it," he said. "Let me know what you find out."

"Will do," I said. I stood up, facing him over the bloodless corpse.

"Watch your back," he said.

"Always."

"If the Master eats you, can I have your nifty coveralls?" Zerbrowski asked.

"Buy your own, you cheap bastard."

"I'd rather have the ones that have enveloped your luscious body."

"Give it a rest, Zerbrowski. I'm not into little choochoos."

"What the hell do trains have to do with anything?" Dolph asked.

Zerbrowski and I looked at each other. We started giggling and couldn't stop. I could claim sleep deprivation. I'd been on my feet for fourteen straight hours, raising the dead and talking to right-wing fruitcakes. The vampire victim was a perfect end to a perfect night. I had a right to be hysterical with laughter. I don't know what Zerbrowski's excuse was.

3

There are a handful of days in October that are nearly perfect. The sky stretches overhead in a clear blue, so deep and perfect that it makes everything else prettier. The trees along the highway are crimson, gold, rust, burgundy, orange. Every color is neon-bright, pulsing in the heavy golden sunlight. The air is cool but not cold; by noon you can wear just a light jacket. It was weather for taking long walks in the woods with someone you wanted to hold hands with. Since I didn't have anyone like that, I was just hoping for a free weekend to go away by myself. The chances of that were slim and none.

October is a big month for raising the dead. Everyone thinks that Halloween is the perfect season for raising zombies. It isn't. Darkness is the only requirement. But everyone wants an appointment for midnight on Halloween. They think spending All Hallows Eve in a cemetery killing chickens and watching zombies crawl out of the ground is great entertainment. I could probably sell tickets.

I was averaging five zombies a night. It was one more zombie than anyone else was doing in one night. I should never have told Bert that four zombies didn't wipe me out. My own fault for being too damn truthful. Of course, truth was, five didn't wipe me out either, but I was damned if I'd tell Bert.

Speaking of my boss, I had to call him when I got home. He was going to love me asking for the night off. It made me smile just thinking about it. Any day I could yank Bert's chain was a good day.

I pulled into my apartment complex at nearly one in the afternoon. All I wanted was a quick shower and seven hours of sleep. I had given up on eight hours; it was too late in the day for that. I had to see Jean-Claude tonight. Joy. But he was the Master Vampire of the City. If there was another master vampire around, he'd know it. I think they can smell each other. Of course, if Jean-Claude had committed the murder, he wasn't likely to confess. But I didn't really believe he'd done it. He was much to good a business vampire to get messy. He was the only master vampire I'd ever met who wasn't crazy in some way: psychotic, or sociopath, take your pick.

Alright, alright, Malcolm wasn't crazy, but I didn't approve of his methods. He headed up the fastest-growing church in America today. The Church of Eternal Life offered exactly that. No leap of faith, no uncertainty, just a guarantee. You could become a vampire and live forever, unless someone like me killed you, or you got caught in a fire, or hit by a bus. I wasn't sure about the bus part, but I'd always wondered. Surely there must be something massive enough to damage even a vampire beyond healing. I hoped someday to test the theory.

I climbed the stairs slowly. My body felt heavy. My eyes burned with the need to sleep. It was three days before Halloween, and the month couldn't end too soon for me. Business would start dropping off before Thanksgiving. The decline would continue until after New Year's, then it'd start picking up. I prayed for a freak snowstorm. Business drops off if the snow is bad. People seem to think we can't raise the dead in deep snow. We can, but don't tell anyone. I need the break.

The hallway was full of the quiet noises of my day-living neighbors. I was fishing my keys out of my coat pocket when the door opposite mine opened. Mrs. Pringle stepped out. She was tall, slender, thinning with age, white hair done in a small bun at the back of her head. The hair was perfectly white. Mrs. Pringle didn't bother with dyes or makeup. She was over sixty-five and didn't care who knew it.

Custard, her Pomeranian, pranced at the end of his leash. He was a round ball of golden fur with little fox ears. Most cats outweighed him, but he's one of those little dogs with a big-dog attitude. In a past life he was a Great Dane.

"Hello, Anita." Mrs. Pringle smiled as she said it. "You're not just getting in from work, are you?" Her pale eyes were disapproving.

I smiled. "Yeah, I had an . . . emergency come up."

She raised an eyebrow, probably wondering what an animator would have for an emergency, but she was too polite to ask. "You don't take good enough care of yourself, Anita. If you keep burning the candle at both ends, you'll be worn out by the time you're my age."

"Probably," I said.

Custard yapped at me. I did not smile at him. I don't believe in encouraging small, pushy dogs. With that peculiar doggy sense, he knew I didn't like him, and he was determined to win me over.

"I saw the painters were in your apartment last week. Is it all repaired?"

I nodded. "Yeah, all the bullet holes have been patched up and painted over."

"I'm really sorry I wasn't home to offer you my apartment. Mr. Giovoni says you had to go to a hotel."

"Yeah."

"I don't understand why one of the other neighbors didn't offer you a couch for the night."

I smiled. I understood. Two months ago I had slaughtered two killer zombies in my apartment and had a police shootout. The walls and one window had been damaged. Some of the bullets had gone through the walls into other apartments. No one else had been hurt, but none of the neighbors wanted anything to do with me now. I suspected strongly that when my two-year lease was up, I would be asked to leave. I guess I couldn't blame them.

"I heard you were wounded."

I nodded. "Just barely." I didn't bother telling her that the bullet wound hadn't been from the shootout. The mistress of a very bad man had shot me in the right arm. It was healed to a smooth, shiny scar, still a little pink.

"How did your visit with your daughter go?" I asked.

Mrs. Pringle's face went all shiny with a smile. "Oh, wonderful. My last and newest grandchild is perfect. I'll show you pictures later, after you've had some sleep." That disapproving look was back in her eyes. Her teacher face. The one that could make you squirm from ten paces, even if you were innocent. And I hadn't been innocent for years.

I held up my hands. "I give up. I'll go to bed. I promise."

"You see you do," she said. "Come along, Custard, we have to go out for our afternoon stroll." The tiny dog danced at the end of his leash, straining forward like a miniature sled dog.

Mrs. Pringle let three pounds of fluffy fur drag her down the hall. I shook my head. Letting a fuzzball boss you around was not my idea of dog ownership. If I ever had another dog, I'd be boss, or one of us wouldn't survive. It was the principle of the thing.

I opened the door and stepped inside the hush of my apartment. The heater whirred, hot air hissing out of the vents. The aquarium clicked on. The sounds of emptiness. It was wonderful.

The new paint was the same off-white as the old. The carpet was grey; couch and matching chair, white. The kitchenette was pale wood with white and gold linoleum. The two-seater breakfast table in the kitchen was a little darker than the cabinets. A modern print was the only color on the white walls.

The space where most people would have put a full-size kitchen set had the thirty-gallon aquarium against the wall, a stereo catty-corner from it.

Heavy white drapes hid the windows and turned the golden sunlight to a pale twilight. When you sleep during the day, you have to have good curtains.

I flung my coat on the couch, kicked my dress shoes off, and just enjoyed the feeling of my bare feet on the carpet. The panty hose came off next, to lie wrinkled and forlorn by the shoes. Barefoot, I padded over to the fish tank.

The angelfish rose to the surface begging for food. The fish are all wider than my outspread hand. They are the biggest angels I've ever seen outside of the pet store I bought them from. The store had breeding angelfish that were nearly a foot long.

I stripped off the shoulder holster and put the Browning in its second home, a specially made holster in the headboard. If any bad guys snuck up on me, I could pull it and shoot them. That was the idea, anyway. So far it had worked.

When the dry-clean-only suit and blouse were hung neatly in the closet, I flopped down on the bed in my bra and undies, still wearing the silver cross that I wore even in the shower. Never know when a pesky vampire is going to try to take a bite out of you. Always prepared, that was my motto, or was that the Boy Scouts? I shrugged and dialed work. Mary, our daytime secretary, answered on the second ring. "Animators, Incorporated. How may we serve you?"

"Hi, Mary, it's Anita."

"Hi, what's up?"

"I need to talk with Bert."

"He's with a prospective client right now. May I ask what this is pertaining to?"

"Him rescheduling my appointments for tonight."

"Ooh, boy. I'll let you tell him. If he yells at someone, it should be you." She was only half-kidding.

"Fine," I said.

She lowered her voice and whispered, "Client is on her way to the front door. He'll be with you in a jiffy."

"Thanks, Mary."

She put me on hold before I could tell her not to. Muzak seeped out of the phone. It was a butchered version of the Beatles' "Tomorrow." I'd have rather listened to static. Mercifully, Bert came on the line and saved me.

"Anita, what time can you come in today?"

"I can't."

"Can't what?"

"Can't come in today."

"At all?" His voice had risen an octave.

"You got it."

"Why the hell not?" Cursing at me already, a bad sign.

"I got beeped by the police after my morning meeting. I haven't even been to bed yet."

"You can sleep in, don't worry about meeting new clients in the afternoon. Just come in for your appointments tonight."

He was being generous, understanding. Something was wrong.

"I can't make the appointments tonight, either."

"Anita, we're overbooked here. You have five clients tonight. Five!"

"Divide them up among the other animators," I said.

"Everybody is already maxed."

"Listen, Bert, you're the one who said yes to the police. You're the one who put me on retainer to them. You thought it would be great publicity."

"It has been great publicity," he said.

"Yeah, but it's like working two full-time jobs sometimes. I can't do both."

"Then drop the retainer. I had no idea it'd take up this much of your time."

"It's a murder investigation, Bert. I can't drop it."

"Let the police do their own dirty work," he said.

He was a fine one to talk about that. Him with his squeaky-clean fingernails and nice safe office. "They need my expertise and my contacts. Most of the monsters won't talk to the police."

He was quiet on the other end of the phone. His breathing came harsh and angry. "You can't do this to me. We've taken money, signed contracts."

"I asked you to hire extra help months ago."

"I hired John Burke. He's been handling some of your vampire slayings, as well as raising the dead."

"Yeah, John's a big help, but we need more. In fact, I bet he could take at least one of my zombies tonight."

"Raise five in one night?"

"I'm doing it," I said.

"Yes, but John isn't you."

That was almost a compliment. "You have two choices, Bert; either reschedule or delegate them to someone else."

"I am your boss. I could just say come in tonight or you're fired." His voice was firm and matter-of-fact.

I was tired and cold sitting on the bed in my bra and undies. I didn't have time for this. "Fire me."

"You don't mean that," he said.

"Look, Bert, I've been on my feet for over twenty hours. If I don't get some sleep soon, I'm not going to be able to work for anybody."

He was silent for a long time, his breathing soft and regular in my ear. Finally, he said, "Alright, you're free for tonight. But you damn well better be back on the job tomorrow."

"I can't promise that, Bert."

"Dammit, Anita, do you want to be fired?"

"This is the best year we've ever had, Bert. Part of that's due to the articles on me in the *Post-Dispatch*."

"They were about zombie rights and that government study you're on. You didn't do them to help promote our business."

"But it worked, didn't it? How many people call up and ask specifically for me? How many people say they've seen me in the paper? How many heard me on the radio? I may be promoting zombie rights, but it's damn good for business. So cut me some slack."

"You don't think I'd do it, do you?" His voice snarled through the phone. He was pissed.

"No, I don't," I said.

His breath was short and harsh. "You damn well better show up tomorrow night, or I'm going to call your bluff." He slammed the receiver in my ear. Childish.

I hung up the phone and stared at it. The Resurrection Company in California had made me a handsome offer a few months back. But I really didn't want to move to the west coast, or the east coast for that matter. I liked St. Louis. But Bert was going to have to break down and hire more help. I couldn't keep this schedule up. Sure, it'd get better after October, but I just seemed to be going from one emergency to another for this entire year.

I had been stabbed, beaten, shot, strangled, and vampire-bit in the space of four months. There comes a point where you just have too many things happening too close together. I had battle fatigue.

I left a message on my judo instructor's machine. I went twice a week at four o'clock, but I wasn't going to make it today. Three hours of sleep just wouldn't have been enough.

I dialed the number for Guilty Pleasures. It was a vampire strip joint. Chippendale's with fangs. Jean-Claude owned and managed it. Jean-Claude's voice came over the line, soft as silk, caressing down my spine even though I knew it was a recording. "You have reached Guilty Pleasures. I would love to make your darkest fantasy come true. Leave a message, and I will get back to you."

I waited for the beep. "Jean-Claude, this is Anita Blake. I need to see you tonight. It's important. Call me back with a time and place." I gave him my home number, then hesitated, listening to the tape scratch. "Thanks." I hung up, and that was that.

He'd either call back or he wouldn't. He probably would. The question was, did I want him to? No. No, I didn't, but for the police, for all those poor people who would die, I had to try. But for me personally, going to the Master was not a good idea.

Jean-Claude had marked me twice already. Two more marks and I would be his human servant. Did I mention that neither mark was voluntary? His servant for eternity. Didn't sound like a good idea to me. He seemed to lust after my body, too, but that was secondary. I could have handled it if all he wanted was physical, but he was after my soul. That he could not have.

I had managed to avoid him for the last two months. Now I was willingly putting myself within reach again.

Stupid. But I remembered the nameless man's hair, soft and mingling with the still-green lawn. The fang marks, the paper-white skin, the fragility of his nude body covered with dew. There would be more bodies to look at, unless we were quick. And quick meant Jean-Claude.

Visions of vampire victims danced in my head. And every one of them was partially my fault, because I was too chickenshit to go see the Master. If I could stop the killings now, with just one dead, I'd risk my soul daily. Guilt is a wonderful motivator.

4

I was swimming in black water, strong smooth strokes. The moon hung huge and shining, making a silver pathway on the lake. There was a black fringe of trees. I was almost to shore. The water was so warm, warm as blood. In that moment I knew why the waters were black. It was blood. I was swimming in a lake of fresh, warm blood.

I woke instantly, gasping for breath. Eyes searching the darkness for . . . what? Something that had caressed my leg just before I woke. Something that lived in blood and darkness.

The phone shrilled, and I had to swallow a scream. I wasn't usually this nervous. It was just a nightmare, dammit. Just a dream.

I fumbled for the receiver and managed, "Yeah."

"Anita?" The voice sounded hesitant, as if its owner might hang up.

"Who is this?"

"It's Willie, Willie McCoy." Even as he said the name, the rhythm of the voice sounded familiar. The phone made it distant and charged with an electric hiss, but I recognized it.

"Willie, how are you?" The minute I said it, I wished I hadn't. Willie was a vampire now; how okay could a dead man be?

"I'm doing real well." His voice had a happy lilt to it. He was pleased that I asked.

I sighed. Truth was, I liked Willie. I wasn't supposed

to like vampires. Any vampire, not even if I'd known him when he was alive.

"How ya doing yourself?"

"Okay, what's up?"

"Jean-Claude got your message. He says ta meet him at the Circus of the Damned at eight o'clock tonight."

"The Circus? What's he doing over there?"

"He owns it now. Ya didn't know?"

I shook my head, realized he couldn't see it, and said, "No, I didn't."

"He says to meet 'im in a show that starts at eight."

"Which show?"

"He said you'd know which one."

"Well, isn't that cryptic," I said.

"Hey, Anita, I just do what I'm told. Ya know how it is?"

I did know. Jean-Claude owned Willie lock, stock, and soul. "It's okay, Willie, it's not your fault."

"Thanks, Anita." His voice sounded cheerful, like a puppy who expected a kick and got patted instead.

Why had I comforted him? Why did I care whether a vampire got its feelings hurt, or not? Answer: I didn't think of him as a dead man. He was still Willie McCoy with his penchant for loud primary-colored suits, clashing ties, and small, nervous hands. Being dead hadn't changed him that much. I wished it had.

"Tell Jean-Claude I'll be there."

"I will." He was quiet for a minute, his breath soft over the phone. "Watch your back tonight, Anita."

"Do you know something I should know?"

"No, but . . . I don't know."

"What's up, Willie?"

"Nuthin', nuthin'." His voice was high and frightened.

"Am I walking into a trap, Willie?"

"No, no, nuthin' like that." I could almost see his small hands waving in the air. "I swear, Anita, nobody's gunnin' for you."

I let that go. Nobody he knew of was all he could swear to. "Then what are you afraid of, Willie?"

"It's just that there's more vampires around here than usual. Some of 'em ain't too careful who they hurt. That's all."

"Why are there more vampires, Willie? Where did they come from?"

"I don't know and I don't want to know, ya know? I got ta go, Anita." He hung up before I could ask anything else. There had been real fear in his voice. Fear for me, or for himself? Maybe both.

I glanced at the radio clock on my bedstand: 6:35. I had to hurry if I was going to make the appointment. The covers were toasty warm over my legs. All I really wanted to do was cuddle back under the blankets, maybe with a certain stuffed toy penguin I knew. Yeah, hiding sounded good.

I threw back the covers and walked into the bathroom. I hit the light switch, and glowing white light filled the small room. My hair stuck up in all directions, a mass of tight black curls. That'd teach me not to sleep on it wet. I ran a brush through the curls and they loosened slightly, turning into a frothing mass of waves. The curls went all over the place and there wasn't a damn thing I could do with it except wash it and start over. There wasn't time for that.

The black hair made my pale skin look deathly, or maybe it was the overhead lighting. My eyes were so dark brown they looked black. Two glittering holes in the pastiness of my face. I looked like I felt; great.

What do you wear to meet the Master of the City? I chose black jeans, a black sweater with bright geometric designs, black Nikes with blue swooshes, and a blue-and-black sport bag clipped around my waist. Color coordination at its best.

The Browning went into its shoulder holster. I put an extra ammo clip in the sport bag along with credit cards, driver's license, money, and a small hairbrush. I slipped on the short leather jacket I'd bought last year. It was the first one I'd ever tried on that didn't make me look like a gorilla. Most leather jackets were so long-sleeved, I could never wear them. The jacket was black, so Bert wouldn't let me wear it to work.

I only zipped the jacket halfway up, leaving room so I could go for my gun if I needed to. The silver cross swung on its long chain, a warm, solid weight between my breasts. The cross would be more help against vampires than the gun, even with silver-coated bullets.

I hesitated at the door. I hadn't seen Jean-Claude in months. I didn't want to see him now. My dream came back to me. Something that lived in blood and darkness. Why the nightmare? Was it Jean-Claude interfering in my dreams again? He had promised to stay out of my dreams. But was his word worth anything? No answer to that.

I flicked off the apartment lights and closed the door behind me. I rattled it to make sure it was locked, and I had nothing left to do but drive to the Circus of the Damned. No more excuses. No more delays. My stomach was so tight it hurt. So I was afraid; so what? I had to go, and the sooner I left, the sooner I could come home. If only I believed that Jean-Claude would make things that simple. Nothing was ever simple where he was concerned. If I learned anything about the murders tonight, I'd pay for it, but not in money. Jean-Claude seemed to have plenty of that. No, his coin was more painful, more intimate, more bloody.

And I had volunteered to go see him. Stupid, Anita, very stupid.

5

There was a bouquet of spotlights on the top of the Circus of the Damned. The lights slashed the black night like swords. The multicolored lights that spelled the name seemed dimmer with the huge white lights whirling overhead. Demonic clowns danced around the sign in frozen pantomime.

I walked past the huge cloth signs that covered the walls. One picture showed a man that had no skin; See the Skinless Man. A movie version of a voodoo ceremony covered another banner. Zombies writhed from open graves. The zombie banner had changed since last I'd visited the Circus. I didn't know if that was good or bad; probably neither. I didn't give a damn what they did here, except...Except it wasn't right to raise the dead just for entertainment.

Who did they have raising zombies for them? I knew it had to be someone new because I had helped kill their last animator. He had been a serial killer and had nearly killed me twice, the second time by ghoul attack, which was a messy way to die. Of course, the way he died had been messy, too, but I wasn't the one who ripped him open. A vampire had done that. You might say I eased him on his way. A mercy killing. Ri-ight.

It was too cold to be standing outside with my jacket half-unzipped. But if I zipped it all the way, I'd never get to my gun in time. Freeze my butt off, or be able to defend myself. The clowns on the roof had fangs. I decided it wasn't that cold after all.

Heat and noise poured out to meet me at the door. Hundreds of bodies pressed together in an enclosed space.

The noise of the crowd was like the ocean, murmurous and large, sound without meaning. A crowd is an elemental thing. A word, a glance, and a crowd becomes a mob. A different being entirely from a group.

There were a lot of families. Mom, Dad, the kiddies. The children had balloons tied to their wrists and cotton candy smeared on their faces and hands. It smelled like a traveling carnival: corn dogs, the cinnamon smell of funnel cakes, snow cones, sweat. The only thing missing was the dust. There was always dust in the air at a summer fair. Dry, choking dust kicked into the air by hundreds of feet. Cars driving over the grass until it is grey-coated with dust.

There was no smell of dirt in the air, but there was something else just as singular. The smell of blood. So faint you'd almost think you dreamed it, but it was there. The sweet copper scent of blood mingled with the smells of cooking food and the sharp smell of a snow cone being made. Who needed dust?

I was hungry, and the corn dogs smelled good. Should I eat first or accuse the Master of the City of murder? Choices, choices.

I didn't get to decide. A man stepped out of the crowd. He was only a little taller than me, with curly blond hair that fell past his shoulders. He was wearing a cornflower-blue shirt with the sleeves rolled up, showing firm, muscular forearms. Jeans no tighter than the skin on a grape showed slender hips. He wore black cowboy boots with blue designs tooled into them. His true-blue eyes matched his shirt.

He smiled, flashing small white teeth. "You're Anita Blake, right?"

I didn't know what to say. It isn't always a good idea to admit who you are.

"Jean-Claude told me to wait for you." His voice was soft, hesitant. There was something about him, an almost childlike appeal. Besides I'm a sucker for a pair of pretty eyes.

"What's your name?" I asked. Always like to know who I'm dealing with.

His smile widened. "Stephen; my name is Stephen." He put out his hand, and I took it. His hand was soft but firm, no manual labor but some weightlifting. Not too much. Enough to firm, not explode. Men my size should not do serious weightlifting. It may look okay in a bathing suit, but in regular clothes you look like a deformed dwarf.

"Follow me, please." He sounded like a waiter, but when he walked into the crowd, I followed him.

He led the way towards a huge blue tent. It was like an old-fashioned circus tent. I'd only seen one in pictures or the movies.

There was a man in a striped coat yelling, "Almost showtime, folks! Present your tickets and come inside! See the world's largest cobra! Watch the fearsome serpent be taken through amazing feats by the beautiful snake charmer Shahar. We guarantee it will be a show you will never forget."

There was a line of people giving their tickets to a young woman. She tore them in half and handed back the stubs.

Stephen walked confidently along the line without waiting. We got some dirty looks, but the girl nodded to us. And in we went.

Tiers of bleachers ran up to the top of the tent. It was huge. Nearly all the seats were full. A sold-out show. Wowee.

There was a blue rail that formed a circle in the middle. A one-ring circus.

Stephen scooted past the knees of about a dozen people to a set of steps. Since we were at the bottom, up was the only way to go. I followed Stephen up the concrete stairs. The tent may have looked like a circus tent, but the bleachers and stairs were permanent. A mini-coliseum.

I have bad knees, which means that I can run on a flat surface but put me on a hill, or stairs, and it hurts. So I didn't try to keep up with Stephen's smooth, running glide.

I did watch the way his jeans fit his snug little behind, though. Looking for clues.

I unzipped the leather jacket but didn't take it off. My gun would show. Sweat glided down my spine. I was going to melt.

Stephen glanced over his shoulder to see if I was following, or maybe for encouragement. He flashed a smile that was just lips curling back from teeth, almost a snarl.

I stopped in the middle of the steps, watching his lithe form glide upward. There was an energy to Stephen as if the air boiled invisibly around him. A shapeshifter. Some lycanthropes are better than others at hiding what they are. Stephen wasn't that good. Or maybe he just didn't care if I knew. Possible.

Lycanthropy was a disease, like AIDS. It was prejudice to mistrust someone for an accident. Most people survived attacks to become shapeshifters. It wasn't a choice. So why didn't I like Stephen as well, now that I knew? Prejudiced, *moi*?

He waited at the top of the stairs, still pretty as a picture, but the air of energy contained in too small a space, like his motor was on high idle, shimmered around him. What was Jean-Claude doing with a shapeshifter on his payroll? Maybe I could ask him.

I stepped up beside Stephen. There must have been something in my face, because he said, "What's wrong?"

I shook my head. "Nothing."

I don't think he believed me. But he smiled and led me towards a booth that was mostly glass with heavy curtains on the inside hiding whatever lay behind. It looked for all the world like a miniature broadcast booth.

Stephen went to the curtained door and opened it. He held it for me, motioning me to go first.

"No, you first," I said.

"I'm being a gentleman here," he said.

"I don't need or want doors opened for me. I'm quite capable, thank you."

"A feminist, my, my."

Truthfully, I just didn't want ol' Stephen at my back. But if he wanted to think I was a hard-core feminist, let him. It was closer to the truth than a lot of things.

He walked through the door. I glanced back to the ring. It looked smaller from up here. Muscular men dressed in glittering loincloths pulled a cart in on their bare shoulders. There were two things in the cart: a huge woven basket and a dark-skinned woman. She was dressed in Hollywood's version of a dancing girl's outfit. Her thick black hair fell like a cloak, sweeping to her ankles. Slender arms, small, dark hands swept the air in graceful curves. She danced in front of the cart. The costume was fake, but she wasn't. She knew how to dance, not for seduction, though it was that, but for power. Dancing was originally an invocation to some god or other; most people forget that.

Goosebumps prickled up the back of my neck, creeping into my hair. I shivered while I stood there and sweated in the heat. What was in the basket? The barker outside had said a giant cobra, but there was no snake in the world that needed a basket that big. Not even the anaconda, the world's heaviest snake, needed a container over ten feet tall and twenty feet wide.

Something touched my shoulder. I jumped and spun. Stephen was standing nearly touching me, smiling.

I swallowed my pulse back into my throat and glared at him. I make a big deal about not wanting him at my back, then let him sneak up behind me. Real swift, Anita, real swift. Because he'd scared me, I was mad at him. Illogical, but it was better to be mad than scared.

"Jean-Claude's just inside," he said. He smiled, but there was a very human glint of laughter in his blue eyes.

I scowled at him, knowing I was being childish, and not caring. "After you, fur-face."

The laughter slipped away. He was very serious as he stared at me. "How did you know?" His voice was uncertain, fragile. A lot of lycanthropes pride themselves on being able to pass for human.

"It was easy," I said. Which wasn't entirely true, but I wanted to hurt him. Childish, unattractive, honest.

His face suddenly looked very young. His eyes filled with uncertainty and pain.

Shit.

"Look, I've spent a lot of time around shapeshifters. I just know what to look for, okay?" Why did I want to reassure him? Because I knew what it was like to be the outsider. Raising the dead makes a lot of people class me with the monsters. There are even days when I agree with them.

He was still staring at me, with his hurt feelings like an open wound in his eyes. If he started to cry, I was leaving.

He turned without another word and walked through the open door. I stared at the door for a minute. There were gasps, screams from the crowd. I whirled and saw it. It was a snake, but it wasn't just the world's biggest cobra, it was the biggest freaking snake I'd ever seen. Its body was banded in dull greyish black and off-white. The scales gleamed under the lights. The head was at least a foot and a half wide. No snake was that big. It flared its hood, and it was the size of a satellite dish. The snake hissed, flicking out a tongue that was like a black whip.

I'd had a semester of herpetology in college. If the snake had been a mere eight feet or less, I would have called it a banded Egyptian cobra. I couldn't remember the scientific name to save myself.

The woman dropped to the ground in front of the snake, forehead to the ground. A mark of obedience from her to the snake. To her god. Sweet Jesus.

The woman stood and began to dance, and the cobra watched her. She'd made herself a living flute for the nearsighted creature to follow. I didn't want to see what would happen if she messed up. The poison wouldn't have time to kill her. The fangs were so damn big they'd spear her like swords. She'd die of shock and blood loss long before the poison kicked in.

Something was growing in the middle of that ring. Magic crawled up my spine. Was it magic that kept the snake safe, or magic that called it up, or was it the snake itself? Did it have power all its own? I didn't even know what to call it. It looked like a cobra, perhaps the world's biggest, yet I didn't even have a word for it. God with a little "g" would do, but it wasn't accurate.

I shook my head and turned away. I didn't want to see the show. I didn't want to stand there with its magic flowing soft and cold over my skin. If the snake wasn't safe, Jean-Claude would have had it caged, right? Right.

I turned away from the snake charmer and the world's biggest cobra. I wanted to talk to Jean-Claude and get the hell out of here.

The open door was filled with darkness. Vampires didn't need lights. Did lycanthropes? I didn't know. Gee, so much to learn. My jacket was unzipped all the way, the better for a fast draw. Though truthfully, if I needed a fast draw tonight, I was in deep shit.

I took a deep breath and let it out. No sense putting it off. I walked through the door into the waiting darkness without looking back. I didn't want to see what was happening in the ring. Truth was, I didn't want to see what was behind the darkness. Was there another choice? Probably not.

6

The room was like a closet with drapes all the way around. There was no one in the curtained darkness but me. Where had Stephen gone? If he had been a vampire, I would have believed the vanishing act, but lycanthropes don't just turn into thin air. So, there had to be a second door.

If I had built this room, where would I put an inner door? Answer: opposite the first door. I swept the drapes aside. The door was there. Elementary, my dear Watson.

The door was heavy wood with some flowering vine carved into it. The doorknob was white with tiny pink flowers in the center of it. It was an awfully feminine door. Of course, no rules against men liking flowers. None at all. It was a sexist comment. Forget I thought it.

I did not draw my gun. See, I'm not completely paranoid.

I turned the doorknob and swung the door inward. I kept pushing until it was flush against the wall. No one was hiding behind it. Good.

The wallpaper was off-white with thin silver, gold, and copper designs running through it. The effect was vaguely oriental. The carpeting was black. I didn't even know carpet came in that color. A canopy bed took up most of one side of the room. Black, gauzy curtains covered it. Made the bed indistinct, misty, like a dream. There was someone asleep in a nest of black covers and crimson sheets. A line of bare chest showed it was a man, but a wave of brown hair covered his face like a shroud. It all looked faintly unreal, as if he was waiting for movie cameras to roll.

A black couch was against the far wall, with blood-red pillows thrown along it. A matching love seat was against the last wall. Stephen was curled up on the love seat. Jean-Claude sat on one corner of the couch. He wore black jeans tucked into knee-high leather boots, dyed a deep, almost velvet black. His shirt had a high lace collar pinned at the neck by a thumb-size ruby pendant. His black hair was just long enough to curl around the lace. The sleeves were loose and billowing, tight at the wrists with lace spilling over his hands until only his fingertips showed.

"Where do you get your shirts?" I asked.

He smiled. "Don't you like it?" His hands caressed down his chest, fingertips hesitating over his nipples. It was an invitation. I could touch that smooth white cloth and see if the lace was as soft as it looked.

I shook my head. Mustn't get distracted. I glanced at Jean-Claude. He was staring at me with those midnight blue eyes. His eyelashes were like black lace.

"She wants you, Master," Stephen said. There was laughter in his voice, derision. "I can smell her desire."

Jean-Claude turned just his head, staring at Stephen. "As can I." The words were innocent, but the feeling behind them wasn't. His voice slithered around the room, low and full of a terrible promise.

"I meant no harm, Master, no harm." Stephen looked scared. I didn't blame him.

Jean-Claude turned back to me as if nothing had happened. His face was still pleasantly handsome, interested, amused.

"I don't need your protection."

"Oh, I think you do."

I whirled and found another vampire standing at my back. I hadn't heard the door open.

She smiled at me, without flashing fang. A trick that the older vampires learn. She was tall and slender with dark skin and long ebony hair that swung around her waist. She wore crimson Lycra bike pants that clung so tight, you knew she wasn't wearing underwear. Her top was red silk, loose and blousy, with thin spaghetti straps holding it in place. It looked like the top to slinky pajamas. Red high-heeled sandals and a thin gold chain set with a single diamond completed the outfit. The word that came to mind was "exotic." She glided towards me, smiling.

"Is that a threat?" I asked.

She stopped in front of me. "Not yet." There was a hint of some other language in her voice. Something darker with rolling, sibilant sounds.

"That is enough," Jean-Claude said.

The dark lady twirled around, black hair like a veil behind her. "I don't think so."

"Yasmeen." The one word was low and dark with warning.

Yasmeen laughed, a harsh sound like breaking glass. She stopped directly in front of me, blocking my view of Jean-Claude. Her hand stretched towards me, and I stepped back, out of reach.

She smiled wide enough to show fangs and reached for me again. I stepped back, and she was suddenly on me, faster than I could blink, faster than I could breathe. Her hand gripped my hair, bending my neck backwards. Her fingertips brushed my skull. Her other hand held my chin, fingers digging in like fleshy metal. My face was immobile between her hands, trapped. Short of taking my gun out and shooting her, there was nothing I could do. And if her movement was any clue, I'd never get the gun out in time.

"I see why you like her. So pretty, so delicate." She half-turned towards Jean-Claude, nearly giving me her back, but still holding my head immobile.

"I never thought you'd take in a human." She made it sound like I was a stray puppy.

Yasmeen turned back to me. I pressed my 9mm into her chest. No matter how fast she was, she would be hurt if I wanted it. I can feel how old a vampire is inside my head. It's part natural ability, and part practice. Yasmeen was old, older than Jean-Claude. I was betting she was over five hundred. If she had been the new dead, high-tech ammo at point-blank range would have shredded her heart, killed her. But over five hundred and a master vampire, it might not kill her. Or then again, it might.

Something flickered over her face; surprise, and maybe just a touch of fear. Her body was statue-still. If she was breathing, I couldn't tell.

My voice sounded strained from the angle she held my neck, but the words were clear. "Very slowly, take your hands away from my face. Put both hands on top of your head and lace your fingers together."

"Jean-Claude, call off your human."

"I'd do what she says, Yasmeen." His voice was pleased. "How many vampires have you killed now, Anita?"

"Eighteen."

Yasmeen's eyes widened just a bit. "I don't believe you."

"Believe this, bitch: I'll pull this trigger and you can kiss your heart good-bye."

"Bullets cannot harm me."

"Silver-plated can. Move off me, now!"

Yasmeen's hand slid away from my hair and jaw.

"Slowly," I said.

She did what I asked. She stood in front of me with her long-fingered hands clasped across her head. I stepped away from her, gun still pointed at her chest.

"Now what?" Yasmeen asked. A smile still curled her lips. Her dark eyes were amused. I didn't like being laughed at, but when tangling with master vampires you let some things slide.

"You can put your hands down," I said.

Yasmeen did, but she continued to stare at me as if I'd sprouted a second head. "Where did you find her, Jean-Claude? The kitten has teeth"

"Tell Yasmeen what the vampires call you, Anita."

It sounded too much like an order, but this didn't seem the time to bitch at him. "The Executioner."

Yasmeen's eyes widened; then she smiled, flashing a lot of fang. "I thought you'd be taller."

"It disappoints me, too, sometimes," I said.

Yasmeen threw back her head and laughed, wild and brittle, with an edge of hysteria. "I like her, Jean-Claude. She's dangerous, like sleeping with a lion."

She glided towards me. I had the gun up and pointed at her. It didn't even slow her down.

"Jean-Claude, tell her I will shoot her if she doesn't back off."

"I promise not to hurt you, Anita. I will be oh so gentle." She swayed over to me, and I wasn't sure what to do. She was playing with me, sadistic but probably not deadly. Could I shoot her for being a pain in the ass? I didn't think so.

"I can taste the heat of your blood, the warmth of your skin on the air like perfume." Her gliding, hip-swinging walk brought her right in front of me. I pointed the gun at her, and she laughed. She pressed her chest against the tip of my gun.

"So soft, wet, but strong." I wasn't sure who she was talking about, her or me. Neither option sounded pleasant. She rubbed her small breasts against the gun, her nipples caressing the gun barrel. "Dainty, but dangerous." The last word was a whispered hiss that flowed over my skin like ice water. She was the first master I'd ever met who had some of Jean-Claude's voice tricks.

I could see her nipples hardening through the thin material of her shirt. Yikes. I pointed the gun at the floor and stepped away from her. "Jesus, are all vampires over two hundred perverts?"

"I am over two hundred," Jean-Claude said.

"I rest my case."

Yasmeen let a warm trickle of laughter spill out of her mouth. The sound caressed my skin like a warm wind. She stalked towards me. I backed up until I hit the wall. She put a hand on either side of the wall near my shoulders and began to lean in like she was doing a pushup. "I'd like to taste her myself."

I shoved the gun into her ribs, too low for her to rub herself against it. "Nobody lays a fang on me," I said.

"Tough girl." She leaned her face over me, lips brushing my forehead. "I like tough girls."

"Jean-Claude, do something with her before one of us gets killed."

Yasmeen pushed away from me, elbows locked, as far away as she could get without moving her hands. Her tongue flicked over her lips, a hint of fang, but mostly wet lips. She leaned back into me, lips half-parted, but she wasn't going for my neck. She was definitely going for my mouth. She didn't want to *taste* me, she wanted to taste me. I couldn't shoot her, not if she just wanted to kiss me. If she'd been a man, I wouldn't have shot her.

Her hair fell forward over my hands, soft like thick silk. Her face was all I could see. Her eyes were a perfect blackness. Her lips hovered just above my mouth. Her breath was warm, and smelled of breath mints, but under the modern smell was something older: the sweet foulness of blood.

"Your breath smells like old blood," I whispered into her mouth.

She whispered back, lips barely caressing my mouth, "I know." Her lips pressed into mine, a gentle kiss. She smiled with our lips still touching.

The door opened, nearly pinning us to the wall. Yasmeen stood up, but kept her hand's around my shoulders. We both looked at the door. A woman with nearly white blond hair looked wildly around the room. Her blue eyes widened as she saw us. She screamed, high and wordless, rage-filled.

"Get off of her!"

I frowned up at Yasmeen. "Is she talking to me?"

"Yes." Yasmeen looked amused.

The woman did not. She ran towards us, hands outstretched, fingers curled into claws. Yasmeen caught her in a blurring moment of pure speed. The woman thrashed and struggled, her hands still reaching for me.

"What the hell is going on?" I asked.

"Marguerite is Yasmeen's human servant," Jean-Claude said. "She thinks you may steal Yasmeen away from her."

"I don't want Yasmeen."

Yasmeen shot me a look of pure anger. Had I hurt her feelings? I hoped so.

"Marguerite, look; she's yours, alright?"

The woman screamed at me, wordless and guttural. What might have been a pretty face was screwed up into something bestial. I'd never seen such instant rage. It was frightening even with a loaded gun in my hand.

Yasmeen had to lift the woman off her feet, holding her struggling in mid-air. "I'm afraid, Jean-Claude, that Marguerite is not going to be satisfied unless she answers the challenge."

"What challenge?" I asked.

"You challenged her claim to me."

"Did not," I said.

Yasmeen smiled. The serpent must have smiled at Eve that way: pleasant, amused, dangerous.

"Jean-Claude, I didn't come here for whatever the hell is going on. I don't want any vampire, let alone a female one," I said.

"If you were my human servant, *ma petite*, there would be no challenge, because once one is bound to a master vampire, it is an unbreakable bond."

"Then what is Marguerite worried about?"

"That Yasmeen may take you as a lover. She does that from time to time to drive Marguerite into jealous rages. For some reason I do not understand, Yasmeen enjoys it."

"Oh, yes, I do enjoy it." Yasmeen turned towards me with the woman still clasped in her arms. She was holding the struggling woman easily, no strain. Of course, vampires can bench press Toyotas. What was one medium-size human to that?

"So what exactly does this mean to me personally?"

Jean-Claude smiled, but there was an edge of tiredness to it. Was he bored? Or angry? Or just tired? "You must fight Marguerite. If you win, then Yasmeen is yours. If you lose, Yasmeen is Marguerite's."

"Wait a minute," I said. "What sort of fight, pistols at dawn?"

"No weapons," Yasmeen said. "My Marguerite is not skilled in weapons. I don't want her hurt."

"Then stop tormenting her," I said.

Yasmeen smiled. "It is part of the fun."

"Sadistic bitch," I said.

"Yes, I am."

Jesus, some people you couldn't even insult. "So you want us to fight bare-handed over Yasmeen?" I couldn't believe I was even asking this question.

"Yes, *ma petite*."

I took a deep breath, looked at my gun, looked back at the screaming woman, then holstered my gun. "Is there any way out of this, besides fighting her?"

"If you admit you are my human servant, then there will be no fight. There will be no need for one." Jean-Claude was watching me, studying my face. His eyes were very still.

"You mean this was a setup," I said. The first warm rumblings of anger chased up my gut.

"A setup, *ma petite*? I had no idea Yasmeen would find you so enticing."

"Bullshit!"

"Admit you are my human servant and all ends here."

"And if I don't?"

"Then you fight Marguerite."

"Fine," I said. "Let's do it."

"What would it cost you to admit what is true, Anita?" Jean-Claude asked.

"I am not your human servant. I will never be your human servant. I wish you'd just accept that and leave me the fuck alone."

He frowned. "*Ma petite*, such language."

"Fuck off."

He smiled then. "As you like, *ma petite*." He sat up on the edge of the couch, maybe so he could see better. "Yasmeen, any time you are ready."

"Wait," I said. I took off my jacket and wasn't sure where to lay it.

The man who had been sleeping on the black-canopied bed reached a hand through the black gauze. "I'll hold it for you," he said.

I stared at him for a minute. He was naked from the waist up. His arms, stomach, chest showed signs of weightlifting, just enough, not too much. He either had a perfect tan or was naturally dark complected. Hair fell in a wavy mass around his shoulders. His eyes were brown and very human. That was nice to see.

I handed him my jacket. He smiled, a quick flash of teeth that chased the last signs of sleep from his face. He sat up with the jacket in one hand, arms encircling his knees that were still hidden under the black and red covers. He laid his cheek on his knees and managed to look winsome.

"Are you quite done, *ma petite*?" Jean-Claude's voice was amused, with an edge of laughter that wasn't humor at all. It was mockery. But whether he was mocking me or himself, I couldn't tell.

"I'm ready, I guess," I said.

"Put her down, Yasmeen. Let us see what happens."

I heard Stephen say, "Twenty on Marguerite."

Yasmeen said, "No fair. I can't bet against my own human servant."

"I'll spot you both twenty that Ms. Blake wins." That came from the man in the bed. I had a second to glance at him, to see him smile at me; then Marguerite was coming.

She slapped at my face, and I blocked it with my forearm. She fought like a girl, all open-handed slaps and fingernails. But she was fast, faster than a human. Maybe she got that from being a human servant, I don't know. Her fingernails raked down my face in a sharp, painful line. That was it: no more Ms. Nice Guy.

I held her off with one hand. She dug her teeth into that hand. I hit her with my right fist as hard as I could, turning my body into it. It was a nice solid hit to the solar plexus.

Marguerite stopped biting my hand and bent over, hands covering her stomach. She was gasping for breath. Good.

My left hand had a bloody imprint of her teeth in it. I touched my left cheek and came away with more blood. Damn, that hurt.

Marguerite knelt on the floor, relearning how to breathe. But she was staring up at me. The look in her blue eyes said the fight wasn't over. As soon as she got her breath back, she would start again.

"Stay down, Marguerite, or I'll hurt you."

She shook her head.

"She can't give up, *ma petite*, or you win Yasmeen's body, if not her heart."

"I don't want her body. I don't want anyone's body."

"Now, that is simply not true, *ma petite*," Jean-Claude said.

"Stop calling me *ma petite*."

"You bear two of my marks, Anita. You are halfway to being my human servant. Admit that, and no one else need suffer tonight."

"Yeah, right," I said.

Marguerite was getting to her feet. I didn't want her on her feet. I moved in before she could stand, and foot-swept her legs out from under her. I forced her shoulders backwards at the same time, and I rode her down. I got her right arm in a joint lock. She tried to get up. I increased the pressure, and she lay back down.

"Give up the fight."

"No." It was only the second coherent thing I'd heard her utter.

"I will break your arm."

"Break it, break it! I don't care." Her face was wild, enraged. God. There was no way to reason with her. Great.

Using the joint lock as a lever, I turned her over on her stomach, increasing the pressure to almost breaking, but not quite. Breaking her arm might not stop the fight. I wanted it over with.

I used my leg and one arm to keep the joint lock on but knelt over her upper body, until my weight would keep her pinned. I took a handful of yellow hair and pulled her neck back. I released her arm and brought my right arm across her neck, with my elbow in front of her Adam's apple and the arm squeezing the arteries on both sides of her neck. I put my right hand on my left wrist and squeezed.

She scratched at my face, but I buried my eyes in her back and she couldn't reach me. She was making small, helpless sounds because she didn't have enough air to make big ones.

Her hands scratched at my right arm, but the sweater was thick. She pushed the sleeve up, exposing my bare arm, and began to shred the skin with her nails. I buried my face deeper into her back and squeezed until my arms shook and I was gritting my teeth. Everything I had was in that one arm, pressing into her slender throat.

Her hands stopped scratching me. They beat against my arm like dying butterflies.

It takes a long time to choke someone into unconsciousness. The movies make it look easy, quick, clean. It isn't easy, it isn't quick, and it sure as hell isn't clean. You can feel the pulse on either side of the neck pounding against your arm while you squeeze the life out of it. The person struggles a lot more than in the movies. And as far as choking someone to death, you better hold on for a long time after they stop moving.

Marguerite went slowly limp, a body part at a time. When she was just dead weight in my arms, I let her go, slowly. She lay on the floor unmoving. I couldn't even see her breathe. Had I squeezed too long?

I touched her neck and found the carotid pulse strong and even. Just out of it, not dead. Good.

I stood and walked back towards the bed.

Yasmeen went to her knees beside Marguerite's still form. "My love, my only one, has she hurt you?"

"She's just unconscious," I said. "She'll come to in a few minutes."

"If you had killed her, I would have torn your throat out."

I shook my head. "Let's not start this shit again. I've had about all the grandstanding I can take for one night."

The man in bed said, "You're bleeding."

Blood was dripping down my right forearm. Marguerite may not have been able to do any real damage, but the scratches were deep enough that some of them might leave scars. Great; I already had a long, thin scar on the underside of my right arm from a knife. Even with the scratches, my right arm had fewer scars than my left. Work-related injuries.

Blood was dripping down my arm rather steadily. The blood didn't show on the black carpeting. A good color if you planned to bleed much in a room.

Yasmeen was helping Marguerite to her feet. The woman had recovered very quickly. Why? Because she was a human servant, of course. Sure.

Yasmeen walked towards the bed, towards me. Her lovely face had thinned until the bones showed through. Her eyes were bright, almost feverish. "Fresh blood, and I haven't fed tonight."

"Control yourself, Yasmeen."

"You have not taught your servant good manners, Jean-Claude," Yasmeen said. She was looking very unkindly at me.

"Leave her alone, Yasmeen." Jean-Claude was standing now.

"Every servant must be tamed, Jean-Claude. You have let it go far too long."

I looked over Yasmeen's shoulder at him. "Tamed?"

"It is an unfortunate stage in the process," he said. His voice was neutral, as if he were talking about taming a horse.

"Damn you." I pulled my gun. I held it two-handed in a teacup grip. Nobody was taming me tonight.

Out of the corner of my eye I saw someone stand up on the other side of the bed. The man was still under the covers. It was a slender woman, her skin the color of coffee with cream. Her black hair was cut very close to her head. She was naked. Where the hell had she come from?

Yasmeen was about a yard from me, tongue playing over her lips, fangs glistening in the overhead light.

"I'll kill you, do you understand that, I'll kill you," I said.

"You'll try."

"Fun and games aren't worth dying for," I said.

"After a few hundred years, that's all that *is* worth dying for."

"Jean-Claude, unless you want to lose her, call her off!" My voice was higher than I wanted it to be, afraid.

At this range the bullet should take out her entire chest. If it worked, there would be no resurrecting her as the undead; her heart would be gone. Of course, she was over five hundred years old. One shot might not do it. Lucky I had more than one bullet.

I caught movement from the corner of my eye. I was half-turned towards it when something flattened me to the ground. The black woman was on top of me. I brought the gun around to fire, not giving a damn if she was human or not. But her hand grabbed my wrists, squeezing. She was going to crush my wrists.

She snarled in my face, all teeth and a low growl. The sound should have had fur around it and pointy teeth. Human faces weren't supposed to look that way.

The woman jerked the Browning out of my hands like taking candy from a baby. She held it wrong, like she didn't know which end of the gun went where.

An arm came around her waist and pulled her backwards off me. It was the man on the bed. The woman turned on him, snarling.

Yasmeen leapt for me. I scooted backwards, putting the wall at my back. She smiled. "Not so tough without your weapon, are you?"

She was suddenly kneeling in front of me. I hadn't seen her come, not even a blur of motion. She appeared beside me like magic.

She had her body up against my knees, pinning me to the wall. Yasmeen dug her fingers into my upper arms and jerked me towards her. Her strength was incredible. She made the black shapeshifter seem fragile.

"Yasmeen, no!" It was Jean-Claude coming to my aid at last. But he was going to be too late. Yasmeen bared her teeth, raised her neck back for the strike, and I couldn't do a damn thing.

She pulled me in tight against her, arms locked behind my back. If I'd been pressed any tighter I'd have come out on the other side.

I screamed, "Jean-Claude!"

Heat; something was burning inside my sweater, over my heart. Yasmeen hesitated. I felt her whole body shudder. What the hell was happening?

A tongue of blue-white flame curled up between us. I screamed and Yasmeen echoed it. We screamed together as we burned.

She fell away from me. Blue-white flame crawled over her shirt. Flames licked around a hole in my sweater. I shrugged out of the shoulder holster and pulled the burning sweater off.

My cross still burned with an intense blue-white flame. I jerked the chain and it snapped. I dropped the cross to the carpet, where the flames smoldered, then died.

There was a perfect cross-shaped burn on my chest, just above my breast, over the beat of my heart. The burn was covered in blisters already. A second-degree burn.

Yasmeen had ripped her own blouse off. She had an identical burn, but lower down between her breasts because she was taller than I was.

I knelt on the floor in just my bra and jeans. Tears were trailing down my face. I had a bigger cross-shaped burn scar on my left forearm. A vampire's human followers had branded me, thinking it was funny. They'd laughed right up to the minute I killed them.

A burn is a bitch. Inch for inch, a burn hurts worse than any other injury.

Jean-Claude stood in front of me. The cross glowed a white-hot light, no flames, but then he wasn't touching it. I looked up to find him shielding his eyes with his arm.

"Put it away, *ma petite*. No one else will harm you tonight, I promise you that."

"Why don't you just back off and let me decide what I'm going to do?"

He sighed. "I was childish to let it get so far out of hand, Anita. Forgive me for my foolishness." It was hard to take the apology seriously while he cowered behind his arm, not daring to look at my glowing cross. But it was an apology. From Jean-Claude, that was a lot.

I picked the cross up by its chain. I had broken the clasp getting it off. I'd need a new chain before it could go around my neck again. I picked my sweater up in my other hand. There was a melted hole bigger than my fist in it. Right over the chest area. The sweater was ruined. No help there. Where do you hide a glowing cross when you aren't wearing a shirt?

The man in the bed handed my leather jacket to me. I met his eyes and saw in them concern, a little fear. His brown eyes were very close to me, and very human. It was comforting, and I wasn't even sure why.

The shoulder holster was flopping down around my waist like suspenders. I shrugged back into the straps. They felt strange next to my bare skin.

The man handed me my gun, butt first. The black shapeshifter stood on the other side of the bed, still naked, glaring at us. I didn't care how he'd gotten my gun from her. I was just glad to have it back.

With the Browning in its holster, I felt safer, though I'd never tried wearing a shoulder holster over bare skin. I suspected it was going to chafe. Oh, well, nothing's perfect.

The man held out a handful of Kleenex to me. The red sheets had slid down, exposing a long nude line of his body to about mid-thigh. The sheet was perilously close to falling off him all together. "Your arm," he said.

I stared down at my right arm. It was still bleeding a little. It hurt so much less than the burn, I had forgotten about it.

I took the Kleenex and wondered what he was doing here. Had he been having sex with the naked woman, the shapeshifter? I hadn't seen her in the bed. Had she been hiding under it?

I cleaned up my arm as best I could; didn't want to bleed too heavily on the leather jacket. I slipped the jacket on, and put the stillglowing cross in my left pocket. Once it was hidden, the glow would stop. The only reason Yasmeen and I had gotten in trouble was that the sweater had a loose weave and her top had left a lot of bare flesh. Vampire flesh touching a blessed cross was always volatile.

Jean-Claude stared down at me, now that the cross was safely hidden. "I am sorry, *ma petite*. I did not mean to frighten you tonight." He held one hand down towards me. The skin was paler than the white lace that covered it.

I ignored his outstretched hand and used the bed to help me stand.

He lowered his hand slowly. His dark blue eyes were very still, looking at me. "It never works as I want it to with you, Anita Blake. Why is that?"

"Maybe you should take the hint, and leave me alone."

He smiled, a bare movement of lips. "I'm afraid it is too late for that."

"What's that supposed to mean?"

The door swung open, banging against the wall and bouncing back. A man stood in the doorway, eyes wide, sweat running down his face. "Jean-Claude . . . the snake." He seemed to be having trouble breathing, as if he had run all the way up the stairs.

"What about the snake?" Jean-Claude asked.

The man swallowed, his breathing slowing. "It's gone crazy."

"What happened?"

The man shook his head. "I don't know. It attacked Shahar, its trainer. She's dead."

"Is it in the crowd?"

"Not yet."

"We will have to finish this discussion later, *ma petite*." He moved for the door, and the rest of the vampires followed at his heels. Stephen went with them. Well trained.

The slender black woman slipped a loose dress, black with red flowers on it, over her head. A pair of red high heels and she was out the door.

The man was out of the bed, naked. There was no time to be embarrassed. He was struggling into a pair of sweats.

This wasn't my problem, but what if the cobra got into the crowd? Not my problem. I zipped the jacket up enough to hide the fact I was shirtless but not so high up I couldn't draw my gun.

I was out the door and into the bright open space of the tent before the nameless man had slipped on his sweat pants. The vampires and shapeshifters were at the edge of the ring, fanning out into a circle around the snake. It filled the small ring with black-and-white coils. The bottom half of a man in a glittering loincloth was disappearing down the cobra's throat. That's what had kept it out of the crowd. It was taking time to feed.

Sweet Jesus.

The man's legs twitched, kicking convulsively. He couldn't be alive. He couldn't be. But the legs twitched as they slid out of sight. Please, God, let it just be a reflex. Don't let him still be alive. The thought was worse than any nightmare I could remember. And I have a lot of material for nightmares.

The monster in the ring wasn't my problem. I didn't have to be the bloody hero this time. People were screaming, running, arms full of children. Popcorn bags and cotton candy were getting crushed underfoot. I waded into the crowd and began pushing my way down. A woman carrying a toddler fell at my feet. A man climbed over them. I dragged the woman to her feet, taking the baby in one arm. People shoved past us. We shuddered just trying to stand still. I felt like a rock in the middle of a raging river.

The woman stared at me, eyes too large for her face. I pushed the toddler into her arms and wedged her between the seats. I grabbed the arms of the nearest large male, sexist that I am, and shouted, "Help them!"

The man's face was startled, as if I had spoken in tongues, but some of the panic faded from his face. He took the woman's arm and began to push his way towards the exit.

I couldn't let the snake get into the crowd. Not if I could stop it. Shit. I was going to play hero, dammit. I started fighting against the tide, to go down when everybody else was coming up and over. An elbow caught me in the mouth and I tasted blood. By the time I fought my way through this mess, it would all be over. God, I hoped so.

7

I stepped out of the crowd like I was flinging aside a curtain. My skin tingled with the memory of shoving bodies, but I stood alone on the last step. The screaming crowd was still up above me, struggling for the exits. But here, just above the ring, there was nothing. The silence lay in thick folds against my face and hands. It was hard to breathe through the thick air. Magic. But whether vampire or cobra, I didn't know.

Stephen stood closest to me, shirtless, slim and somehow elegant. Yasmeen had on his blue shirt, hiding her naked upper body. She had tied the shirt up to expose a tanned expanse of tummy. Marguerite stood beside her. The black woman stood on Stephen's right. She had kicked off her high heels and stood flat-footed in the ring.

Jean-Claude stood on the far side of the circle with two new blond vampires on either side. He turned and stared at me across the distance. I felt his touch inside me where no hand was ever meant to go. My throat tightened; sweat broke on my body. Nothing at that moment would have made me go closer to him. He was trying to tell me something. Something private and too intimate for words.

A hoarse scream brought my attention to the center of the ring. Two men lay broken and bleeding to one side. The cobra reared over them. It was like a moving tower of muscle and scale. It hissed at us. The sound was loud, echoing.

The men lay on the ground at its . . . feet? tail? One of them twitched. Was he alive? My hands squeezed the guard-

rail until my fingers ached. I was so scared I could taste
bile at the back of my throat. My skin was cold with it.
You ever have those dreams where snakes are everywhere,
so thick on the ground you can't walk unless you step on
them? It's almost claustrophobic. The dream always ends
with me standing in the middle of the trees with snakes
dripping down on me, and all I can do is scream.

Jean-Claude held out one slender hand towards me. The
lace covered everything but the tips of his fingers. Everyone else was staring at the snake. Jean-Claude was staring
at me.

One of the wounded men moved. A soft moan escaped
his lips and seemed to echo in the huge tent. Was it illusion
or had the sound really echoed? It didn't matter. He was
alive, and we had to keep him that way.

We? What was this "we" stuff? I stared into Jean-Claude's
deep blue eyes. His face was utterly blank, wiped clean of
any emotion I understood. He couldn't trick me with his
eyes. His own marks had seen to that, but mind tricks—if
he worked at it—were still possible. He was working at it.

It wasn't words, but a compulsion. I wanted to go to him.
To run to him. To feel the smooth, solid grip of his hand.
The softness of lace against my skin. I leaned against the
railing, dizzy. I gripped it to keep from falling. What the
hell were these mind games now? We had other problems,
didn't we? Or didn't he care about the snake? Maybe it had
all been a trick. Maybe he had told the cobra to run amuck.
But why?

Every hair on my body raised, as if some invisible finger
had just brushed it. I shivered and couldn't stop.

I was staring down at a pair of very nice black boots,
high and soft. I looked up and met Jean-Claude's eyes. He
had left his place around the cobra to come to me. It beat
the hell out of me going to him.

"Join with me, Anita, and we have enough power to stop
the creature."

I shook my head. "I don't know what you're talking
about."

He brushed his fingertips down my arm. Even through the leather jacket I could feel his touch like a line of ice, or was it fire?

"How can you be hot and cold at the same time?" I asked.

He smiled, a bare movement of lips. "*Ma petite*, stop fighting me, and we can tame the creature. We can save the men."

He had me there. A moment of personal weakness against the lives of two people. What a choice.

"Once I let you inside my head that far, it'll be easier for you to come in next time. My soul is not up for grabs for anybody's life."

He sighed. "Very well, it is your choice." He started to turn away from me. I grabbed his arm, and it was warm and firm and very, very real.

He turned to me, eyes large and drowning deep, like the bottom of the ocean, and just as deadly. His own power kept me from falling in; alone I would have been lost.

I swallowed hard enough for it to hurt, and pulled my hand away from him. I had the urge to wipe my hand against my pants, as if I had touched something bad. Maybe I had.

"Will silver bullets hurt it?"

He seemed to think about that for a second. "I do not know."

I took a deep breath. "If you stop trying to hijack my mind, I'll help you."

"You'll face it with a gun, rather than with me?" His voice sounded amused.

"You got it."

He stepped away from me and motioned me towards the ring.

I vaulted the rail and landed beside him. I ignored him as much as I was able and started walking towards the creature. I pulled the Browning out. It was nice and solid in my hand. A comforting weight.

"The ancient Egyptians worshipped it as a god, *ma petite*.

She was Edjo, the royal serpent. Cared for, sacrificed to, adored."

"It isn't a god, Jean-Claude."

"Are you so sure?"

"I'm a monotheist, remember. It's just another supernatural creepycrawlie to me."

"As you like, *ma petite*."

I turned back to him. "How the hell did you get it past quarantine?"

He shook his head. "Does it matter?"

I glanced back at the thing in the middle of the ring. The snake charmer lay in a bloody heap to one side of the snake. It hadn't eaten her. Was that a sign of respect, affection, dumb luck?

The cobra pushed towards us, belly scales clenching and unclenching. It made a dry, whispering sound against the ring's floor.

He was right; it didn't matter how the thing had gotten into the country. It was here now. "How are we going to stop it?"

He smiled wide enough to flash fangs. Maybe it was the "we." "If you could disable its mouth, I think we could deal with it."

The snake's body was thicker than a telephone pole. I shook my head. "If you say so."

"Can you injure the mouth?"

I nodded. "If silver bullets work on it, yeah."

"My little marksman," he said.

"Can the sarcasm," I said.

He nodded. "If you are going to try to shoot it, I would hurry, *ma petite*. Once it wades into my people, it will be too late." His face was unreadable. I couldn't tell if he wanted me to do it, or not.

I turned and started walking across the ring. The cobra stopped moving forward. It waited, like a swaying tower. It stood there, if something without legs could stand, and waited for me, whiplike tongue flicking out, tasting the air. Tasting me.

Jean-Claude was suddenly beside me. I hadn't heard him come, hadn't felt him come. Just another mind trick. I had other things to worry about right now.

He spoke, low and urgent; I think only I heard. "I will do my best to protect you, *ma petite*."

"You were doing a great job up in your office."

He stopped walking. I didn't.

"I know you are afraid of it, Anita. Your fear crawls through my belly," he called, soft and faint as wind.

I whispered back, not sure he would even be able to hear me. "Stay the fuck out of my mind."

The cobra watched me. I held the Browning in a two-handed grip, pointed at the thing's head. I thought I was out of striking distance, but I wasn't sure. How far away is safe distance from a snake that's bigger than a Mack truck? Two states away, three? I was close enough to see the snake's flat black eyes, empty as a doll's.

Jean-Claude's words blew through my mind like flower petals. I could even have sworn I smelled flowers. His voice had never held the scent of perfume before. "Force it to follow you, and give us its back before you shoot."

The pulse in my neck was beating so hard, it hurt to breathe. My mouth was so dry I couldn't swallow right. I began to move, ever so slowly, away from the vampires and shapeshifters. The snake's head followed me, as it had followed the snake charmer. If it started to strike, I'd shoot it, but if it would just keep moving with me, I'd give Jean-Claude a chance at its back.

Of course, silver bullets might not hurt it. In fact, the thing was so damn big, the ammo I had in the Browning might not do more than irritate it. I felt like I was trapped in one of those monster movies where the giant slime monster keeps coming no matter how much you shoot it. I hoped that was just a Hollywood invention.

If the bullets didn't hurt it, I was going to die. I flashed on the image of the man's legs kicking as they went down. The lump was still visible in the snake's body, like it had fed on a really big rat.

The tongue flicked out and I gasped, swallowing a scream. God, Anita, control yourself. It's just a snake. A giant man-eating cobra snake, but still only a snake. Yeah, right.

Every hair on my body stood at attention. The power that I'd felt the snake charmer calling up was still here. It wasn't enough that the thing was poisonous and had teeth big enough to spear me with. It had to be magic, too. Great, just great.

The smell of flowers was thicker, closer. It hadn't been Jean-Claude at all. The cobra was filling the air with perfume. Snakes don't smell like flowers. They smell musty, and once you know what they smell like, you never forget it. Nothing with fur ever smelled like that. A vampire's coffin smells a bit like snakes.

The cobra turned its giant head with me. "Come on, just a little farther," I was speaking to the snake. Which is pretty stupid, since they're deaf. The smell of flowers was thick and sweet. I shuffled around the ring, and the snake shadowed me. Maybe it was habit. I was small and had long, dark hair, though not nearly as long as the dead snake charmer. Maybe the beastie wanted someone to follow?

"Come on, pretty girl, come to mama," I whispered so low my lips barely moved. Just me and the snake and my voice. I didn't dare look across the ring at Jean-Claude. Nothing mattered but my feet shuffling over the ground, the snake's movements, the gun in my hands. It was like some kind of dance.

The cobra parted its mouth, tongue flicking, giving me a glimpse of scythelike fangs. Cobras have fixed fangs, not retractable like a rattlesnake's. Nice to know I remembered some of my herpetology. Though I bet Dr. Greenburg had never seen anything like this.

I had a horrible impulse to giggle. Instead, I sighted down my arm at the thing's mouth. The scent of flowers was strong enough to touch. I squeezed the trigger.

The snake's head jerked backwards, blood splattering the floor. I fired again and again. The jaws exploded into bits of flesh and bone. The cobra opened its ruined jaws, hissing. I think it was screaming.

Its telephone-pole body slashed the ground, whipping back and forth. Could I kill it? Could just bullets kill it? I fired three more shots into the head. The body turned on itself in a huge wondrous knot. The black and white scales boiled over each other, frenzied, bloodspattered.

A loop of body rolled out and punched my legs out from under me. I came up on knees and one hand, gun in the other hand ready to point. Another coil smashed into me. It was like being hit by a whale. I lay half-stunned under several hundred pounds of snake. One striped coil pinned me to the ground. The beast reared over me, blood and pale drops of poison running down its shattered jaws. If the poison hit my skin, it would kill me. There was too much of it not to.

I lay flat on my back with the snake writhing across me and fired at it. I just kept squeezing the trigger as the head rushed down on me.

Something hit the snake. Something covered in fur dug teeth and claws into the snake's neck. It was a werewolf with furry, man-shaped arms. The cobra reared, pressing me under its weight. The smooth belly scales pushed at my nearly naked upper body like a giant hand, squeezing. It wasn't going to eat me, it was going to crush me to death.

I screamed and fired into the snake's body. The gun clicked empty. Shit!

Jean-Claude appeared over me. His pale, lace-covered hands lifted the coil off me as if it wasn't a thousand pounds of muscle. I scooted backwards on hands and feet. I crab-walked until I hit the edge of the ring, then I popped the empty clip and got the extra out of my sport bag. I didn't remember firing all thirteen rounds, but I must have. I jacked a round into the chamber, and I was ready to rock and roll.

Jean-Claude was elbow deep in snake. He pulled a piece of glistening spine out of the meat, splitting the snake apart.

Yasmeen was tearing at the giant snake like a kid with taffy. Her face and upper body were bathed in blood. She pulled a long piece of snake intestine out and laughed.

I had never really seen vampires use every bit of their inhuman strength. I sat on the edge of the ring with my loaded gun and just watched.

The black shapeshifter was still in human form. She had gotten a knife from somewhere and was happily carving the snake up.

The cobra whipped its head into the ground, sending the werewolf rolling. The snake reared and came smashing down. Its ruined jaws plunged into the black woman's shoulder. She screamed. One fang came out the back of her dress. Poison squirted from the fang, splashing onto the ground. Poison and blood soaked into the back of her dress.

I moved forward, gun ready, but I hesitated. The cobra was flinging its head from side to side, trying to shake the woman off. The fang was too deeply imbedded and the mouth too damaged. The cobra was trapped, and so was the woman.

I wasn't sure I could hit the snake's head without hitting her. The woman was screaming, shrieking. Her hands clawed helplessly at the snake. She'd dropped her knife somewhere.

A blond vampire grabbed the black woman. The snake reared back, lifting the woman in his jaws, worrying her like a dog with a toy. She shrieked.

The werewolf jumped on the snake's neck, riding it like a wild horse. There was no way to shoot without hitting someone now. Dammit. I had to just stand there, watching.

The man from the bed was running across the ring. Had it taken him that long to slip into the grey sweat pants and zippered jacket? The jacket was unzipped and flapped as he ran, exposing most of his tanned chest. He was unarmed as far as I could tell. What the hell did he think he could do? Dammit.

He knelt beside the two men who had been alive when all the shit started. He dragged one of them away from the fight. It was good thinking.

Jean-Claude grabbed the woman. He gripped the fang that speared her shoulder and snapped it off. The crack was loud as a rifle shot. The woman's shoulder stretched away from her body, bones and ligaments snapping. She gave one last shriek and went limp. He carried her towards me, laying her on the ground. Her right arm was hanging by strands of muscle. He had freed her from the snake, and damn near pulled her arm off.

"Help her, *ma petite*." He left her at my feet, bleeding and unconscious. I knew some first aid, but Jesus. There was no way to put a tourniquet on the wound. I couldn't splint the arm. It wasn't just broken, it was ripped apart.

A breath of wind oozed through the tent. Something tugged at my gut. I gasped and looked up away from the dying girl. Jean-Claude stood beside the snake. All the vampires were tearing at the body, and still it lived. A wind ruffled the lace on his collar, the black waves of his hair. The wind whispered against my face, pulling my heart up into my throat. The only sound I could hear was the thunder of my own blood beating against my ears.

Jean-Claude moved forward almost gently. And I felt something inside me move with him. It was almost like he held an invisible line to my heart, pulse, blood. My pulse was so fast, I couldn't breathe. What was happening?

He was on the snake, hands digging in the flesh just below the mouth. I felt *my* hands dig into the writhing flesh. *My* hands digging at bone, snapping it. *My* hands shoving in almost to the elbow. It was slick, wet, but not warm. Our hands pushed, then pulled, until our shoulders strained with the effort.

The head tore away to land across the ring. The head flopped, mouth snapping at empty air. The body still struggled, but it was dying now.

I had fallen to the ground beside the wounded woman. The Browning was still in my hand, but it wouldn't have helped me. I could hear again, feel again. My hands weren't covered in blood and gore. They had been Jean-Claude's hands, not mine. Dear God, what was happening to me?

I could still feel the blood on my hands. It was an incredibly powerful sensory memory. God!

Something touched my shoulder. I whirled, gun nearly shoved into the man's face. It was the man in the grey sweats. He was kneeling beside me, hands in the air, his eyes staring at the gun in my hands.

"I'm on your side," he said.

My pulse was still thumping in my throat. I didn't trust myself to speak, so I just nodded and stopped pointing the gun at him.

He took off his sweat jacket. "Maybe we can stop some of the blood with this." He wadded the jacket up and shoved it against the wound.

"She's probably in shock," I said. My voice sounded strange, hollow.

"You don't look so good yourself."

I didn't feel so good either. Jean-Claude had entered my mind, my body. It had been like we were one person. I started to shiver and couldn't stop. Maybe it was shock.

"I called the police and an ambulance," he said.

I stared at him. His face was very strong, high cheekbones, square jaw, but his lips were softer, making it a very sympathetic face. His wavy brown hair fell forward like a curtain around his face. I remembered another man with long brown hair. Another human tied to the vampires. He had died badly, and I hadn't been able to save him.

I caught sight of Marguerite on the far side of the ring, watching. Her eyes were wide, her lips half-parted. She was enjoying herself. God.

The werewolf pulled back from the snake. The shapeshifter looked like a very classy version of every wolfman that had ever stalked the streets of London, except it was naked and had genitalia between its legs. Movie wolfmen were always smooth, sexless as a Barbie doll.

The werewolf's fur was a dark honey color. A blond

werewolf? Was it Stephen? If it wasn't, then he had disappeared, and I didn't think Jean-Claude would allow that.

A voice yelled, "Everybody freeze!" Across the ring were two patrol cops with their guns out. One of them said, "Jesus Christ!"

I put my gun away while they were staring at the dead snake. The body was still twitching, but it was dead. It just takes longer for a reptile's body to know it's dead than most mammals.

I felt light and empty as air. Everything had a faintly unreal quality. It wasn't the snake. It was whatever Jean-Claude had done to me. I shook my head, trying to clear it, to think. The cops were here. I had things I needed to do.

I fished the little plastic ID card out of my sport bag and clipped it to the collar of my jacket. It identified me as a member of the Regional Preternatural Investigation Team. It was almost as good as a badge.

"Let's go talk to the cops before they start shooting."

"The snake's dead," he said.

The wolfman was tearing at the dead thing with a long pointed muzzle, ripping off chunks of meat. I swallowed hard and looked away. "They may not think the snake is the only monster in the ring."

"Oh." He said it very softly, as if the thought had never occurred to him before. What the hell was he doing with the monsters?

I walked towards the police, smiling. Jean-Claude stood there in the middle of the ring, his white shirt so bloody it clung to him like water, outlining the point of one nipple hard against the cloth. Blood was smeared down one side of his face. His arms were crimson to the elbows. The youngest vampire, a woman, had buried her face in the snake's blood. She was scooping the bloody meat into her mouth and sucking on it. The sounds were wet and seemed louder than they should have been.

"My name's Anita Blake. I work with the Regional Preternatural Investigation Team. I've got ID."

"Who's that with you?" The uniform nodded his head

in the man's direction. His gun was still pointed vaguely towards the ring.

I whispered out of the corner of my mouth, "What is your name?"

"Richard Zeeman," he said softly.

Out loud I said, "Richard Zeeman, just an innocent bystander." That last was probably a lie. How innocent could a man be who woke up in a bed surrounded by vampires and shapeshifters?

But the uniform nodded. "What about the rest of them?"

I glanced where he was staring. It didn't look any better. "The manager and some of his people. They waded into the thing to keep it out of the crowd."

"But they ain't human, right?" he said.

"No," I said, "they aren't human."

"Jesus H. Christ, the guys back at the station aren't going to believe this one," his partner said.

He was probably right. I had been here, and I almost didn't believe it. A giant man-eating cobra. Jesus H. Christ indeed.

8

I was sitting in a small hallway that served as the performers' entrance to the big tent. The lighting was permanently dim, as if some of the things rolling through wouldn't like a lot of light. Big surprise there. There were no chairs, and I was getting a little tired of sitting on the floor. I'd given a statement first to a uniform, then to a detective. Then RPIT had arrived and the questioning started all over again. Dolph nodded to me, and Zerbrowski shot at me with his thumb and forefinger. That had been an hour and fifteen minutes ago. I was getting a wee bit tired of being ignored.

Richard Zeeman and Stephen the Werewolf were sitting across from me. Richard's hands were clasped loosely around one knee. He was wearing white Nikes with a blue swoosh, and no socks. Even his ankles were tan. His thick hair brushed the tops of his naked shoulders. His eyes were closed. I could gaze at his muscular upper body as long as I wanted to. His stomach was flat with a triangle of dark hair peeking above the sweat pants. His upper chest was smooth, perfect, no hair at all. I approved.

Stephen was cuddled on the floor, asleep. Bruises blossomed up the left side of his face, black-purple and that raw red color a really bad bruise gets. His left arm was in a sling, but he'd refused to go to the hospital. He was wrapped in a grey blanket that the paramedics had given him. As far as I could tell, it was all he was wearing. I guess he'd lost his clothes when he shapeshifted. The wolfman had been bigger than he was, and the legs had been a very different shape. So the skin-tight jeans and the beautiful cowboy boots were history. Maybe that was why the black shapeshifter had been naked. Had that been why Richard Zeeman was naked, as well? Was he a shapeshifter?

I didn't think so. If he was, he hid it better than anybody I'd ever been around. Besides, if he had been a shapeshifter, why didn't he join the fight against the cobra? He'd done a sensible thing for an unarmed human being; he'd stayed out of the way.

Stephen, who had started out the night looking scrumptious, looked like shit. The long, blond curls clung to his face, wet with sweat. There were dark smudges under his closed eyes. His breathing was rapid and shallow. His eyes were struggling underneath his closed lids. Dream? Nightmare? Do werewolves dream of shapeshifted sheep?

Richard still looked scrumptious, but then a giant cobra hadn't been slamming him into a concrete floor. He opened his eyes, as if he had felt me staring at him. He stared back, brown eyes neutral. We stared at each other without saying anything.

His face was all angles, high-sculpted cheekbones, and firm jaw. A dimple softened the lines of his face and made him a little too perfect for my taste. I've never been comfortable around men that are beautiful. Low self-esteem, maybe. Or maybe Jean-Claude's lovely face had made me appreciate the very human quality of imperfection.

"Is he alright?" I asked.

"Who?"

"Stephen."

He glanced down at the sleeping man. Stephen made a small noise in his sleep, helpless, frightened. Definitely a nightmare.

"Should you wake him?"

"You mean from the dream?" he asked.

I nodded.

He smiled. "Nice thought, but he won't wake up for hours. We could burn the place down around him and he wouldn't move."

"Why not?"

"You really want to know?"

"Sure, I've got nothing better to do right now."

He glanced up the silent hallway. "Good point." He settled back against the wall, bare back searching for a more comfortable piece of wall. He frowned; so much for a comfortable wall.

"Stephen changed back from wolfman to human in less than a two-hour time span." He said it like it explained everything. It didn't.

"So?" I asked.

"Usually a shapeshifter stays in animal form for eight to ten hours, then collapses and changes back to human form. It takes a lot of energy to shapeshift early."

I glanced down at the dreaming shapeshifter. "So this collapse is normal?"

Richard nodded. "He'll be out for the rest of the night."

"Not a great survival method," I said.

"A lot of werewolves bite the dust after collapsing. The human hunters come upon them after they've passed out."

"How do you know so much about lycanthropes?"

"It's my job," he said, "I teach science at a local junior high."

I just stared at him. "You're a junior high science teacher?"

"Yes." He was smiling. "You looked shocked."

I shook my head. "What's a school teacher doing messed up with vampires and werewolves?"

"Just lucky, I guess."

I had to smile. "That doesn't explain how you know about lycanthropes."

"I had a class in college."

I shook my head. "So did I, but I didn't know about shapeshifters collapsing."

"You've got a degree in preternatural biology?" he asked.

"Yep."

"Me, too."

"So how do you know more about lycanthropes than I do?" I said.

Stephen moved in his sleep, flinging his good arm outward. The blanket slid off his shoulder, exposing his stomach and part of a thigh.

Richard drew the blanket back over the sleeping man, covering him, like tucking in a child. "Stephen and I have been friends a long time. I bet you know things about zombies that I never learned in college."

"Probably," I said.

"Stephen's not a teacher, is he?"

"No." He smiled, but it wasn't pleasant. "School boards frown on lycanthropes being teachers."

"Legally, they can't stop you."

"Yeah, right," he said. "They fire-bombed the last teacher who dared to teach their precious children. Lycanthropy isn't contagious while in human form."

"I know that," I said.

He shook his head. "Sorry, it's just a sore topic with me."

My pet project was rights for zombies; why shouldn't Richard have a pet project? Fair hiring practices for the furry. It worked for me.

"You are being tactful, *ma petite*. I would not have thought it of you." Jean-Claude was in the hallway. I hadn't heard him walk up. But I'd been distracted, talking with Richard. Yeah, that was it.

"Could you stamp your feet next time? I'm getting sick of you sneaking up on me."

"I wasn't sneaking, *ma petite*. You were distracted talking to our handsome Mr. Zeeman." His voice was pleasant, mild as honey, and yet there was a threat to it. You could feel it like a cold wind down your spine.

"What's wrong, Jean-Claude?" I asked.

"Wrong? What could possibly be wrong?" Anger and some bitter amusement flowed through his voice.

"Cut it out, Jean-Claude."

"Whatever could be the matter, *ma petite*?"

"You're angry; why?"

"My human servant does not know my every mood.

Shameful." He knelt beside me. The blood on his white shirt had dried to a brownish stain that took up most of the shirt front. The lace at his sleeves looked like crumpled brown flowers. "Do you lust after Richard because he's handsome, or because he's human?" His voice was almost a whisper, intimate as if he'd said something entirely different. Jean-Claude whispered better than anyone else I knew.

"I don't lust after him."

"Come, come, *ma petite*. No lies." He leaned towards me, long-fingered hand reaching for my cheek. There was dried blood on his hand.

"You've got blood under your fingernails," I said.

He flinched, his hand squeezing into a fist. Point for my side. "You reject me at every turn. Why do I put up with it?"

"I don't know," I said, truthfully. "I keep hoping you'll get tired of me."

"I am hoping to have you with me forever, *ma petite*. I would not make the offer if I thought I would grow bored."

"I think I would get tired of you," I said.

His eyes widened a bit. I think it was real surprise. "You are trying to taunt me."

I shrugged. "Yes, but it's still the truth. I'm attracted to you, but I don't love you. We don't have stimulating conversations. I don't go through my day saying 'I must remember to share that joke with Jean-Claude, or tell him about what happened at work tonight.' I ignore you when you let me. The only things we have in common are violence and the dead. I don't think that's much to base a relationship on."

"My, aren't we the philosopher tonight." His midnight blue eyes were only inches from mine. The eyelashes looked like black lace.

"Just being honest."

"We wouldn't want you to be less than honest," he said. "I know how you despise lies." He glanced at Richard. "How you despise monsters."

"Why are you angry with Richard?"

"Am I?" he said.

"You know damn well you are."

"Perhaps, Anita, I am realizing that the one thing you want is the one thing I cannot give you."

"And what do I want?"

"Me to be human," he said softly.

I shook my head. "If you think your only shortcoming is being a vampire, you're wrong."

"Really?"

"Yeah. You're an egotistical, overbearing bully."

"A bully?" He sounded genuinely surprised.

"You want me, so you can't believe that I don't want you. Your needs, your desires are more important than anyone else's."

"You are my human servant, *ma petite*. It makes our lives complicated."

"I am not your human servant."

"I have marked you, Anita Blake. You are my human servant."

"No," I said. It was a very firm no, but my stomach was tight with the thought that he was right, and I would never be free of him.

He stared at me. His eyes were as normal as they ever got, dark, blue, lovely. "If you had not been my human servant, I could not have defeated the snake god so easily."

"You mind-raped me, Jean-Claude. I don't care why you did it."

A look of distaste spread across his face. "If you choose the word rape, then you know that I am not guilty of that particular crime. Nikolaos forced herself on you. She tore at your mind, *ma petite*. If you had not carried two of my marks, she would have destroyed you."

Anger was bubbling up from my gut, spreading up my back and into my arms. I had this horrible urge to hit him. "And because of the marks you can enter my mind, take me over. You told me it made mind games harder on me, not easier. Did you lie about that, too?"

"My need was great tonight, Anita. Many people would have died if the creature had not been stopped. I drew power where I could find it."

"From me."

"Yes, you are my human servant. Just by being near me you increase my power. You know that."

I had known that, but I hadn't known he could channel power through me like an amplifier. "I know I'm some sort of witch's familiar for you."

"If you would allow the last two marks, it would be more than that. It would be a marriage of flesh, blood, and spirit."

"I notice you didn't say soul," I said.

He made an exasperated sound low in his throat. "You are insufferable." He sounded genuinely angry. Goody.

"Don't you ever force your way into my mind again."

"Or what?" The words were a challenge, angry, confused.

I was on my knees beside him nearly spitting into his face. I had to stop and take a few deep breaths to keep from screaming at him. I spoke very calmly, low and angry. "If you ever touch me like that again, I will kill you."

"You will try." His face was nearly pressed against mine. As if when he inhaled, he would bring me to him. Our lips would touch. I remembered how soft his lips were. How it felt to be pressed against his chest. The roughness of his cross-shaped burn under my fingers. I jerked back, and felt almost dizzy.

It had only been one kiss, but the memory of it burned along my body like every bad romance novel you'd ever read. "Leave me alone!" I hissed it in his face, hands balled into fists. "Damn you! Damn you!"

The office door opened, and a uniformed officer stuck his head out. "There a problem out here?"

We turned and stared at him. I opened my mouth to tell him exactly what was wrong, but Jean-Claude spoke first. "No problem, officer."

It was a lie, but what was the truth? That I had two

vampire marks on me and was losing my soul a piece
at a time. Not something I really wanted to be common
knowledge. The police sort of frown on people who have
close ties with the monsters.

The officer was looking at us, waiting. I shook my head.
"Nothing's wrong, officer. It's just late. Could you ask
Sergeant Storr if I can go home now?"

"What's the name?"

"Anita Blake."

"Storr's pet animator?"

I sighed. "Yeah, that Anita Blake."

"I'll ask." The uniform stared at the three of us for a
minute. "You got anything to add to this?" He was speaking
to Richard.

"No."

The uniform nodded. "Okay, but keep whatever isn't
happening to a dull roar."

"Of course. Always glad to cooperate with the police,"
Jean-Claude said.

He nodded his thanks and went back into the office.
We were left kneeling in the hallway. The shapeshifter
was still asleep on the floor. His breathing made a quiet
noise that didn't so much fill the silence as emphasize it.
Richard was motionless, dark eyes staring at Jean-Claude.
I was suddenly very aware that Jean-Claude and I were only
inches apart. I could feel the line of his body like warmth
against my skin. His eyes flicked from my face down my
body. I was still wearing only a bra underneath the unzipped
jacket.

Goosebumps rolled up my arms and down my chest. My
nipples hardened as if he had touched them. My stomach
clenched with a need that had nothing to do with blood.

"Stop it!"

"I am doing nothing, *ma petite*. It is your own desire that
rolls over your skin, not mine."

I swallowed and had to look away from him. Okay, I
lusted after him. Great, fine, it didn't mean a thing. Ri-ight.
I scooted away from him, putting my back to the wall, not

looking at him as I spoke. "I came here tonight for information, not to play footsie with the Master of the City."

Richard was just sitting there, meeting my eyes. There was no embarrassment, just interest, as if he didn't know quite what I was. It wasn't an unfriendly look.

"Footsie," Jean-Claude said. I didn't need to see his face to hear the smile in his voice.

"You know what I mean."

"I've never heard it called 'footsie' before."

"Stop doing that."

"What?"

I glared at him, but his eyes were sparkling with laughter. A slow smile touched his lips. He looked very human just then.

"What did you want to discuss, *ma petite*? It must be something very important to make you come near me voluntarily."

I searched his face for mockery, or anger, or anything, but his face was as smooth and pleasant as carved marble. The smile, the sparkling humor in his eyes, was like a mask. I had no way of telling what lay underneath. I wasn't even sure I wanted to know.

I took a deep breath and let it out slowly through my mouth. "Alright. Where were you last night?" I looked at his face, trying to catch any change of expression.

"Here," he said.

"All night?"

He smiled. "Yes."

"Can you prove it?"

The smile widened. "Do I need to?"

"Maybe," I said.

He shook his head. "Coyness, from you, *ma petite*. It does not become you."

So much for being slick and trying to pull information from the Master. "Are you sure you want this discussed in public?"

"You mean Richard?"

"Yes."

"Richard and I have no secrets from one another, *ma petite*. He is my human hands and eyes, since you refuse to be."

"What's that mean? I thought you could only have one human servant at a time."

"So you admit it." His voice held a slow curl of triumph.

"This isn't a game, Jean-Claude. People died tonight."

"Believe me, *ma petite*, whether you take the last marks and become my servant in more than name is no game to me."

"There was a murder last night," I said. Maybe if I concentrated just on the crime, on my job, I could avoid the verbal pitfalls.

"And?" he prompted.

"It was a vampire victim."

"Ah," he said, "my part in this becomes clear."

"I'm glad you find it funny," I said.

"Dying from vampire bites is only temporarily fatal, *ma petite*. Wait until the third night when the victim rises, then question him." The humor died from his eyes. "What is it that you are not telling me?"

"I found at least five different bite radiuses on the victim."

Something flickered behind his eyes. I wasn't sure what, but it was real emotion. Surprise, fear, guilt? Something.

"So you are looking for a rogue master vampire."

"Yep. Know any?"

He laughed. His whole face lit up from the inside, as if someone had lit a candle behind his skin. In one wild moment he was so beautiful, it made my chest ache. But it wasn't a beauty that made me want to touch it. I remembered a Bengal tiger that I'd seen once in a zoo. It was big enough to ride on like a pony. Its fur was orange, black, cream, oyster-shell white. Its eyes were gold. The heavy paws wider than my outspread hand paced, paced, back and forth, back and forth, until it had worn a path in the dirt. Some genius had put one barred wall so close to the fence that held back the crowd, I could have reached through and touched the tiger easily. I had to ball my hands into fists and shove them in my pockets to keep from reaching through those bars and petting that tiger. It was so close, so beautiful, so wild, so . . . tempting.

I hugged my knees to my chest, hands clasped tight together. The tiger would have taken my hand off, and yet there was that small part of me that regretted not reaching through the bars. I watched Jean-Claude's face, felt his laughter like velvet running down my spine. Would part of me always wonder what it would have been like if I had just said yes? Probably. But I could live with it.

He was staring at me, the laughter dying from his eyes like the last bit of light seeping from the sky. "What are you thinking, *ma petite*?"

"Can't you read my mind?" I asked.

"You know I cannot."

"I don't know anything about you, Jean-Claude, not a bloody thing."

"You know more about me than anyone else in the city."

"Yasmeen included?"

He lowered his eyes, almost embarrassed. "We are very old friends."

"How old?"

He met my eyes, but his face was empty, blank. "Old enough."

"That's not an answer," I said.

"No," he said, "it is an evasion."

So he wasn't going to answer my question; what else was new? "Are there any other master vampires in town besides you, Malcolm, and Yasmeen?"

He shook his head. "Not to my knowledge."

I frowned. "What's that supposed to mean?"

"Exactly what I said."

"You're the Master of the City. Aren't you supposed to know?"

"Things are a little unsettled, *ma petite*."

"Explain that."

He shrugged, and even in the bloodstained shirt it looked graceful. "Normally, as Master of the City, all other lesser master vampires would need my permission to stay in the city, but"—he shrugged again—"there are those who think I am not strong enough to hold the city."

"You've been challenged?"

"Let us just say I am expecting to be challenged."

"Why?" I asked.

"The other masters were afraid of Nikolaos," he said.

"And they're not afraid of you." It wasn't a question.

"Unfortunately, no."

"Why not?"

"They are not as easily impressed as you are, *ma petite*."

I started to say I wasn't impressed, but it wasn't true. Jean-Claude could smell it when I lied, so why bother?

"So there could be another master in the city without your knowledge."

"Yes."

"Wouldn't you sort of sense each other?"

"Perhaps, perhaps not."

"Thanks for clearing that up."

He rubbed fingertips across his forehead as if he had a headache. Did vampires get headaches? "I cannot tell you what I do not know."

"Would the . . ." I groped for a word, and couldn't find one—"more mundane vampires be able to kill someone without your permission?"

"Mundane?"

"Just answer the damn question."

"Yes, they could."

"Would five vampires hunt in a pack without a master vampire to referee?"

He nodded. "Very nice choice of word, *ma petite*, and the answer is no. We are solitary hunters, given a choice."

I nodded. "So either you, Malcolm, Yasmeen, or some mysterious master is behind it."

"Not Yasmeen. She is not strong enough."

"Okay, then you, Malcolm, or a mysterious master."

"Do you really think I have gone rogue?" He was smiling at me, but his eyes held something more serious. Did it matter to him what I thought of him? I hoped not.

"I don't know."

"You would confront me, thinking I might be insane? How indiscreet of you."

"If you don't like the answer, you shouldn't have asked the question," I said.

"Very true."

The office door opened. Dolph came out, notebook in hand. "You can go home, Anita. I'll check the statements with you tomorrow."

I nodded. "Thanks."

"Heh, I know where you live." He smiled.

I smiled back. "Thanks, Dolph." I stood up.

Jean-Claude stood in one smooth motion like he was a puppet pulled up by invisible strings. Richard stood slower, using the wall to stand, as if he were stiff. Standing, Richard was taller than Jean-Claude by at least three inches. Which made Richard six-one. Almost too tall for my taste, but no one was asking me.

"And could we talk to you some more, Jean-Claude?" Dolph said.

Jean-Claude said, "Of course, detective." He walked down the hall. There was a stiffness in the way he moved. Did vampires bruise? Had he been hurt in the fight? Did it matter? No, no, it didn't. In a way Jean-Claude was right; if he had been human, even an egotistical son of a bitch, there might have been possibilities. I'm not prejudiced, but God help me, the man has to at least be alive. Walking corpses, no matter how pretty, are just not my cup of tea.

Dolph held the door for Jean-Claude. Dolph looked back at us. "You're free to go, too, Mr. Zeeman."

"What about my friend Stephen?"

Dolph glanced at the sleeping shapeshifter. "Take him home. Let him sleep it off. I'll talk to him tomorrow." He glanced at his wristwatch. "Make that later today."

"I'll tell Stephen when he wakes up."

Dolph nodded and closed the door. We were alone in the buzzing silence of the hallway. Of course, maybe it was just my own ears buzzing.

"Now what?" Richard said.

"We go home," I said.

"Rashida drove."

I frowned. "Who?"

"The other shapeshifter, the woman whose arm was torn up."

I nodded. "Take Stephen's car."

"Rashida drove us both."

I shook my head. "So you're stranded."

"Looks that way."

"You could call a cab," I said.

"No money." He almost smiled.

"Fine; I'll drive you home."

"And Stephen?"

"And Stephen," I said. I was smiling and I didn't know why, but it was better than crying.

"You don't even know where I live. It could be Kansas City."

"If it's a ten-hour drive, you're on your own," I said. "But if it's reasonable, I'll drive you."

"Is Meramec Heights reasonable?"

"Sure."

"Let me get the rest of my clothes," he asked.

"You look fully dressed to me," I said.

"I've got a coat around here somewhere."

"I'll wait here," I said.

"You'll watch Stephen?" Something like fear crossed his face, filled his eyes.

"What are you afraid of?" I asked.

"Airplanes, guns, large predators, and master vampires."

"I agree with two out of four," I said.

"I'll go get my coat."

I slid down to sit beside the sleeping werewolf. "We'll be waiting."

"Then I'll hurry." He smiled when he said it. He had a very nice smile.

Richard came back wearing a long black coat. It looked like real leather. It flapped like a cape around his bare chest. I liked the way the leather framed his chest. He buttoned the coat and tied the leather belt tight. The black leather went with the long hair and handsome face; the grey sweats and Nikes did not. He knelt and picked Stephen up in his arms, then stood. The leather creaked as his upper arms strained. Stephen was my height and probably didn't weigh twenty pounds more than I did. Petite. Richard carried him like he wasn't heavy.

"My, my, grandmother, what strong arms you have."

"Is my line, 'The better to hold you with'?" He was looking at me very steadily.

I felt heat creeping up my face. I hadn't meant to flirt, not on purpose. "You want a ride, or not?" My voice was rough, angry with embarrassment.

"I want a ride," he said quietly.

"Then can the sarcasm."

"I wasn't being sarcastic."

I stared up at him. His eyes were perfectly brown like chocolate. I didn't know what to say, so I didn't say anything. A tactic I should probably use more often.

I turned and walked away, fishing my car keys out as I moved. Richard followed behind. Stephen snuffled against his chest, pulling the blanket close in his sleep.

"Is your car very far?"

"A few blocks; why?"

"Stephen isn't dressed for the cold."

I frowned at him. "What, you want me to drive the car around and pick you up?"

"That would be very nice," he said.

I opened my mouth to say no, then closed it. The thin blanket wasn't much protection, and some of Stephen's injuries were from saving my life. I could drive the car around.

I satisfied myself with grumbling under my breath, "I

can't believe I'm a door-to-door taxi for a werewolf."

Richard either didn't hear me, or chose to ignore it. Smart, handsome, junior high science teacher, degree in preternatural biology, what more can I ask for? Give me a minute and I'd think of something.

9

The car rode in its own tunnel of darkness. The headlights were a moving circle of light. The October night closed behind the car like a door.

Stephen was asleep in the back seat of my Nova. Richard sat in the passenger seat, half-turned in his seat belt to look at me. It was just polite to look at someone when you talk to them. But I felt at a disadvantage because I had to watch the road. All he had to do was stare at me.

"What do you do in your spare time?" Richard asked.

I shook my head. "I don't have spare time."

"Hobbies?"

"I don't think I have any of those, either."

"You must do something besides shoot large snakes in the head," he said.

I smiled and glanced at him. He leaned towards me as much as the seat belt would allow. He was smiling, too, but there was something in his eyes, or his posture, that said he was serious. Interested in what I would say.

"I'm an animator," I said.

He clasped his hands together, left elbow propped on the back of the seat. "Okay, when you're not raising the dead, what do you do?"

"Work on preternatural crimes with the police, mostly murders."

"And?" he said.

"And I execute rogue vampires."

"And?"

"And nothing," I said. I glanced at him again. In the dark I couldn't see his eyes, their color was too dark for that, but I could feel his gaze. Probably imagination. Yeah. I'd been hanging around Jean-Claude too long. The smell of Richard's leather coat mingled with a faint whiff of his cologne. Something expensive and sweet. It went very nicely with the smell of leather.

"I work. I exercise. I go out with friends." I shrugged. "What do you do when you're not teaching?"

"Scuba diving, caving, bird watching, gardening, astronomy." His smile was a dim whiteness in the near dark.

"You must have a lot more free time than I do."

"Actually, the teacher always has more homework than the students," he said.

"Sorry to hear that."

He shrugged, the leather creaked and slithered over his skin. Good leather always moved like it was still alive.

"Do you watch TV?" he asked.

"My television broke two years ago, and I never replaced it."

"You must do something for fun."

I thought about it. "I collect toy penguins." The minute I said it, I wished I hadn't.

He grinned at me. "Now we're getting somewhere. The Executioner collects stuffed toys. I like it."

"Glad to hear it." My voice sounded grumpy even to me.

"What's wrong?" he said.

"I'm not very good at small talk," I said.

"You were doing fine."

No, I wasn't, but I wasn't sure how to explain it to him. I didn't like talking about myself to strangers. Especially strangers with ties to Jean-Claude.

"What do you want from me?" I said.

"I'm just passing the time."

"No, you weren't." His shoulder-length hair had fallen around his face. He was taller, thicker, but the outline was familiar. He looked like Phillip in the shadowed dark.

Phillip was the only other human being I'd ever seen with the monsters.

Phillip sagged in the chains. Blood poured in a bright red flood down his chest. It splattered onto the floor, like rain. Torchlight glittered on the wet bone of his spine. Someone had ripped his throat out.

I staggered against the wall as if someone had hit me. I couldn't get enough air. Someone kept whispering, "Oh, God, oh, God," over and over, and it was me. I walked down the steps with my back pressed against the wall. I couldn't take my eyes from him. Couldn't look away. Couldn't breathe. Couldn't cry.

The torchlight reflected in his eyes, giving the illusion of movement. A scream built in my gut and spilled out my throat. "Phillip!"

Something cold slithered up my spine. I was sitting in my car with the ghost of guilty conscience. It hadn't been my fault that Phillip died. I certainly didn't kill him, but...but I still felt guilty. Someone should have saved him, and since I was the last one with a chance to do it, it should have been me. Guilt is a many splendored thing.

"What do you want from me, Richard?" I asked.

"I don't want anything," he said.

"Lies are ugly things, Richard."

"What makes you think I'm lying?"

"Finely honed instinct," I said.

"Has it really been that long since a man tried to make polite small talk with you?"

I started to look at him, and decided not to. It had been that long. "The last person who flirted with me was murdered. It makes a girl a little cautious."

He was quiet for a minute. "Fair enough, but I still want to know more about you."

"Why?"

"Why not?"

He had me there. "How do I know Jean-Claude didn't tell you to make friends?"

"Why would he do that?"

I shrugged.

"Okay, let's start over. Pretend we met at the health club."

"Health club?" I said.

He smiled. "Health club. I thought you looked great in your swimsuit."

"Sweats," I said.

He nodded. "You looked cute in your sweats."

"I liked looking great better."

"If I get to imagine you in a swimsuit, you can look great; sweats only get cute."

"Fair enough."

"We made pleasant small talk and I asked you out."

I had to look at him. "Are you asking me out?"

"Yes, I am."

I shook my head and turned back to the road. "I don't think that's a good idea."

"Why not?" he asked.

"I told you."

"Just because one person got killed on you doesn't mean everyone will."

I gripped the steering wheel tight enough to make my hands hurt. "I was eight when my mother died. My father remarried when I was ten." I shook my head. "People go away and they don't come back."

"Sounds scary." His voice was soft and low.

I didn't know what had made me say that. I didn't usually talk about my mother to strangers, or anybody else for that matter. "Scary," I said softly. "You could say that."

"If you never let anyone get close to you, you don't get hurt, is that it?"

"There are also a lot of very jerky men in the twenty-one-to-thirty age group," I said.

He grinned. "I'll give you that. Nice-looking, intelligent, independent women are not exactly plentiful either."

"Stop with the compliments, or you'll have me blushing."

"You don't strike me as someone who blushes easily."

A picture flashed in my mind. Richard Zeeman naked beside the bed, struggling into his sweat pants. It hadn't embarrassed me at the time. It was only now, with him so warm and close in the car, that I thought about it. A warm flush crept up my face. I blushed in the dark, glad he couldn't see. I didn't want him to know I was thinking about what he looked like without his clothes on. I don't usually do that. Of course, I don't usually see a man buck naked before I've even gone out on a date. Come to think of it, I didn't see men naked on dates either.

"We're in the health club, sipping fruit juice, and I ask you out."

I stared very hard at the road. I kept flashing on the smooth line of his thigh and lower things. It was embarrassing, but the harder I tried not to think about it, the clearer the picture seemed to get.

"Movies and dinner?" I said.

"No," he said. "Something unique. Caving."

"You mean crawling around in a cave on a first date?"

"Have you ever been caving?"

"Once."

"Did you enjoy it?"

"We were sneaking up on bad guys at the time. I didn't think much about enjoying it."

"Then you have to give it another chance. I go caving at least twice a month. You get to wear your oldest clothes and get really dirty, and no one tells you not to play in the mud."

"Mud?" I said.

"Too messy for you?"

"I was a bio-lab assistant in college; nothing's too messy for me."

"At least you can say you get to use your degree in your work."

I laughed. "True."

"I use my degree, too, but I went in for educating the munchkins."

"Do you like teaching?"

"Very much." Those two words held a warmth and excitement that you didn't hear much when people talked about their work.

"I like my job, too."

"Even when it forces you to play with vampires and zombies?"

I nodded. "Yeah."

"We're sitting in the juice bar, and I've just asked you out. What do you say?"

"I should say no."

"Why?"

"I don't know."

"You sound suspicious."

"Always," I said.

"Never taking a chance is the worst failure of all, Anita."

"Not dating is a choice, not a failure." I was feeling a wee bit defensive.

"Say you'll go caving this weekend." The leather coat crinkled and moved as he tried to move closer to me than the seat belt would allow. He could have reached out and touched me. Part of me wanted him to, which was sort of embarrassing all on its own.

I started to say no, then realized I wanted to say yes. Which was silly. But I was enjoying sitting in the dark with the smell of leather and cologne. Call it chemistry, instant lust, whatever. I liked Richard. He flipped my switch. It had been a long time since I had liked anybody.

Jean-Claude didn't count. I wasn't sure why, but he didn't. Being dead might have something to do with that.

"Alright, I'll go caving. When and where?"

"Great. Meet in front of my house at, say, ten o'clock on Saturday."

"Ten in the morning?" I said.

"Not a morning person?" he asked.

"Not particularly."

"We have to start early, or we won't get to the end of the cave in one day."

"What do I wear?"

"Your oldest clothes. I'll be dressed in coveralls over jeans."

"I've got coveralls." I didn't mention that I used my coveralls to keep blood off my clothes. Mud sounded a lot more friendly.

"Great. I'll bring the rest of the equipment you need."

"How much more equipment do I need?"

"A hard hat, a light, maybe knee pads."

"Sounds like a boffo first date," I said.

"It will be," he said. His voice was soft, low, and somehow more private than just sitting in my car. It wasn't Jean-Claude's magical voice, but then what was?

"Turn right here," he said, pointing to a side street. "Third house on the right."

I pulled into a short, blacktopped driveway. The house was half brick and some pale color. It was hard to tell in the dark. There were no streetlights to help you see. You forget how dark the night can be without electricity.

Richard unbuckled his seat belt and opened the door. "Thanks for the ride."

"Do you need help getting him inside?" My hand was on the key as I asked.

"No, I got it. Thanks, though."

"Don't mention it."

He stared at me. "Did I do something wrong?"

"Not yet," I said.

He smiled, a quick flash in the darkness. "Good." He unlocked the back door behind him, and got out of the car. He leaned in and scooped Stephen up, holding the blanket close so it didn't slide off. He lifted with his legs more than his back; weightlifting will teach you that. A human body is a lot harder to lift than even free weights. A body just isn't balanced as well as a barbell.

Richard shut the car door with his back. The back door clicked shut, and I unbuckled my seat belt so I could lock the doors. Through the still-open passenger side door Richard was watching me. Over the idling of the car's engine his voice carried, "Locking out the boogeymen?"

"You never know," I said.

He nodded. "Yeah." There was something in that one word that was sad, wistful, innocence lost. It was nice to talk with another person who understood. Dolph and Zerbrowski understood the violence and the nearness of death, but they didn't understand the monsters.

I closed the door and scooted back behind the steering wheel. I buckled my seat belt and put the car in gear. The headlights sparkled over Richard, Stephen's hair like a yellow splash in his arms. Richard was still staring at me. I left him in the dark in front of his house with the singing of autumn crickets the only sound.

10

I pulled up in front of my apartment building at a little after 2:00 A.M. I'd planned to be in bed a long time before this. The new cross-shaped burn was a burning, acid-eating ache. It made my whole chest hurt. My ribs and stomach were sore, stiff. I turned on the dome light in the car and unzipped the leather jacket. In the yellow light bruises were blossoming across my skin. For a minute I couldn't think how I'd gotten hurt; then I remembered the crushing weight of the snake crawling over me. Jesus. I was lucky it was bruises and not broken ribs.

I clicked off the light and zipped the jacket back up. The shoulder straps were chafing on my bare skin, but the burn hurt so much more that the bruises and the chafing seemed pretty darn minor. A good burn will take your mind off everything else.

The light that usually burned over the stairs was out. Not the first time. I'd have to call the office once it opened for the day and report it, though. If you didn't report it, it didn't get fixed.

I was three steps up before I saw the man. He was sitting at the head of the stairs waiting for me. Short blond hair, pale in the darkness. His hands sat on the top of his knees, palms up to show that he didn't have a weapon. Well, that he didn't have a weapon *in his hands*. Edward always had a weapon unless someone had taken it away from him.

Come to think of it, so did I.

"Long time no see, Edward."

"Three months," he said. "Long enough for my broken arm to heal completely."

I nodded. "I got my stitches out about two months ago."

He just sat on the steps looking down at me.

"What do you want, Edward?"

"Couldn't it be a social call?" He was laughing at me, quietly.

"It's two o'clock in the freaking morning; it better not be a social call."

"Would you rather it was business?" His voice was soft, but it carried.

I shook my head. "No, no." I never wanted to be business for Edward. He specialized in killing lycanthropes, vampires, anything that used to be human and wasn't anymore. He'd gotten bored with killing people. Too easy.

"Is it business?" My voice was steady, no tremble. Good for me. I could draw the Browning, but if we ever drew down on each other for real, he'd kill me. Being friends with Edward was like being friends with a tame leopard. You could pet it and it seemed to like you, but you knew deep down that if it ever got hungry enough, or angry enough, it would kill you. Kill you and eat the flesh from your bones.

"Just information tonight, Anita, no problems."

"What sort of information?" I asked.

He smiled again. Friendly ol' Edward. Ri-ight.

"Can we go inside and talk about it? It's freezing out here," he said.

"The last time you were in town you didn't seem to need an invitation to break into my apartment."

"You've got a new lock."

I grinned. "You couldn't pick it, could you?" I was genuinely pleased.

He shrugged; maybe it was the darkness, but if it hadn't been Edward, I'd have said he was embarrassed.

"The locksmith told me it was burglarproof," I said.

"I didn't bring my battering ram with me," he said.

"Come on up. I'll fix coffee." I stepped around him. He

stood and followed me. I turned my back on him without worrying. Edward might shoot me someday, but he wouldn't do it in the back after telling me he was just here to talk. Edward wasn't honorable, but he had rules. If he planned to kill me, he'd have announced it. Told me how much people were paying him to off me. Watched the fear slide through my eyes.

Yeah, Edward had rules. He just had fewer of them than most people did. But he never broke a rule, never betrayed his own skewed sense of honor. If he said I was safe for tonight, he meant it. It would have been nice if Jean-Claude had had rules.

The hallway was middle-of-the-night, middle-of-the-week, had-to-get-up-in-the-morning quiet. My day living neighbors were all asnooze in their beds without care. I unlocked the new locks on my door and ushered Edward inside.

"That's a new look for you, isn't it?" he asked.

"What?"

"What happened to your shirt?"

"Oh." Suave comebacks, that's me. I didn't know what to say, or rather, how much to say.

"You've been playing with vampires again," he said.

"What makes you think so?" I asked.

"The cross-shaped burn on your, ah, chest."

Oh, that. Fine. I unzipped the jacket and folded it over the back of the couch. I stood there in my bra and shoulder holster and met his eyes without blushing. Brownie point for me. I undid the belt and slipped out of the shoulder holster, then took it into the kitchen with me. I laid the gun still in its holster on the countertop and got coffee beans out of the freezer, wearing just my bra and jeans. In front of any other male, alive or dead, I would have been embarrassed, but not Edward. There had never been sexual tension between us. We might shoot each other one fine day, but we'd never sleep together. He was more interested in the fresh burn than my breasts.

"How'd it happen?" he asked.

I ground the beans in the little electric spice mill I'd bought for the occasion. Just the smell of freshly ground coffee made me feel better. I put a filter in my Mr. Coffee, poured the coffee in, poured the water in, and pushed the button. This was about as fancy as my cooking skills got.

"I'm going to get a shirt to throw on," I said.

"The burn won't like anything touching it," Edward said.

"I won't button it, then."

"Are you going to tell me how you got burned?"

"Yes." I took my gun and walked into the bedroom. In the back of my closet I had a long-sleeved shirt that had once been purple but had faded to a soft lilac. It was a man's dress shirt and hung down nearly to my knees, but it was comfortable. I rolled the sleeves up to my elbows and buttoned it halfway up. I left it gapping over the burn. I glanced in the mirror and found that most of my cleavage was covered. Perfect.

I hesitated but finally put the Browning Hi-Power in its holster behind the headboard. Edward and I weren't fighting tonight, and anything that came through the door, with its new locks, would have to go through Edward first. I felt pretty safe.

He was sitting on my couch, legs out in front of him crossed at the ankle. He'd sunk down until the top of his shoulders rested on the couch's arm.

"Make yourself at home," I said.

He just smiled. "Are you going to tell me about the vampires?"

"Yes, but I'm having trouble deciding exactly how much to tell you."

The smile widened. "Naturally."

I set out two mugs, sugar, and real cream from the refrigerator. The coffee dripped into the little glass pot. The smell was rich, warm, and thick enough to wrap your arms around.

"How do you like your coffee?"

"Fix it the way you'd fix it for yourself."

I glanced back at him. "No preference?"

He shook his head, still resting against the couch arm.

"Okay." I poured the coffee into the mugs, added three sugars and a lot of cream to each, stirred, and sat them on the two-seater breakfast table.

"You're not going to bring it to me?"

"You don't drink coffee on a white couch," I said.

"Ah." He got up in one smooth motion, all grace and energy. He'd have been very impressive if I hadn't spent most of the night with vampires.

We sat across from each other. His eyes were the color of spring skies, that warm pale blue that still manages to look cold. His face was pleasant, his eyes neutral and watching everything I did.

I told him about Yasmeen and Marguerite. I left out Jean-Claude, the vampire murder, the giant cobra, Stephen the Werewolf, and Rick Zeeman. Which meant it was a very short story.

When I finished Edward sat there, sipping his coffee and staring at me.

I sipped coffee and stared back.

"That does explain the burn," he said.

"Great," I said.

"But you left out a lot."

"How do you know?"

"Because I was following you."

I stared at him, choking on my coffee. When I could talk without coughing, I said, "You were what?"

"Following you," he said. His eyes were still neutral, smile still pleasant.

"Why?"

"I've been hired to kill the Master of the City."

"You were hired for that three months ago."

"Nikolaos is dead; the new master isn't."

"You didn't kill Nikolaos," I said. "I did."

"True; you want half the money?"

I shook my head.

"Then what's your complaint? I got my arm broken helping you kill her."

"And I got fourteen stitches, and we both got vampire bit," I said.

"And cleansed ourselves with holy water," Edward said.

"Which burns likes acid," I said.

Edward nodded, sipped his coffee. Something moved behind his eyes, something liquid and dangerous. His expression hadn't changed, I'd swear to it, but it was suddenly all I could do to meet his eyes.

"Why were you following me, Edward?"

"I was told you would be meeting with the new Master tonight."

"Who told you that?"

He shook his head, that inscrutable smile curling his lips. "I was inside the Circus tonight, Anita. I saw who you were with. You played with the vampires, then you went home, so one of them has to be the Master."

I fought to keep my face blank, too blank, so the effort showed, but the panic didn't show. Edward had been following me, and I hadn't known it. He knew all the vampires I had seen tonight. It wasn't that big a list. He'd figure it out.

"Wait a minute," I said. "You let me go up against that snake without helping me?"

"I came in after the crowd ran out. It was almost over by the time I peeked into the tent."

I drank coffee and tried to think of a way to make this better. He had a contract to kill the Master, and I had led him right to him. I had betrayed Jean-Claude. Why did that bother me?

Edward was watching my face as if he would memorize it. He was waiting for my face to betray me. I worked hard at being blank and inscrutable. He smiled that close, canary-eating grin of his. He was enjoying himself. I was not.

"You only saw four vampires tonight: Jean-Claude, the dark exotic one who must be Yasmeen, and the two blonds. You got names for the blonds?"

I shook my head.

His smile widened. "Would you tell me if you had?"

"Maybe."

"The blonds aren't important," he said. "Neither of them were master vamps."

I stared at him, forcing my face to be neutral, pleasant, attentive, blank. Blank is not one of my better expressions, but maybe if I practiced enough . . .

"That leaves Jean-Claude and Yasmeen. Yasmeen's new in town; that just leaves Jean-Claude."

"Do you really think that the Master of the freaking City would show himself like that?" I put all the scorn I could find into my voice. I wasn't the best actor in the world, but maybe I could learn.

Edward stared at me. "It's Jean-Claude, isn't it?"

"Jean-Claude isn't powerful enough to hold the city. You know that. He's, what, a little over two hundred? Not old enough."

He frowned at me. Good. "It's not Yasmeen."

"True."

"You didn't talk to any other vampires tonight?"

"You may have followed me into the Circus, Edward, but you didn't listen at the door when I met the Master. You couldn't have. The vamps or the shapeshifters would have heard you."

He acknowledged it with a nod.

"I saw the Master tonight, but it wasn't anyone who came down to fight the snake."

"The Master let his people risk their lives and didn't help?" His smile was back.

"The Master of the City doesn't have to be physically present to lend his power, you know that."

"No," he said, "I don't."

I shrugged. "Believe it or not." I prayed, please let him believe.

He was frowning. "You're not usually this good a liar."

"I'm not lying." My voice sounded calm, normal, truthful. Honesty-R-Us.

"If Jean-Claude really isn't the Master, then you know who is?"

The question was a trap. I couldn't answer yes to both questions, but hell, I'd been lying; why stop now? "Yes, I know who it is."

"Tell me," he said.

I shook my head. "The Master would kill me if he knew I talked to you."

"We can kill him together like we did the last one." His voice was terribly reasonable.

I thought about it for a minute. I thought about telling him the truth. Humans First might not be up to tangling with the Master, but Edward was. We could kill him together, a team. My life would be a lot simpler. I shook my head and sighed. Shit.

"I can't, Edward."

"Won't," he said.

I nodded. "Won't."

"If I believe you, Anita, it means I need the name of the Master. It means you are the only human who knows that name." The friendly banter seeped out of his face like melting ice. His eyes were as empty and pitiless as a winter sky. There was no one home that I could talk to.

"You don't want to be the only human who knows the name, Anita."

He was right. I didn't, but what could I say? "Take it or leave it, Edward."

"Save yourself a lot of pain, Anita; tell me the name."

He believed. Hot damn. I lowered my eyes to look down into my coffee so he wouldn't see the flash of triumph in my eyes. When I looked back up, I had my face under control. Me and Meryl Streep.

"I don't give in to threats, you know that."

He nodded. He finished his coffee and sat the mug in the middle of the table. "I will do whatever is necessary to finish this job."

"I never doubted that," I said. He was talking about torturing me for information. He sounded almost regretful, but that wouldn't stop him. One of Edward's primary rules was "Always finish a job."

He wouldn't let a little thing like friendship ruin his perfect record.

"You saved my life, and I saved yours," he said. "It doesn't buy you anything now. You understand that?"

I nodded. "I understand."

"Good." He stood up. I stood up. We looked at each other. He shook his head. "I'll find you tonight, and I'll ask again."

"I won't be bullied, Edward." I was finally getting a little mad. He had come in here asking for information; now he was threatening me. I let the anger show. No acting needed.

"You're tough, Anita, but not that tough." His eyes were neutral, but wary, like those of a wolf I'd seen once in California. I'd just walked around a tree and there it had been, standing. I froze. I had never really understood what neutral meant until then. The wolf didn't give a damn if it hurt me or not. My choice. Threaten it, and the shit hit the fan. Give it room to run, and it would run. But the wolf didn't care; it was prepared either way. I was the one with my pulse in my throat, so startled that I'd stopped breathing. I held my breath and wondered what the wolf would decide. It finally loped off through the trees.

I'd relearned how to breathe and gone back down to the campsite. I had been scared, but I could still close my eyes and see the wolf's pale grey eyes. The wonder of staring at a large predator without any cage bars between us. It had been wonderful.

I stared up at Edward now and knew that this, too, was wonderful in its way. Whether I had known the information or not, I wouldn't have told him. No one bullied me. No one. That was one of *my* rules.

"I don't want to have to kill you, Edward."

He smiled then. "You kill me?" He was laughing at me.

"You bet," I said.

The laughter seeped out of his eyes, his lips, his face, until he stared at me with his neutral, predator eyes.

I swallowed and remembered to take slow, even breaths. He would kill me. Maybe. Maybe not.

"Is the Master worth one of us dying?" I asked.

"It's a matter of principle," he said.

I nodded. "Me, too."

"We know where we stand, then." he said.

"Yeah."

He walked towards the door. I followed, and unlocked the door for him. He paused in the doorway. "You've got until full dark tonight."

"The answer will be the same."

"I know," he said. He walked out without even glancing back. I watched him until he disappeared down the stairs. Then I shut the door and locked it. I stood leaning my back against the door and tried to think of a way out.

If I told Jean-Claude, he might be able to kill Edward, but I didn't give humans to the monsters. Not for any reason. I could tell Edward about Jean-Claude. He might even be able to kill the Master. I could even help him.

I tried picturing Jean-Claude's perfect body riddled with bullets, covered in blood. His face blown away by a shotgun. I shook my head. I couldn't do it. I didn't know why exactly, but I couldn't hand Jean-Claude over to Edward.

I couldn't betray either of them. Which left me ass-deep in alligators. So what else was new?

11

I stood on the shore under a black fringe of trees. The black lake lapped and rolled away into the dark. The moon hung huge and silver in the sky. The moonlight made glittering patterns on the water. Jean-Claude rose from the water. Water was streaming in silver lines from his hair and shirt. His short black hair was in tight curls from being wet. The white shirt clung to his body, making his nipples clear and hard against the cloth. He held out his hand to me.

I was wearing a long, dark dress. It was heavy and hung around me like a weight. Something inside the skirt made it stick out to either side like a tiny malformed hoop. A heavy cloak was pushed back over my shoulders. It was autumn, and the moon was harvest-full.

Jean-Claude said, "Come to me."

I stepped off the shore and sank into the water. It filled the skirt, soaking into the cloak. I tore the cloak off, letting it sink out of sight. The water was warm as bath water, warm as blood. I raised my hand to the moonlight, and the liquid that streamed down it was thick and dark and had never been water.

I stood in the shallows in a dress that I had never imagined, by a shore I did not know, and stared at the beautiful monster as he moved towards me, graceful and covered in blood.

I woke gasping for air, hands clutching at the sheets like a lifeline. "You promised to stay out of my dreams, you son of a bitch," I whispered.

The radio clock beside the bed read 2:00 P.M. I'd been asleep for ten hours. I should have felt better, but I didn't. It was as if I'd been running from nightmare to nightmare, and hadn't really gotten to rest. The only dream I remembered was the last one. If they had all been that bad, I didn't want to remember the rest.

Why was Jean-Claude haunting my dreams again? He'd given his word, but maybe his word wasn't worth anything. Maybe.

I stripped in front of the bathroom mirror. My ribs and stomach were covered in deep, nearly purple bruises. My chest was tight when I breathed, but nothing was broken. The burn on my chest was raw, the skin blackened where it wasn't covered in blisters. A burn hurts all the way down, as if the pain burrows from the skin down to the bone. A burn is the only injury where I am convinced I have nerve endings below skin level. How could it hurt so damn bad, otherwise?

I was meeting Ronnie at the health club at three. Ronnie was short for Veronica. She said it helped her get more work as a private detective if people assumed she was male. Sad but true. We would lift weights and jog. I slipped a black sports bra very carefully over the burn. The elastic pressed in on the bruises, but everything else was okay. I rubbed the burn with antiseptic cream and taped a piece of gauze over it. A man's red t-shirt with the sleeves and neck cut out went over everything else. Black biker pants, jogging socks with a thin red stripe, and black Nike Airs completed the outfit.

The t-shirt showed the gauze, but it hid the bruises. Most of the regulars at the health club were accustomed to my coming in bruised or worse. They didn't ask a lot of questions anymore. Ronnie says I was grumpy at them. Fine with me. I like to be left alone.

I had my coat on, gym bag in hand, when the phone rang. I debated but finally picked it up. "Talk to me," I said.

"It's Dolph."

My stomach tightened. Was it another murder? "What's up, Dolph?"

"We got an ID on the John Doe you looked at."

"The vampire victim?"

"Yeah."

I let out the breath I'd been holding. No more murders, and we were making progress; what could be better?

"Calvin Barnabas Rupert, friends called him Cal. Twenty-six years old, married to Denise Smythe Rupert for four years. No children. He was an insurance broker. We haven't been able to turn up any ties with the vampire community."

"Maybe Mr. Rupert was just in the right place at the wrong time."

"Random violence?" He made it a question.

"Maybe."

"If it was random, we got no pattern, nothing to look at."

"So you're wondering if I can find out if Cal Rupert had any ties to the monsters?"

"Yes," he said.

I sighed. "I'll try. Is that it? I'm late for an appointment."

"That's it. Call me if you find out anything." His voice sounded positively grim.

"You'd tell me if you found another body, wouldn't you?"

He gave a snort of laughter. "Make you come down and measure the damn bites, yeah. Why?"

"Your voice sounds grim."

The laughter dribbled out of his voice. "You're the one who said there'd be more bodies. You changed your mind on that?"

I wanted to say, yes, I've changed my mind, but I didn't. "If there is a pack of rogue vampires, we'll be seeing more bodies."

"Can you think of anything else it could be besides vampires?" he asked.

I thought about it for a minute, and shook my head. "Not a damn thing."

"Fine, talk to you later." The phone buzzed dead in my hand before I could say anything. Dolph wasn't much on hello and good-bye.

I had my back-up gun, a Firestar 9mm, in the pocket of my jacket. There was just no way to wear a holster in exercise clothes. The Firestar only held eight bullets to the Browning's thirteen, but the Browning tended to stick out of my pocket and make people stare. Besides, if I couldn't get the bad guys with eight bullets, another five probably wouldn't help. Of course, there was an extra clip in the zipper pocket of my gym bag. A girl couldn't be too cautious in these crime-ridden times.

12

Ronnie and I were doing power circuits at Vic Tanny's. There were two full sets of machines and no waiting at 3:14 on a Thursday afternoon. I was doing the Hip Abduction/Hip Adduction machine. You pulled a lever on the side and the machine went to different positions. The Hip Adduction position looked vaguely obscene, like a gynecological torture device. It was one of the reasons I never wore shorts when we lifted weights. Ronnie either.

I was concentrating on pressing my thighs together without making the weights clink. Weights clinking means you're not controlling the exercise, or it means you're working with too much weight. I was using sixty pounds. It wasn't too heavy.

Ronnie lay on her stomach using the Leg Curl, flexing her calves over her back, heels nearly touching her butt. The muscles under her calves bunched and coiled under her skin. Neither of us is bulky, but we're solid. Think Linda Hamilton in *Terminator 2*.

Ronnie finished before I did and paced around the machines waiting for me. I let the weights ease back with only the slightest clink. It's okay to clink the weights when you're finished.

We eased out from the machines and started running on the oval track. The track was bordered by a glass wall that showed the blue pool. A lone man was doing laps in goggles and a black bathing cap. The other side was bordered by the free weight room and the aerobics studio. The ends of the track were mirrored so you could always see yourself running face on. On bad days I could have done without watching myself; on good days it was kind of fun. A way to make sure your stride was even, arms pumping.

I told Ronnie about the vampire victim as we ran. Which meant we weren't running fast enough. I increased my pace and could still talk. When you routinely do four miles outside in the St. Louis heat, the padded track at Vic Tanny is just not that big a challenge. We did two laps and went back to the machines.

"What did you say the victim's name was again?" She sounded normal, no strain. I increased our pace to a flat-out run. All talking ceased.

Arm machines this time. Regular Pull-over for me, Overhead Press for Ronnie, then two laps of the track, then trade machines.

When I could talk, I answered her question. "Calvin Rupert," I said. I did twelve pull-overs with 100 pounds. Of all the machines, this one is easiest for me. Weird, huh?

"Cal Rupert?" she asked.

"That's what his friends called him," I said, "Why?"

She shook her head. "I know a Cal Rupert."

I watched her and let my body do the exercise without me. I was holding my breath, which is bad. I remembered to breathe and said, "Tell me."

"When I was asking questions around Humans Against Vampires during those rash of vampire deaths. Cal Rupert belonged to HAV."

"Describe him for me."

"Blond, blue or grey eyes, not too tall, well built, attractive."

There might be more than one Cal Rupert in St. Louis, but what were the odds that they'd look that much alike? "I'll have Dolph check it out, but if he was a member of HAV, it might mean the vampire kill was an execution."

"What do you mean?"

"Some of HAV thinks the only good vampire is a dead vampire." I was thinking of Humans First, Mr. Jeremy

Ruebens's little group. Had they killed a vampire already? Was this retaliation?

"I need to know if Cal was still a member of HAV or if he'd joined a new, more radical group called Humans First."

"Catchy," Ronnie said.

"Can you find out for me? If I go down there asking questions, they'll burn me at the stake."

"Always glad to help my best friend and the police at the same time. A private detective never knows when having the police owe you one may come in handy."

"True," I said.

I got to wait for Ronnie this time. On leg machines she was faster. Upper body was my area. "I'll call Dolph as soon as we're finished here. Maybe it's a pattern? A hell of a coincidence if it's not."

We started around the track and Ronnie said, "So, have you decided what you're wearing to Catherine's Halloween party?"

I glanced at her, nearly stumbling. "Shit," I said.

"I take that to mean you forgot about the party. You were bitching about it only two days ago."

"I've been a little busy, okay?" I said. But it wasn't alright. Catherine Maison-Gillett was one of my best friends. I'd worn a pink prom dress with puff sleeves in her wedding. It had been humiliating. We'd all told the great lie of all bridesmaids. We could cut the dress short and wear it in normal life. No way. Or I could wear it at the next formal occasion I was invited to. How many formals are you invited to once you graduate college? None. At least none where I'd willingly wear a pink, puff-sleeved, hoop-skirted, reject from *Gone With the Wind*.

Catherine was throwing her very first party since the wedding. The Halloween festivities started long before dark so that I could make an appearance. When someone goes to that much trouble, you have to show up. Dammit.

"I made a date for Saturday," I said.

Ronnie stopped running and stared at me in the mirror. I kept running; if she wanted to ask questions she'd have to catch me first. She caught me.

"Did you say date?"

I nodded, saving my breath for running.

"Talk, Anita." Her voice was vaguely threatening.

I grinned at her and told her an edited version of my meeting with Richard Zeeman. I didn't leave out much, though.

"He was naked in a bed the first time you saw him?" She was cheerfully outraged.

I nodded.

"You do meet men in the most interesting places," she said.

We were jogging on the track again. "When's the last time I met a man?"

"What about John Burke?"

"Other than him." Jerks did not count.

She thought about that for a minute. She shook her head. "Too long."

"Yep," I said.

We were on our last machine, the last two laps, then stretching, showers, and done. I didn't really enjoy exercising. Neither did Ronnie. But we both needed to be in good shape so we could run away from the bad guys, or run them down. Though I hadn't chased after many villains lately. I seemed to do a lot more running away.

We moved over to the open area near the racquetball courts and the tanning rooms. It was the only place with enough room to stretch out. I always stretched before and after exercising. I'd had too many injuries not to be careful.

I started rotating the neck slowly; Ronnie followed me. "I guess I'll have to cancel the date."

"Don't you dare," Ronnie said. "Invite him to the party."

I looked at her. "You've got to be kidding. A first date surrounded by people he doesn't know."

"Who do you know besides Catherine?" she asked.

She had a point there. "I've met her new husband."

"You were in the wedding," Ronnie said.

"Oh, yeah."

Ronnie frowned at me. "Be serious, ask him to the party, make plans for the caving next week."

"Two dates with the same man?" I shook my head. "What if we don't like each other?"

"No excuses," Ronnie said. "This is the closest you've been to a date in months. Don't blow it."

"I don't date because I don't have time to date."

"You don't have time to sleep, either, but you manage it," she said.

"I'll do it, but he may say no to the party. I would rather not go myself."

"Why not?"

I gave her a long look. She looked innocent enough. "I'm an animator, a zombie-queen. Having me at a Halloween party is redundant."

"You don't have to tell people what you do for a living."

"I'm not ashamed of it."

"I didn't say you were," Ronnie said.

I shook my head. "Just forget it. I'll make the counteroffer to Richard, then we'll go from there."

"You'll want a sexy outfit for the party now," she said.

"Do not," I said.

She laughed. "Do too."

"Alright, alright, a sexy outfit if I can find one in my size three days before Halloween."

"I'll help you. We'll find something."

She'd help me. We'd find something. It sounded sort of ominous. Pre-date jitters. Who, me?

13

At 5:15 that afternoon I was on the phone to Richard Zeeman. "Hi, Richard, this is Anita Blake."

"Nice to hear your voice." His voice was smiling over the phone; I could almost feel it.

"I forgot that I've got a Halloween party to go to Saturday afternoon. They started the party during daylight so I could make an appearance. I can't not show up."

"I understand," he said. His voice was very carefully neutral—neutral cheerful.

"Would you like to be my date for the party? I have to work Halloween night, of course, but the day could be ours."

"And the caving?"

"A rain check," I said.

"Two dates; this could be serious."

"You're laughing at me," I said.

"Never."

"Shit, do you want to go or not?"

"If you promise to go caving a week from Saturday."

"My solemn word," I said.

"It's a deal." He was quiet on the phone for a minute. "I don't have to wear a costume for this party, do I?"

"Unfortunately, yes," I said.

He sighed.

"Backing out?"

"No, but you owe me two dates for humiliating myself in front of strangers."

I grinned and was glad he couldn't see it. I was entirely too pleased. "Deal."

"What costume are you wearing?" he asked.

"I haven't got one yet. I told you I forgot the party; I meant it."

"Hmm," he said. "I think picking out costumes should tell a lot about a person, don't you?"

"This close to Halloween we'll be lucky to find anything in our size."

He laughed. "I might have an ace up my sleeve."

"What?"

He laughed again. "Don't sound so damn suspicious. I've got a friend who's a Civil War buff. He and his wife do re-creations."

"You mean like dress up?"

"Yes."

"Will they have the right sizes?"

"What size dress do you wear?"

That was a personal question for someone who'd never even kissed me. "Seven," I said.

"I would have guessed smaller."

"I'm too chesty for a six, and they don't make six and a halfs."

"Chesty, woo, woo."

"Stop it."

"Sorry, couldn't resist," he said.

My beeper went off. "Damn."

"What's that sound?"

"My beeper," I said. I pressed the button and it flashed the number—the police. "I have to take it. Can I call you back in a few minutes, Richard?"

"I'll wait with bated breath."

"I'm frowning at the phone, I hope you know that."

"Thanks for sharing that. I'll wait here by the phone. Call me when you're done with (sob) work."

"Cut it out, Richard."

"What'd I do?"

"Bye, Richard, talk to you soon."

"I'll be waiting," he said.

"Bye, Richard." I hung up before he could make any more "pitiful me" jokes. The really sad part was I thought it was cute. Gag me with a spoon.

I called Dolph's number. "Anita?"

"Yeah."

"We got another vampire victim. Looks the same as the first one, except it's a woman."

"Damn," I said softly.

"Yeah, we're over here at DeSoto."

"That's farther south than Arnold," I said.

"So?" he said.

"Nothing, just give me the directions."

He did.

"It'll take me at least an hour to get there," I said.

"The stiff's not going anywhere, and neither are we." He sounded discouraged.

"Cheer up, Dolph, I may have found a clue."

"Talk."

"Veronica Sims recognized the name Cal Rupert. Description matches."

"What are you doing talking to a private detective?" He sounded suspicious.

"She's my workout partner, and since she just gave us our first clue, I'd sound a little more grateful, if I were you."

"Yeah, yeah. Hurrah for the private sector. Now talk."

"A Cal Rupert was a member of HAV about two months ago. The description matches."

"Revenge killings?" he asked.

"Maybe."

"Half of me hopes it's a pattern. At least we'd have some place to start looking." He made a sound between a laugh and a snort. "I'll tell Zerbrowski you found a clue. He'll like that."

"All us Dick Tracy Crimebusters speak police lingo," I said.

"Police lingo?" I could feel the grin over the phone. "You find any more clues, you let us know."

"Aye, aye, Sergeant."

"Can the sarcasm," he said.

"Please, I always use fresh sarcasm, never canned."

He groaned. "Just get your butt out here so we can all go home." The phone went dead. I hung up.

Richard Zeeman answered on the second ring. "Hello."

"It's Anita."

"What's up?"

"The message was from the police. They need my expertise."

"A preternatural crime?" he asked.

"Yeah."

"Is it dangerous?"

"To the person who was killed, yeah."

"You know that's not what I meant," he said.

"It's my job, Richard. If you can't deal with it, maybe we shouldn't date at all."

"Hey, don't get defensive. I just wanted to know if you would be in any personal danger." His voice was indignant.

"Fine. I've got to go."

"What about the costumes? Do you want me call my friend?"

"Sure."

"Will you trust me to pick your costume?" he asked.

I thought about that for a few heartbeats. Did I trust him to get me a costume? No. Did I have time to hunt up a costume on my own? Probably not. "Why not?" I said. "Beggars can't be choosers."

"We'll survive the party and then next week we'll go crawl in the mud."

"I can't wait," I said.

He laughed. "Neither can I."

"I've got to go, Richard."

"I'll have the costumes at your apartment for inspection. I'll need directions."

I gave him directions.

"I hope you like your costume."

"Me too. Talk to you later." I hung the receiver on the pay phone's cradle and stared at it. That had been too easy. Too smooth. He'd probably pick out a terrible costume for me. We'd both have a miserable time and be trapped into a second date with each other. Eek!

Ronnie handed me a can of fruit juice and took a sip of her own. She had cranberry and I had ruby red grapefruit. I couldn't stand cranberry.

"What'd cutesie pie say?"

"Please don't call him that," I said.

She shrugged. "Sorry, it just sort of slipped out." She had the grace to look embarrassed.

"I forgive you, this once."

She grinned, and I knew she wasn't repentant. But I'd ribbed her often enough about her dates. Turnabout is fair play. Payback is a bitch.

14

The sun was sinking in a slash of crimson like a fresh, bleeding wound. Purple clouds were piling up to the west. The wind was strong and smelled like rain.

Ruffo Lane was a narrow gravel road. Barely wide enough for two cars to pass each other. The reddish gravel crunched underfoot. Wind rustled the tall, dry weeds in the ditch. The road disappeared over the rise of a hill. Police cars, marked and plain, were lined up along one side of the road as far as I could see. The road disappeared over the rise of a hill. There were a lot of hills in Jefferson County.

I was already dressed in a clean pair of overalls, black Nikes, and surgical gloves when my beeper went off. I had to scramble at the zipper and drag the damn thing out into the dying light. I didn't have to see the number. I knew it was Bert. It was only a half hour until full dark, if that. My boss was wondering where I was, and why I wasn't at work. I wondered if Bert would really fire me. I stared down at the corpse and wasn't sure I cared.

The woman was curled on her side, arms shielding her naked breasts, as if even in death she was modest. Violent death is the ultimate invasion. She would be photographed, videotaped, measured, cut open, sewn back up. No part of her, inside or out, would be left untouched. It was wrong. We should have been able to toss a blanket over her and leave her in peace, but that wouldn't help us prevent the next killing. And there would be a next one; the second body was proof of that.

I glanced around at the police and the ambulance team,

waiting to take the body away. Except for the body, I
was the only woman. I usually was, but tonight, for some
reason, it bothered me. Her waist-length hair spilled out
into the weeds in a pale flood. Another blonde. Was that
coincidence? Or not? Two was a pretty small sample. If the
next victim was blond, then we'd have a trend.

If all the victims were caucasian, blond, and members of
Humans Against Vampires, we'd have our pattern. Patterns
helped solve the crime. I was hoping for a pattern.

I held a penlight in my mouth and measured the bite
marks. There were no bite marks on the wrists this time.
There were rope burns instead. They'd tied her up, maybe
hung her from the ceiling like a side of beef. There is no
such thing as a good vampire who feeds off humans. Never
believe that a vampire will only take a little. That it won't
hurt. That's like believing your date will pull out in time.
Just trust him. Yeah, right.

There was a neat puncture wound on either side of the
neck. There was a bit of flesh missing from her left breast,
as if something had taken a bite out of her just above the
heart. The bend of her right arm was torn apart. The ball
joint was naked in the thin beam of light. Pinkish ligaments
strained to hold the arm together.

The last serial murderer that I'd worked on had torn the
victims into pieces. I had walked on carpet so drenched
with blood that it squelched underfoot. I had held pieces
of intestine in my hand, looking for clues. It was the new
worst-thing-I'd-ever-seen.

I stared down at the dead woman and was glad she hadn't
been torn apart. And it wasn't because I figured it had been
an easier death, though I hoped it had. And it wasn't
because there were more clues, because there weren't. It
was just that I didn't want to see any more slaughtered
people. I'd had my quota for the year.

There is an art to holding a penlight in your mouth and
measuring wounds without drooling on yourself. I managed. The secret was sucking on the end of the flashlight
from time to time.

The thin beam of the flashlight shone on her thighs. I wanted to see if she had a groin wound like the man. I wanted to be sure this was the work of the same killers. It would be a hell of a coincidence if there were two vampire packs hunting separately, but it was possible. I needed to be as sure as I could that we had just one rogue pack. One was plenty, two was a screaming nightmare. Surely, God would not be that unkind, but just in case . . . I wanted to see if she had a groin wound. The man's hands had shown no rope marks. Either the vampires were getting more organized, or it was a different group.

Her arms had been glued over her chest, tied in place by rigor mortis. Nothing short of an axe was going to move her legs, not until final rigor went away, which would be forty-eight hours or so. I couldn't wait two days, but I didn't want to chop the body into pieces either.

I got down on all fours in front of the corpse. I apologized for what I was about to do, but couldn't think of anything better.

The flashlight's thin beam trembled over her thighs, like a tiny spotlight. I touched the line that separated her legs and pushed my fingers in that line, trying to feel by fingertip if there was a wound there.

It must have looked like I was groping the corpse, but I couldn't think of a more dignified way to do it. I glanced up, trying not to feel the solid rubberiness of her skin. The sun was just a splash of crimson in the west like dying coals. True darkness slipped over the sky like a flood of ink. And the woman's legs moved under my hands.

I jumped. Nearly swallowing the flashlight. Nervous, me? The woman's flesh was soft. It hadn't been a moment ago. The woman's lips were halfparted. Hadn't they been closed before?

This was crazy. Even if she had been a vampire, she wouldn't rise until the third night after death. And she'd died from multiple vampire bites in one massive blood feast. She was dead, just dead.

Her skin shimmered white in the darkness. The sky was

black; if the moon was up in those black-purple clouds, I couldn't see it. Yet her skin shimmered as if touched by moonlight. She wasn't exactly glowing, but it was close. Her hair glimmered like spider silk spread over the grass. She'd just been dead a minute ago; now she was . . . beautiful.

Dolph loomed over me. At six-nine he loomed even when I was standing up; with me kneeling he was gigantic. I stood up, peeled off one surgical glove, and took the penlight out of my mouth. Never touch anything you're likely to put in your mouth after touching the open wounds of a stranger. AIDS, you know. I shoved the penlight into the breast pocket of the coveralls. I took off the other glove and crumpled them both into a side pocket.

"Well?" Dolph said.

"Does she look different to you?" I asked.

He frowned. "What?"

"The corpse; does it look different to you?"

He stared down at the pale body. "Now that you mention it. It looks like she's asleep." He shook his head. "We're going to have to call an ambulance and have a doctor pronounce her dead."

"She's not breathing."

"Would you want the fact that you weren't breathing to be the only criterion?"

I thought about that for a minute. "No, I guess not."

Dolph leafed through his notebook. "You said a person who dies of multiple vampire bites can't rise from the dead as a vampire." He was reading my own words back at me. I was hoist on my petard.

"That's true in most cases."

He stared down at the woman. "But not in this one."

"Unfortunately no," I said.

"Explain this, Anita." He didn't sound happy. I didn't blame him.

"Sometimes even one bite can make a corpse rise as a vampire. I've only read a couple of articles about it. A very powerful master vamp can sometimes contaminate every corpse it touches."

"Where'd you read the articles?"

"The *Vampire Quarterly*."

"Never heard of it," he said.

I shrugged. "I have a degree in preternatural biology; I must be on someone's list for stuff like that." A thought came to me that wasn't pleasant at all. "Dolph."

"Yeah."

"The man, the first corpse, this is its third night."

"It didn't glow in the dark," Dolph said.

"The woman's corpse didn't look bad until full dark."

"You think the man's going to rise?" he asked.

I nodded.

"Shit," he said.

"Exactly," I said.

He shook his head. "Wait a minute. He can still tell us who killed him."

"He won't come back as a normal vamp," I said. "He died of multiple wounds, Dolph; he'll come back as more animal than human."

"Explain that."

"If they took the body to St. Louis City Hospital, then it's safe behind reinforced steel, but if they listened to me, then it's at the regular morgue. Call the morgue and tell them to evacuate the building."

"You're serious," he said.

"Absolutely."

He didn't even argue with me. I was his preternatural expert, and what I said was pretty much gospel until proven otherwise. Dolph didn't ask for your opinion unless he was prepared to act upon it. He was a good boss.

He slipped into his car, nearest to the murder scene of course, and called the morgue.

He leaned out the open car door. "The body was sent to St. Louis City Hospital, routine for all vampire victims. Even ones our preternatural expert tells us are safe." He smiled at me when he said it.

"Call St. Louis City and make sure they've got the body in the vault room."

"Why would they transport the body to the vampire morgue and not put the body in the vault room?" he asked.

I shook my head. "I don't know. But I'll feel better after you call them."

He took a deep breath and let it go. "Okay." He got back on the phone and dialed the number from memory. Shows what kind of year Dolph's been having.

I stood at the open car door and listened. There wasn't much to hear. No one answered.

Dolph sat there listening to the distant ring of the phone. He stared up at me. His eyes asked the question.

"Somebody should be there," I said.

"Yeah," he said.

"The man will rise like a beast," I said. "It'll slaughter everything in its path unless the master that made it comes back to pick it up, or until it's really dead. They're called animalistic vampires. There's no colloquial term for them. They're too rare for that."

Dolph hung up the phone and surged out of the car, yelling, "Zerbrowski!"

"Here, Sarge." Zerbrowski came at a trot. When Dolph yelled, you came running, or else. "How's it going, Blake?"

What was I supposed to say, terrible? I shrugged and said, "Fine."

My beeper went off again. "Dammit, Bert!"

"Talk to your boss," Dolph said. "Tell him to leave you the fuck alone."

Sounded good to me.

Dolph went off yelling orders. The men scrambled to obey. I slid into Dolph's car and called Bert.

He answered on the first ring; not a good sign. "This better be you, Anita."

"And if it's not?" I said.

"Where the hell are you?"

"Murder scene with a fresh body," I said.

That stopped him for a second. "You're missing your first appointment."

"Yeah."

"But I'm not going to yell."

"You're being reasonable," I said. "What's wrong?"

"Nothing except that the newest member of Animators, Inc., is taking your first two appointments. His name is Lawrence Kirkland. Just meet him at the third appointment, and you can take the last three appointments and show him the ropes."

"You hired someone? How'd you find someone so fast? Animators are pretty rare. Especially one who could do two zombies in one night."

"It's my job to find talent."

Dolph slid into the car, and I slid into the passenger seat.

"Tell your boss you've got to go."

"I've got to go, Bert."

"Wait, you have an emergency vampire staking at St. Louis City Hospital."

My stomach clenched up. "What name?"

He paused, reading the name, "Calvin Rupert."

"Shit."

"What's wrong?" he asked.

"When did the call come in?"

"Around three this afternoon, why?"

"Shit, shit, shit."

"What's wrong, Anita?" Bert asked.

"Why was it marked urgent?" Zerbrowski slipped into the back of the unmarked car. Dolph put the car in gear and hit the sirens and lights. A marked car fell into line behind us, lights strobing into the dark. Lights and sirens, wowee.

"Rupert had one of those dying wills," Bert said. "If he even had one vampire bite, he wanted to be staked."

That was consistent with someone who was a member of HAV. Hell, I had it in my will. "Do we have a court order of execution?"

"You only need that after the guy rises as a vampire. We've got permission from the next of kin; just go stake him."

I grabbed the dashboard as we bounced over the narrow road. Gravel pinged against the underside of the car. I cradled the phone receiver between shoulder and chin and slipped into a seat belt.

"I'm on my way to the morgue now," I said.

"I sent John ahead when I couldn't get you," Bert said.

"How long ago?"

"I called him after you didn't answer your beeper."

"Call him back, tell him not to go."

There must have been something in my voice, because he said, "What's wrong, Anita?"

"We can't get any answer at the morgue, Bert."

"So?"

"The vampire may have already risen and killed everybody, and John's walking right into it."

"I'll call him," Bert said. The connection broke, and I shoved the receiver down as we spilled out onto New Highway 21.

"We can kill the vampire when we get there," I said.

"That's murder," Dolph said.

I shook my head. "Not if Calvin Rupert had a dying will."

"Did he?"

"Yeah."

Zerbrowski slammed his fist into the back of the seat. "Then we'll pop the son of a bitch."

"Yeah," I said.

Dolph just nodded.

Zerbrowski was grinning. He had a shotgun in his hands.

"Does that thing have silver shot in it?" I asked.

Zerbrowski glanced at the gun. "No."

"Please, tell me I'm not the only one in this car with silver bullets."

Zerbrowski grinned. Dolph said, "Silver's more expensive than gold. City doesn't have that kind of money."

I knew that, but I was hoping I was wrong. "What do you do when you're up against vampires and lycanthropes?"

Zerbrowski leaned over the back seat. "Same thing we

do when we're up against a gang with Uzi pistols."

"Which is?" I said.

"Be outgunned," he said. He didn't look happy about it. I wasn't too happy about it, either. I was hoping that the morgue attendants had just run, gotten out, but I wasn't counting on it.

15

My vampire kit included a sawed-off shotgun with silver shot, stakes, mallet, and enough crosses and holy water to drown a vampire. Unfortunately, my vampire kit was sitting in my bedroom closet. I used to carry it in the trunk, minus the sawed-off shotgun, which has always been illegal. If I was caught carrying the vampire kit without a court order of execution on me, it was an automatic jail term. The new law had kicked in only weeks before. It was to keep certain overzealous executioners from killing someone and saying, "Gee, sorry." I, by the way, am not one of the overzealous. Honest.

Dolph had cut the sirens about a mile from the hospital. We cruised into the parking lot dark and quiet. The marked car behind us had followed our lead. There was already one marked car waiting for us. The two officers were crouched beside the car, guns in hand.

We all spilled out of the dark cars, guns out. I felt like I'd been shanghaied into a Clint Eastwood movie. I couldn't see John Burke's car. Which meant John checked his beeper more than I did. If the vampire was safely behind metal walls, I promised to answer all beeper messages immediately. Please, just don't let me have cost lives. Amen.

One of the uniforms who had been waiting for us duck-walked to Dolph and said, "Nothing's moved since we got here, Sergeant."

Dolph nodded. "Good. Special forces will be here when they can get to it. We're on the list."

"What do you mean, we're on the list?" I asked.

Dolph looked at me. "Special forces has the silver bullets, and they'll get here as soon as they can."

"We're going to wait for them?" I said.

"No."

"Sergeant, we are supposed to wait for special forces when going into a preternatural situation," the uniform said.

"Not if you're the Regional Preternatural Investigation Team," he said.

"You should have silver bullets," I said.

"I've got a requisition in," Dolph said.

"A requisition, that's real helpful."

"You're a civvie. You get to wait outside. So don't bitch," he said.

"I'm also the legal vampire executioner for the State of Missouri. If I'd answered my beeper instead of ignoring it to irritate Bert, the vampire would be staked already, and we wouldn't be doing this. You can't leave me out of it. It's more my job than it is yours."

Dolph stared at me for a minute or two, then nodded very slowly.

"You should have kept your mouth shut," Zerbrowski said. "And you'd get to wait in the car."

"I don't want to wait in the car."

He just looked at me. "I do."

Dolph started walking towards the doors. Zerbrowski followed. I brought up the rear. I was the police's preternatural expert. If things went badly tonight, I'd earn my retainer.

All vampire victims were brought to the basement of the old St. Louis City Hospital, even those who die in a different county. There just aren't that many morgues equipped to handle freshly risen vampires. They've got a special vault room with a steel reinforced everything and crosses laid on the outside of the door. There's even a feeding tank to take the edge off that first blood lust. Rats, rabbits, guinea pigs. Just a snack to calm the newly risen.

Under normal circumstances the man's body would have been in the vampire room, and there would have been no problem, but I had promised them that he was safe. I was their expert, the one they called to stake the dead. If I said a body was safe, they believed me. And I'd been wrong. God help me, I'd been wrong.

16

St. Louis City Hospital sat like a stubby brick giant in the middle of a combat zone. Walk a few blocks south and you could see Tony Award–winning musicals straight from Broadway. But here we could have been on the dark side of the moon. If the moon had slums.

Broken windows decorated the ground like shattered teeth.

The hospital, like a lot of inner-city hospitals, had lost money, so they had closed it down. But the morgue stayed open because they couldn't afford to move the vampire room.

The room had been designed in the early 1900s when people still thought they could find a cure for vampirism. Lock a vampire in the vault, watch it rise and try to "cure" it. A lot of vamps cooperated because they wanted to be cured. Dr. Henry Mulligan had pioneered the search for a cure. The program was discontinued when one of the patients ate Dr. Mulligan's face.

So much for helping the poor misunderstood vampire.

But the vault room was still used for most vampire victims. Mostly as a precaution, because these days when a vamp rose there was a vampire counsellor waiting to guide the newly risen to civilized vampirehood.

I had forgotten about the vampire counsellor. It was a pioneer program that'd only been in effect a little over a month. Would an older vampire be able to control an animalistic vampire, or would it take a master vampire to control it? I didn't know. I just didn't know.

Dolph had his gun out and ready. Without silver-plated bullets, it was better than spitting at the monster, but barely. Zerbrowski held the shotgun like he knew how to use it. There were four uniformed officers at my back. All with guns, all ready to blast undead ass. So why wasn't I comforted? Because nobody else had any freaking silver bullets, expect me.

The double glass doors swooshed open automatically. Seven guns were trained on the door as it moved. My fingers were all cramped up trying not to shoot the damn door.

One of the uniforms swallowed a laugh. Nervous, who us?

"Alright," Dolph said, "there are civilians in here. Don't shoot any of them."

One of the uniforms was blond. His partner was black and much older. The other two uniforms were in their twenties: one skinny and tall with a prominent Adam's apple; the other short with pale skin and eyes nearly glassy with fear.

Each policeman had a cross-shaped tie tack. They were the latest style and standard issue for the St. Louis police. The crosses would help, maybe even keep them alive.

I hadn't had time to get my crucifix's chain replaced. I was wearing a charm bracelet that dangled with tiny crosses. I was also wearing an anklet chain, not just because it matched the bracelet, but if anything unusual happened tonight, I wanted to have a backup.

It's sort of a tossup which I'd least like to live without, cross or gun. Better to have both.

"You got any suggestions about how we should do this, Anita?" Dolph asked.

It wasn't too long ago that the police wouldn't have been called in at all. The good ol' days when vampires were left to a handful of dedicated experts. Back when you could just stake a vamp and be done with it. I had been one of the few, the proud, the brave, the Executioner.

"We could form a circle, guns pointing out. It would up our chances of not getting snuck up on."

The blond cop said, "Won't we hear it coming?"

"The undead make no noise," I said.

His eyes widened.

"I'm kidding, officer," I said.

"Hey," he said softly. He sounded offended. I guess I didn't blame him.

"Sorry," I said.

Dolph frowned at me.

"I said I was sorry."

"Don't tease the rookies," Zerbrowski said. "I bet this is his first vampire."

The black cop made a sound between a laugh and a snort. "His first day, period."

"Jesus," I said. "Can he wait out in the car?"

"I can handle myself," the blond said.

"It's not that, " I said, "but isn't there some kind of union rule against vampires on the first day?"

"I can take it," he said.

I shook my head. His first fucking day. He should have been out directing traffic somewhere, not playing tag with the walking dead.

"I'll take point," Dolph said. "Anita to my right." He pointed two fingers at the black cop and the blond. "You two on my left." He pointed at the last two uniforms. "Behind Ms. Blake. Zerbrowski, take the back."

"Gee, thanks, Sarge," he muttered.

I almost let it go, but I couldn't. "I'm the only one with silver ammo. I should have point," I said.

"You're a civvie, Anita," Dolph said.

"I haven't been a civvie for years and you know it."

He looked at me for a long second, then nodded. "Take point, but if you get killed, my ass is grass."

I smiled. "I'll try to remember that."

I stepped out in front, a little ahead of the others. They formed a rough circle behind me. Zerbrowski gave me a thumbs-up sign. It made me smile. Dolph gave the barest of nods. It was time to go inside. Time to stalk the monster.

17

The walls were two-tone green. Dark khaki on the bottom, puke green on top. Institutional green, as charming as a sore tooth. Huge steam pipes, higher than my head, covered the walls. The pipes were painted green, too. They narrowed the hallway to a thin passageway.

Electrical conduit pipes were a thinner silver shadow to the steam pipes. Hard to put electricity in a building never designed for it.

The walls were lumpy where they'd been painted over without being scraped first. If you dug at the walls, layer after layer of different color would come up, like the strata in an archaeological dig. Each color had its own history, its own memories of pain.

It was like being in the belly of a great ship. Except instead of the roar of engines, you had the beat of nearly perfect silence. There are some places where silence hangs in heavy folds. St. Louis City Hospital was one of those places.

If I'd been superstitious, which I am not, I would have said the hospital was the perfect place for ghosts. There are different kinds of ghosts. The regular kind are spirits of the dead left behind when they should have gone to Heaven or Hell. Theologians had been arguing over what the existence of ghosts meant for God and the church for centuries. I don't think God is particularly bothered by it, but the church is.

Enough people had died in this place to make it thick with real ghosts, but I'd never seen any personally. Until a ghost wraps its cold arms around me, I'd just as soon not believe in it.

But there is another kind of ghost. Psychic impressions, strong emotions, soak into the walls and floors of a building. It's like an emotional tape recorder. Sometimes with video images, sometimes just sound, sometimes just a shiver down your spine when you walk over a certain spot.

The old hospital was thick with shivery places. I personally had never seen or heard anything, but walking down the hallway you knew somewhere, near at hand, there was something. Something waiting just out of sight, just out of hearing, just out of reach. Tonight it was probably a vampire.

The only sounds were the scrape of feet, the brush of cloth, us moving. There was no other sound. When it's really quiet you start hearing things even if it's just the buzz of your own blood pounding in your ears.

The first corner loomed before me. I was point. I'd volunteered to be point. I had to go around the corner first. Whatever lay around the bend, it was mine. I hate it when I play hero.

I went down on one knee, gun held in both hands, pointing up. It didn't do any good to stick my gun around the corner first. I couldn't shoot what I couldn't see. There are a variety of ways to go around blind corners, none of them foolproof. It mostly matters whether you're more afraid of getting shot or getting grabbed. Since this was a vampire I was more worried about being grabbed and having my throat ripped out.

I pressed my right shoulder against the wall, took a deep breath, and threw myself forward. I didn't do a neat shoulder roll into the hallway. I just sort of fell on my left side with the gun held two-handed out in front of me. Trust me, this is the fastest way to be able to aim around a corner. I wouldn't necessarily advise it if the monsters were shooting back.

I lay in the hallway, heart pounding in my ears. The

good news was there was no vampire. The bad news was that there was a body.

I came up to one knee, still searching the shadowed hallway for hints of movement. Sometimes with a vampire you don't see anything, you don't even hear it, you feel it in your shoulders and back, the fine hairs on the back of your neck. Your body responds to rhythms older than thought. In fact, thinking instead of doing can get you dead.

"It's clear," I said. I was still kneeling in the middle of the hallway, gun out, ready for bear.

"You through rolling around on the floor?" Dolph asked.

I glanced at him, then back to the hallway. There was nothing there. It was alright. Really.

The body was wearing a pale blue uniform. A gold and black patch on the sleeve said "Security." The man's hair was white. Heavy jowls, a thick nose, his eyelashes like grey lace against his pale cheeks. His throat was just so much raw meat. The spine glistened wetly in the overhead lights. Blood splashed the green walls like a macabre Christmas card.

There was a gun in the man's right hand. I put my back to the left-hand wall and watched the corridor to either side until the corners cut my view. Let the police investigate the body. My job tonight was to keep us alive.

Dolph crouched beside the body. He leaned forward, doing a sort of push-up to bring his face close to the gun. "It's been fired."

"I don't smell any powder near the body," I said. I didn't look at Dolph when I said it. I was too busy watching the corridor for movement.

"The gun's been fired," he said. His voice sounded rough, clogged.

I glanced down at him. His shoulders were stiff, his body rigid with some kind of pain.

"You know him, don't you?" I said.

Dolph nodded. "Jimmy Dugan. He was my partner for a few months when I was younger than you are. He retired and couldn't make it on the pension, so he got a job here." Dolph shook his head. "Shit."

What could I say? "I'm sorry" didn't cut it. "I'm sorry as hell" was a little better but it still wasn't enough. Nothing I could think of to say was adequate. Nothing I could do would make it better. So I stood there in the blood-spattered hall and did nothing, said nothing.

Zerbrowski knelt beside Dolph. He put a hand on his arm. Dolph looked up. There was a flash of some strong emotion in his eyes; anger, pain, sadness. All the above, none of the above. I stared down at the dead man, gun still clasped tight in his hand, and thought of something useful to say.

"Do they give the guards here silver bullets?"

Dolph glanced up at me. No guessing this time; it was anger. "Why?"

"The guards should have silver bullets. One of you take it, and we'll have two guns with silver bullets."

Dolph just stared at the gun. "Zerbrowski."

Zerbrowski took the gun gently, as if afraid of waking the man. But this vampire victim wasn't going to rise. His head lolled to one side, muscles and tendons snapped. It looked like somebody had scooped out the meat and skin around his spine with a big spoon.

Zerbrowski checked the cylinder. "Silver." He rolled the cylinder into the revolver and stood up, gun in his right hand. The shotgun he held loosely in his left hand.

"Extra ammo?" I asked.

Zerbrowski started to kneel back down, but Dolph shook his head. He searched the dead man. His hands were candy-coated in blood when he was done. He tried to wipe the drying blood onto a white handkerchief but the blood stained the lines in his hands, gathered around his fingernails. Only soap and scrubbing would get it off.

He said, softly, "Sorry, Jimmy." He still didn't cry. I would have cried. But then, women have more chemicals in their tear ducts. It makes us tear up easier than men. Honest.

"No extra ammo. Guess Jimmy thought five'd be enough for some dumb-ass security job." His voice was warm with anger. Anger was better than crying. If you can manage it.

I kept checking the corridor, but my eyes kept going to the dead man. He was dead because I hadn't done my job. If I hadn't told the ambulance drivers that the body was safe, they'd have put him in the vault, and Jimmy Dugan wouldn't have died.

I hate it when things are my fault.

"Go," Dolph said.

I took the lead. There was another corner. I did my little kneel-and-roll routine again. I lay half on my side, gun pointed two-handed down the hallway. Nothing moved in the long, green hallway. There was something lying in the floor. I saw the lower part of the guard first. Legs in pale blue, blood-drenched pants. A head with a long brown ponytail lay to one side of the body like a forgotten lump of meat.

I got to my feet, gun still hovering, looking for something to aim at. Nothing moved except the blood that was still dripping down the walls. The blood dripped slowly like rain at the end of the day, thickening, congealing as it moved.

"Jesus!" I wasn't sure which uniform said it, but I agreed.

The upper body had been ripped apart as if the vampire had plunged both hands into her chest and pulled. Her spine had shattered like Tinkertoys. Gobbets of flesh, blood, and bone sprinkled the hallway like gruesome flower petals.

I could taste bile at the back of my throat. I breathed through my mouth in deep, even breaths. Mistake. The air tasted like blood—thick, warm, faintly salty. There was an underlying sourness where the upper intestine and stomach had been broken open. Fresh death smells like a cross between a slaughterhouse and an outhouse. Shit and blood is what death smells like.

Zerbrowski was scanning the hallway, borrowed gun in hand. He had four bullets. I had thirteen, plus an extra clip in my sport bag. Where was the second guard's gun?

"Where's her gun?" I asked.

Zerbrowski's eyes flicked to me, then to the corpse, then back to scanning the hallway. "I don't see it."

I'd never met a vampire that used a gun, but there was

always a first time. "Dolph, where's the guard's gun?"

Dolph knelt in the blood and tried to search the body. He moved the bloody flesh and pieces of cloth around, like you'd stir it with a spoon. Once the sight would have made me lose my lunch, but it didn't anymore. Was it a bad sign that I didn't throw up on the corpses anymore? Maybe.

"Spread out, look for the gun," Dolph said.

The four uniforms spread out and searched. The blond was pasty and swallowed convulsively, but he was making it. Good for him. It was the tall one with the prominent Adam's apple that broke first. He slid on a piece of meat that set him down hard on his butt in a pool of congealed blood. He scrambled to his knees and vomited against the wall.

I was breathing quick, shallow breaths. The blood and carnage hadn't been enough, but the sound of someone else throwing up just might be.

I pressed my shoulders into the wall and moved towards the next corner. I will not throw up. I will not throw up. Oh, God, please don't let me throw up. Have you ever tried to aim a gun while throwing your guts up? It's damn near impossible. You're helpless until you're finished. After seeing the guards, I didn't want to be helpless.

The blond cop was leaning against the wall. His face was shiny with a sick sweat. He looked at me and I could read it in his eyes. "Don't," I whispered, "please don't."

The rookie fell to his knees and that was it. I lost everything I'd eaten that day. At least I didn't throw up on the corpse. I'd one that once, and Zerbrowski had never let me live it down. On that particular case, the complaint was that I'd tampered with evidence.

If I'd been the vampire, I would have come then while half of us were vomiting our guts out. But nothing slithered around the corner. Nothing came screaming out of the darkness. Lucky us.

"If you're all done," Dolph said, "we need to find her gun and what did this."

I wiped my mouth on the sleeve of my coveralls. I was

sweating, but there hadn't been time to take them off. My black Nikes stuck to the floor with little squeech sounds. There was blood on the bottom of my shoes. Maybe the coverall wasn't such a bad idea.

What I wanted was a cool cloth. What I got was to continue down the green hallway, making little bloody footprints behind me. I scanned the floor and there it was, footprints going away from the body, back down the hall towards the first guard.

"Dolph?"

"I see them," he said.

The faint footprints walked through the carnage and down the corner, away from us. Away sounded good, but I knew better. We were here to get up close and personal. Dammit.

Dolph knelt by the largest piece of the body. "Anita."

I walked over to him, avoiding the bloody footprints. Never step on clues. The police don't like it.

Dolph pointed at a blackened piece of cloth. I knelt carefully, glad that I was still in my overalls. I could kneel in all the blood I wanted without messing my clothes. Always prepared, like a good Boy Scout.

The woman's shirt was charred and blackened. Dolph touched the material with the tip of his pencil. The cloth flaked in heavy layers, cracking like stale bread. Dolph poked a hole through one of the layers. It crumbled. A burst of ash and a sharp acrid smell came up from the body.

"What the hell happened to her?" Dolph asked.

I swallowed, still tasting vomit at the back of my throat. This wasn't helping. "It's not cloth."

"What is it, then?"

"Flesh."

Dolph just looked at me. He held the pencil like it might break. "You're serious."

"Third-degree burn," I said.

"What caused this?"

"Can I borrow your pencil?" I asked.

He handed it to me without a word.

I dug at what was left of her chest. The flesh was so badly fried that her shirt melted into it. I pushed the layers aside, digging downward with the pencil. The body felt horribly light, and crisp like the burned skin of a chicken. When I'd plunged half the length of the pencil into the burn, I touched something solid. I used the pencil to pry it upward. When it was almost at the surface I put fingers inside the hole and pulled a lump of twisted metal from the burned flesh.

"What is it?" Dolph asked.

"It's what's left of her cross."

"No," he said.

The lump of melted silver glinted through the black ash. "This was her cross, Dolph. It melted into her chest, caught her clothing on fire. What I don't understand is why the vampire kept contact with the burning metal. The vampire should be nearly as burned as she is, but it's not here."

"Explain that," he said.

"Animalistic vampires are like PCP addicts. They don't feel pain. I think the vampire crushed her to his chest, the cross touched him, burst into flames, and the vampire stayed against her, tearing her apart while they burned. Against any normal vampire, she would have been safe."

"So crosses can't stop this one," he said.

I stared at the lump of metal. "Apparently not."

The four uniforms were looking at the dim hallway, a little frantically. They hadn't bargained on the crosses not working. Neither had I. The bit about not feeling pain had been a small footnote to one article. No one had theorized that that would mean crosses didn't protect you. If I survived, I'd have to work up a little article for the *Vampire Quarterly*. Crosses melting into flesh, wowee.

Dolph stood up. "Keep together, people."

"The crosses don't work," one uniform said. "We gotta go back and wait for special teams."

Dolph just looked at him. "You can go back if you want to." He glanced down at the dead guard. "It's volunteer only. The rest of you go back outside and wait for special teams."

The tall one nodded and touched his partner's arm. His partner swallowed hard, his eyes flicking to Dolph, then to the guard's crispy-crittered body. He let his partner drag him away down the hall. Back to safety and sanity. Wouldn't it have been nice if we all could have gone? But we couldn't let something like this escape. Even if I hadn't had an order of execution, we would have had to kill it, rather than take the risk of letting it get outside.

"What about you and the rookie?" Dolph asked the black cop.

"I've never run from the monsters. He's free to go back with the others."

The blond shook his head, gun in hand, fingers mottled with tension. "I'm staying."

The black cop gave him a smile that meant more than words. He'd made a man's choice. Or would that be a mature person's choice? Whatever, he was staying.

"One more corner and the vault should be in sight," I said.

Dolph glanced at the last corner. His eyes met mine and I shrugged. I didn't know what was going to be around the corner. This vampire was doing things that I would have said were impossible. The rules had been changed, and not in our favor.

I hesitated on the wall farthest from the corner. I pushed my back into the wall and slid slowly into sight, around the corner. I was staring down a short, straight hallway. There was a gun lying in the middle of the floor. The second guard's gun? Maybe. On the left-hand wall there should have been a big steel door with crosses hanging on it. The steel had exploded outward in a twisted silver mess. They'd put the body in the vault after all. I hadn't gotten the guards killed. They should have been safe. Nothing moved. There was no light in the vault. It was just a blasted darkness. If there was a vampire waiting in the room, I couldn't see it. Of course, I wasn't all that close, either. Close did not seem to be a good idea.

"Clear, as far as I can see," I said.

"You don't sound sure," Dolph said.

"I'm not," I said. "Peek around the corner at what's left of the vault."

He didn't peek, but he looked. He let out a soft whistle. Zerbrowski said, "Je-sus."

I nodded. "Yeah."

"Is it in there?" Dolph asked.

"I think so."

"You're our expert. Why don't you sound sure?" Dolph asked.

"If you would have asked me if a vampire could plow through five feet of silver-steel with crosses hung all over the damn place, I'd have said no way." I stared into the black hole. "But there it is."

"Does this mean you're as confused as we are?" Zerbrowski asked.

"Yep."

"Then we're in deep shit," he said.

Unfortunately, I agreed.

18

The vault loomed up before us. Pitch black with a crazy vampire waiting inside; just my cup of tea Ri-ight.

"I'll take point now," Dolph said. He had the second guard's gun in his hands. His own gun was tucked out of sight. He had silver bullets now; he'd go first. Dolph was good about that. He'd never order one of his men to do something he wouldn't do himself. Wish Bert was like that. Bert was more likely to promise your first-born child, then ask if it was alright with you.

Dolph hesitated at the open mouth of the vault. The darkness was thick enough to cut. It was the absolute darkness of a cave. The kind where you can touch your eyeballs with your fingers and not blink.

He motioned us forward with the gun, but he went past the darkness, farther down the hallway. The bloody footprints entered the darkness and came back out. Bloody footprints going down the hall, around the corner. I was getting tired of corners.

Zerbrowski and I moved up to stand on either side of Dolph. The tension slid along my neck, shoulders. I took a deep breath and let it out, slowly. Better. Look, my hand's not even shaking.

Dolph didn't roll around on the floor to clear the corner. He just went around back to the wall, two-handed aim, ready for bear.

A voice said, "Don't shoot, I'm not dead."

I knew the voice.

"It's John Burke. He's with me."

Dolph glanced back at me. "I remember him."

I shrugged; better safe then sorry. I trusted Dolph not to shoot John by accident, but there were two cops here I'd never met. Always err on the side of caution when it comes to firearms. Words to survive by.

John was tall, slender, dark complected. His short hair was perfectly black with a broad white streak in front. It was a startling combination. He'd always been handsome, but now that he'd shaved off his beard, he looked less like a Hollywood villain and more like a leading man. Tall, dark, and handsome, and knew how to kill vampires. What more could you ask for? Plenty, but that's another story.

John came around the corner smiling. He had a gun out, and better yet, he had his vampire kit in one hand. "I came ahead to make sure the vampire didn't get loose while you were en route."

"Thanks, John," I said.

He shrugged. "Just protecting the public welfare."

It was my turn to shrug. "Anything you say."

"Where's the vampire?" Dolph asked.

"I was tracking it," John said.

"How?" I asked.

"Bloody bare footprints."

Bare footprints. Sweet Jesus. The corpse didn't have shoes, but John did. I turned towards the vault. Too late, too slow, too damn bad.

The vampire came out of the darkness, moving too fast to see. It was just a blur that smashed into the rookie, driving him into the wall. He screamed, gun pressed to the vampire's chest. The gun was loud in the hallway, echoing in the pipes. The bullets came out the back of the vampire like they'd hit mist. Magic.

I moved forward, trying to aim without hitting the rookie. He was screaming, one continuous sound. Blood sprayed in a warm rain. I shot at the thing's head but it moved, incredibly fast, tossing the man against the other wall, tearing at him. There was a lot of yelling and movement, but it all seemed far away, slowed down. It would all be

over in a matter of moments. I was the only one close
enough with silver bullets. I stepped in, body brushing
the vampire, and put the barrel to the back of its skull.
A normal vampire wouldn't have let me do it. I pulled
the trigger, but the vampire whirled, lifting the man off
his feet, throwing him into me. The bullet went wide and
we crashed to the floor. The air was knocked out of me
for a second with the weight of two adult males on my
chest. The rookie was on top of me, screaming, bleeding,
dying.

I wedged the gun against the back of the vamp's skull and
fired. The back of the head exploded outward in a fine spray
of blood, bone, and heavier, wetter things. The vampire kept
digging at the man's throat. It should have been dead, but it
wasn't.

The vampire reared back, blood-clotted teeth straining.
It had paused like a man breathing between swallows. I
shoved the barrel in its mouth. The teeth grated on the
metal. The face exploded from the upper lip to the top
of the head. The lower teeth mouthed the air but couldn't
get a bite. The headless body raised up on its hands, as if
trying to get up. I touched the gun to its chest and pulled
the trigger. At this distance I might be able to take out its
heart. I'd never actually tried to take out a vampire using
just a pistol. I wondered if it would work. I wondered what
would happen to me if it didn't.

A shudder ran through the thing's body. It breathed outward in a long, wordless sigh.

Dolph and Zerbrowski were there dragging the thing
backwards. I think it was dead already, but just in case,
the help was appreciated. John splashed the vampire with
holy water. The liquid bubbled and fizzed on the dying
vampire. It was dying. It really was.

The rookie wasn't moving. His partner dragged him off
me, cradling him against his chest like a child. Blood
plastered the blond hair to his face. The pale eyes were
wide open, staring at nothing. The dead are always blind,
one way or another.

He'd been brave, a good kid, though he wasn't that much younger than me. But I felt about a million years old staring into his pale, dead face. He was dead, just like that. Being brave doesn't save you from the monsters. It just ups your chances.

Dolph and Zerbrowski had taken the vampire to the floor. John was actually straddling the body with a stake and mallet in hand. I hadn't used a stake in years. Shotgun was my choice. But then, I was a progressive vampire slayer.

The vampire was dead. It didn't need to be staked, but I just sat against the wall and watched. Better safe than sorry. The stake went in easier than normal because I'd made a hole for it. My gun was still in my hand. No need to put it up yet. The vault was still an empty blackness; where there was one vampire there were often more. I'd keep the gun out.

Dolph and Zerbrowski went to the ruined vault, guns out. I should have gotten up and gone with them, but it seemed very important right now just to breathe. I could feel the blood pumping through my veins; every pulse in my body was loud. It was good to be alive; too bad I hadn't been able to save the kid. Yeah, too bad.

John knelt beside me. "You alright?"

I nodded. "Sure."

He looked at me like he didn't believe it, but he let it go. Smart man.

The light flashed on in the vault. Rich, yellow light, warm as a summer's day. "Je-sus," Zerbrowski said.

I stood up, and nearly fell; my legs were shaky. John caught my arm, and I stared at him until he let go. He gave a half-smile. "Still a hard case."

"Always," I said.

There had been two dates between us. Mistake. It made working together more awkward, and he couldn't cope with me being a female version of him. He had this old southern idea of what a lady should be. A lady should not carry a gun and spend most of her time covered in blood and corpses. I had two words for that attitude. Yeah, those are the words.

There was a large fish tank smashed against one wall. It had held guinea pigs, or rats, or rabbits. All it held now were bright splashes of blood and bits of fur. Vampires don't eat meat, but if you put small animals in a glass container, then throw it against the wall, you get diced small animals. There wasn't enough left to scoop up with a spoon.

There was a head near the glass mess, probably male, judging from the short hair and style. I didn't go any closer to check. I didn't want to see the face. I'd have been brave tonight. I had nothing left to prove.

The body was in one piece, barely. It looked like the vampire had shoved both hands into the chest, grabbed a handful of ribs and pulled. The chest was nearly torn in two, but a band of pink muscle tissue and intestine held it together.

"The head's got fangs," Zerbrowski said.

"It's the vampire counsellor," I said.

"What happened?"

I shrugged. "At a guess, the counsellor was leaning over the vamp when it rose. It killed him, quick and messy."

"Why'd it kill the vampire counsellor?" Dolph asked.

I shrugged. "It was more animal than human, Dolph. It woke up in a strange place with a strange vampire leaning over it. It reacted like any trapped animal and protected itself."

"Why couldn't the counsellor control it? That's what he was here for."

"The only person who can control an animalistic vampire is the master who made it. The counsellor wasn't powerful enough to control it."

"Now what?" John asked. He'd put up his gun. I still hadn't. I felt better with it out for some reason.

"Now I go make my third animation appointment of the evening."

"Just like that?"

I looked up at him, ready to be angry at somebody. "What do you want me to do, John? Fall into a screaming fit? That wouldn't bring back the dead, and it would annoy the hell out of me."

He sighed. "If you only matched your packaging."

I put my gun back in the shoulder holster, smiled at him, and said, "Fuck you."

Yeah, those are the words.

19

I had washed most of the blood off my face and hands in the bathroom at the morgue. The bloodstained coveralls were in my trunk. I was clean and presentable, or as presentable as I was going to get tonight. Bert had said to meet the new guy at my third appointment for the night. Oakglen Cemetery, ten o'clock. The theory was that the new man already raised two zombies and would just watch me raise the third one. Fine with me.

It was 10:35 before I pulled into Oakglen Cemetery. Late. Dammit. It'd make a great impression on the new animator, not to mention my client. Mrs. Doughal was a recent widow. Like five days recent. Her dearly departed husband had left no will. He'd always meant to get around to it, but you know how it is, just kept putting it off. I was to raise Mr. Doughal in front of two lawyers, two witnesses, the Doughals' three grown children, and a partridge in a pear tree. They'd made a ruling just last month that the newly dead, a week or less, could be raised and verbally order a will. It would save the Doughals half their inheritance. Minus lawyer fees, of course.

There was a line of cars pulled over to the side of the narrow gravel road. The tires were playing hell with the grass, but if you didn't park off to one side, nobody could use the road. Of course, how many people needed to use a cemetery road at 10:30 at night? Animators, voodoo priests, pot-smoking teenagers, necrophiliacs, satanists. You had to be a member of a legitimate religion and have a permit to worship in a cemetery after dark. Or be an animator.

We didn't need a permit. Mainly because we didn't have a reputation for human sacrifice. A few bad apples have really given voodooists a bad name. Being Christian, I sort of frown on satanism. I mean, they are, after all, the bad guys. Right?

As soon as my foot hit the road, I felt it. Magic. Someone was trying to raise the dead, and they were very near at hand.

The new guy had already raised two zombies. Could he do a third? Charles and Jamison could only do two a night. Where had Bert found someone this powerful on such short notice?

I walked past five cars, not counting my own. There were nearly a dozen people pressed around the grave. The women were in skirt-suits; the men all wore ties. It was amazing how many people dressed up to come to the graveyard. The only reason most people come to the graveyard is for a funeral. A lot of clients dress for one, semi-formal, basic black.

It was a man's voice leading the mourners in rising calls of, "Andrew Doughal, arise. Come to us, Andrew Doughal, come to us."

The magic built on the air until it pressed against me like a weight. It was hard to get a full breath. His magic rode the air, and it was strong, but uncertain. I could feel his hesitation like a touch of cold air. He would be powerful, but he was young. His magic tasted untried, undisciplined. If he wasn't under twenty-one, I'd eat my hat.

That's how Bert had found him. He was a baby, a powerful baby. And he was raising his third zombie of the night. Hot damn.

I stayed in the shadows under the tall trees. He was short, maybe an inch or two taller than me, which made him five-four at best. He wore a white dress shirt and dark slacks. Blood had dried on the shirt in nearly black stains. I'd have to teach him how to dress, as Manny had taught me. Animating is still on an informal apprenticeship. There are no college courses to teach you how to raise the dead.

He was very earnest as he stood there calling Andrew Doughal from the grave. The crowd of lawyers and relatives huddled at the foot of the grave. There was no family member inside the blood circle with the new animator. Normally, you put a family member behind the tombstone so he or she could control the zombie. This way, only the animator could control it. But it wasn't an oversight, it was the law. The dead could be raised to request and dictate a will but only if the animator, or some neutral party, had control of it.

The mound of flowers shuddered and a pale hand shot upward, grabbing at the air. Two hands, the top of a head. The zombie spilled from the grave like it was being pulled by strings.

The new animator stumbled. He fell to his knees in the soft dirt and dying flowers. The magic stuttered, wavering. He'd bitten off one zombie more than he could finish. The dead man was still struggling from the grave. Still trying to get its legs free, but there was no one controlling it. Lawrence Kirkland had raised the zombie, but he couldn't control it. The zombie would be on its own with no one to make it mind. Uncontrolled zombies give animators a bad name.

One of the lawyers was saying, "Are you all right?"

Lawrence Kirkland nodded his head, but he was too exhausted to speak. Did he even now realize what he'd done? I didn't think so. He wasn't scared enough.

I walked up to the huddled group. "Ms. Blake, we missed you," the lawyer said. "Your . . . associate seems to be ill."

I gave them my best professional smile. See nothing wrong. A zombie isn't about to go amuck. Trust me.

I walked to the edge of the blood circle. I could feel it like a wind pushing me back. The circle was shut, and I was on the outside. I couldn't get in unless Lawrence asked me in.

He was on all fours, hands lost in the flowers of the grave. His head hung down, as if he was too tired to raise it. He probably was.

"Lawrence," I said softly, "Lawrence Kirkland."

He turned his head in slow motion. Even in the dark I could see the exhaustion in his pale eyes. His arms were trembling. God, help us.

I leaned in close so the audience couldn't hear what I said. We'd try to keep the illusion that this was just business as usual, as long as I could. If we were lucky, the zombie would just wander away. If we weren't lucky, it would hurt someone. The dead are usually pretty forgiving of the living, but not always. If Andrew Doughal hated one of his relatives, it would be a long night.

"Lawrence, you have to break the circle and let me in," I said.

He just stared at me, eyes dull, no glimmer of understanding. Shit.

"Break the circle, Lawrence, now."

The zombie was free to its knees. Its white dress shirt gleamed against the darkness of the burial suit. Uncomfortable for all eternity. Doughal looked pretty good for the walking dead. He was pale with thick grey hair. The skin was wavy, pale, but there were no signs of rot. The kid had done a good job for the third zombie of the night. Now if only I could control it, we were home free.

"Lawrence, break the circle, please!"

He said something, too low for me to hear. I leaned as close as the blood would let me get and said, "What?"

"Larry, name's Larry."

I smiled, it was too ridiculous. He was worried about me calling him Lawrence instead of Larry with a rogue zombie climbing out of the dirt. Maybe he'd snapped under the pressure. Naw.

"Open the circle, Larry," I said.

He crawled forward, nearly falling face first into the flowers. He scraped his hand across the line of blood. The magic snapped. The circle of power was gone, just like that. Now it was just me.

"Where's your knife?"

He tried to look back over his shoulder but couldn't

manage it. I saw the blade gleam in the moonlight on the other side of the grave.

"Just rest," I said. "I'll take care of it."

He collapsed into a little ball, hugging his arms around himself, as if he was cold. I let him go, for now. The first order of business had to be the zombie.

The knife was lying beside the gutted chicken he'd used to call the zombie. I grabbed the knife and faced the zombie over the grave. Andrew Doughal was leaning against his own tombstone, trying to orient himself. It's hard on a person, being dead; it takes a few minutes to wake up the dead brain cells. The mind doesn't quite believe that it should work. But it will, eventually.

I pushed back the sleeve of my leather jacket and took a deep breath. It was the only way, but I didn't have to like it. I drew the blade across my wrist. A thin, dark line appeared. The skin split and blood trickled out, nearly black in the moonlight. The pain was sharp, stinging. Small wounds always felt worse than big ones . . . at first.

The wound was small and wouldn't leave a scar. Short of slitting my wrist, or someone else's, I couldn't remake the blood circle. It was too late in the ceremony to get another chicken and start over. I had to salvage this ceremony, or the zombie would be free with no boss. Zombies without bosses tended to eat people.

The zombie was still sitting on its tombstone. It stared at nothing with empty eyes. If Larry had been strong enough, Andrew Doughal might have been able to talk, to reason on his own. Now he was just a corpse waiting for orders, or a stray thought.

I climbed onto the mound of gladioluses, chrysanthemums, carnations. The perfume of flowers mixed with the stale smell of the corpse. I stood knee-deep in dying flowers and waved my bleeding wrist in front of the zombie's face.

The pale eyes followed my hand, flat and dead as day-old fish. Andrew Doughal was not home, but something was, something that smelled blood and knew its worth.

I know that zombies don't have souls. In fact, I can only raise the dead after three days. It takes that long for the soul to leave. Incidentally, the same amount of time it takes for vampires to rise. Fancy that.

But if it isn't the soul reanimating the corpse, then what is it? Magic, my magic, or Larry's. Maybe. But there was something in the corpse. If the soul was gone, something filled the void. In an animation that worked, magic filled it. Now? Now I didn't know. I wasn't even sure I wanted to know. What did it matter as long as I pulled the fat out of the fire? Yeah. Maybe if I kept repeating that, I'd even believe it.

I offered the corpse my bleeding wrist. The thing hesitated for a second. If it refused, I was out of options.

The zombie stared at me. I dropped the knife and squeezed the skin around the wound. Blood welled out, thick and viscous. The zombie snatched at my hand. Its pale hands were cold and strong. Its head bowed over the wound, mouth sucking. It fed at my wrist, jaws working convulsively, swallowing as hard and as fast as it could. I was going to have the world's worst hickey. But at least it hurt.

I tried to draw my hand away, but the zombie just sucked harder. It didn't want to let go. Great.

"Larry, can you stand?" I asked softly. We were still trying to pretend that nothing had gone wrong. The zombie had accepted blood. I controlled it now, if I could get it to let go.

Larry looked up at me in slow motion. "Sure," he said. He got to his feet using the burial mound for support. When he was standing, he asked, "What now?"

Good question. "Help me get it loose." I tried to pull my wrist free, but the thing hung on for dear life.

Larry wrapped his arms around the corpse and pulled. It didn't help.

"Try the head," I said.

He tried pulling back on the corpse's hair, but zombies don't feel pain. Larry pried a finger along the corpse's mouth, breaking the suction with a little pop. Larry looked like he was going to be sick. Poor him; it was my arm.

He wiped his finger on his dress slacks, as if he had touched something slimy. I wasn't sympathetic.

The knife wound was already red. It would be a hell of a bruise tomorrow.

The zombie stood on top of its grave, staring at me. There was life in the eyes; someone was home. The trick was, was it the right someone?

"Are you Andrew Doughal?" I asked.

He licked his lips and said, "I am." It was a rough voice. A voice for ordering people about. I wasn't impressed. It was my blood that gave him the voice. The dead really are mute, really do forget who and what they are, until they taste fresh blood. Homer was right; makes you wonder what else was true in the *Iliad*.

I put pressure on the knife wound with my other hand and stepped back, off the grave. "He'll answer your questions now," I said. "But keep them simple. He's been mostly dead all day."

The lawyers didn't smile. I guess I didn't blame them. I waved them forward. They hung back. Squeamish lawyers? Surely not.

Mrs. Doughal poked her lawyer in the arm. "Get on with it. This is costing a fortune."

I started to say we don't charge by the minute, but for all I knew Bert had arranged for the longer the corpse was up, the more expensive it was. That actually was a good idea. Andrew Doughal was fine tonight. He answered questions in his cultured, articulate voice. If you ignored the way his skin glistened in the moonlight, he looked alive. But give it a few days, or weeks. He'd rot; they all rotted. If Bert had figured out a way to make clients put the dead back in their graves before pieces started to fall off, so much the better.

There were few things as sad as the family bringing dear old mom back to the cemetery with expensive perfume covering up the smell of decay. The worst was the client who had bathed her husband before bringing him back. She had to bring most of his flesh in a plastic garbage sack. The meat had just slid off the bone in the warm water.

Larry moved back, stumbling over a flowerpot. I caught him, and he fell against me, still unsteady.

He smiled. "Thanks . . . for everything." He stared at me, our faces inches apart. A trickle of sweat oozed down his face in the cold October night.

"You got a coat?"

"In my car."

"Get it and put it on. You'll catch your death sweating in this cold."

His smile flashed into a grin. "Anything you say, boss." His eyes were bigger than they should have been, a lot of white showing. "You pulled me back from the edge. I won't forget."

"Gratitude is great, kid, but go get your coat. You can't work if you're home sick with the flu."

Larry nodded and started slowly towards the cars. He was still unsteady, but he was moving. The flow of blood had almost stopped on my wrist. I wondered if I had a Band-Aid in my car big enough to cover it. I shrugged and started to follow Larry towards the cars. The lawyers' deep, courtroom voices filled the October dark. Words echoing against the trees. Who the hell were they trying to impress? The corpse didn't care.

20

Larry and I sat on the cool autumn grass watching the lawyers draw up the will. "They're so serious," he said.

"It's their job to be serious," I said.

"Being a lawyer means you can't have a sense of humor?"

"Absolutely," I said.

He grinned. His short, curly hair was a red so bright, it was nearly orange. His eyes were blue and soft as a spring sky. I'd seen both hair and eyes in the dome light from our cars. Back in the dark he looked grey-eyed and brown-haired. I'd hate to have to give a witness description of someone I only saw in the dark.

Larry Kirkland had that milk-pale complexion of some redheads. A thick sprinkling of golden freckles completed the look. He looked like an overgrown Howdy Doody puppet. I mean that in a cute way. Being short, really short for a man, I was sure he wouldn't like being called cute. It was one of my least favorite endearments. I think if all short people could vote, the word "cute" would be stricken from the English language. I know it would get my vote.

"How long have you been an animator?" I asked.

He glanced at the luminous dial of his watch. "About eight hours."

I stared at him. "This is your first job, anywhere?"

He nodded. "Didn't Mr. Vaughn tell you about me?"

"Bert just said he'd hired another animator named Lawrence Kirkland."

"I'm in my senior year at Washington University, and this is my semester of job co-op."

"How old are you?"

"Twenty; why?"

"You're not even legal," I said.

"So I can't drink or go in porno theaters. No big loss, unless the job takes us to places like that." He looked at me and leaned in. "Does the job take us to porno theaters?" His face was neutrally pleasant, and I couldn't tell if he was teasing or not. I gambled that he was kidding.

"Twenty is fine." I shook my head.

"You don't look like twenty's fine," he said.

"It's not your age that bothers me," I said.

"But something bothers you."

I wasn't sure how to put it into words, but there was something pleasant and humorous in his face. It was a face that laughed more often than it cried. He looked bright and clean as a new penny, and I didn't want that to change. I didn't want to be the one who forced him to get down in the dirt and roll.

"Have you ever lost someone close to you? Family, I mean?"

The humor slipped away from his face. He looked like a solemn little boy. "You're serious."

"Deadly," I said.

He shook his head. "I don't understand."

"Just answer the question. Have you ever lost someone close to you?"

He shook his head. "I've even got all my grandparents."

"Have you ever seen violence up close and personal?"

"I got into fights in high school."

"Why?"

He grinned. "They thought short meant weak."

I had to smile. "And you showed them different."

"Hell, no; they beat the crap out of me for four years." He smiled.

"You ever win a fight?"

"Sometimes," he said.

"But the winning's not the important part," I said.

He looked very steadily at me, eyes serious. "No, it's not."

There was a moment of nearly perfect understanding between us. A shared history of being the smallest kid in class. Years of being the last picked for sports. Being the automatic victim for bullies. Being short can make you mean. I was sure that we understood each other but, being female, I had to verbalize it. Men do a lot of this mind-reading shit, but sometimes you're wrong. I needed to know.

"The important part is taking the beating and not giving up," I said.

He nodded. "Takes a beating and keeps on ticking."

Now that I'd spoiled our first moment of perfect understanding by making us both verbalize, I was happy. "Other than school fights, you've never seen violence?"

"I go to rock concerts."

I shook my head. "Not the same."

"You got a point to make?" he asked.

"You should never have tried to raise a third zombie."

"I did it, didn't I?" He sounded defensive, but I pressed on. When I have a point to make, I may not be graceful, but I'm relentless.

"You raised and lost control of it. If I hadn't come along, the zombie would have broken free and hurt someone."

"It's just a zombie. They don't attack people."

I stared at him, trying to see if he was kidding. He wasn't. Shit. "You really don't know, do you?"

"Know what?"

I covered my face with my hands and counted to ten, slowly. It wasn't Larry I was mad at, it was Bert, but Larry was so convenient for yelling. I'd have to wait until tomorrow to yell at Bert, but Larry was right here. How lucky.

"The zombie had broken free of your control, Larry. If I hadn't come along and fed it blood, it would have found blood on its own. Do you understand?"

"I don't think so."

I sighed. "The zombie would have attacked someone. Taken a bite out of someone."

"Zombies attacking humans is just superstition, ghost stories."

"Is that what they're teaching in college now?" I asked.

"Yes."

"I'll loan you some back copies of *The Animator*. Trust me, Larry, zombies do attack people. I've seen people killed by them."

"You're just trying to scare me," he said.

"Scared would be better than stupid."

"I raised it. What do you want from me?" He looked completely baffled.

"I want you to understand what nearly happened here tonight. I want you to understand that what we do isn't a game. It's not parlor tricks. It's real, and it can be dangerous."

"Alright," he said. He'd given in too easily. He didn't really believe. He was humoring me. But there are some things you can't tell someone. He, or she, has to learn some things in person. I wished I could wrap Larry up in cellophane and keep him on a shelf, all safe and secure and untouched, but life didn't work that way. If he stayed in this business long enough, the new would wear off. But you can't tell someone who's reached twenty and never been touched by death. They don't believe in the boogeyman.

At twenty I'd believed in everything. I suddenly felt old.

Larry pulled a pack of cigarettes out of his coat pocket.

"Please tell me you don't smoke," I said.

He looked up at me, eyes sort of wide and startled. "You don't smoke?"

"No."

"You don't like people to smoke around you?" He made it a question.

"No," I said.

"Look, I feel pretty awful right now. I need the cigarette, okay?"

"Need it?"

"Yeah, need it." He had one slender white cigarette between two fingers of his right hand. The pack had disappeared back into his pocket. A disposable lighter had appeared. He looked at me very steadily. His hands were shaking just a bit.

Shit. He'd raised three zombies on his first night out, and I was going to be talking to Bert about the wisdom of sending Larry out on his own.

Besides, we were outside. "Go ahead."

"Thanks."

He lit the cigarette and drew a deep breath of nicotine and tar. Smoke curled out of his mouth and nose, like pale ghosts. "Feel better already," he said.

I shrugged. "Just so you don't smoke in the car with me."

"No problem," he said. The tip of his cigarette pulsed orange in the dark as he sucked on it. He looked past me, letting smoke curl from his lips as he said, "We're being paged."

I turned and, sure enough, the lawyers were waving at us. I felt like a janitor being called in to clean up the messy necessities. I stood up, and Larry followed me.

"You sure you feel well enough for this?" I asked.

"I couldn't raise a dead ant, but I think I'm up to watching you do it."

There were bruises under his eyes and the skin was too tight around his mouth, but if he wanted to play macho man who was I to stop him? "Great; let's do it."

I got salt out of my trunk. It was perfectly legal to carry zombie-raising supplies. I suppose the machete that I used for beheading chickens could be used as a weapon, but the rest of the stuff was considered harmless. Shows you what the legal system knows about zombies.

Andrew Doughal had recovered himself. He still looked a little waxy, but his face was serious, concerned, alive. He smoothed a hand down the stylish lapel of his suit coat. He looked down at me, not just because he was taller but because he was good at looking down. Some people have a real talent for being condescending.

"Do you know what's happening, Mr. Doughal?" I asked the zombie.

He looked down his narrow patrician nose. "I am going home with my wife."

I sighed. I hated it when zombies didn't realize they were dead. They acted so . . . human.

"Mr. Doughal, do you know why you're in a cemetery?"

What's happening?" one of the lawyers asked.

"He's forgotten that he's dead," I said softly.

The zombie stared at me, perfectly arrogant. He must have been a real pain in the ass when he was alive, but even assholes are piteous once in awhile.

"I don't know what you are babbling about," the zombie said. "You obviously are suffering from some delusion."

"Can you explain why you are here in a cemetery?" I asked.

"I don't have to explain anything to you."

"Do you remember how you got to the cemetery?"

"We . . . we drove, of course." The first hint of unease wavered through his voice.

"You're guessing, Mr. Doughal. You don't really remember driving to the cemetery, do you?"

"I . . . I . . . " He looked at his wife, his grown children, but they were walking to their cars. No one even looked back. He was dead, no getting around that, but most families didn't just walk away. They might be horrified, or saddened, or even sickened, but they were never neutral. The Doughals had gotten the will signed, and they were leaving. They had their inheritance. Let good ol' dad crawl back into his grave.

He called, "Emily?"

She hesitated, stiffening, but one of her sons grabbed her arm and hurried her toward the cars. Was he embarrassed, or scared?

"I want to go home," he yelled after them. The arrogance had leaked away, and all that was left was that sickening fear, the desperate need not to believe. He felt so alive. How could he possibly be dead?

His wife half-turned. "Andrew, I'm sorry." Her grown children hustled her into the nearest car. You would have thought they were the getaway drivers for a bank robbery, they peeled out so fast.

The lawyers and secretaries left as fast as was decent. Everybody had what they'd come for. They were done with the corpse. The trouble was that the "corpse" was staring after them like a child who was left in the dark.

Why couldn't he have stayed an arrogant SOB?

"Why are they leaving me?" he asked.

"You died, Mr. Doughal, nearly a week ago."

"No, it's not true."

Larry moved up beside me. "You really are dead, Mr. Doughal. I raised you from the dead myself."

He stared from one to the other of us. He was beginning to run out of excuses. "I don't feel dead."

"Trust us, Mr. Doughal, you are dead," I said.

"Will it hurt?"

A lot of zombies asked that; will it hurt to go back into the grave? "No, Mr. Doughal, it doesn't hurt. I promise."

He took a deep, shaking breath and nodded. "I'm dead, really dead?"

"Yes."

"Then put me back, please." He had rallied and found his dignity. It was nightmarish when the zombie refused to believe. You could still lay them to rest, but the clients had to hold them down on the grave while they screamed. I'd only had that happen twice, but I remembered each time as if it had happened last night. Some things don't dim with time.

I threw salt against his chest. It sounded like sleet hitting a roof. "With salt I bind you to your grave."

I had the still-bloody knife in my hand. I wiped the gelling blood across his lips. He didn't jerk away. He believed. "With blood and steel I bind you to your grave, Andrew Doughal. Be at peace, and walk no more."

The zombie laid full length on the mound of flowers. The flowers seemed to flow over him like quicksand, and just like that he was swallowed back into the grave.

We stood there a minute in the empty graveyard. The only sounds were the wind sighing high up in the trees and the melancholy song of the year's last crickets. In *Charlotte's Web,* the crickets sang, "Summer is over and gone. Over and gone, over and gone. Summer is dying, dying." The first hard frost, and the crickets would be dying. They were like Chicken Little, who told everyone the sky was falling; except in this case, the crickets were right.

The crickets stopped suddenly like someone had turned a switch. I held my breath, straining to hear. There was nothing but the wind, and yet . . . My shoulders were so tight they hurt. "Larry?"

He turned innocent eyes to me. "What?"

There, three trees to our left, a man's figure was silhouetted against the moonlight. I caught movement out of the corner of my eye, on the right side. More than one. The darkness felt alive with eyes. More than two.

I used Larry's body to shield me from the eyes, drawing my gun, holding it along my leg so it wouldn't be obvious.

Larry's eyes widened. "Jesus, what's wrong?" His voice was a hoarse whisper. He didn't give us away. Good for him. I started herding him towards the cars, slowly, just your friendly neighborhood animators finished with their night's work and going home to a well-deserved rest.

"There are people out here."

"After us?"

"After me, more likely," I said.

"Why?"

I shook my head. "No time for explanations. When I say run, run like hell for the cars."

"How do you know they mean to hurt us?" His eyes were flashing a lot of white. He saw them now, too. Shadows moving closer, people out in the dark.

"How do you know they don't mean to hurt us?" I asked.

"Good point," he said. His breathing was fast and shallow. We were maybe twenty feet from the cars.

"Run," I said.

"What?" his voice sounded startled.

I grabbed his arm and dragged him into a run for the cars. I pointed the gun at the ground, still hoping whoever it was wouldn't be prepared for a gun.

Larry was running on his own, puffing a little from fear, smoking, and maybe he didn't run four miles every other day.

A man stepped in front of the cars. He brought up a large revolver. The Browning was already moving. It fired before my aim was steady. The muzzle flashed brilliant in the dark. The man jumped, not used to being shot at. His shot whined into the darkness to our left. He froze for the seconds it took me to aim and fire again. Then he crumpled to the ground and didn't get up again.

"Shit." Larry breathed it like a sigh.

A voice yelled, "She's got a gun."

"Where's Martin?"

"She shot him."

I guess Martin was the one with the gun. He still wasn't moving. I didn't know if I killed him or not. I wasn't sure I cared, as long as he didn't get up and shoot at us again.

My car was closer. I shoved car keys into Larry's hands. "Open the door, open the passenger side door, then start the car. Do you understand me?"

He nodded, freckles standing out in the pale circle of his face. I had to trust that he wouldn't panic and take off without me. He wouldn't do it out of malice, just fear.

Figures were converging from all directions. There had to be a dozen or more. The sound of running feet whispering on grass came over the wind.

Larry stepped over the body. I kicked a .45 away from the limp hand. The gun slid out of sight under the car. If I hadn't been pressed for time, I'd have checked his pulse. I always like to know if I've killed someone. Makes the police report go so much smoother.

Larry had the car door open and was leaning over to unlock the passenger side door. I aimed at one of the running figures and pulled the trigger. The figure stumbled, fell, and started screaming. The others hesitated. They weren't used to being shot at. Poor babies.

I slid into the car and yelled, "Drive, drive, drive!"

Larry peeled out in a spray of gravel. The car fishtailed, headlights swaying crazily. "Don't wrap us around a tree, Larry."

His eyes flicked to me. "Sorry." The car slowed from stomach-turning speed to grab-the-door-handle-and-hold-on speed. We were staying between the trees; that was something.

The headlights bounced off trees; tombstones flashed white. The car skidded around a curve, gravel spitting. A man stood framed in the middle of the road. Jeremy Ruebens of Humans First stood pale and shining in the lights. He stood in the middle of a flat stretch of road. If we could make the turn beyond him, we'd be out on the highway and safe.

The car was slowing down.

"What are you doing?" I asked.

"I can't just hit him," Larry said.

"The hell you can't."

"I can't!" His voice wasn't outraged, it was scared.

"He's just playing chicken with us, Larry. He'll move."

"Are you sure?" A little boy's voice asking if there really was a monster in the closet.

"I'm sure; now floor it and get us out of here."

He pressed down on the accelerator. The car jumped forward, rushing toward the small, straight figure of Jeremy Ruebens.

"He's not moving," Larry said.

"He'll move," I said.

"Are you sure?"

"Trust me."

His eyes flicked to me, then back to the road. "You better be right," he whispered.

I believed Ruebens would move. Honest. But even if he wasn't bluffing, the only way out was either past him or through him. It was Ruebens's choice.

The headlights bathed him in glaring white light. His small, dark features glared at us. He wasn't moving.

"He isn't moving," Larry said.

"He'll move," I said.

"Shit," Larry said. I couldn't have agreed more.

The headlights roared up onto Jeremy Ruebens, and he threw himself to one side. There was the sound of brushing cloth as his coat slid along the car's side. Close, damn close.

Larry picked up speed and swung us around the last corner and into the last straight stretch. We spilled out onto the highway in a shower of gravel and spinning tires. But we were out of the cemetery. We'd made it. Thank you, God.

Larry's hands were white on the steering wheel. "You can ease down now," I said. "We're safe."

He swallowed hard enough for me to hear it, then nodded. The car started gradually approaching the speed limit. His face was beaded with sweat that had nothing to do with the cool October evening.

"You alright?"

"I don't know." His voice sounded sort of hollow. Shock.

"You did good back there."

"I thought I was going to run over him. I thought I was going to kill him with the car."

"He thought so, too, or he wouldn't have moved," I said.

He looked at me. "What if he hadn't moved?"

"He did move."

"But what if he hadn't?"

"Then we would have gone over him, and we'd still be on the highway, safe."

"You would have let me run him down, wouldn't you?"

"Survival is the name of the game, Larry. If you can't deal with that, find another business to be in."

"Animators don't get shot at."

"Those were members of Humans First, a right-wing fanatic group that hates anything to do with the supernatural." So I was leaving out about the personal visit from Jeremy Ruebens. What the kid didn't know might not hurt him.

I stared at his pale face. He looked hollow-eyed. He'd met the dragon, a little dragon as dragons go, but once you've seen violence, you're never the same again. The first time you have to decide, live or die, us or them, it changes you forever. No going back. I stared at Larry's shocked face and wished it could have been different. I wished I could have kept him shining, new, and hopeful. But as my Grandmother Blake used to say, "If wishes were horses, we'd all ride."

Larry had had his first taste of my world. The only question was, would he want a second dose, or would he run? Run or go, stay or fight, age-old questions. I wasn't sure which way I wanted Larry to choose. He might live longer if he got the hell away from me, but then again maybe he wouldn't. Heads they win, tails you lose.

21

"What about my car?" Larry asked.

I shrugged. "You've got insurance, right?"

"Yes, but . . ."

"Since they couldn't trash us, they may decide to trash your car."

He looked at me as if he wasn't sure whether I was kidding. I wasn't.

There was a bicycle in front of us suddenly, out of the dark. A child's pale face flashed in the headlights. "Watch out!"

Larry's eyes flicked back to the road in time to see the kid's wide, startled eyes. The brakes squealed, and the child vanished from the narrow arch of lights. There was a crunch and a bump before the car skidded to a stop. Larry was breathing heavy; I wasn't breathing at all.

The cemetery was just on our right. We were too close to stop, but . . . but, shit, it was a kid.

I stared out the back window. The bicycle was a crumpled mess. The child lay in a very still heap. God, please don't let him be dead.

I didn't think Humans First had enough imagination to have a child in reserve as bait. If it was a trap, it was a good one, because I couldn't leave the tiny figure crumpled by the road.

Larry was gripping the steering wheel so hard his arms shook. If I thought he'd been pale before, I'd been wrong. He looked like a sick ghost.

"Is he . . . hurt?" His voice squeezed out deep and rough

with something like tears. It wasn't hurt he'd wanted to say. He just couldn't bring himself to use the big "D" word. Not yet, not if he could help it.

"Stay in the car," I said.

Larry didn't answer. He just sat there staring at his hands. He wouldn't look at me. But, dammit, this wasn't my fault. The fact that he'd lost his cherry tonight was not my fault. So why did it feel like it was?

I got out of the car, Browning ready in case the crazies decided to chase us onto the road. They could have gotten the .45 and be coming to shoot us. The child hadn't moved. I was just too far away to see the chest rise and fall. Yeah, that was it. I was maybe a yard away.

Please be alive.

The child lay sprawled on its stomach, one arm trapped underneath, probably broken. I scanned the dark cemetery as I knelt by the child. No right-wing crazies came swarming out of the darkness. The child was dressed in the proverbial little boy's outfit of striped shirt, shorts, and tiny running shoes. Who had sent him out dressed for summer on this cold night? His mother. Had some woman dressed him, loved him, sent him out to die?

His curly brown hair was silken, baby-fine. The skin of his neck was cool to the touch. Shock? It was too soon to be cold from death. I waited for the big pulse in his neck, but nothing happened. Dead. Please, God, please.

His head raised up, and a soft sound came out of his mouth. Alive. Thank you, God.

He tried to roll over but fell back against the road. He cried out.

Larry was out of the car, coming towards us. "Is he alright?"

"He's alive," I said.

The boy was determined to roll over, so I grabbed his shoulders and helped. I tried to keep his right arm in against his body. I had a glimpse of huge brown eyes, round baby face, and in his right hand was a knife bigger than he was. He whispered, "Tell him to come help move me." Tiny little fangs showed between baby lips. The knife pressed against my stomach over the sport bag. The point slid underneath the leather jacket to touch the shirt underneath. I had one of those frozen moments when time stretches out in slow-mo nightmare. I had all the time in the world to decide whether to betray Larry, or die. Never give anyone to the monsters; it's a rule. I opened my mouth and screamed, "Run!"

The vampire didn't stab me. He just froze. He wanted me alive; that's why the knife and not fangs. I stood up, and the vampire just stared up at me. He didn't have a backup plan. Great.

The car stood, open doors spilling light out into the darkness. The headlights made a wide theatrical swash. Larry was just standing there, frozen, undecided. I yelled, "Get in the car!"

He moved towards the open car door. A woman was standing in the glare of the headlights. She was dressed in a long white coat open over the cream and tan of a very nice pants suit. She opened her mouth and snarled into the light, fangs glistening.

I was running, screaming, "Behind you!"

Larry stared at me; his gaze went past me. His eyes widened. I could hear the patter of little feet behind me. Terror spread across Larry's face. Was this the first vampire he'd ever seen?

I drew my gun, but was still running. You can't hit shit when you're running. I had a vampire in front and behind. Coin toss.

The female vampire bounded onto the hood of the car and propelled herself in a long, graceful leap that carried her into Larry and sent them tumbling across the road.

I couldn't shoot her without risking Larry. I whirled at the last second and put the gun point-blank into the child-vampire's face.

His eyes widened. I squeezed the trigger. Something hit me from behind. The shot went wild and I was on the road, flat on my stomach with something bigger than a bread box on top of me.

The air was knocked out of me. But I turned, trying to point the gun back at the thing on my back. If I didn't do something now, I might never have to worry about breathing again.

The boy came up on me, knife flashing downward. The gun was turning, but too slowly. I would have screamed if I'd had air. The knife buried into the sleeve of my jacket. I felt the blade bite into the road underneath. My arm was pinned. I squeezed the trigger and the shot went harmlessly off into the dark.

I twisted my neck to try to see who, or what, was straddling me. It was a what. In the red glow of the rear car lights his face was all flat, high cheekbones with narrow, almost slanted eyes and long, straight hair. If he'd been any more ethnic, he'd have been carved in stone, surrounded by snakes and Aztec gods.

He reached over me and encircled my right hand, the one that was pinned, the one that was still holding the gun. He pressed the bones of my hand into the metal. His voice was deep and soft. "Drop the gun or I'll crush your hand." He squeezed until I gasped.

Larry screamed, high and mournful.

Screaming was for when you didn't have anything better to do. I scraped my left sleeve against the road, baring my watch and the charm bracelet. The three tiny crosses glinted in the moonlight. The vampire hissed but didn't let go of my gun hand. I dragged the bracelet across his hand. A sharp smell of burning flesh; then he used his free hand to drag at my left sleeve. Holding onto just the sleeve, he held my left hand back, so I couldn't touch him with the crosses.

If he'd been the new dead, just the sight of the crosses would have sent him screaming; but he wasn't just old dead, he was ancient. It was going to take more than blessed crosses to get him off my back.

Larry screamed again.

I screamed, too, because I couldn't do anything else, except hold onto the gun and make him crush my hand. Not productive. They didn't want me dead, but hurt, hurt was okay. He could crush my hand into bloody pulp. I gave up my gun, screaming, tugging at the knife that held my arm pinned, trying to jerk my left sleeve free of his hand so I could plunge the crosses into his flesh.

A shot exploded above our heads. We all froze and stared back at the cemetery. Jeremy Ruebens and company had recovered their gun and were shooting at us. Did they think we were in cahoots with the monsters? Did they care who they shot?

A woman screamed, "Alejandro, help me!" The scream was from behind us. The vampire on my back was suddenly gone. I didn't know why, and I didn't care. I was left with the child-monster looming over me, staring at me with large dark eyes.

"Doesn't it hurt?" he asked.

It was such an unexpected question that I answered it. "No."

He looked disappointed. He squatted down beside me, hands on his small thighs. "I meant to cut you so I could lick the blood." His voice was still a little boy's voice, would always be a little boy's voice, but the knowledge in his eyes beat down on my skin like heat. He was older than Jean-Claude, much older.

A bullet smashed into the rear light of my car, just above the boy's head. He turned towards the fanatics with a very unchildlike snarl. I tried to pull the knife out of the road, but it was imbedded. I couldn't budge it.

The boy crawled into the darkness, vanishing with a backwash of wind. He was going for the fanatics. God help them.

I looked back over my shoulder. Larry was on the ground with a woman with long, waving brown hair on top of him. The man who'd been on top of me, Alejandro, and another woman were struggling with the vampire on Larry. She wanted to kill him, and they were trying to stop her. It seemed like a good plan to me.

Another bullet whined towards us. It didn't come close. A half-strangled scream, and then no more gunshots. Had the boy gotten him? Was Larry hurt? And what the hell could I do to help him, and me?

The vampires seemed to have their hands full. Whatever I was going to do, now was the time. I tried unzipping the leather jacket left-handed, but it stuck halfway down. Great. I bit the side of the jacket, using my teeth in place of the trapped hand. Unzipped; now what?

I pulled the sleeve off my left hand with my teeth, then put the sleeve under my hip and wiggled out of it. Slipping my right hand free of the pinned sleeve was the easy part.

Alejandro picked up the brown-haired woman and threw her over the car. She sailed into the darkness, but I didn't hear her hit the ground. Maybe she could fly. If she could, I didn't want to know.

Larry was nearly lost to sight behind a curtain of pale hair. The second female was bending over him like a prince about to bestow the magic kiss. Alejandro got a handful of that long, long hair and jerked her to her feet. He flung her into the side of the car. She staggered but didn't go down, snapping at him like a dog on a leash.

I went wide around them, holding the crosses out in front like every old movie you've ever seen. Except I'd never seen a vampire hunter with a charm bracelet.

Larry was on his hands and knees, swaying ever so slightly. His voice was high, nearly hysterical. He just kept repeating, "I'm bleeding, I'm bleeding."

I touched his arm, and he jumped like I'd bit him. His eyes flashed white. Blood was welling down his neck, black in the moonlight. She'd bit him, Jesus help us, she'd bit him.

The pale female was still fighting to get to Larry. "Can't you smell the blood?" It was a plea.

"Control yourself, or I'll do it for you." Alejandro's voice was a low scream. The anger in his voice cut and sliced. The pale woman went very still.

"I'm alright now." Her voice held fear. I'd never heard one vampire be scared to . . . death of another. Let them fight it out. I had better things to do. Like figuring out how to get us past the remaining vampires and into the car.

Alejandro had the female shoved against the car with one hand. My gun was in his left hand. I unsnapped the anklet with its matching crosses. You can't sneak up on a vampire. Even the new dead are jumpier than a long-tailed cat in a room full of rocking chairs. Since I had no chance of sneaking up on him, I tried the direct approach.

"She bit him, you son of a bitch. She bit him!" I pulled the back of his shirt as if to get his attention. I dropped the crosses down his back.

He screamed.

I brushed the bracelet crosses across his hand. He dropped the gun. I caught it. A tongue of blue flame licked up his back. He clawed and scrambled, but he couldn't reach the crosses. Burn, baby, burn.

He whirled, shrieking. His open hand caught me on the side of the head. I was airborne. I slammed back-first into the road. I tried to take as much of the impact as I could with my arms, but my head rocked back, slamming into the road.

The world swam with black spots. When my vision cleared, I was staring up into a pale face; long, yellow-white hair the color of corn silk traced over my cheek as the vampire knelt to feed.

I still had the Browning in my right hand. I pulled the trigger. Her body jerked backwards like someone had shoved her. She fell back onto the road, blood pouring out of a hole in her stomach that was nothing compared to the wound in her back. I hoped I'd shattered her spine.

I staggered to my feet.

The male vampire, Alejandro, tore off his shirt. The crosses fell to the road in a little pool of molten blue fire. His back was burned black, with blisters here and there to add color. He whirled on me, and I shot him once in the chest. The shot was rushed, and he didn't go down.

Larry grabbed the vampire's ankle. Still Alejandro kept coming, dragging Larry across the blacktop like a child. He grabbed Larry's arm, jerking him to his feet. Larry threw a chain over the vampire's head. The heavy silver cross burst into flame. Alejandro screamed.

I yelled, "Get in the car, now!"

Larry slid into the driver's seat and kept sliding until he was in the passenger seat. He slammed the passenger side door shut and locked it, for what good it would do. The vampire tore the chain and threw the cross end over end into the roadside trees. The cross winked out of sight like a falling star.

I slid into the car, slamming the door and locking it. I clicked the safety on the Browning and shoved it between my legs.

The vampire, Alejandro, was huddled around his pain, too hurt to give chase right that second. Goodie.

I shoved the car in gear and gunned it. The car fishtailed. I slowed to the speed of light, and the car straightened out on the road. We poured down the dark tunnel in a circle of flickering light and tree shadows. And down at the end of our tunnel was a figure in white with long, brown hair spilling in the wind. It was the vampire that had jumped Larry. She was just standing there in the middle of the road. Just standing there. We were about to find out if vampires played chicken. I was about to take my own advice. I put the gas pedal to the floorboards. The car lurched forward. The vampire just stood there while we barreled down at her.

At the last second I realized she wasn't going to move, and I didn't have time to. We were about to test my theory about cars and vampiric flesh. Where's a silver car when you need one?

22

The headlights flashed on the vampire like a spotlight. I had an image of pale face, brown hair, fangs stretched wide. We hit her going sixty. The car shuddered. She rolled in painful slow motion up over the hood, and yet it was happening too fast for me to do anything. She hit the windshield with a sharp, crackling sound. Metal screamed.

The windshield crumbled into a mass of spiderweb cracks. I was suddenly trying to see through the wrong end of a smashed prism. The safety glass had done its job. It hadn't shattered and cut us to ribbons. It had just cracked all to hell, and I couldn't see to drive. I stamped down on the brakes.

An arm shot through the glass, raining glittering shards down on Larry. He screamed. The hand closed on his shirt, pulling him into the broken teeth of the windshield.

I turned the wheel to the left as hard as I could. The car spun out and all I could do was let off the gas, not touch the brake, and ride.

Larry had a death grip on the door arm and the headrest. He was screaming, fighting not to be pulled through the jagged glass. I said a quick prayer and let go of the wheel. The car spun helplessly. I shoved a cross against the hand. It smoked and bubbled. The hand let go of Larry and vanished through the hole in the crumbled glass.

I grabbed at the steering wheel, but it was too little too late. The car careened off the road into the ditch. Metal screamed as something under the car broke, something large. I was slammed into the driver's side door. Larry was suddenly on top of me; then we were both tumbling to the other side. Then it was over. The silence was startling. It was as if I'd gone deaf. There was a great roaring whiteness in my ears.

Someone said, "Thank God," and it was me.

The passenger side door peeled open like the shell of a nut. I scrambled back away from the opening. Larry was left stranded and staring. He was jerked out of the car. I slid into the front floorboard, aiming where Larry had vanished.

I was staring up at Larry's body with a dark hand clamped so tight on his throat, I didn't know if he could breathe. I stared down the barrel of my gun at the dark face of the vampire, Alejandro. His face was unreadable as he said, "I will tear his throat out."

"I'll blow your head off," I said. A hand came fishing through the broken windshield. "Back off or you lose that pretty face."

"He will die first," the vampire said. But the hand vanished back through the hole. There was the sound of some other language in the vampire's English. Emotion gave him an accent.

Larry's eyes were too wide, showing too much white. He was breathing, shallow and too fast. He'd hyperventilate, if he lived that long.

"Decide," the vampire said. His voice was flat, empty of everything. Larry's terror-filled eyes were eloquent enough for both of them.

I hit the safety on the gun and handed it butt-first to his outstretched hand. It was a mistake, I knew that, but I also knew I couldn't sit here and watch Larry's throat be ripped out. There are some things that are more important than physical survival. You gotta be able to look at yourself in the mirror. I gave up my gun for the same reason I'd stopped for the child. There was no choice. I was one of the good guys. Good guys were self-sacrificing. It was a rule somewhere.

23

Larry's face was a bloody mask. No single cut seemed to be serious, but nothing bleeds like a shallow scalp wound. Safety glass was not designed to be vampire-proof. Maybe I could write in and suggest it.

Blood trickled over Alejandro's hand, still gripping Larry's throat. The vampire had stuffed my gun in the back of his pants. He handled the gun like he knew how to use one. Pity. Some vampires were technophobes. It gave you an edge, sometimes.

Larry's blood flowed over the vampire's hand. Sticky and warm like barely solid Jell-O. The vampire didn't react to the blood. Iron self-control. I stared into his nearly black eyes and felt the pull of centuries like monstrous wings unfolding in his eyes. The world swam. The inside of my head was sinking, expanding. I reached out to touch something, anything to keep from falling. A hand gripped mine. The skin was cool and smooth. I jerked back, falling against the car.

"Don't touch me! Don't ever touch me!"

The vampire stood uncertainly, Larry's throat gripped in one blood-streaked hand, holding his other hand out towards me. It was a very human gesture. Larry's eyes were bugging out.

"You're choking him," I said.

"Sorry," the vampire said. He released him.

Larry fell to his knees, gasping. His first breath was a hissing scream for air.

I wanted to ask Larry how he was, but I didn't. My job

was to get us out of here alive, if possible. Besides, I had an idea how Larry felt. Hurt. No need to ask stupid questions.

Well, maybe one stupid question. "What do you want?" I asked.

Alejandro looked at me, and I fought the urge to look at his face while I talked to him. It was hard. I ended up staring at the hole my bullet had made in the side of his chest. It was a very small hole, and had already stopped bleeding. Was he healing that fast? Shit. I stared at the wound as hard as I could. To fight the urge for eye contact. It's hard to be tough when you're staring at someone's chest. But I'd had years of practice before Jean-Claude decided to share his "gift" with me. Practice makes . . . well, you know.

The vampire hadn't answered me, so I asked again, voice steady and low. I didn't sound like someone who was afraid. Bully for me. "What do you want?"

I felt the vampire look at me, almost as if he'd run a finger down my body. I shivered and couldn't stop. Larry crawled to me, head hanging, dripping blood as he moved.

I knelt beside him. And before I could stop myself, the stupid question popped out. "Are you alright?"

His eyes raised to me through a mask of blood. He finally said, "Nothing a few stitches wouldn't cure." He was trying to make a joke. I wanted to hug him and promise the worst was over. Never make promises you can't keep.

The vampire didn't exactly move, but something brought my attention back to him. He stood knee-deep in autumn weeds. My eyes were on a level with his belt buckle, which made him about my height. Short for a man. A white, Anglo-Saxon, twentieth-century man. The belt buckle glinted gold and was carved into a blocky, stylized human figure. The carving, like the vampire's face, was straight out of an Aztec calendar.

The urge to look upward and meet his eyes crawled over my skin. My chin had actually risen an inch or so before I realized what I was doing. Shit. The vamp was messing with my mind, and I couldn't feel it. Even now, knowing he had to be doing something to me, I couldn't sense it. I was blind and deaf just like every other tourist.

Well, maybe not every tourist. I hadn't been munched on yet, which probably meant they wanted something more than just blood. I'd be dead otherwise, and so would Larry. Of course, I was still wearing blessed crosses. What could this creature do once I was stripped of crosses? I did not want to find out.

We were alive. It meant they wanted something that we couldn't give them dead. But what?

"What in the hell do you want?"

His hand came into view. He was offering his hand to help me stand. I stood without help, putting myself a little in front of Larry.

"Tell me who your master is, girl, and I won't hurt you."

"Who else will, then?" I asked.

"Clever, but I swear you will leave here in safety if you give me the name."

"First of all, I don't have a master. I'm not even sure I have an equal." I fought the urge to glance at his face, see if he got the joke. Jean-Claude would have gotten it.

"You stand before me, making jokes?" His voice sounded surprised, nearly outraged. Good, I think.

"I don't have a master," I said. Master vampires can smell truth or lies.

"If you truly believe that, you are deluding yourself. You bear two master signs. Give me the name and I will destroy him for you. I will free you of this . . . problem."

I hesitated. He was older than Jean-Claude. A lot older. He might be able to kill the Master of the City. Of course, that would leave this master vampire in control of the city. He and his three helpers. Four vampires, one less than were killing people, but I was willing to bet there was a fifth vamp around here somewhere. You couldn't have that many rogue master vampires running around one medium-size city.

Any master that was slaughtering civilians would be a bad thing to have in charge of all the vampires in the area. Just call it a feeling.

I shook my head. "I can't."

"You want free of him, do you not?"

"Very much."

"Let me free you, Ms. Blake. Let me help you."

"Like you helped the man and woman you murdered?"

"I did not murder them," he said. His voice sounded very reasonable. His eyes were powerful enough to drown in but the voice wasn't as good. There was no magic to the voice. Jean-Claude's was better. Or Yasmeen's, for that matter. Nice to know that not every talent came equally with time. Ancient wasn't everything.

"So you didn't strike the fatal blow. So what? Your flunkies do your will, not their own."

"You'd be surprised how much free will we have."

"Stop it," I said.

"What?"

"Sounding so damn reasonable."

There was laughter in his voice. "You would rather I rant and rave?"

Yes, actually, but I didn't say it out loud. "I won't give you the name. Now what?"

There was a rush of wind at my back. I tried to turn, to face the wind. The woman in white rushed at me. Fangs straining, hands clawing, spattered with other people's blood, the vampire smashed into me. We fell backwards into the weeds with her on top. She darted towards my neck like a snake. I shoved my left wrist into her face. One cross brushed her lips. A flash of light, the stench of burning flesh, and the vampire was gone, screaming into the darkness. I had never seen any vampire move that fast. Had it been mind-magic? Had she tricked me that badly even with a blessed cross? How many over-five-hundred-year-old vamps can you have in one pack? Two, I hoped. Any more than that and they'd have us outnumbered.

I scrambled to my feet. The master vampire was on his

hands and knees beside the remains of my car. Larry was
nowhere in sight. A flutter of panic clawed at my chest;
then I realized Larry had crawled underneath the car so the
vampire couldn't make him a hostage again. When all else
fails, hide. It works for rabbits.

The vampire's blistered back was bent at a painful angle
as he tried to pull Larry out from under the car. "I will pull
this arm out of its socket, if you do not come here!"

"You sound like you've got a kitten under the bed,"
I said.

Alejandro whirled around. He flinched, like it hurt. Great.

I felt something move behind me. I didn't argue with
the sensation. Say it was nerves; I turned, crosses ready.
Two vampires behind me. One was the pale-haired female.
I guess the shot had missed her spine; pity. The other
vampire could have been her male twin. They both hissed
and cowered from the crosses. Nice to see someone was
bothered.

The master came at me from the back, but I heard him.
Either the burn was making him clumsy, or the crosses
were helping me. I stood halfway between the three vampires, crosses sort of pointed at both groups. The blonds
peered over their arms, but the crosses had them well
and truly scared. The master never hesitated. He came
in a rushing burst of speed. I backpedaled, tried to keep
the crosses between us, but he grabbed my left forearm.
With the crosses dangling inches from his flesh, he held
on.

I pulled, getting as much distance from him as I could,
then hit him in the solar plexus with everything I had. He
made an "umph" sound, then flicked his hand at my face.
I rocked back and tasted blood. He'd barely touched me,
but he'd proven his point. If I wanted to exchange blows,
he'd beat the crap out of me.

I hit him in the throat. He gagged and looked surprised.
Beaten to snot was still a hell of a lot better than being
bitten. I'd rather be dead than have pointy teeth.

His fist closed over my right fist, squeezing just enough

to let me feel his strength. He was still trying to warn me off rather than hurt me. Bully for him.

He raised both his arms, drawing me closer into his body. I didn't want closer, but there didn't seem to be a hell of a lot I could do about it. Unless, of course, vampires had testicles. The throat shot had hurt. I glanced at his face, almost close enough to kiss. I leaned into him, getting as much room as I could. He just kept drawing me closer. His own momentum helped.

My knee hit him hard, and I ground it up and into him. It was not a glancing blow. He crumpled forward but didn't let go of my hands. I wasn't loose, but it was a start, and I'd answered an age-old question. Vampires did have balls.

He jerked my hands behind my back, pinning me between his arms and his body. His body felt wooden, stiff, and unyielding as stone. It had been warm and soft and hurtable only a second before. What had happened?

"Take the things off her wrist," he said. He wasn't talking to me.

I tried to crane my head around to see what was coming up behind me. I couldn't see anything. The two pale vampires were still huddled in the face of the naked crosses.

Something touched my wrist. I jerked, but he held me still. "If you struggle, he will cut you."

I turned my head as far back as I could, and was staring into the round eyes of the boy vampire. He'd recovered his knife and was using it to poke at the bracelet.

The master vampire's hands squeezed my arms until I thought they'd pop from the pressure like shaken soda pop. I must have made some sound, because he said, "I did not mean to hurt you tonight." His mouth was pressed against my ear, lost in my hair. "This was your choice."

The bracelet broke with a small snap. I felt it fall away into the weeds. The master vampire drew a deep breath, as if it were easier to breathe now. He was only an inch or two taller than I was, but he held both my wrists in one small hand, fingers squeezing to make the grip tight. It hurt, and I fought not to make small, helpless noises.

He stroked his free hand through my hair, then grabbed a handful and pulled my head backwards so he could see my eyes. His eyes were solid, absolute black; the whites had drowned. "I will have his name, Anita, one way or another."

I spit in his face.

He screamed, tightening his grip on my wrists until I cried out. "I could have made this pleasant, but now I think I want you to hurt. Look into my eyes, mortal, and despair. Taste of my eyes, and there will be no secrets between us." His voice dropped to the barest of whispers. "Perhaps I will drink your mind like others drink blood, and leave nothing behind but your mindless husk."

I stared into the darkness that was his eyes and felt myself fall, forward, impossibly forward, and down, down into a blackness that was pure and total, and had never known light.

24

I was staring up into a face I didn't know. The face was
holding a bloody handkerchief to its forehead. Short hair,
pale eyes, freckles. "Hi, Larry," I said. My voice sounded
distant and strange. I couldn't remember why.

It was still dark. Larry's face had been cleaned up a
little, but the wound was still bleeding. I couldn't have
been out that long. Out? Where had I been out to? All
I could remember was eyes, black eyes. I sat up too fast.
Larry caught my arm or I would have fallen.

"Where are the . . . "

"Vampires," he finished for me.

I leaned into his arm and whispered, "Yeah."

There were people all around us in the dark, huddled in
little whispering groups. The lights of a police car strobed
the darkness. Two uniforms were standing quietly next to
the car, talking with a man whose name wouldn't come
to me.

"Karl," I said.

"What?" Larry asked.

"Karl Inger, the tall man talking to the police."

Larry nodded. "That's right."

A small, dark man knelt beside us. Jeremy Ruebens of
Humans First, who last I knew had been shooting at us.
What the hell was going on?

Jeremy smiled at me. It looked genuine.

"What makes you my friend all of a sudden?"

His smile broadened. "We saved you."

I pushed away from Larry to sit on my own. A moment of dizziness and I was fine. Yeah, right. "Talk to me, Larry."

He glanced at Jeremy Ruebens, then back to me. "They saved us."

"How?"

"They threw holy water on the one who bit me." He touched his throat with his free hand, an unconscious gesture, but he noticed me watching. "Is she going to have control over me?"

"Did she enter your mind at the same time as she bit you?"

"I don't know," he said. "How can you tell?"

I opened my mouth to explain, then closed it. How to explain the unexplainable? "If Alejandro, the master vampire, had bitten me at the same time he rolled my mind, I'd be under his power now."

"Alejandro?"

"That's what the other vampires called the master."

I shook my head, but the world swam in black waves and I had to swallow hard not to vomit. What had he done to me? I'd had mind games played on me before, but I'd never had a reaction like this.

"There's an ambulance coming," Larry said.

"I don't need one."

"You've been unconscious for over an hour, Ms. Blake," Ruebens said. "We had the police call an ambulance when we couldn't wake you."

Ruebens was close enough for me to reach out and touch him. He looked friendly, positively radiant, like a bride on her big day. Why was I suddenly his favorite person? "So they threw holy water on the vamp that bit you; what then?" I asked Larry.

"They drove the rest of them off with crosses and charms."

"Charms?"

Ruebens pulled out a chain with two miniature metal-faced books hanging on it. Both books would have fit in the palm of my hand with room to spare. "They aren't charms, Larry. They're tiny Jewish Holy Books."

"I thought a Star of David."

"The star doesn't work, because it's a racial symbol, not really a religious symbol."

"So it's like miniature Bibles?"

I raised my eyebrows. "The Torah contains the Old Testament, so yeah, it's like miniature Bibles."

"Would the Bible work for us Christians?"

"I don't know. Probably, I've just never been attacked by vampires while carrying a Bible." That was probably my fault. In fact, when was the last time I'd read the Bible? Was I becoming a Sunday Christian? I'd worry about my soul later, after my body felt a little better.

"Cancel the ambulance; I'm fine."

"You are not fine," Ruebens said. He reached out as if to touch me. I looked at him. He stopped in mid-motion. "Let us help you, Ms. Blake. We share common enemies."

The police were walking towards us over the dark grass. Karl Inger was coming, too, talking softly to the police as they moved.

"Do the police know you were shooting at us first?"

Something passed over Ruebens's face.

"They don't know, do they?"

"We saved you, Ms. Blake, from a fate worse than death. I was wrong to try and hurt you. You raise the dead, but if you are truly enemies with the vampires, then we are allies."

"The enemy of my enemy is my friend, huh?"

He nodded.

The police were almost here, almost within earshot. "Alright, but you ever point a gun at me again and I'll forget you saved me."

"It will never happen again, Ms. Blake; you have my word."

I wanted to say something disparaging, but the police were there. They'd hear. I wasn't going to tell on Ruebens and Humans First, so I had to save my smart alec comebacks for later use. Knowing Ruebens, I'd get another chance.

I lied to the police about what Humans First had done, and I lied about what Alejandro had wanted from me. It was just another of those mindless attacks that had happened twice already. Later, to Dolph and Zerbrowski, I'd tell the truth, but right now I just didn't feel like explaining the entire mess to strangers. I wasn't even sure Dolph would get the whole story. Like the fact that I was almost assuredly Jean-Claude's human servant.

Nope, no need to mention that.

25

Larry's car was a late-model Mazda. The vampires had kept Humans First so busy they hadn't had time to trash the car. Lucky for us, since my car was totaled. Oh, I'd have to go through the insurance company and let them tell me the car was totaled, but there was something large broken underneath the car; fluids darker than blood were leaking out. The front end looked like we'd hit an elephant. I knew totaled when I saw it.

We'd spent the last several hours at the emergency room. The ambulance attendants insisted I see a doctor, and Larry needed three small stitches in his forehead. His orangey hair fell forward and hid the wound. His first scar. The first of many if he stayed in this business and hung around me.

"You've been on the job, what, fourteen hours? What do you think so far?" I asked.

He glanced at me sideways, then back to the road. He smiled, but it didn't look funny. "I don't know."

"Do you want to be an animator when you graduate?"

"I thought I did," he said.

Honesty; a rare talent. "Not sure now?"

"Not really."

I let it rest there. My instinct was to talk him out of it. To tell him to go into some sane, normal business. But I knew that raising the dead wasn't just a job choice. If your "talent" was strong enough, you had to raise the dead or risk the power coming out at odd moments. Does the term roadkill mean anything to you? It meant something to my stepmother Judith. Of course, she wasn't pleased with my job. She thought it was gruesome. What could I say? She was right.

"There are other job choices for a preternatural biology degree."

"What? A zoo, exterminator?"

"Teacher," I said, "park ranger, naturalist, field biologist, researcher."

"And which of those jobs can make you this kind of money?" he asked.

"Is money the only reason you want to be an animator?" I was disappointed.

"I want to do something to help people. What better than using my specialized skills to rid the world of dangerous undead?"

I stared at him. All I could see was his profile in the darkened car, face underlit from the dashboard. "You want to be a vampire executioner, not an animator." I didn't try to keep the surprise out of my voice.

"My ultimate goal, yes."

"Why?"

"Why do you do it?"

I shook my head. "Answer the question, Larry."

"I want to help people."

"Then be a policeman; they need people on the force who know preternatural creatures."

"I thought I did pretty good tonight."

"You did."

"Then what's wrong?"

I tried to think how to phrase it in fifty convincing words or less. "What happened tonight was awful, but it gets worse."

"Olive's coming up; which way do I turn?"

"Left."

The car took the exit and slid into the turning lane. We sat at the light with the turn signal blinking in the dark.

"You don't know what you're getting into," I said.

"Then tell me," he said.

"I'll do better than that. I'll show you."

"What's that supposed to mean?"

"Turn right at the third light."

We rolled into the parking lot. "First building on the right."

Larry slid into the only open space he could find. My parking space. My poor little Nova wouldn't be coming back to it.

I took off my jacket in the darkness of the car. "Hit the overhead light," I said.

He did as he was told. He was better at following orders than I was. Which, since he'd be following my orders, was fine.

I showed him the scars on my arms. "The cross-shaped burn is from human servants who thought it was funny. The mound of scar tissue at the bend of my arm is where a vampire tore my arm to pieces. Physical therapist says it's a miracle that I got full use of my arm back. Fourteen stitches from a human servant, and that's just my arms."

"There's more?" His face looked pale and strange in the dome light.

"A vampire shoved the broken end of a stake in my back."

He winced.

"And my collarbone was broken at the same time my arm got chewed up."

"You're trying to scare me."

"You bet," I said.

"I won't be scared off."

Tonight should have scared him off without my showing him my scars. But it hadn't. Dammit, he'd stick, if he didn't get killed first. "Alright, you're staying for the rest of the semester, great, but promise me you won't go hunting vampires without me."

"But Mr. Burke . . . "

"He helps execute vampires, but he doesn't hunt them alone."

"What's the difference between an execution and a hunt?"

"An execution just means a body that needs staking, or a vampire that's all nice and chained up waiting for the final stroke."

"Than what's a hunt?" he asked.

"When I go back out after the vampires that nearly killed us tonight, that's a hunt."

"And you don't trust Mr. Burke to teach me to hunt?"

"I don't trust Mr. Burke to keep you alive."

Larry's eyes widened.

"I don't mean he'd deliberately hurt you. I mean I don't trust anybody but me with your life."

"You think it'll come down to that?"

"It damn near did."

He was quiet for a handful of minutes. He stared down at his hands that were smoothing back and forth over the steering wheel. "I promise not to go vampire hunting with anybody but you." He stared at me, blue, blue eyes studying my face. "Not even Mr. Rodriguez? Mr. Vaughn said he taught you."

"Manny did teach me, but he doesn't hunt vampires anymore."

"Why not?"

I met his true-blue eyes and said, "His wife's too afraid, and he's got four kids."

"You and Mr. Burke aren't married and don't have kids."

"That's right."

"Neither do I," he said.

I had to smile. Had I ever been this eager? Naw. "No one likes a smart alec, Larry."

He grinned, and it made him look about thirteen. Jesus, why wasn't he running for cover after tonight? Why wasn't I? No answers, at least none that made sense. Why did I do it? Because I was good at it, came the answer. Maybe Larry could be good at it, too. Maybe, or maybe he'd just get dead.

I got out of the car and leaned back in the open door. "Go straight home, and if you don't have an extra cross, buy one tomorrow."

"Okay," he said.

I shut the door on his solemn, earnest face. I walked up the stairs and didn't look back. I didn't watch him drive away, still alive, still eager after his first brush with the monsters. I was only four years older than he was. Four years. It felt like centuries. I had never been that green. My mother's death when I was eight saw to that. It takes the edge off the shiny brightness to lose a parent early.

I was still going to try to talk Larry out of being a vampire executioner, but if all else failed, I'd work with him. There are only two kinds of vampire hunters: good ones and dead ones. Maybe I could make Larry one of the good ones. It beat the hell out of the alternative.

26

It was 3:34, Friday morning. It had been a long week. Of course, when hadn't it been a long week this year? I had told Bert to hire more help. He hired Larry. Why didn't that make me happy? Because Larry was just another victim waiting for the right monster. Please keep him safe, God, please. I'd had about as many innocents die on me as I thought I could handle.

The hallway had that middle-of-the-night feel to it. The only sounds were the hush of the heating vents, the muffled sound of my Nike Airs on the carpeting. It was too late for my day-living neighbors to stay up, and too early for them to get up. Two hours before dawn, you get privacy.

I opened my brand-new burglarproof lock and stepped into the darkness of my apartment. I hit the lights and flooded the white walls, carpet, couch, and chair with bright light. No matter how good your night vision is, everyone likes light. We're creatures of the daylight, no matter what we do for a living.

I threw my jacket on the kitchen counter. It was too dirty to toss on the white couch. I had mud and bits of weed plastered all over me. But very little blood; the night had turned out alright.

I was slipping out of the shoulder holster when I felt it. The air currents had moved, as if something had moved through them. Just like that I knew I wasn't alone.

My hand was on the gun butt when Edward's voice came out of the darkness of my bedroom. "Don't, Anita."

I hesitated, fingers touching the gun. "And if I do?"

"I'll shoot you. You know I'll do it." His voice was that soft, sure predatory sound. I'd seen him use flamethrowers when his voice sounded like that. Smooth and calm as the road to Hell.

I eased away from my gun. Edward would shoot me if I forced him to. Better not to force it, not yet. Not yet.

I clasped my hands on top of my head without waiting for him to tell me. Maybe I'd get brownie points for being a cooperative prisoner. Naw.

Edward stepped out of the darkness like a blond ghost. He was dressed all in black except for his short hair and pale face. His black-gloved hands held a Beretta 9mm pointed very steadily at my chest.

"New gun?" I asked.

The ghost of a smile curled his lips. "Yes, like it?"

"Beretta's a nice gun, but you know me."

"A Browning fan," he said.

I smiled at him. Just two ol' buddies talking shop.

He pressed the gun barrel against my body while he took the Browning from me. "Lean and spread it."

I leaned on the back of the couch while he patted me down. There was nothing to find, but Edward didn't know that. He was never careless. That was one of the reasons he was still alive. That, and the fact that he was very, very good.

"You said you couldn't pick my lock," I said.

"I brought better tools," he said.

"So it's not burglarproof."

"It would be to most people."

"But not to you."

He stared at me, his eyes as empty and dead as winter's sky. "I am not most people."

I had to smile. "You can say that again."

He frowned at me. "Give me the master's name, and we don't have to do this." The gun never wavered. My Browning stuck out of the front of his belt. I hoped he'd remembered the safety. Or maybe I didn't.

I opened my mouth, closed it, and just looked at him. I couldn't give Jean-Claude over to Edward. I was the Executioner, but the vampires called Edward Death. He'd earned the name.

"I thought you'd be following me tonight."

"I went home after watching you raise the zombie. Guess I should have stayed around. Who bloodied your mouth?"

"I'm not going to tell you a bloody thing. You know that."

"Everyone breaks, Anita, everyone."

"Even you?"

That ghost of a smile was back again. "Even me."

"Someone got the better of Death? Tell, tell."

The smile widened. "Some other time."

"Nice to know there'll be another time," I said.

"I'm not here to kill you."

"Just to frighten or torture me into revealing the master's name, right?"

"Right," he said, voice soft and low.

"I was hoping you'd say wrong."

He almost shrugged. "Give me the Master of the City, Anita, and I'll go away."

"You know I can't do that."

"I know you have to, or it's going to be a very long night."

"Then it's going to be a long night, because I'm not going to give you shit."

"You won't be bullied," he said.

"Nope."

He shook his head. "Turn around, lean your waist up against the couch, and put your hands behind your back."

"Why?"

"Just do it."

"So you can tie my hands?"

"Do it, now."

"I don't think so."

The frown was back. "Do you want me to shoot you?"

"No, but I'm not going to just stand here while you tie me up, either."

"The tying up doesn't hurt."

"It's what comes after that I'm worried about."

"You knew what I'd do if you didn't help me."

"Then do it," I said.

"You're not cooperating."

"So sorry."

"Anita."

"I just don't believe in helping people who are going to torture me. Though I don't see any bamboo slivers. How can you possibly torture someone without bamboo slivers?"

"Stop it." He sounded angry.

"Stop what?" I widened my eyes and tried to look innocent and harmless, me and Kermit the Frog.

Edward laughed, a soft chuckle that rolled and expanded until he squatted on the floor, gun loose in his hands, staring up at me. His eyes were shiny.

"How can I torture you when you keep making me laugh?"

"You can't; that was the plan."

He shook his head. "No, it wasn't. You were just being a smartass. You're always a smartass."

"Nice of you to notice."

He held up his hand. "No more, please."

"I'll make you laugh until you beg for mercy."

"Just tell me the damn name. Please, Anita. Help me." The laughter drained from his eyes like the sun slipping out of the sky. I watched the humor, the humanity, slip away, until his eyes were as cold and empty as a doll's. "Don't make me hurt you," he said.

I think I was Edward's only friend, but that wouldn't stop him from hurting me. Edward had one rule: do whatever it takes to get the job done. If I forced him to torture me, he would, but he didn't want to.

"Now that you've asked nicely, try the first question again," I said.

His eyes narrowed, then he said, "Who hit you in the mouth?"

"A master vampire," I said softly.

"Tell me what happened." It was too much like an order for my taste, but he did have both the guns.

I told him everything that had happened. All about Alejandro. Alejandro who felt so old inside my head, it made my bones ache. I added one tiny lie, lost in all that truth. I told him Alejandro was Master of the City. One of my better ideas, heh?

"You really don't know where his daytime resting place is, do you?"

I shook my head. "I'd give it to you if I had it."

"Why this change of heart?"

"He tried to kill me tonight. All bets are off."

"I don't believe that."

It was too good a lie to waste, so I tried salvaging it. "He's also gone rogue. It's him and his flunkies that have been killing innocent citizens."

Edward smirked at the innocent, but he let it go. "An altruistic motive, that I believe. If you weren't such a damn bleeding heart, you'd be dangerous."

"I kill my share, Edward."

His empty, blue eyes stared at me; then he nodded, slowly. "True."

He handed me back my gun, butt first. A tight, clenched ball in my stomach unrolled. I could breathe deep, long sighs of relief.

"If I find out where this Alejandro stays, you want in on it?"

I thought about that for a minute. Did I want to go after five rogue vampires, two of them over five hundred years old? I did not. Did I want to send even Edward after them alone? No, I did not. Which meant . . .

"Yeah, I want a piece of them."

Edward smiled, broad and shining. "I love my work."

I smiled back. "Me, too."

27

Jean-Claude lay in the middle of a white canopied bed. His skin was only slightly less white than the sheets. He was dressed in a nightshirt. Lace fell down the low collar, forming a lace window around his chest. Lace flowed from the sleeves, nearly hiding his hands. It should have looked feminine, but Jean-Claude made it utterly masculine. How could any man wear a white lace gown and not look silly? Of course, he wasn't a man. That must be it.

His black hair curled in the lace collar. Touchable. I shook my head. Not even in my dreams. I was dressed in something long and silky. It was a shade of blue almost as dark as his eyes. My arms looked very white against it. Jean-Claude got to his knees and reached his hand out to me. An invitation.

I shook my head.

"It is only a dream, *ma petite*. Will you not come to me even here?"

"It's never just a dream with you. It always means more."

His hand fell to the sheets, fingertips caressing the cloth.

"What are you trying to do to me, Jean-Claude?"

He looked very steadily at me. "Seduce you, of course."

Of course. Silly me.

The phone beside the bed rang. It was one of those white princess phones with lots of gold on it. There hadn't been a telephone a second before. It rang again, and the dream fell to shreds. I came awake grabbing for the phone.

"Hello."

"Hey, did I wake you?" Irving Griswold asked.

I blinked at the phone. "Yeah, what time is it?"

"It's ten o'clock. I know better than to call early."

"What do you want, Irving?"

"Grouchy."

"I got in late. Can we skip the sarcasm?"

"I, your true-blue reporter friend, will forgive you that grumpy hello, if you answer a few questions."

"Questions?" I sat up, hugging the phone to me. "What are you talking about?"

"Is it true that Humans First saved you last night, as they're claiming?"

"Claiming? Can you talk in complete sentences, Irving?"

"The morning news had Jeremy Ruebens on it. Channel five. He claimed that he and Humans First saved your life last night. Saved you from the Master Vampire of the City."

"Oh, he did not."

"May I quote you?"

I thought about that for a minute. "No."

"I need a quote for the paper. I'm trying to give a chance for a rebuttal."

"A rebuttal?"

"Hey, I was an English major."

"That explains so much."

"Can you give me your side of the story, or not?"

I thought about that for a minute. Irving was a friend and a good reporter. If Ruebens was already on the morning news with the story, I needed to get my side out. "Can you give me fifteen minutes to make coffee and get dressed?"

"For an exclusive, you bet."

"Talk to you then." I hung up and went straight for the coffeemaker. I was wearing jogging socks, jeans, and the oversized t-shirt I'd slept in when Irving called back. I had a steaming cup of coffee on the bedside table beside the phone. Cinnamon hazelnut coffee from V. J.'s Tea and Spice Shop over on Olive. Mornings didn't get much better than this.

"Okay, spill it," he said.

"Gee, Irving, no foreplay?"

"Get to it, Blake, I've got a deadline."

I told him everything. I had to admit that Humans First had saved my cookies. Darn. "I can't confirm that the vampire they ran off was the Master of the City."

"Hey, I know Jean-Claude is the master. I interviewed him, remember?"

"I remember."

"I know this Indian guy was not Jean-Claude."

"But Humans First doesn't know that."

"A double exclusive, wowee."

"No, don't say that Alejandro isn't the master."

"Why not?"

"I'd clear it with Jean-Claude first, if I were you."

He cleared his throat. "Yeah, not a bad idea." He sounded nervous.

"Is Jean-Claude giving you trouble?"

"No, why do you ask?"

"For a reporter you lie badly."

"Jean-Claude and I got business just between us. It doesn't concern The Executioner."

"Fine; just watch your back, okay?"

"I'm flattered that you're worried about me, Anita, but trust me, I can handle it."

I didn't argue with that. I must have been in a good mood. "Anything you say, Irving."

He let it go, so I did, too. No one could handle Jean-Claude, but it wasn't my business. Irving had been the one hot for the interview. So there were strings attached; not a big surprise, and not my business. Really.

"This'll be on the front page of the morning paper. I'll check with Jean-Claude about whether to mention this new vamp isn't the master."

"I'd really appreciate it if you could hold off on that."

"Why?" He sounded suspicious.

"Maybe it wouldn't be such a bad idea for Humans First to believe Alejandro is the master."

"Why?"

"So they don't kill Jean-Claude," I said.

"Oh," he said.

"Yeah," I said.

"I'll bear that in mind," he said.

"You do that."

"Gotta go; deadline calls."

"Okay, Irving, talk to you later."

"Bye, Anita, thanks." He hung up.

I sipped the still-steaming coffee, slowly. The first cup of the day should never be rushed. If I could get Humans First to believe the same lie Edward bought, then no one would be hunting Jean-Claude. They'd be hunting Alejandro. The master that was slaughtering humans. Put the police on the case, and we had the rogue vamps outnumbered. Yeah, I liked it.

The trick was, would everyone buy it? Never know until you try.

28

I had finished a pot of coffee and managed to get dressed when the phone rang again. One of those mornings.

"Yeah," I said.

"Ms. Blake?" the voice sounded very uncertain.

"Speaking."

"This is Karl Inger."

"Sorry if I sounded abrupt. What's up, Mr. Inger?"

"You said you'd speak to me again if we had a better plan. I have a better plan," he said.

"For killing the Master of the City?" I made it a question.

"Yes."

I took a deep breath and let it out slow, away from the phone. Didn't want him to think I was heavy breathing at him. "Mr. Inger . . ."

"Please, hear me out. We saved your life last night. That must be worth something."

He had me there. "What's your plan, Mr. Inger?"

"I'd rather tell you in person."

"I'm not going to my office for some hours yet."

"Could I come to your home?"

"No." It was automatic.

"You don't bring business home?"

"Not when I can help it," I said.

"Suspicious of you."

"Always," I said.

"Can we meet somewhere else? There's someone I want you to meet."

"Who, and why?"

"The name won't mean anything to you."

"Try me."

"Mr. Oliver."

"First name?"

"I don't know it."

"Okay, then why should I meet him?"

"He has a good plan for killing the Master of the City."

"What?"

"No, I think it will be better if Mr. Oliver explains it in person. He's much more persuasive than I am."

"You're doing okay," I said.

"Then you'll meet me?"

"Sure, why not?"

"That's wonderful. Do you know where Arnold is?"

"Yes."

"There's a pay fishing lake just outside of Arnold on Tesson Ferry Road. Do you know it?"

I had an impression that I had driven by it on the way to two murders. All roads led to Arnold. "I can find it."

"How soon can you meet me there?" he asked.

"An hour."

"Great; I'll be waiting."

"Is this Mr. Oliver going to be at the lake?"

"No, I'll drive you from there."

"Why all the secrecy?"

"Not secrecy," he said, his voice dropped, embarrassed. "I'm just not very good at giving directions. It'll be easier if I just take you."

"I can follow you in my car."

"Why, Ms. Blake, I don't think you entirely trust me."

"I don't entirely trust anybody, Mr. Inger, nothing personal."

"Not even people who save your life?"

"Not even."

He let that drop, probably for the best, and said, "I'll meet you at the lake in an hour."

"Sure."

"Thank you for coming, Ms. Blake."

"I owe you. You've made sure I'm aware of that."

"You sound defensive, Ms. Blake. I did not mean to offend you."

I sighed. "I'm not offended, Mr. Inger. I just don't like owing people."

"Visiting Mr. Oliver today will clear the slate between us. I promise that."

"I'll hold you to that, Inger."

"I'll meet you in an hour," he said.

"I'll be there," I said.

We hung up. "Damn." I'd forgotten I hadn't gotten to eat yet today. If I'd remembered, I'd have said two hours. Now I'd have to literally grab something on the way. I hated eating in the car. But, heh, what's a little mess between friends? Or even between people who've saved your life? Why did it bother me so much that I owed Inger?

Because he was a right-wing fruitcake. A zealot. I didn't like doing business with zealots. And I certainly didn't like owing my life to one.

Ah, well; I'd meet him, then we'd be square. He had said so. Why didn't I believe it?

29

Chip-Away Lake was about half an acre of man-made water and thin, raised man-made bank. There was a little shed that sold bait and food. It was surrounded by a flat gravel parking lot. A late-model car sat near the road with a sign that read, "For Sale." A pay fishing lake and a used car lot combined; how clever.

An expanse of grass spread out to the right of the parking lot. A small, ramshackle shed and what looked like the remains of some large industrial barbecue. A fringe of woods edged the grass, rising higher into a wooded hill. The Meramec River edged the left side of the lake. It seemed funny to have free-flowing water so close to the man-made lake.

There were only three cars in the parking lot this cool autumn afternoon. Beside a shiny burgundy Chrysler Le Baron stood Inger. A handful of fishermen had bundled up and put poles in the water. Fishing must be good to get people out in the cold.

I parked beside Inger's car. He strode towards me smiling, hand out like a real estate salesman who was happy I'd come to see the property. Whatever he was selling, I didn't want. I was almost sure of that.

"Ms. Blake, so glad you came." He clasped my hand with both of his, hearty, good-natured, insincere.

"What do you want, Mr. Inger?"

His smile faded around the edges. "I don't know what you mean, Ms. Blake."

"Yes, you do."

"No, I really don't."

I stared into his puzzled face. Maybe I spent too much time with slimeballs. After a while you forget that not everyone in the world is a slimeball. It just saves so much time to assume the worst.

"I'm sorry, Mr. Inger. I . . . I've been spending too much time looking for criminals. It makes you cynical."

He still looked puzzled.

"Never mind, Mr. Inger; just take me to see this Oliver."

"Mr. Oliver," he said.

"Sure"

"Shall we take my car?" He motioned towards his car.

"I'll follow you in mine."

"You don't trust me." He looked hurt. I guess most people aren't used to being suspected of wrongdoing before they've done anything wrong. The law says innocent until proven guilty, but the truth is, if you see enough pain and death, it's guilty until proven innocent.

"Alright, you drive."

He looked very pleased. Heartwarming.

Besides I was carrying two knives, three crosses, and a gun. Innocent or guilty, I was prepared. I didn't expect to need the weaponry with Mr. Oliver, but later, I might need it later. It was time to go armed to the teeth, ready for bear, or dragon, or vampire.

30

Inger drove down Old Highway 21 to East Rock Creek.
Rock Creek was a narrow, winding road barely wide enough
for two cars to pass. Inger drove slow enough for the curves,
but fast enough so you didn't get bored.

There were farmhouses that had stood for years and new
houses in subdivisions where the earth was raw and red as
a wound. Inger turned into one of those new subdivisions.
It was full of large, expensive-looking houses, very modern.
Thin, spindly trees were tied to stakes along the gravel
road. The pitiful trees trembled in the autumn wind, a
few surprised leaves still clinging to the spider-thin limbs.
This area had been a forest before they bulldozed it. Why
do developers destroy all the mature trees, then plant new
trees that won't look good for decades?

We pulled up in front of a fake log cabin that was bigger
than any real cabin had ever been. Too much glass, the yard
naked dirt the color of rust. The white gravel that made up
the driveway had to have been brought in from miles away.
All the native gravel was as red as the dirt.

Inger started to go around the car, to open my door I
think. I opened my own door. Inger seemed a little lost,
but he'd get over it. I'd never seen the sense in perfectly
healthy people not opening their own doors. Especially car
doors where the man had to walk all the way around the
car, and the woman just waited like a . . . a lump.

Inger led the way up the porch steps. It was a nice porch,
wide enough to sit on come summer evenings. Right now it
was all bare wood and a huge picture window with closed

drapes in a barn-red design with wagon wheels drawn all over it. Very rustic.

He knocked on the carved wooden door. A pane of leaded glass decorated the center of the door, high up and sparkling, more for decoration then for seeing through. He didn't wait for the door to be opened, but used a key and walked in. He didn't seem to expect an answer, so why knock?

The house was in a thick twilight of really nice drapes, all closed against the syrup-heavy sunlight. The polished wood floors were utterly bare. The mantel of the heavy fireplace was naked, the fireplace cold. The place smelled new and unused, like new toys on Christmas. Inger never hesitated. I followed his broad back into the wooden hallway. He didn't look behind to see if I was keeping up. Apparently when I'd decided not to let him open my door for me, he seemed to have decided that no further courtesy was necessary.

Fine with me.

There were doors at widely spaced intervals along the hallway. Inger knocked at the third door on the left. A voice said, "Enter."

Inger opened the door and went inside. He held the door for me, standing very straight by the door. It wasn't courtesy. He stood like a soldier at attention. Who was in the room to make Inger toe the line? One way to find out.

I went into the room.

There was a bank of windows to the north with heavy drapes pulled across them. A thin line of sunlight cut across the room, bisecting a large, clean desk. A man sat in a large chair behind the desk.

He was a small man, almost a midget or a dwarf. I wanted to say dwarf, but he didn't have the jaw or the shortened arms. He looked well formed under his tailored suit. He had almost no chin and a sloping forehead, which drew attention to the wide nose and the prominent eyebrow ridge. There was something familiar about his face, as if I'd seen it somewhere else before. Yet I knew I'd never met a person who looked just like him. It was a very singular face.

I was staring at him. I was embarrassed and didn't like it. I met his eyes; they were perfectly brown and smiling. His dark hair was cut one hair at a time, expensive and blow-dried. He sat in his chair behind the clean polished desk and smiled at me.

"Mr. Oliver, this is Anita Blake," Inger said, still standing stiffly by the door.

He got out of his chair and came around the desk to offer me his small, well-formed hand. He was four feet tall, not an inch more. His handshake was firm and much stronger than he looked. A brief squeeze, and I could feel the strength in his small frame. He didn't look musclebound, but that easy strength was there, in his face, hand, stance.

He was small, but he didn't think it was a defect. I liked that. I felt the same way.

He gave a close-lipped smile and sat back down in his big chair. Inger brought a chair from the corner and put it facing the desk. I took the chair. Inger remained standing by the now-closed door. He was defiantly at attention. He respected the man in the chair. I was willing to like him. That was a first for me. I'm more likely to instantly mistrust than like someone.

I realized that I was smiling. I felt warm and comfortable facing him, like he was a favorite and trusted uncle. I frowned at him; what the hell was happening to me?

"What's going on?" I said.

He smiled, his eyes sparkling warmly at me. "Whatever do you mean, Ms. Blake?"

His voice was soft, low, rich, like cream in coffee. You could almost taste it. A comforting warmth to your ears. I only knew one other voice that could do similar things.

I stared at the thin band of sunlight only inches from Oliver's arm. It was broad daylight. He couldn't be. Could he?

I stared at his very alive face. There was no trace of that otherness that vampires gave off. And yet, his voice, this warm cosy feeling, none of it was natural. I'd never liked and trusted anyone instantly. I wasn't about to start now.

"You're good," I said "Very good."

"Whatever do you mean, Ms. Blake?" You could have cuddled into the warm fuzziness of his voice like a favorite blanket.

"Stop it."

He looked quizzically at me, as if confused. The act was perfect, and I realized why; it wasn't an act. I'd been around ancient vampires, but never one that had been able to pass for human, not like this. You could have taken him anywhere and no one would have known. Well, almost no one.

"Believe me, Ms. Blake, I'm not trying to do anything."

I swallowed hard. Was that true? Was he so damn powerful that the mind tricks and the voice were automatic? No; if Jean-Claude could control it, this thing could, too.

"Cut the mind tricks, and curb the voice, okay? If you want to talk business, talk, but cut the games."

His smile widened, still not enough to show fangs. After a few hundred years, you must get really good at smiling like that.

He laughed then; it was wonderful, like warm water falling from a great height. You could have jumped into it and bathed, and felt good.

"Stop it, stop it!"

Fangs flashed as he finished chuckling at me. "It isn't the vampire marks that allowed you to see through my, as you call them, games. It is natural talent, isn't it?"

I nodded. "Most animators have it."

"But not to the degree you do, Ms. Blake. You have power, too. It crawls along my skin. You are a necromancer."

I started to deny it, but stopped. Lying to something like this was useless. He was older than anything I'd ever dreamed of, older than any nightmare I'd ever had. But he didn't make my bones ache; he felt good, better than Jean-Claude, better than anything.

"I could be a necromancer. I choose not to be."

"No, Ms. Blake, the dead respond to you, all the dead. Even I feel the pull."

"You mean I have a sort of power over vampires, too?"

"If you could learn to harness your talents, Ms. Blake, yes, you have a certain power over all the dead, in their many guises."

I wanted to ask how to do that, but stopped myself. A master vampire wasn't likely to help me gain power over his followers. "You're taunting me."

"I assure you, Ms. Blake, that I am very serious. It is your potential power that has drawn the Master of the City to you. He wants to control that emerging power, for fear it will be turned against him."

"How do you know that?"

"I can taste him through the marks he has laid upon you."

I just stared at him. He could taste Jean-Claude. Shit.

"What do you want from me?"

"Very direct; I like that. Human lives are too short to waste in trivialities."

Was that a threat? Staring into his smiling face, I couldn't tell. His eyes were still sparkling, and I was still feeling very warm and fuzzy towards him. Eye contact. I knew better than that. I stared at the top of his desk and felt better, or worse. I could be scared now.

"Inger said you had a plan for taking out the Master of the City. What is it?" I spoke staring at his desk. My skin crawled with the desire to look up. To meet his eyes, to let the warmth and comfort wash over me. Make all the decisions easy.

I shook my head. "Stay out of my mind or this interview is over."

He laughed again, warm and real. It raised goose bumps on my arms. "You really are good. I haven't met a human in centuries that rivaled you. A necromancer; do you realize how rare that talent is?"

Really I didn't, but I said, "Yes."

"Lies, Ms. Blake, to me, please don't bother."

"We're not here to talk about me. Either state your plan or I'm leaving."

"I am the plan, Ms. Blake. You can feel my powers, the ebb and flow of more centuries than your little master has ever dreamed of. I am older than time itself."

That I didn't believe, but I let it go. He was old enough; I wasn't going to argue with him, not if I could help it.

"Give me your master and I will free you of his marks."

I glanced up, then quickly down. He was still smiling at me, but the smile didn't look real anymore. It was an act like everything else. It was just a very good act.

"If you can taste my master in the marks, can't you just find him yourself?"

"I can taste his power, judge how worthy a foe he would be, but not his name and not where he lies; that is hidden." His voice was very serious now, not trying to trick me. Or at least I didn't think it was; maybe that was a trick, too.

"What do you want from me?"

"His name and his daytime resting place."

"I don't know the daytime resting place." I was glad it was the truth, because he would smell a lie.

"Then his name, give me his name."

"Why should I?"

"Because I wish to be Master of the City, Ms. Blake."

"Why?"

"So many questions. Is it not enough that I would free you from his power?"

I shook my head. "No."

"Why should you care about what happens to the other vampires?"

"I don't, but before I hand you the power to control every vampire in the immediate area, I'd like to know what you intend to do with all that power."

He laughed again. This time it was just a laugh. He was trying.

"You are the most stubborn human I have met in a very long time. I like stubborn people; they get things done."

"Answer my question."

"I think it is wrong to have vampires as legal citizens. I wish to put things back as they were."

"Why should you want vampires to be hunted again?"

"They are too powerful to be allowed to spread unchecked. They will take over the human race much quicker through legislation and voting rights than they ever could through violence."

I remembered the Church of Eternal Life, the fastest-growing denomination in the country. "Say you're right; how would you stop it?"

"By forbidding the vampires to vote, or take part in any legislation."

"There are other master vampires in town."

"You mean Malcolm, the head of the Church of Eternal Life."

"Yes."

"I have observed him. He will not be able to continue his one-man crusade to make vampires legitimate. I shall forbid it and dismantle his church. Surely you see the church as the larger danger, as I do."

I did, but I hated agreeing with an ancient master vampire. It seemed wrong somehow.

"St. Louis is a hotbed of political activity and entrepreneurial vampires. They must be stopped. We are predators, Ms. Blake; nothing we do can change that. We must go back to being hunted or the human race is doomed. Surely you see that."

I did see that. I believed that. "Why would you care if the human race is doomed? You're not part of it anymore."

"As the oldest living vampire, it is my duty to keep us in check, Ms. Blake. These new rights are getting out of hand and must be stopped. We are too powerful to be allowed such freedom. Humans have their right to be human. In the olden days only the strongest, smartest, or luckiest vampires survived. The human vampire hunters weeded out the stupid, the careless, the violent. Without that check-and-balance system, I fear what will happen in a few decades."

I agreed, wholeheartedly; it was sorta scary. I agreed with the oldest living thing I'd ever met. He was right. Could I give him Jean-Claude? Should I give him Jean-Claude?

"I agree with you, Mr. Oliver, but I can't just give him up, just like that. I don't know why really, but I can't."

"Loyalty; I admire that. Think upon it, Ms. Blake, but do not take too long. I need to put my plan into action as soon as possible."

I nodded. "I understand. I . . . I'll give you an answer within a couple of days. How do I reach you?"

"Inger will give you a card with a number on it. You may safely speak to him as to me."

I turned and looked at Inger, still standing at attention beside the door. "You're his human servant, aren't you?"

"I have that honor."

I shook my head. "I need to leave now."

"Do not feel badly that you could not recognize Inger as my human servant. It is not a mark which shows; otherwise how could they be our human ears and eyes and hands, if everyone knew they were ours?"

He had a point. He had a lot of points. I stood up. He stood up, too. He offered me his hand.

"I'm sorry, but I know that touching makes the mind games easier."

The hand dropped back to his side. I do not need to touch you to play mind games, Ms. Blake." The voice was wonderful, shining and bright as Christmas morning. My throat was tight, and the warmth of tears filled my eyes. Shit, shit, shit, shit.

I backed for the door, and Inger opened it for me. They were just going to let me leave. He wasn't going to mind-rape me and get the name. He was really going to let me walk away. That did more to prove him a good guy than anything else. Because he could have squeezed my mind dry. But he let me go.

Inger closed the door behind us, slowly, reverently.

"How old is he?" I asked.

"You couldn't tell?"

I shook my head. "How old?"

Inger smiled. "I am over seven hundred years old. Mr. Oliver was ancient when I met him."

"He's older than a thousand years."

"Why do you say that?"

"I've met a vampire that was a little over a thousand. She was scary, but she didn't have that kind of power."

He smiled. "If you wish to know his true age, then you must ask him yourself."

I stared up at Inger's smiling face for a minute. I remembered where I'd seen a face like Oliver's. I'd had one anthropology class in college. There'd been a drawing that looked just like Oliver. It had been a reconstruction of a *Homo erectus* skull. Which made Oliver about a million years old.

"My God," I said.

"What's wrong, Ms. Blake?"

I shook my head. "He can't be that old."

"How old is that?"

I didn't want to say it out loud, as if that would make it real. A million years. How powerful would a vampire grow in a million years?

A woman walked up the hallway towards us, coming from deeper in the house. She swayed on bare feet, toenails painted a bright scarlet that matched her fingernails. The belted dress she wore matched the nail polish. Her legs were long and pale, but it was that kind of paleness that promised to tan if it ever got enough sunlight. Her hair fell past her waist, thick and absolute black. Her makeup was perfect, her lips scarlet. She smiled at me; fangs showed below her lips.

But she wasn't a vampire. I didn't know what the hell she was, but I knew what she wasn't. I glanced at Inger. He didn't look happy.

"Shouldn't we be going?" I said.

"Yes," he said. He backed towards the front door and I backed behind him. Neither of us took our eyes off the fanged beauty slinking down the hall towards us.

She moved in a liquid run that was almost too fast to follow. Lycanthropes could move like that, but that wasn't what she was, either.

She was around Inger and coming for me. I gave up being cool and sort of ran backwards towards the front door. But she was too fast for me, too fast for any human.

She grabbed my right forearm. She looked puzzled. She could feel the knife sheath on my arm. She didn't seem to know what it was. Bully for me.

"What are you?" My voice was steady. Not afraid. Heap big vampire slayer. Yeah, right.

She opened her mouth wider, tongue caressing the fangs. The fangs were longer than a vampire's; she'd never be able to close her mouth around them.

"Where do the fangs go when you close your mouth?" I said.

She blinked at me, the smile slipping away from her face. She ran her tongue over them, then they folded back into the roof of her mouth.

"Retractable fangs. Cool," I said.

Her face was very solemn. "I'm glad you enjoyed the show, but there's so much more to see." The fangs unfolded again. She widened her jaws, almost a yawn, flashing the fangs nicely in the dim beams of sunlight that got around the drapes.

"Mr. Oliver will not like you threatening her," Inger said.

"He grows weak, sentimental." Her fingers dug into my arm stronger than she should have been.

She was holding my right arm, so I couldn't go for the gun. The knives were out for similar reasons. Maybe I should wear more guns.

She hissed at me, a violent explosion of air that no human throat ever made. The tongue that flicked out was forked.

"Sweet Jesus, what are you?"

She laughed, but it didn't sound right now; maybe the split tongue. Her pupils had narrowed to slits, her irises turned a golden yellow while I watched.

I tugged on my arm but her fingers were like steel. I dropped to the floor. She lowered my arm but didn't let go.

I leaned back on my left side, drew my legs up under me, and kicked her right kneecap with everything I had. The leg crumpled. She screamed and fell to the floor, but she let my arm go.

Something was happening to her legs. They seemed to be growing together, the skin spreading. I'd never seen anything like it, and I didn't want to now.

"Melanie, what are you doing?" The voice was behind us. Oliver stood in the hallway just short of the brighter light of the living room. His voice was the sound of rocks falling, trees breaking. A storm that was just words but seemed to cut and slash.

The thing on the floor cringed from the voice. Her lower body was becoming serpentine. A snake of some kind. Jesus.

"She's a lamia," I said softly. I backed away, putting the outside door to my back, hand on the door knob. "I thought they were extinct."

"She is the last one," Oliver said. "I keep her with me because I fear what she would do left to her own desires."

"Your creature that you can call, what is it?" I asked.

He sighed, and I felt the years of sadness in that one sound. A regret too deep for words. "Snakes, I can call snakes."

I nodded my head. "Sure." I opened the door and backed out onto the sunny porch. No one tried to stop me.

The door shut behind me and after a few minutes Inger came out. He was stiff with anger. "We most humbly apologize for her. She is an animal."

"Oliver needs to keep her on a tighter leash."

"He tries."

I nodded. I knew about trying. Doing your best, but anything that could control a lamia could play mind games with me all day, and I might never know it. How much of my trust and good wishes was real and how much of it was manufactured by Oliver?

"I'll drive you back."

"Please."

And away we went. I'd met my first lamia and perhaps the oldest living creature in the world. A red-fucking-letter day.

31

The phone was ringing as I unlocked the apartment door. I shoved the door open with my shoulder and ran for the phone. I got it on the fifth ring and nearly yelled, "Hello."

"Anita?" Ronnie made it a question.

"Yeah, it's me."

"You sound out of breath."

"I had to run for the phone. What's up?"

"I remembered where I knew Cal Rupert from."

It took me a minute to remember who she was talking about. The first vampire victim. I'd forgotten, just for a moment, that there was a murder investigation going on. I was a little ashamed of that. "Talk to me, Ronnie."

"I was doing some work for a local law firm last year. One of the lawyers specialized in drawing up dying wills."

"I know that Rupert had a dying will. That's how I could stake him without waiting for an order of execution."

"But did you also know that Reba Baker had a dying will with the same lawyer?"

"Who's Reba Baker?"

"It may be the female victim."

My stomach tightened. A clue, a real live clue. "What makes you think so?"

"Reba Baker was young, blond, and missed an appointment. She doesn't answer her phone. They called her at work, and she hasn't been in for two days."

"The length of time she'd have been dead," I said.

"Exactly."

"Call Sergeant Rudolf Storr. Tell him what you just told me. Use my name to get to him."

"You don't want to check it out ourselves?"

"Not on your life. This is police business. They're good at it. Let 'em earn their paychecks."

"Shucks, you're no fun."

"Ronnie, call Dolph. Give it to the police. I've met the vampires that are killing these people. We don't want to make ourselves targets."

"You what!"

I sighed. I'd forgotten that Ronnie didn't know. I told her the shortest version that would make any sense. "I'll fill you in on everything Saturday morning when we work out."

"You going to be alright?"

"So far, so good."

"Watch your back, okay?"

"Always; you too."

"I never seem to have as many people after my back as you do."

"Be thankful," I said.

"I am." She hung up.

We had a clue. Maybe a pattern, except for the attack on me. I didn't fit any pattern. They'd come after me to get Jean-Claude. Everybody wanted Jean-Claude's job. The trouble was, you couldn't abdicate; you could only die. I liked what Oliver had had to say. I agreed with him, but could I sacrifice Jean-Claude on the altar of good sense? Dammit.

I just didn't know.

32

Bert's office was small and painted pale blue. He thought it was soothing to the clients. I thought it was cold, but that fit Bert, too. He was six feet tall with the broad shoulders and build of an ex-college football player. His stomach was moving a little south with too much food and not enough exercise, but he carried it well in his seven-hundred-dollar suits. For that kind of money, the suits should have carried the Taj Mahal.

He was tanned, grey-eyed, with a buzz haircut that was nearly white. Not age, his natural hair color.

I was sitting across from his desk in work clothes. A red skirt, matching jacket, and a blouse that was so close to scarlet I'd had to put on a little makeup so that my face didn't seem ghostly. The jacket was tailored so that my shoulder holster didn't show.

Larry sat in the chair beside me in a blue suit, white shirt, and blue-on-blue tie. The skin around his stitches had blossomed into a multicolored bruise across his forehead. His short red hair couldn't hide it. It looked like someone had hit him in the head with a baseball bat.

"You could have gotten him killed, Bert," I said.

"He wasn't in any danger until you showed up. The vampires wanted you, not him."

He was right, and I didn't like it. "He tried to raise a third zombie."

Bert's cold little eyes lit up. "You can do three in a night?"

Larry had the grace to look embarrassed. "Almost."

Bert frowned. "What's 'almost' mean?"

"It means he raised it, but lost control of it. If I hadn't been there to fix things, we'd have had a rampaging zombie on our hands."

He leaned forward, hands folded on his desk, small eyes very serious. "Is this true, Larry?"

"I'm afraid so, Mr. Vaughn."

"That could have been very serious, Larry. You understand that?"

"Serious?" I said. "It would have been a bloody disaster. The zombie could have eaten one of our clients!"

"Now, Anita, no reason to frighten the boy."

I stood up. "Yes, there is."

Bert frowned at me. "If you hadn't been late, he wouldn't have tried to raise the last zombie."

"No, Bert. You are not making this all my fault. You sent him out on his first night alone. Alone, Bert."

"And he handled himself well," Bert said.

I fought the urge to scream, because it wouldn't help. "Bert, he's a twenty-year-old college student. This is a freaking seminar for him. If you get him killed, it's gonna look sorta bad."

"May I say something?" Larry asked.

I said, "No."

Bert said, "Certainly."

"I'm a big boy. I can take care of myself."

I wanted to argue that, but looking into his true-blue eyes I couldn't say it. He was twenty. I remembered twenty. I'd known everything at twenty. It took me another year to realize I knew nothing. I was still hoping to learn something before I hit thirty, but I wasn't holding my breath.

"How old were you when you started working for me?" Bert said.

"What?"

"How old were you?"

"Twenty-one; I'd just graduated college."

"When will you turn twenty-one, Larry?" Bert asked.

"March."

"See, Anita, he's just a few months younger. He's the same age you were."

"That was different."

"Why?" Bert said.

I couldn't put it into words. Larry still had all his grand-parents. He'd never seen death and violence up close and personal. I had. He was an innocent, and I hadn't been innocent for years. But how to explain that to Bert without hurting Larry's feelings? No twenty-year-old man likes to hear that a woman knows more about the world than he does. Some cultural fables die hard.

"You sent me out with Manny, not alone."

"He was supposed to go out with you, but you had police business to handle."

"That's not fair, Bert, and you know it."

He shrugged. "If you'd been doing your job, he wouldn't have been alone."

"There've been two murders. What am I supposed to do? Say sorry, folks, I've got to babysit a new animator. Sorry about the murders."

"Nobody has to babysit me," Larry said.

We both ignored him.

"You have a full time job here with Animators, Inc."

"We've had this argument before, Bert."

"Too many times," he said.

"You're my boss, Bert. Do what you think best."

"Don't tempt me."

"Hey, guys," Larry said, "I'm getting the feeling that you're using me for an excuse to fight. Don't get carried away, okay?"

We both glared at him. He didn't back down, just stared at us. Point for him.

"If you don't like the way I do my job, Bert, fire me, but stop yanking my chain."

Bert stood up, slowly, like a leviathan rising from the waves. "Anita . . ."

The phone rang. We all stared at it for a minute. Bert finally picked it up and growled, "Yeah, what is it?"

He listened for a minute, then glared at me. "It's for you." His voice was incredibly mild as he said it. "Detective Sergeant Storr, police business."

Bert's face was smiling, butter wouldn't have melted in his mouth.

I held out my hand for the phone without another word. He handed me the receiver. He was still smiling, his tiny grey eyes warm and sparkling. It was a bad sign.

"Hi, Dolph, what's up?"

"We're at the lawyer's office that your friend Veronica Sims gave us. Nice that she called you first and not us."

"She called you second, didn't she?"

"Yeah."

"What have you found out?" I didn't bother to keep my voice down. If you're careful, one side of a conversation isn't very enlightening.

"Reba Baker is the dead woman. They identified her from morgue photos."

"Pleasant way to end the work week," I said.

Dolph ignored that. "Both victims were clients with dying wills. If they died by vampire bite, they wanted to be staked, then cremated."

"Sounds like a pattern to me," I said.

"But how did the vampires find out that they had dying wills?"

"Is this a trick question, Dolph? Someone told them."

"I know that," he said. He sounded disgusted.

I was missing something. "What do you want from me, Dolph?"

"I've questioned everyone, and I'd swear they were all telling the truth. Could someone have been giving the information and not remember?"

"You mean could the vampire have played mind games, so that the traitor wouldn't know afterwards?"

"Yeah," he said.

"Sure," I said.

"Could you tell which one the vampire got to if you were here?"

I glanced at my boss's face. If I missed another night during our busiest season, he might fire me. There were days when I didn't think I'd care. This wasn't one of them. "Look for memory losses; hours, or even entire nights."

"Anything else?"

"If someone has been feeding info to the vampires, they may not remember it, but a good hypnotist will be able to raise the memory."

"The lawyer is screaming about rights and warrants. We've only got a warrant for the files, not for their minds."

"Ask him if he wants to be responsible for tonight's murder victim, one of his own clients?"

"She; the lawyer's a woman," he said.

How embarrassing and how sexist of me. "Ask her if she's willing to explain to her client's family why she obstructed your investigation."

"The clients won't know unless we let it out," he said.

"That's true," I said.

"Why, that would be blackmail, Ms. Blake."

"Isn't it, though?" I said.

"You had to be a cop in a past life," he said. "You're too devious not to be."

"Thanks for the compliment."

"Any hypnotists you'd recommend?"

"Alvin Thormund. Wait a sec and I'll get his number for you." I got out my thin business card holder. I tried to only keep cards I wanted to refer to from time to time. We'd used Alvin for several cases of vampire victims with amnesia. I gave Dolph the number.

"Thanks, Anita."

"Let me know what you find out. I might be able to identify the vampire involved."

"You want to be there when we put them under?"

I glanced at Bert. His face was still relaxed, pleasant. Bert at his most dangerous.

"I don't think so. Just make a recording of the session. If I need to, I'll listen to it later."

"Later may mean another body," he said. "Your boss giving you trouble again?"

"Yeah," I said.

"You want me to talk to him?" Dolph asked.

"I don't think so."

"He being a real bastard about it?"

"The usual."

"Okay, I'll call this Thormund and record the sessions. I'll let you know if we find out anything."

"Beep me."

"You got it." He hung up. I didn't bother to say good-bye. Dolph never did.

I handed the phone back to Bert. He hung it up still staring at me with his pleasant, threatening eyes. "You have to go out for the police tonight?"

"No."

"How did we merit this honor?"

"Cut the sarcasm, Bert." I turned to Larry. "You ready to go, kid?"

"How old are you?" he asked.

Bert grinned.

"What difference does it make?" I asked.

"Just answer the question, okay?"

I shrugged. "Twenty-four."

"You're only four years older than me. Don't call me kid."

I had to smile. "Deal, but we better be going. We have dead to raise, money to make." I glanced at Bert.

He was leaning back in his chair, blunt-fingered hands clasped over his belly. He was grinning.

I wanted to wipe the grin off his face with a fist. I resisted the urge. Who says I have no self-control?

33

It was an hour before dawn. When all the Whos down in Whoville were asnooze in their beds without care. Sorry, wrong book. If I get to stay awake until dawn, I get just a tad slaphappy. I'd been up all night teaching Larry how to be a good, law-abiding animator. I wasn't sure Bert would appreciate the last, but I knew I would.

The cemetery was small. A family plot with pretensions. A narrow two-lane road rounded a hill, and suddenly there it was, a swathe of gravel beside the road. You had seconds to decide to turn in, that this was it. Tombstones climbed up the hill. The angle was so steep, it looked like the coffins should have slid downhill.

We stood in the dark with a canopy of trees whispering overhead. The woods were thick on either side of the road. The little plot was just a narrow space beside the road, but it was well cared for. There were still-living family members to see to the upkeep. I didn't even want to imagine how they mowed the hillside. Maybe a rope-and-pulley system to make sure the mower didn't roll over and add another corpse.

Our last clients of the night had just driven away back to civilization. I'd raised five zombies. Larry had raised one. Yeah, he could have raised two, but we just ran out of darkness. It doesn't take that long to raise a zombie, at least for me, but there's travel time included. In four years I'd only had two zombies in the same cemetery on the same night. Most of the time you were driving like a maniac to make all the appointments.

My poor car had been towed to a service station, but the insurance people hadn't seen it yet. It would take days or weeks for them to tell me it was totaled. There hadn't been time to rent a car for the night, so Larry was driving. He'd have been with me even if I'd had the car. I was the one bitching about not having enough help, so I got to train him. It was only fair, I guessed.

The wind rushed through the trees. Dry leaves scurried across the road. The night was full of small, hurried noises. Rushing, rushing, towards...what? All Hallows Eve. You could feel Halloween on the air.

"I love nights like this," Larry said.

I glanced over at him. We were both standing with our hands in our pockets staring out into the darkness. Enjoying the evening. We were also both covered in dried chicken blood. Just a nice, normal night.

My beeper went off. The high-pitched beep sounded very wrong in the quiet, windswept night. I hit the button. Mercifully, the noise stopped. The little light flashed a phone number at me. I didn't recognize the number. I hoped it wasn't Dolph, because an unfamiliar number this late at night, or early in the morning, meant another murder. Another body.

"Come on, we gotta get to a phone."

"Who is it?"

"I'm not sure." I started down the hill.

He followed me and asked, "Who do you think it is?"

"Maybe the police."

"The murders you're working on?"

I glanced back at him and rammed my knee into a tombstone. I stood there for a few seconds, holding my breath while the pain ran through me. "Shiiit!" I said softly and with feeling.

"Are you alright?" Larry touched my arm.

I drew away from his hand, and he let his hand drop. I wasn't much into casual touching. "I'm fine." Truth was, it still hurt, but what the hell? I needed to get to a phone, and the pain would get better the more I walked on it. Honest.

I stared carefully ahead to avoid other hard objects. "What do you know about the murders?"

"Just that you're helping the police on a preternatural crime, and that it's taking you away from your animating jobs."

"Bert told you that."

"Mr. Vaughn, yes."

We were at the car. "Look, Larry, if you're going to work for Animators, Inc., you've got to drop all this Mr. and Ms. stuff. We aren't your professors. We're coworkers."

He smiled, a flash of white in the dark. "Alright, Ms. . . . . Anita."

"That's better. Now let's go find a phone."

We drove into Chesterfield on the theory that, as the closest town, it would have the closest phone. We ended up at a bank of pay phones in the parking lot of a closed service station. The station glowed softly in the dark, but a halogen streetlight beamed over the pay phones, turning night into day. Insects and moths danced around the light. The swift, flitting shapes of bats swam in and out of the light, eating the insects.

I dialed the number while Larry waited in the car. Give him a point for discretion. The phone rang twice; then a voice said, "Anita, is that you?"

It was Irving Griswold, reporter and friend. "Irving, what in blazes are you doing paging me at this hour?"

"Jean-Claude wants to see you tonight, now." His voice sounded rushed and uncertain.

"Why are you delivering the message?" I was afraid I wasn't going to like the answer.

"I'm a werewolf," he said.

"What's that got to do with anything?"

"You didn't know." He sounded surprised.

"Know what?" I was getting angry. I hate twenty questions.

"Jean-Claude's animal is a wolf."

That explained Stephen the Werewolf and the black woman. "Why weren't you there the other night, Irving? Did he let you off your leash?"

"That's not fair."

He was right. It wasn't. "I'm sorry, Irving. I'm just feeling guilty because I introduced the two of you."

"I wanted to interview the Master of the City. I got my interview."

"Was it worth the price?" I said.

"No comment."

"That's my line."

He laughed. "Can you come to the Circus of the Damned? Jean-Claude has some information on the master vampire that jumped you."

"Alejandro?"

"That's the one."

"We'll be there as soon as we can, but it's going to be damn close to dawn before we can get to the Riverfront."

"Who's we?"

"A new animator I'm breaking in. He's driving." I hesitated. "Tell Jean-Claude no rough stuff tonight."

"Tell him yourself."

"Coward."

"Yes, ma'am. See you as soon as you can get here. Bye."

"Bye, Irving." I held the buzzing receiver for a few seconds, then hung up. Irving was Jean-Claude's creature. Jean-Claude could call wolves the way Mr. Oliver called snakes. The way Nikolaos had called rats, and wererats. They were all monsters. It was just a choice of flavors.

I slid back into the car. "You wanted more experience with vampires, right?" I buckled the seat belt.

"Of course," Larry said.

"Well, you're going to get it tonight."

"What do you mean?"

"I'll explain while you drive. We don't have much time before dawn."

Larry threw the car in gear and peeled out of the parking lot. He looked eager in the dim glow of the dashboard. Eager and very, very young.

34

The Circus of the Damned had closed down for the night, or would that be morning? It was still dark, but there was a wash of lightness to the east as we parked in front of the warehouse. An hour earlier, and there wouldn't have been a parking place even close to the Circus. But the tourists leave as the vampires fold down for the night.

I glanced at Larry. His face was smeared with dried blood. So was mine. It hadn't occurred to me until just now to find some place to clean up first. I glanced up at the eastern sky and shook my head. There was no time. Dawn was coming.

The toothed clowns still glowed and twirled atop the marquee, but it was a tired dance. Or maybe I was the one who was tired.

"Follow my lead in here, Larry. Never forget that they are monsters; no matter how human they look, they aren't. Don't take off your cross, don't let them touch you, and don't stare directly into their eyes."

"I know that from class. I had two semesters of Vampire Studies."

I shook my head. "Class is nothing, Larry. This is the real thing. Reading about it doesn't prepare you for it."

"We had guest speakers. Some of them were vampires."

I sighed and let it go. He'd have to learn on his own. Like everybody else did. Like I had.

The big doors were locked. I knocked. The door opened a moment later. Irving stood there. He wasn't smiling. He looked like a chubby cherub with soft, curling hair in a fringe over his ears, and a big bald spot in the middle. Round, wire-framed glasses perched on a round little nose. His eyes widened a little as we stepped inside. The blood looked like what it was in the light.

"What have you been doing tonight?" he asked.

"Raising the dead," I said.

"This the new animator?"

"Larry Kirkland, Irving Griswold. He's a reporter, so everything you say can be used against you."

"Hey, Blake, I've never quoted you when you said not to. Give me that."

I nodded. "Given."

"He's waiting for you downstairs," Irving said.

"Downstairs?" I said.

"It is almost dawn. He needs to be underground."

Ah. "Sure," I said, but my stomach clenched tight. The last time I'd gone downstairs at the Circus, it had been to kill Nikolaos. There had been a lot of killing that morning. A lot of blood. Some of it mine.

Irving led the way through the silent midway. Someone had hit the switch, and the lights were dull. The fronts of the games had been shut and locked down, covers thrown over the stuffed animals. The scent of corn dogs and cotton candy hung on the air like aromatic ghosts, but the smells were dim and tired.

We passed the haunted house with its life-size witch on top, standing silent and staring with bulging eyes. She was green and had a wart on her nose. I'd never met a witch that looked anything but normal. They certainly weren't green, and warts could always be surgically removed.

The glass house was next. The darkened Ferris wheel towered over everything. "I feel like one, / Who treads alone / Some banquet hall deserted, / Whose lights are fled, / Whose garlands dead, / And all but he departed," I said.

Irving glanced back to me. "Thomas Moore, *Oft in the Stilly Night*."

I smiled. "I couldn't remember the title to save myself. I'll just have to agree with you."

"Double major, journalism and English literature."

"I bet that last comes in handy as a reporter," I said.

"Hey, I slip a little culture in when I can." He sounded offended, but I knew he was pretending. It made me feel better to have Irving joking with me. It was nice and normal. I needed all the nice I could get tonight.

It was an hour until dawn. What harm could Jean-Claude do in an hour? Better not to ask.

The door in the wall was heavy and wooden with a sign reading, "Authorized Personnel Only Beyond This Point." For once I wished I wasn't authorized.

The little room beyond was just a small storage room with a bare light bulb hanging from the ceiling. A second door led down the stairs. The stairs were almost wide enough for the three of us to walk abreast, but not quite. Irving walked ahead of us, as if we still needed leading. There was nowhere to go but down. Prophetic, that.

There was a sharp bend to the stairs. There was a brush of cloth, the sensation of movement. I had my gun out and ready. No thought necessary, just lots and lots of practice.

"You won't need that," Irving said.

"Says you."

"I thought the Master was a friend of yours," Larry said.

"Vampires don't have friends."

"How about junior high science teachers?" Richard Zeeman walked around the corner. He was wearing a forest-green sweater with a lighter green and brown forest woven into it. The sweater hung down nearly to his knees. On me it would have been a dress. The sleeves were pushed back over his forearms. Jeans and the same pair of white Nikes completed the outfit. "Jean-Claude sent me up to wait for you."

"Why?" I asked.

He shrugged. "He seems nervous. I didn't ask questions."

"Smart man," I said.

"Let's keep moving," Irving said.

"You sound nervous, too, Irving."

"He calls and I obey, Anita. I'm his animal."

I reached out to touch Irving's arm, but he moved away. "I thought I could play human, but he's shown me that I'm an animal. Just an animal."

"Don't let him do that to you," I said.

He stared at me, his eyes filled with tears. "I can't stop him."

"We better get moving. It's almost dawn," Richard said.

I glared at him for saying it.

He shrugged. "It'll be better if we don't keep the master waiting. You know that."

I did know that. I nodded. "You're right. I don't have any right to get mad at you."

"Thanks."

I shook my head. "Let's do it."

"You can put the gun up," he said.

I stared at the Browning. I liked having it out. For security it beat the hell out of a teddy bear. I put the gun away. I could always get it out again later.

At the end of the stairs there was one last door—smaller, rounded with a heavy iron lock. Irving took out a huge black key and slipped it into the door. The lock gave a well-oiled click, and he pushed it forward. Irving was trusted with the key to below the stairs. How deep was he in, and could I get him out?

"Wait a minute," I said.

Everyone turned to me. I was the center of attention. Great. "I don't want Larry to meet the Master, or even know who he is."

"Anita . . ." Larry started.

"No, Larry, I've been attacked twice for the information. It is definitely on a need-to-know basis. You don't need to know."

"I don't need you to protect me," he said.

"Listen to her," Irving said. "She told me to stay away from the Master. I said I could handle myself. I was wrong, real wrong."

Larry crossed his arms over his chest, a stubborn set to his bloodstained cheeks. "I can take care of myself."

"Irving, Richard, I want a promise on this. The less he knows, the safer he'll be."

They both nodded.

"Doesn't anyone care what I think?" Larry asked.

"No," I said.

"Dammit, I'm not a child."

"You two can fight later," Irving said. "The Master's waiting."

Larry started to say something; I raised my hand. "Lesson number one; never keep a nervous master vampire waiting."

Larry opened his mouth to argue, then stopped. "Okay, we'll argue later."

I wasn't looking forward to later, but arguing with Larry over whether I was being overprotective beat the hell out of what lay beyond the door. I knew that. Larry didn't, but he was about to learn, and there wasn't a damn thing I could do to stop it.

35

The ceiling stretched upward into the darkness. Huge drapes of silky material fell in white and black, forming cloth walls. Minimalist chairs in black and silver formed a small conversation group. A glass and dark wood coffee table took up the center of the room. A black vase with a bouquet of white lilies was the only decoration. The room looked half-finished, as if it needed paintings hung on the walls. But how do you hang paintings on cloth walls? I was sure Jean-Claude would figure it out eventually.

I knew the rest of the room was a huge cavernous ware-house made of stone, but the only thing left of that was the high ceiling. There was even black carpeting on the floor, soft and cushioned.

Jean-Claude sat in one of the black chairs. He was slumped in the chair, ankles crossed, hands clasped across his stomach. His white shirt was plain, just a simple dress shirt except for the fact that the front sides were sheer. The line of buttons, cuffs, and collar was solid, but the chest was laid bare through a film of gauze. His cross-shaped burn was brown and clear against the pale skin.

Marguerite sat at his feet, head laid on his knee like an obedient dog. Her blond hair and pale pink pants suit seemed out of place in the black-and-white room.

"You've redecorated," I said.

"A few comforts," Jean-Claude said.

"I'm ready to meet the Master of the City," I said.

His eyes widened, a question forming on his face.

"I don't want my new coworker to meet the Master. It

seems to be dangerous information right now."

Jean-Claude never moved. He just stared at me, one hand absently rubbing Marguerite's hair. Where was Yasmeen? In a coffin somewhere, tucked safely away from the coming dawn.

"I will take you alone to meet . . . the Master," he said at last. His voice was neutral, but I could detect a hint of laughter underneath the words. It wasn't the first time Jean-Claude had found me funny, and it probably wouldn't be the last.

He stood in one graceful movement, leaving Marguerite kneeling beside the empty chair. She looked displeased. I smiled at her, and she glared at me. Baiting Marguerite was childish, but it made me feel better. Everyone needs a hobby.

Jean-Claude swept the curtains aside to show darkness. I realized then that there was discreet electric light in the room, indirect lighting set in the walls themselves. There was nothing but the flicker of torches beyond the curtains. It was like that one piece of cloth held back the modern world with all its comforts. Beyond lay stone and fire and secrets best whispered in the dark.

"Anita?" Larry called after me. He looked uncertain, maybe even scared. But I was taking the most dangerous thing in the room with me. He'd be safe with Irving and Richard. I didn't think Marguerite was a danger without Yasmeen to hold her leash.

"Stay here, Larry, please. I'll be back as soon as I can."

"Be careful," he said.

I smiled. "Always."

He grinned. "Yeah, sure."

Jean-Claude motioned me through and I went, following the sweep of his pale hand. The curtain fell behind us, cutting off the light. Darkness closed around us like a fist. Torches sparked against the far wall but couldn't touch the swelling dark.

Jean-Claude led the way into the dark. "We wouldn't want your coworker to overhear us." His voice whispered in the dark, growing like a wind to beat against the curtains.

My heart hammered against my rib cage. How the hell did he do that? "Save the dramatics for someone you can impress."

"Brave words, *ma petite*, but I taste your heartbeat in my mouth." The last word breathed over my skin as if his lips had passed just over the nape of my neck. Goosebumps marched down my arms.

"If you want to play games until after dawn, that's fine with me, but Irving told me that you had information on the master vampire that attacked me. Do you, or was it a lie?"

"I have never lied to you, *my petite*."

"Oh, come on."

"Partial truths are not the same thing as lies."

"I guess that depends on where you're sitting," I said.

He acknowledged that with a nod. "Shall we sit against the far wall, out of hearing range?"

"Sure."

He knelt in the thin circle of a torch's light. The light was for my benefit, and I appreciated it. But no sense telling him that.

I sat across from him, back to the wall. "So, what do you know about Alejandro?"

He was staring at me, a peculiar look on his face.

"What?" I asked.

"Tell me everything that happened last night, *ma petite*, everything about Alejandro."

It was too much like an order for my tastes, but there was something in his eyes, his face; uneasiness, almost fear. Which was silly. What did Jean-Claude have to fear from Alejandro? What indeed? I told him everything I remembered.

His face went carefully blank, beautiful and unreal like a painting. The colors were still there, but the life, the movement, had fled. He put one finger between his lips and slowly slid it out of sight. The finger came glistening back to the light. He extended that wet finger towards me. I scooted away from him.

"What are you trying to do?"

"Wash the blood off of your cheek. Nothing more."

"I don't think so."

He sighed, the barest of sounds, but it slithered over my skin like air. "You make everything so difficult."

"Glad you noticed."

"I need to touch you, *ma petite*. I believe Alejandro has done something to you."

"What?"

He shook his head. "Something impossible."

"No riddles, Jean-Claude."

"I believe he has marked you."

I stared at him. "What do you mean?"

"Marked you, Anita Blake, marked you with the first mark, just as I have."

I shook my head. "That's not possible. Two vampires can't have the same human servant."

"Exactly," he said. He moved towards me. "Let me test the theory, *ma petite*, please."

"What does testing the theory mean?"

He said something soft and harsh in French. I'd never heard him curse before. "It is after dawn and I am tired. Your questions will make something simple last all bloody day." There was real anger in his voice, but under that was tiredness and that thread of fear. The fear scared me. He was supposed to be some untouchable monster. Monsters weren't afraid of other monsters.

I sighed. Was it better to just get it over with, like a shot? Maybe. "Alright, in the interest of time. But give me some idea of what to expect. You know I don't like surprises."

"I must touch you to search first for my marks, then for his. You should not have fallen so easily into his eyes. That should not have happened."

"Get it over with," I said.

"Is my touch so repulsive that you must prepare yourself as for pain?"

Since that was almost exactly what I was doing, I wasn't

sure what to say. "Just do it, Jean-Claude, before I change my mind."

He slid his finger between his lips again.

"Do you have to do it that way?"

"*Ma petite*, please."

I squirmed against the cool stone wall. "Alright, no more interruptions."

"Good." He knelt in front of me. His fingertip traced my right cheek, leaving a line of wetness down my skin. The dried blood was gritty under his touch. He leaned into me, as if he was going to kiss me. I put my hands on his chest to keep him from touching me. His skin was hard and smooth under the gauze of his shirt.

I jerked away and hit my head against the wall. "Dammit."

He smiled. His eyes glinted blue in the torchlight. "Trust me." He moved in, lips hovering over my mouth. "I won't hurt you." The words whispered into my mouth, a soft push of air.

"Yeah, right," I said, but the words came out soft and uncertain.

His lips brushed mine, then pressed gently against my mouth. The kiss moved from my lips to my cheek. His lips were soft as silk, gentle as marigold petals, hot as the noonday sun. They worked down my skin until his mouth hovered over the pulse in my neck.

"Jean-Claude?"

"Alejandro was alive when the Aztec empire was just a dream." He whispered it against my skin. "He was there to greet the Spaniards and watch the Aztecs fall. He has survived when others have died or gone mad." His tongue flicked out, hot and wet.

"Stop it." I pushed against him. His heart beat against my hands. I pushed my hands upward to his throat. The big pulse in his throat fluttered against my skin. I placed a thumb over the smoothness of one of his eyelids. "Move it or lose it," I said. My voice was breathy with panic, and something worse . . . desire.

The feel of his body against me, under my hands, his lips touching me—some hidden part of me wanted it. Wanted him. So I lusted after the Master; so what? Nothing new. His eyeball trembled under my thumb, and I wondered if I could do it. Could I blank out one of those midnight-blue orbs? Could I blind him?

His lips moved against my skin. Teeth brushed my skin, the hard brush of fangs rubbed against my throat. And the answer was, suddenly, yes. I tensed to press inward, and he was gone like a dream, or a nightmare.

He stood in front of me, looking down, his eyes all dark, no white showing. His lips had drawn back from his teeth to expose glistening fangs. His skin was marble-white and seemed to glow from inside, and still he was beautiful.

"Alejandro has given you the first mark, *ma petite*. We share you. I do not know how, but we do. Two more marks and you are mine. Three more and you are his. Would it not be better to be mine?"

He knelt in front of me again, but was careful not to touch me. "You desire me as a woman desires a man. Is that not better than some stranger taking you by force?"

"You didn't ask my permission for the first two marks. They weren't by choice."

"I am asking permission now. Let me share with you the third mark."

"No."

"You would rather serve Alejandro?"

"I'm not going to serve anyone," I said.

"This is a war, Anita. You cannot be neutral."

"Why not?"

He stood up and paced a tight circle. "Don't you understand? The killings are a challenge to my authority, and his marking you is another challenge. He will take you from me if he can."

"I don't belong to you, or to him."

"What I have tried to get you to believe, to accept, he will shove down your throat."

"So I'm in the middle of an undead turf war because of your marks."

He blinked, opened his mouth, then closed it. Finally, "Yes."

I stood up. "Thanks a lot." I walked past him. "If you have any more info on Alejandro, send me a letter."

"This will not go away just because you wish it to."

I stopped in front of the curtain. "Hell, I knew that. I've wished hard enough for you to leave me alone."

"You would miss me if I were not here."

"Don't flatter yourself."

"And do not lie to yourself, *ma petite*. I would give you a partnership. He will give you slavery."

"If you really believed this partnership crap, you wouldn't have forced the first two marks on me. You would have asked. For all I know, the third mark can't be given without my cooperation." I stared at him. "That's it, isn't it? You need my help or something for the third mark. It's different from the first two. You son of a bitch."

"The third mark without your . . . help would be like rape to making love. You would hate me for all eternity if I took you by force."

I turned my back on him and grabbed the curtain. "You got that right."

"Alejandro will not care if you hate him. He wants only to hurt me. He will not ask your permission. He will simply take you."

"I can take care of myself."

"Like you took care last night?"

Alejandro had rolled me under and over and I hadn't even known it. What protection did I have against something like that? I shook my head and jerked back the curtain. The light was so bright, I was blind. I stood in the glare waiting for my eyes to adjust. The cool darkness blew against my back. The light was hot and intrusive after the darkness, but anything was better than whispers in the night. Blinded by the light or blinded by darkness; I'd take light every time.

36

Larry was lying on the floor, head cradled in Yasmeen's lap. She held his wrists. Marguerite had pinned his body under her own. She was licking the blood off his face with long, lingering strokes of her tongue. Richard lay in a crumpled heap, blood running down his face. There was something on the floor. It writhed and moved. Grey fur flowed over it like water. A hand reached skyward, then shrank like a dying flower, bones glistening, shoving upward through the flesh. The fingers shrank, flesh rolling over the nubs of raw flesh. All that raw meat and no blood. The bones slid in and out with wet, sucking noises. Drops of clear fluid spattered the black rug. But no blood.

I drew the Browning and moved so I could point it somewhere between Yasmeen and the thing on the floor. I had my back to the curtain but moved away from it. Too easy for something to reach through.

"Let him go, now."

"We haven't hurt him," Yasmeen said.

Marguerite leaned into Larry's body; one hand cupped his groin, massaging.

"Anita!" His eyes were wide, skin pale; freckles stood out like ink spots.

I fired a shot inches from Yasmeen's head. The sound was sharp and echoed. Yasmeen snarled at me. "I can rip his throat out before you squeeze that trigger again."

I aimed for Marguerite's head, right over one blue eye. "You kill him, I kill Marguerite. You willing to make the trade?"

"Yasmeen, what are you doing?" Jean-Claude came in at my back. My eyes flicked to him, then back to Marguerite. Jean-Claude wasn't the danger, not now.

The thing on the floor rose on four shaky legs and shook itself like a dog after a bath. It was a huge wolf. Thick grey-brown fur covered the animal, fluffy and dry as if the wolf had been freshly washed and blow-dried. Liquid formed a thick puddle on the carpet. Bits of clothing were scattered around. The wolf had emerged from the mess newly formed, reborn.

A pair of round wire-framed glasses sat on the glass and black coffee table, neatly folded.

"Irving?"

The wolf gave a small half-growl, half-bark. Was that a yes?

I had always known that Irving was a werewolf, but seeing it was something else entirely. Until just that moment I hadn't really believed, not really. Staring into the wolf's pale brown eyes, I believed.

Marguerite lay on the ground behind Larry now. Her arms wrapped around his chest, legs wrapping his waist. Most of her was hidden behind him, shielded.

I had spent too much time gazing at Irving. I couldn't shoot Marguerite without risking Larry. Yasmeen was kneeling beside them, one hand gripping a handful of Larry's hair. "I will snap his neck."

"You will not harm him, Yasmeen," Jean-Claude said. He stood beside the coffee table. The wolf moved up beside him, growling softly. His fingers brushed the top of the wolf's head.

"Call off your dogs, Jean-Claude, or this one dies." She stretched Larry's throat into one straining pale line to emphasize her point. The Band-Aid that had been hiding his vampire bite had been removed. Marguerite's tongue flicked out, touching the straining flesh.

I was betting that I could shoot Marguerite in the forehead while she licked Larry's neck, but Yasmeen could, and might, break his neck. I couldn't take the chance.

"Do something, Jean-Claude," I said. "You're the Master of the City. She's supposed to take your orders."

"Yes, Jean-Claude, order me."

"What's going on here, Jean-Claude?" I asked.

"She is testing me."

"Why?"

"Yasmeen wants to be Master of the City. But she isn't strong enough."

"I was strong enough to keep you and your servant from hearing this one's screams. Richard called your name, and you heard nothing because I kept you from it."

Richard stood just behind Jean-Claude. Blood was smeared from the corner of his mouth. There was a small cut on his right cheek that trickled blood down his face. "I tried to stop her."

"You did not try hard enough," Jean-Claude said.

"Argue amongst yourselves later," I said. "Right now, we have a problem."

Yasmeen laughed. The sound wriggled down my spine like someone had spilled a can of worms. I shuddered, and decided then and there that I'd shoot Yasmeen first. We'd find out if a master vampire was really faster than a speeding bullet.

She released Larry with a laugh and stood. Marguerite still clung to him. He got to his hands and knees with the woman riding him like a horse, arms and legs still clamped around him. She was laughing, kissing his neck.

I kicked her in the face as hard as I could. She slid off Larry and lay dazed on the floor. Yasmeen started forward and I fired at her chest. Jean-Claude hit my arm, and the shot went wide.

"I need her alive, Anita."

I jerked away from him. "She's crazy."

"But he needs my assistance to combat the other masters," Yasmeen said.

"She'll betray you if she can," I said.

"But I still need her."

"If you can't control Yasmeen, then how in the hell are you going to fight Alejandro?"

"I don't know," he said. "Is that what you wanted to hear? I do not know."

Larry was still huddled by our feet.

"Can you get up?"

He looked up at me, eyes shiny with unshed tears. He used one of the chairs to brace himself and almost fell. I grabbed his arm, gun still in my right hand. "Come on, Larry, we're getting out of here."

"Sounds great to me." His voice was incredibly breathless, straining not to cry.

We worked our way towards the door, me helping Larry walk, gun still out pointed vaguely at everything in the room.

"Go with them, Richard. See them safely to their car. And do not fail me again like you did today."

Richard ignored the threat and walked around us to hold the door open. We walked through without turning our backs on the vampires or the werewolf. When the door closed, I let out a breath I hadn't even known I was holding.

"I can walk now," Larry said.

I let go of his arm. He put a hand against the wall but otherwise seemed okay. The first slow tear trailed down his cheek. "Get me out of here."

I put my gun up. It wouldn't help now. Richard and I both pretended not to notice Larry's tears. They were very quiet. If you hadn't been looking directly at him, you wouldn't have known he was crying.

I tried to think of something to say, anything. But what could I say? He had seen the monsters, and they had scared the shit out of him. They scared the shit out of me. They scared the shit out of everybody. Now Larry knew that. Maybe it was worth the pain. Maybe not.

37

Early-morning light lay heavy and golden on the street outside. The air was cool and misty. You couldn't see the river from here, but you could feel it; that sense of water on the air that made every breath fresher, cleaner.

Larry got out his car keys.

"You okay to drive?" I asked.

He nodded. The tears had dried in thin tracks down his face. He hadn't bothered to wipe them away. He wasn't crying anymore. He was as grim-faced as you could be and still look like an overgrown Howdy Doody. He opened his door and got in, sliding across to unlock the passenger side.

Richard stood there. The cool wind blew his hair across his face. He ran fingers through it to keep it from his face. The gesture was achingly familiar. Phillip had always been doing that. Richard smiled at me, and it wasn't Phillip's smile. It was bright and open, and there was nothing hidden in his brown eyes.

Blood had started to dry at the corner of his mouth, and on his cheek.

"Get out while you still can, Richard."

"Out from what?"

"There's going to be an undead war. You don't want to be caught in the middle."

"I don't think Jean-Claude would let me walk away," he said. He wasn't smiling when he said it. I couldn't decide whether he was handsomer smiling or solemn.

"Humans don't do too well in the middle of the monsters, Richard. Get out if you can."

"You're human."

I shrugged. "Some people would argue that."

"Not me." He reached out to touch me. I stood my ground and didn't move away. His fingertips brushed the side of my face, warm and very alive.

"See you at three o'clock this afternoon, unless you're going to be too tired."

I shook my head, and his hand dropped away from my face. "Wouldn't miss it," I said.

He smiled again. His hair blew in a tangle across his face. I kept the front of my own hair cut short enough so that it stayed out of my eyes, most of the time. Layering was a wonderful thing.

I opened the passenger side door. "I'll see you this afternoon."

"I'll bring your costume with me."

"What am I going to be dressed as?"

"A Civil War bride," he said.

"Does that mean a hoop skirt?"

"Probably."

I frowned. "And what are you going to be?"

"A Confederate officer."

"You get to wear pants," I said.

"I don't think the dress would fit me."

I sighed. "It's not that I'm not grateful, Richard, but . . ."

"Hoop skirts aren't your style?"

"Not hardly."

"My offer was grubbies and all the mud we could crawl in. The party was your idea."

"I'd get out of it if I could."

"It might be worth all the trouble just to see you dressed up. I get the feeling it's a rarity."

Larry leaned across the seat, and said, "Can we get a move on? I need a cigarette and some sleep."

"I'll be right there." I turned back to Richard but suddenly didn't know what to say. "See you later."

He nodded. "Later."

I got in the car, and Larry pulled away before I got my seat belt fastened. "What's the rush?"

"I want to get as far away from this place as I can."

I looked at him. He still looked pale.

"You alright?"

"No, I'm not alright." He looked at me, blue eyes bright with anger. "How can you be so casual after what just happened?"

"You were calm after last night. You got bitten last night."

"But that was different," he said. "That woman sucked on the bite. She . . ." His hands clenched the steering wheel so tightly his hands shook.

"You were hurt worse last night; what makes this tougher?"

"Last night was violent, but it wasn't . . . perverted. The vampires last night wanted something. The name of the Master. The ones tonight didn't want anything, they were just being . . ."

"Cruel," I offered.

"Yes, cruel."

"They're vampires, Larry. They aren't human. They don't have the same rules."

"She would have killed me tonight on a whim."

"Yes, she would have," I said.

"How can you bear to be around them?"

I shrugged. "It's my job."

"And my job, too."

"It doesn't have to be, Larry. Just refuse to work on vampire cases. Most of the rest of the animators do."

He shook his head. "No, I won't give up."

"Why not?" I asked.

He didn't say anything for a minute. He pulled onto 270 headed south. "How could you talk about a date this afternoon after what just happened?"

"You have to have a life, Larry. If you let this business eat you alive, you'll never make it." I studied his face. "And you never answered my question."

"What question?"

"Why won't you give up the idea of being a vampire executioner?"

Larry hesitated, concentrating on driving. He suddenly seemed very interested in passing cars. We drove under a railroad bridge, warehouses on either side. Many of the windows were broken or missing. Rust dripped down the bridge overpass.

"Nice section of town," he said.

"You're avoiding the question. Why?"

"I don't want to talk about it."

"I asked about your family; you said they were all alive. What about friends? You lose a friend to the vamps?"

He glanced at me "Why ask that?"

"I know the signs, Larry. You're determined to kill the monsters because you've got a grudge, don't you?"

He hunched his shoulders and stared straight ahead. The muscles in his jaws clenched and unclenched.

"Talk to me, Larry," I said.

"The town I come from is small, fifteen hundred people. While I was away at college my freshman year, twelve people were murdered by a pack of vampires. I didn't know them, any of them, really. I knew them to say hi to, but that was it."

"Go on."

He glanced at me. "I went to the funerals over Christmas break. All those coffins, all those families. My dad was a doctor, but he couldn't help them. Nobody could help them."

"I remember the case," I said. "Elbert, Wisconsin, three years ago, right?"

"Yes, how did you know?"

"Twelve people is a lot for a single vampire kill. It made the papers. Brett Colby was the vampire hunter they got for the job."

"I never met him, but my parents told me about him. They made him sound like a cowboy riding into town to take down the bad guys. He found and killed five vampires.

He helped the town when nobody else could."

"If you just want to help people, Larry, be a social worker, or a doctor."

"I'm an animator; I've got a built-in resistance to vampires. I think God meant for me to hunt them."

"Geez Louise, Larry, don't go on a holy crusade, you'll end up dead."

"You can teach me."

I shook my head. "Larry, this isn't personal. It can't be personal. If you let your emotions get in the way, you'll either get killed or go stark raving mad."

"I'll learn, Anita."

I stared at his profile. He looked so stubborn. "Larry . . ." I stopped. What could I say? What brought any of us into this business? Maybe his reasons were as good as my own, maybe better. It wasn't just love of killing, like with Edward. And heaven knew I needed help. There were getting to be too many vampires for just little ol' me.

"Alright, I'll teach you, but you do what I say, when I say it. No arguments."

"Anything you say, boss." He grinned at me briefly, then turned back to the road. He looked determined and relieved, and young.

But we were all young once. It passes, like innocence and a sense of fair play. The only thing left in the end is a good instinct for survival. Could I teach Larry that? Could I teach him how to survive? Please, God, let me teach him, and don't let him die on me.

38

Larry dropped me off in front of my apartment building at 9:05. It was way past my bedtime. I got my gym bag out of the back seat. Didn't want to leave my animating equipment behind. I locked and shut the door, then leaned in the passenger side door. "I'll see you tonight at five o'clock back here, Larry. You're designated driver until I get a new car."

He nodded.

"If I'm late getting home, don't let Bert send you out alone, okay?"

He looked at me then. His face was full of some deep thought that I couldn't read. "You think I can't handle myself?"

I knew he couldn't handle himself, but I didn't say that out loud. "It's only your second night on the job. Give yourself and me a break. I'll teach you how to hunt vampires, but our primary job is raising the dead. Try to remember that."

He nodded.

"Larry, if you have bad dreams, don't worry. I have them too sometimes."

"Sure," he said. He put the car in gear, and I had to close the door. Guess he didn't want to talk anymore. Nothing we'd seen yet would give me nightmares, but I wanted Larry to be prepared, if mere words could prepare anyone for what we do.

A family was loading up a grey van with coolers and a picnic hamper. The man smiled. "I don't think we'll get many more days like this."

"I think you're right." It was that pleasant small talk that you use with people whose names you don't know but whose faces you keep seeing. We were neighbors, so we said hello and good-bye to each other, but nothing else. That was the way I liked it. When I came home, I didn't want someone coming over to borrow a cup of sugar.

The only exception I made was Mrs. Pringle, and she understood my need for privacy.

The apartment was warm and quiet inside. I locked the door and leaned against it. Home, ah. I tossed the leather jacket on the back of the couch and smelled perfume. It was flowery and delicate with a powdery undertaste that only the really expensive ones have. It wasn't my brand.

I pulled the Browning and put my back to the door. A man stepped around the corner from the dining room area. He was tall, thin, with black hair cut short in front, long in back, the latest style. He just stood there, leaning against the wall, arms crossed over his chest, smiling at me.

A second man came up from behind the couch, shorter, more muscular, blond, smiling. He sat on the couch, hands where I could see them. Nobody had any weapons, or none that I could see.

"Who the hell are you?"

A tall black man came out of the bedroom. He had a neat mustache, and dark sunglasses hid his eyes.

The lamia stepped out beside him. She was in human form, in the same red dress as yesterday. She wore scarlet high heels today, but nothing else had changed.

"We've been waiting for you, Ms. Blake."

"Who are the men?"

"My harem."

"I don't understand."

"They belong to me." She trailed red nails down the black man's hand hard enough to leave a thin line of blood. He just smiled.

"What do you want?"

"Mr. Oliver wants to see you. He sent us to fetch you."

"I know where the house is. I can drive there on my own."

"Oh, no, we've had to move," she said, swaying into the room. "Some nasty bounty hunter tried to kill Oliver yesterday."

"What bounty hunter?" Had it been Edward?

She waved a hand. "We were never formally introduced. Oliver wouldn't let me kill him, so he escaped, and we had to move."

It sounded reasonable, but . . . "Where is he now?"

"We'll take you to him. We've got a car waiting outside."

"Why didn't Inger come for me?"

She shrugged. "Oliver gives orders and I follow them." A look passed over her lovely face—hatred.

"How long has he been your master?"

"Too long," she said.

I stared at them all, gun still out but not pointed at anyone. They hadn't offered to hurt me. So why didn't I want to put the gun up? Because I'd seen what the lamia changed into, and it had scared me.

"Why does Oliver need to see me so soon?"

"He wants your answer."

"I haven't decided yet whether to give him the Master of the City."

"All I know is that I was told to bring you. If I don't, he'll be angry. I don't want to be punished, Ms. Blake; please come with us."

How do you punish a lamia? Only one way to find out. "How does he punish you?"

The lamia stared at me. "That is a very personal question."

"I didn't mean it to be."

"Forget it." She swayed towards me. "Shall we go?" She had stopped just in front of me, close enough to touch.

I was beginning to feel silly with the gun out, so I put it up. Nobody was threatening me. A novel approach.

Normally, I still would have offered to follow them in my car, but my car was dead. So . . . if I wanted to meet Oliver, I had to go with them.

I wanted to meet Oliver. I wasn't willing to give him Jean-Claude, but I was willing to give him Alejandro. Or at least enlist his aid against Alejandro. I also wanted to know if it was Edward who had tried to kill him. There weren't that many of us in the business. Who else could it be?

"Alright, let's go," I said. I got my leather jacket from the couch and opened the door. I motioned them all out the door. The men went without a word, the lamia last.

I locked the door behind us. They waited politely out in the hall for me. The lamia took the tall black man's arm. She smiled. "Boys, one of you offer the lady your arm."

Blondie and black-hair turned to look at me. Black-hair smiled. I hadn't been with this many smiling people since I bought my last used car.

They both offered me their arms, like in some late movie. "Sorry, guys, I don't need an escort."

"I've trained them to be gentlemen, Ms. Blake; take advantage of it. There are precious few gentlemen around these days."

I couldn't argue with that, but I also didn't need help down the stairs. "I appreciate it, but I'm fine."

"As you like, Ms. Blake." She turned to the two men. "You two are to take special care of Ms. Blake." She turned back to me. "A woman should always have more than one man."

I fought the urge to shrug. "Anything you say."

She gave a brilliant smile and strutted down the hall on her man's arm. The two men sort of fell in beside me. The lamia spoke back over her shoulder, "Ronald here is my special beau. I don't share him; sorry."

I had to smile. "That's fine, I'm not greedy."

She laughed, a high-pitched delighted sound with an edge of giggle to it. "Not greedy; oh, that's very good, Ms. Blake, or may I call you Anita?"

"Anita's fine."

"Then you must call me Melanie."

"Sure," I said. I followed her and Ronald down the hall. Blondie and Smiley hovered on either side of me, lest I trip and stub my toe. We'd never get down the stairs without one of us falling.

I turned to Blondie. "I believe I will take your arm." I smiled back at Smiley. "Could we have a little room here?"

He frowned, but he stepped back. I slipped my left hand through Blondie's waiting arm. His forearm swelled under my hand. I couldn't tell if he was flexing or was just that musclebound. But we all made it down the stairs safely with lonely Smiley bringing up the rear.

The lamia and Ronald were waiting by a large black Lincoln Continental. Ronald held the door for the lamia, then slid into the driver's seat.

Smiley rushed forward to open the door for me. How had I known he would? Usually I complain about things like that, but the whole thing was too strange. If the worst thing that happened to me today was having overzealous men open doors for me, I'd be doing fine.

Blondie slid into the seat next to me, sliding me to the middle of the seat. The other one had run around and was getting in the other side. I was going to end up sandwiched between them. No big surprise.

The lamia named Melanie turned around in her seat, propping her chin on her arm. "Feel free to make out on the way. They're both very good."

I stared into her cheerful eyes. She seemed to be serious. Smiley put his arm across the back of the seat, brushing my shoulders. Blondie tried to take my hand, but I eluded him. He settled for touching my knee. Not an improvement.

"I'm really not into public sex," I said. I moved Blondie's hand back to his own lap.

Smiley's hand slid around my shoulder. I moved up in the seat away from both of them. "Call them off," I said.

"Boys, she's not interested."

The men scooted back from me, as close to their sides of the car as they could get. Their legs still gently touched mine, but at least nothing else was touching.

"Thank you," I said.

"If you change your mind during the drive, just tell them. They love taking orders, don't you, boys?"

The two men nodded, smiling. My, weren't we a happy little bunch? "I don't think I'll change my mind."

The lamia shrugged. "As you like, Anita, but the boys will be sorely disappointed if you don't at least give them a good-bye kiss."

This was getting weird; cancel that, weirder. "I never kiss on the first date."

She laughed. "Oh, I like it. Don't we, boys?" All three men made appreciative sounds. I had the feeling they'd have sat up and begged if she'd told them to. Arf, arf. Gag me with a spoon.

39

We drove south on 270. Steep, grassy ditches and small trees lined the road. Identical houses sat up on the hills, fences separating the small yards from the next small yard. Tall trees took up many yards. Twoseventy was the major highway that ran through St. Louis, but there was almost always a feeling of green nature, open spaces; the gentle roll of the land was never completely lost.

We took 70 West heading towards St. Charles. The land opened up on either side to long, flat fields. Corn stretched tall and golden, ready to be harvested. Behind the field was a modern glass building that advertised pianos and an indoor golf range. An abandoned SAM's Wholesale and a used-car lot led up to the Blanchette bridge.

The left side of the road was crisscrossed by water-filled dikes to keep the land from flooding. Industry had moved in with tall glass buildings. An Omni Hotel complete with fountain was nearest the road.

A stand of woods that still flooded too often to be torn down and turned into buildings bordered the left-hand side of the road until the trees met the Missouri River. Trees continued on the other bank as we entered St. Charles.

St. Charles didn't flood, so there were apartment buildings, strip malls, a deluxe pet supermarket, a movie theater, Drug Emporium, Old Country Buffet, and Appleby's. The land vanished behind billboards and Red Roof Inns. It was hard to remember that the Missouri River was just behind you, and this had once been forest. Hard to see the land for the buildings.

Sitting in the warm car with only the sound of wheels on pavement and the murmur of voices from the front seat, I realized how tired I was. Even stuck between the two men, I was ready for a nap. I yawned.

"How much farther?" I asked.

The lamia turned in her seat. "Bored?"

"I haven't been to sleep yet. I just want to know how much longer the ride is going to take."

"So sorry to inconvenience you," she said. "It isn't much farther, is it, Ronald?"

He shook his head. He hadn't said a word since I'd met him. Could he talk?

"Exactly where are we going?" They didn't seem to want to answer the question, but maybe if I phrased it differently.

"About forty-five minutes outside of St. Peters."

"Near Wentzville?" I asked.

She nodded.

An hour to get there and nearly two hours back. Which would make it around 1:00 when I got home. Two hours of sleep. Great.

We left St. Charles behind, and the land reappeared— fields on either side behind well-tended barbed-wire fences. Cattle grazed on the low, rolling hills. The only sign of civilization was a gas station close to the highway. There was a large house set far back from the road with a perfect expanse of grass stretching to the road. Horses moved gracefully over the grass. I kept waiting for us to pull into one of the gracious estates, but we passed them all by.

We finally turned onto a narrow road with a street sign that was so rusted and bent, that I couldn't read it. The road was narrow and instant rustic. Ditches crowded in on either side. Grass, weeds, the year's last goldenrod, grew head-high and gave the road a wild look. A field of beans gone dry and yellow waited to be harvested. Narrow gravel driveways appeared out of the weeds with rusted mailboxes that showed that there were houses. But most of the houses were just glimpses through the trees. Barn swallows dipped and dived over the road. The pavement ended abruptly, spilling the car onto gravel.

Gravel pinged and clattered under the car. Wooded hills crowded the gravel road. There was still an occasional house, but they were getting few and far between. Where were we going?

The gravel ended, and the road was only bare reddish dirt with large reddish rocks studded in it. Deep ruts swallowed the car's tires. The car bounced and fought its way down the dirt. It was their car. If they wanted to ruin it driving over wagon tracks, that was their business.

Finally, even the dirt road ended in a rough circle of rock. Some of the rocks were nearly as big as the car. The car stopped. I was relieved that there were some things even Ronald wouldn't drive a car over.

The lamia turned around to face me. She was smiling, positively beaming. She was too damn cheerful. Something was wrong. Nobody was this cheery unless they wanted something. Something big. What did the lamia want? What did Oliver want?

She got out of the car. The men followed her like well-trained dogs. I hesitated, but I'd come this far; might as well see what Oliver wanted. I could always say no.

The lamia took Ronald's arm again. In high heels on the rocky ground, it was a sensible precaution. I in my little Nikes didn't need help. Blondie and Smiley offered an arm apiece; I ignored them. Enough of this play-acting. I was tired and didn't like being dragged to the edge of the world. Even Jean-Claude had never dragged me to some forsaken backwoods area. He was a city boy. Of course, Oliver had struck me as a city boy, too. Shows that you can't judge a vampire by one meeting.

The rocky ground led up to a hillside. More boulders had crashed down the side of the hill to lie in crumbled, broken heaps. Ronald actually picked Melanie up and carried her over the worst of the ground.

I stopped the men before they could offer. "I can make it myself; thanks anyway."

They looked disappointed. The blond said, "Melanie has told us to look after you. If you trip and fall in the rocks, she'll be unhappy with us."

The brunette nodded.

"I'll be fine, boys, really." I went ahead of them, not waiting to see what they'd do. The ground was treacherous with small rocks. I scrambled over a rock bigger than I was. The men were right behind me, hands extended ready to catch me if I fell. I'd never even had a date who was this paranoid.

Someone cursed, and I turned to see the brunette sprawled on the ground. I had to smile. I didn't wait for them to catch up. I'd had enough nursemaiding, and the thought of getting no sleep today had put me in a bad mood. Our biggest night of the year, and I was going to be wasted. Oliver better have something important to say.

Around a tall pile of rubble was a slash of black opening, a cave. Ronald carried the lamia inside without waiting for me. A cave? Oliver had moved to a cave? Somehow it didn't fit my picture of him in his modern, sunlit study.

Light hovered at the entrance to the cave, but a few feet in the darkness was thick. I waited at the edge of the light, unsure what to do. My two caretakers came in behind me. They pulled small penlights out of their pockets. The beams seemed pitifully small against the darkness.

Blondie took the lead; Smiley brought up the rear. I walked in the middle of their thin strings of light. A faint pool followed my feet and kept me from tripping over stray bits of rock, but most of the tunnel was smooth and perfect. A thin trickle of water took up the center of the floor, working its patient way through the stone. I stared up at the ceiling lost in darkness. All this had been done by water. Impressive.

The air was cool and moist against my face. I was glad I had the leather jacket on. It'd never get warm here, but it'd never get really cold either. That's why our ancestors lived in caves. Year-round temperature control.

A wide passage branched to the left. The deep sound of water gurgled and bumped in the darkness. A lot of water. Blondie ran his light over a stream that filled most of the left passage. It was black, and looked deep and cold.

"I didn't bring my wading boots," I said.

"We follow the main passage," Smiley said. "Don't tease her. The mistress will not like it." His face looked very serious in the half-light.

The blond shrugged, then moved his light straight ahead. The trickle of water spread in a thin fan pattern on the rock but there was still plenty of dry rock on either side. I wasn't going to have to get my feet wet, yet.

We took the left-hand side of the wall. I touched it to keep my balance and jerked away. The walls were slimy with water and melting minerals.

Smiley laughed at me. I guess laughing was allowed.

I glanced back at him, frowning, then put my hand back on the wall. It wasn't that icky. It had just surprised me. I'd touched worse.

The sound of water thundering from a great height filled the darkness. There was a waterfall up ahead; I didn't need my eyes to tell me that.

"How tall do you think the waterfall is?" Blondie asked.

The thundering filled the darkness. Surrounded us. I shrugged. "Ten, twenty feet, maybe more."

He shone his light on a trickle of water that fell about five inches. The tiny waterfall was what fed the thin stream. "The cave magnifies the sound and makes it sound like thunder," he said.

"Neat trick," I said.

A wide shelf of rock led in a series of tiny waterfalls up to a wide base of stone. The lamia sat on the edge of the shelf, high-heeled feet dangling over the edge. Maybe a rise of eight feet, but the ceiling soared overhead into blackness. That was what made the water echo.

Ronald stood at her back, like a good bodyguard, hands clasped in front of him. There was a wide opening near them that led farther into the cave towards the source of the little stream.

Blondie climbed up and offered me a hand.

"Where's Oliver?"

"Just ahead," the lamia said. There was an edge of laughter to her voice, as if there was some joke I wasn't getting. It was probably going to be at my expense.

I ignored Blondie's hand and made it up to the shelf by myself. My hands were covered with a thin coat of pale brown mud and water, a perfect recipe for slime. I fought the urge to wipe them on my jeans and knelt by the small pool of water that fed the waterfalls. The water was ice-cold, but I washed my hands in it and felt better. I dried them on my jeans.

The lamia sat with her men grouped around her as if they were posing for a family photo. They were waiting on someone. Oliver. Where was he?

"Where's Oliver?"

"I'm afraid he won't be coming." The voice came from ahead of me farther into the cave. I stepped back but couldn't go far without stepping off the edge.

The two flashlights turned on the opening like tiny spotlights. Alejandro stepped into the thin beam of lights. "You won't be meeting Oliver tonight, Ms. Blake."

I went for my gun before anything else could happen. The lights went out, and I was left in the absolute dark with a master vampire, a lamia, and three hostile men. Not one of my better days.

40

I dropped to my knees, gun ready, close to my body. The darkness was thick as velvet. I couldn't see my hand in front of my face. I closed my eyes, trying to concentrate on hearing. There; the scrape of shoes on stone. The movement of air as someone moved closer to me. I had thirteen silver bullets. We were about to find out if silver would hurt a lamia. Alejandro had already taken a silver bullet in the chest and didn't look much the worse for it.

I was in very deep shit.

The footsteps were almost on top of me. I could feel the body close to me. I opened my eyes. It was like looking inside a ball of ebonite, utterly black. But I could feel someone standing over me. I raised the gun to gut or lower chest level and fired still on my knees.

The flashes were like lightning in the darkness, blue-flame lightning. Smiley fell backwards in the flash of light. I heard him fall over the edge, then nothing. Nothing but darkness.

Hands grabbed my forearms, and I hadn't heard a thing. It was Alejandro. I screamed as he dragged me to my feet.

"Your little gun cannot hurt me," he said. His voice was soft and close. He hadn't taken my gun away. He wasn't afraid of it. He should have been.

"I have offered Melanie her freedom once Oliver and the city's Master are dead. I offer you eternal life, eternal youth, and you may live."

"You did give me the first mark."

"Tonight I will give you the second," he said. His voice was soft and ordinary compared to Jean-Claude's, but the intimacy of the dark and his hands on me made the words more than they should have been.

"And if I don't want to be your human servant?"

"Then I will take you anyway, Anita. Your loss will damage the Master. It will lose him followers, confidence. Oh, yes, Anita, I will have you. Join with me willingly, and it will be pleasure. Fight me, and it will be agony."

I used his voice to aim the gun at his throat. If I could sever his spine, a thousand years and more old or not, he might die. Might. Please, God.

I fired. The bullet took him in the throat. He jerked backwards but didn't let go of my arms. Two more bullets into his throat, one into his jaw, and he threw me away from him, shrieking.

I ended on my back in the ice-cold water.

A flashlight cut through the dark. Blondie stood there, a perfect target. I fired at it and the light went out, but there was no scream. I'd rushed the shot and missed. Damn.

I couldn't climb down the rock in the dark. I'd fall and break a leg. So the only way left was deeper into the cave, if I could get there.

Alejandro was still screaming, wordless, rage-filled. The screams echoed and bounced on the rock walls until I was deaf as well as blind.

I scrambled through the water, putting a wall at my back. If I couldn't hear them, maybe they couldn't hear me.

"Get that gun away from her," the lamia said. She had moved and seemed to be beside the wounded vampire.

I waited in the dark for some clue that they were coming for me. There was a rush of cool air against my face. It wasn't them moving. Was I that close to the opening that led deeper into the cave? Could I just slip away? In the dark, not knowing if there were pits, or water deep enough to drown in? Didn't sound like a good idea. Maybe I could just kill them all here. Fat chance.

Through the echoes of Alejandro's shrieks was another sound, a highpitched hissing, like that of a giant snake. The lamia was shapechanging. I had to get away before she finished. Water splashed almost on top of me. I looked up, and there was nothing to see, just the solid blackness.

I couldn't feel anything, but the water splashed again. I pointed up and fired. The flash of light revealed Ronald's face. The dark glasses were gone. His eyes were yellow with slitted pupils. I saw all that in the lightning flash of the gun. I fired twice more into that slit-eyed face. He screamed, and fangs showed below his teeth. God. What was he?

Whatever Ronald was, he fell backwards. I heard him hit the water in a splash that was much too loud for the shallow pool. I didn't hear him move after he fell. Was he dead?

Alejandro's screams had stopped. Was he dead, too? Was he creeping closer? Was he even now almost on top of me? I held the gun out in front of me and tried to feel something, anything, in the darkness.

Something heavy dragged across the rock. My stomach clenched tight. The lamia. Shit.

That was it. I eased my shoulder around the corner into the opening. I crept along on knees and one hand. I didn't want to run if I didn't have to. I'd brain myself on a stalactite or drop into some bottomless pit. Alright, maybe not bottomless, but if I fell thirty feet or so, it wouldn't have to be bottomless. Dead is dead.

Icy water soaked through my jeans and shoes. The rock was slick under my hand. I crawled as fast as I could, hand searching for some drop-off, some danger that my eyes couldn't see.

The heavy, sliding sound filled the blackness. It was the lamia. She'd already changed. Would her scales be quicker over the slick rocks, or would I be quicker? I wanted to get up and run. Run as far and as fast as I could. My shoulders tightened with the need to get away.

A loud splash announced she'd entered the water. She could move faster than I could crawl; I was betting on that.

And if I ran . . . and fell or knocked myself silly? Well, better to have tried than to be caught crawling in the cold like a mouse.

I scrambled to my feet and started to run. I kept my left hand out in front of me to protect my face, but the rest I left to chance. I couldn't see shit. I was running full out, blind as a bat, my stomach tight with anticipation of some pit opening up under my feet.

The sounds of sliding scales was getting farther away. I was outrunning her. Great.

A piece of rock slammed into my right shoulder. The impact spun me into the other wall. My arm was numb from shoulder to fingertips. I'd dropped the gun. Three bullets left, but that had been better than nothing. I leaned into the wall, cradling my arm, waiting for the feeling to return, wondering if I could find my gun in the dark, wondering if I had time.

A light bobbed towards me down the tunnel. Blondie was coming; risking himself, if I'd had my gun. But I didn't have my gun. I could have broken my arm ramming into that ledge. The feeling was coming back in a painful wash of prickles and a throbbing ache where the rock had hit me. I needed a flashlight. What if I hid and got Blondie's light? I had two knives. As far as I knew, Blondie wasn't armed. It had possibilities.

The light was going slowly, sweeping from side to side. I had time, maybe. I got to my feet and felt for the rock that had nearly taken my arm off. It was a shelf with an opening behind it. Cool air blew against my face. It was a small tunnel. It was shoulder level to me, which made it about face level for Blondie. Perfect.

I placed my hands palm down and pushed up. My right arm protested, but it was doable. I crawled into the tunnel, hands out in front searching for stalactites or more rock shelves. Nothing but small, empty space. If I'd been much bigger, I wouldn't have fit at all. Hurray for being petite.

I got out the knife for my left hand. The right was still trembling. I was better right-handed, like most right-handed people, but I practiced left-handed, too—ever since a vampire broke my right arm and using my left had been the only thing that saved me. Nothing like near death to get you to practice.

I crouched on my knees in the tunnel, knife gripped, using my right hand for balance. I would only get one chance at this. I had no illusions about my chances against an athletic man who outweighed me by at least a hundred pounds. If the first rush didn't work, he'd beat me to a pulp or give me to the lamia. I'd rather be beaten.

I waited in the dark with my knife and prepared to slit someone's throat. Not pretty when you think of it that way. But necessary, wasn't it?

He was almost here. The thin penlight looked bright after the darkness. If he shone the light in the direction of my hiding place before he got beside it, I was sunk. Or if he passed close to the left-hand side of the tunnel, and not under me . . . Stop it. The light was almost underneath me. I heard his feet wade through the water, coming closer. He was hugging the right-hand side of the wall, just like I wanted him to.

His pale hair came into sight nearly even with my knees. I moved forward and he turned. His mouth made a little "O" of surprise; then the blade plunged into the side of his neck. Fangs flicked from behind his teeth. The blade snicked on his spine. I grabbed his long hair in my right hand, bowing his neck, and tore the knife out the front of his throat. Blood splashed outward in a surprised shower. The knife and my left hand were slick with it.

He fell to the tunnel floor with a loud splash. I scrambled off the ledge and landed beside his body. The light had rolled into the water, still glowing. I fished it out. Lying almost under Blondie's hand was the Browning. It was wet, but that didn't matter. You could shoot most modern guns underwater and they worked fine. That was one of the things that made terrorism so easy.

Blood turned the stream dark. I shone the light back down the tunnel. The lamia was framed in the small light.

Her long black hair spilled over her pale upper body. Her breasts were high and prominent with deep, nearly reddish nipples. From the waist down she was ivory-white with zigzags of pale gold. The long belly scales were white speckled with black. She reared on that long, hard tail and flicked her forked tongue at me.

Alejandro stood up behind her, covered in blood but walking, moving. I wanted to shout, "Why don't you die" but it wouldn't help; maybe nothing would help.

The lamia pushed onward down the tunnel. The gun had killed her men with their fangs, Ronald with his snake eyes. I hadn't tried it on her yet. What did I have to lose?

I kept the light on her pale chest and raised the gun.

"I am immortal. Your little bullets will not harm me."

"Come a little closer and let's test the theory," I said.

She slid towards me, arms moving as if in time with legs. Her whole body moved with the muscular thrusts of the tail. It looked curiously natural.

Alejandro stayed leaning against the wall. He was hurt. Yippee.

I let her get within ten feet; close enough to hit her, far enough away to run like hell if it didn't work.

The first bullet took her just above the left breast. She staggered. It hit her, but the hole closed like water, smooth and unblemished. She smiled.

I raised the gun, just a little, and fired just above the bridge of her perfect nose. Again she staggered, but the hole didn't even bleed. It just healed. Normal bullets had about as much effect on vampires.

I put the gun in the shoulder holster, turned, and ran.

A wide crack led off from the main tunnel. I'd have to take off my jacket to squeeze through. The last thing I wanted was to get stuck with the lamia able to work her way through to me. I stayed with the main tunnel.

The tunnel was smooth and straight as far as I could see. Shelves projected out at angles, some with water trickling out of them, but crawling on my belly with a snake after me wasn't my idea of a good time.

I could run faster than she could move. Snakes, even giant snakes, just weren't that fast. As long as I didn't hit a dead end, I'd be fine. God, I wished I believed that.

The stream was ankle-deep now. The water was so cold, I had trouble feeling my feet. Running helped. Concentrating on my body, moving, running, trying not to fall, trying not to think about what was behind me. The real trick would be, was there another way out? If I couldn't kill them and couldn't get past them and there was only one way out, I was going to lose.

I kept running. I did four miles three times a week, plus a little extra. I could keep running. Besides, what choice did I have?

The water was filling the passageway and growing deeper. I was knee-deep in water. It was slowing me down. Could she move faster in water than I could? I didn't know. I just didn't know.

A rush of air blew against my back. I turned, and there was nothing there. The air was warm and smelled faintly of flowers. Was it the lamia? Did she have other ways of catching me besides just chasing? No; lamias could perform illusions only on men. That was their power. I wasn't male, so I was safe.

The wind touched my face, gently, warm and fragrant with a rich, green smell like freshly dug roots. What was happening?

"Anita."

I whirled, but there was no one there. The circle of light showed only tunnel and water. There was no sound but the lapping of water. Yet . . . the warm wind blew against my cheek, and the smell of flowers was growing stronger.

Suddenly, I knew what it was. I remembered being chased up the stairs by a wind that couldn't have been there, the glow of blue fire like free-floating eyes. The second mark.

It had been different, no smell of flowers, but I knew that was it. Alejandro didn't have to touch me to give me the mark, no more than Jean-Claude had.

I slipped on the slick stones and fell neck-deep in water. I scrambled to my feet, thigh-deep in water. My jeans were soaked and heavy. I sloshed forward, trying to run, but the water was too deep for running. It'd be quicker to swim.

I dove into the water, flashlight grasped in one hand. The leather jacket dragged at me, slowed me down. I stood up and stripped it off and let it float with the current. I hated to lose the jacket, but if I survived, I could buy more.

I was glad I was wearing a long-sleeved shirt and not a sweater. It was too damn cold to strip down anymore. It was faster swimming. The warm wind tickled down my face, hot after the chill of the water.

I don't know what made me look behind me, just a feeling. Two pinpoints of blackness were floating towards me in the air. If blackness could burn, then that's what it was: black flame coming for me on the warm, flower-scented breeze.

A rock wall loomed ahead. The stream ran under it. I held onto the wall and found there was maybe an inch of air space between the water and the roof of the tunnel. It looked like a good way to drown.

I treaded water and shone the flashlight around the passage. There; a narrow shelf of rock to climb out on, and blessed be, another tunnel. A dry one.

I pulled myself up on the shelf, but the wind hit me like a warm hand. It felt good and safe, and it was a lie.

I turned, and the black flames hovered over me like demonic fireflies. "Anita, accept it."

"Go to hell!" I pressed my back to the wall, surrounded by the warm tropical wind. "Please, don't do this," but it was a whisper.

The flames descended slowly. I hit at them. The flames passed through my hands like ghosts. The smell of flowers was almost chokingly sweet. The flames passed into my eyes, and for an instant I could see the world through bits of colored flame and a blackness that was a kind of light.

Then nothing. My vision was my own. The warm breeze died slowly away. The scent of flowers clung to me like some expensive perfume.

There was the sound of something large moving in the dark. I brought the flashlight up slowly into the dark-skinned face of a nightmare.

Straight, black hair was cut short and smooth around a thin face. Golden eyes with pupils like slits stared at me unblinking, immobile. His slender upper body dragged his useless lower body closer to me.

From the waist down he was all translucent skin. You could still see his legs and genitals, but they were all blending together to form a rough snakelike shape. Where do little lamias come from when there are no male lamias? I stared at what had once been a human being and screamed.

He opened his mouth, and fangs flicked into sight. He hissed, and spit dribbled down his chin. There was nothing human left in those slitted eyes. The lamia was more human than he was, but if I was changing into a snake maybe I'd be crazy, too. Maybe crazy was a blessing.

I drew the Browning and fired point-blank into his mouth. He jerked back, shrieking, but no blood, no dying. Dammit.

There was a scream from farther away, echoing towards us. "Raju!" The lamia was screaming for her mate, or warning him.

"Anita, don't hurt him." This from Alejandro. At least he had to yell. He couldn't whisper in my mind anymore.

The thing pulled itself towards me, mouth gaping, fangs straining.

"Tell him not to hurt me!" I yelled back.

The Browning was safely in its holster, and I was out of bullets anyway. Flashlight in one hand, knife in the other, I waited. If they got here in time to call him off, fine. I didn't have much faith in silver knives if silver bullets didn't harm him, but I wasn't going down without a fight.

His hands were bloody from dragging his body over the rocks. I never thought I'd see anything that was worse than being changed into a vampire, but there it was, crawling towards me.

It was between me and the dry tunnel, but it was moving agonizingly slow. I pressed my back to the wall and got to my feet. He—it—moved faster, definitely after me. I ran past it, but a hand closed on my ankle, yanked me to the ground.

The creature grabbed my legs and started to pull me towards it. I sat up and plunged the knife into its shoulder. It screamed, blood spilling down its arm. The knife stuck in the bone, and the monster jerked it out of my hand.

Then it reared back and struck my calf, fangs sinking in. I screamed and drew the second knife.

It raised its face, blood trickling down its mouth, heavy yellow drops clinging to its fangs.

I plunged the blade into one golden eye. The creature shrieked, drowning us in echoes. It rolled onto its back, lower body thrashing, hands clawing. I rolled with it and pushed the knife in with everything I had.

I felt the tip of the knife scrape on its skull. The monster continued to thrash and fight, but it was as hurt as I could make it. I left the knife in its eye but jerked the one free of its shoulder.

"Raju, no!"

I flashed the light on the lamia. Her pale upper body gleamed wet in the light. Alejandro was beside her. He looked nearly healed. I'd never seen a vampire that could heal that fast.

"I will kill you for their deaths," the lamia said.

"No, the girl is mine."

"She has killed my mate. She must die!"

"I will give her the third mark tonight. She will be my servant. That is revenge enough."

"No!" she screamed.

I was waiting for the poison to start working, but so far the bite just hurt, no burning, no nothing. I stared at the dry tunnel, but they'd just follow me and I couldn't kill them, not like this, not today. But there'd be other days.

I slipped back into the stream. There was still only an inch of air space. Risk drowning, or stay, and either be killed by a lamia or enslaved by a vampire. Choices, choices.

I slipped into the tunnel, mouth pressed near the wet roof. I could breathe. I might survive the day. Miracles do happen.

Small waves began to slosh through the tunnel. A wave washed over my face, and I swallowed water. I treaded water as gently as I could. It was my movements that were making the waves. I was going to drown myself.

I stayed very still until the water calmed, then took a deep breath, hyperventilating to expand the lungs and take in as much air as I could. I dunked under the water and kicked. It was too narrow for anything but a scissor kick. My chest was tight, throat aching with the need to breathe. I surfaced and kissed rock. There wasn't even an inch of air. Water splashed into my nose and I coughed, swallowing more water. I pressed as close to the ceiling as I could, taking small shallow breaths, then under again, kicking, kicking for all I was worth. If the tunnel filled completely before I was through it, I was going to die.

What if the tunnel didn't end? What if it was all water? I panicked, kicking furiously, flashlight bouncing crazily off the walls, hovering in the water like a prayer.

Please, God, please, don't let me die here like this.

My chest burned, throat bursting with the need to breathe. The light was dimming, and I realized it was my eyes that were losing the light. I was going to pass out and drown. I pushed for the surface and my hands touched empty air.

I took a gasping breath that hurt all the way down. There was a rocky shore and one bright line of sunlight. There was a hole up in the wall. The sunlight formed a misty haze in the air. I crawled onto the rock, coughing and relearning how to breathe.

I still had the flashlight and knife in my hands. I didn't remember holding onto them. The rock was covered in a thin sheet of grey mud. I crawled through it towards the rockslide that had opened the hole in the wall.

If I could make it through the tunnel, maybe they could, too. I didn't wait to feel better. I put the knife back in its sheath, slid the flashlight in my pocket, and started crawling.

I was covered in mud, hands scraped raw, but I was at the opening. It was a thin crack, but through it I could see trees and a hill. God, it looked good.

Something surfaced behind me.

I turned.

Alejandro rose from the water into the sunlight. His skin burst into flame, and he shrieked, diving into the water away from the burning sun.

"Burn, you son of bitch, burn."

The lamia surfaced.

I slipped into the crack and stuck. I pulled with my hands and pushed with my feet, but the mud slid and I couldn't get through.

"I will kill you."

I wrenched my back and put everything I had into wriggling free of that damn hole. The rock scraped along my back and I knew I was bleeding. I fell out onto the hill and rolled until a tree stopped me.

The lamia came to the crack. Sunlight didn't hurt her. She struggled to get through, tearing at the rock, but her ample chest wasn't going to fit. Her snake body might be narrowable, but the human part wasn't.

But just in case, I got to my feet and started down the hill. It was steep enough that I had to walk from tree to tree, trying not to fall down the hill. The whoosh of cars was just ahead. A road; a busy one by the sound of it.

I started to run, letting the momentum of the hill take me faster and faster towards the sounds of cars. I could glimpse the road through the trees.

I stumbled out onto the edge of the road, covered in grey mud, slimy, wet to the bone, shivering in the autumn air. I'd never felt better. Two cars wheezed by, ignoring my waving arms. Maybe it was the gun in the shoulder holster.

A green Mazda pulled up and stopped. The driver leaned across and opened the passenger side door. "Hop in."

It was Edward.

I stared into his blue eyes, and his face was as blank and unreadable as a cat's, and just as self-satisfied. I didn't give a damn. I slid into the seat and locked the door behind me.

"Where to?" he asked.

"Home."

"You don't need a hospital?"

I shook my head. "You were following me again."

He smiled. "I lost you in the woods."

"City boy," I said.

His smile widened. "No name-calling. You look like you flunked your Girl Scout exam."

I started to say something, then stopped. He was right, and I was too tired to argue.

41

I was sitting on the edge of my bathtub in nothing but a large beach towel. I had showered and shampooed and washed the mud and blood down the drain. Except for the blood that was still seeping out of the deep scrape on my back. Edward held a smaller towel to the cut, putting pressure on it.

"When the bleeding stops, I'll bandage it up for you," he said.

"Thanks."

"I seem to always be patching you up."

I glanced over my shoulder at him and winced. "I've returned the favor."

He smiled. "True."

The cuts on my hands had already been bandaged. I looked like a tan version of the mummy's hand.

He touched the fang marks on my calf gently. "This worries me."

"Me, too."

"There's no discoloration." He looked up at me. "No pain?"

"None. It wasn't a full lamia, maybe it wasn't that poisonous. Besides, you think anywhere in St. Louis is going to have lamia antivenom? They've been listed extinct for over two hundred years."

Edward palpated the wound. "I can't feel any swelling."

"It's been over an hour, Edward. If poison was going to kick in, it would have by now."

"Yeah." He stared at the bite. "Just keep an eye on it."

"I didn't know you cared," I said.

His face was blank, empty. "It would be a lot less interesting world without you in it." The voice was flat, unemotional. It was like he wasn't there at all. Yet it was a compliment. From Edward, it was a huge compliment.

"Gee whiz, Edward, contain your excitement."

He gave a small smile that left his eyes blue and distant as winter skies. We were friends of a sort, good friends, but I would never really understand him. There was too much of Edward that you couldn't touch, or even see.

I used to believe that if it came to it, he'd kill me, if it were necessary. Now, I wasn't sure. How could you be friends with someone who you suspected might kill you? Another mystery of life.

"The bleeding's stopped," he said. He smeared antiseptic on the wound, then started taping bandages in place. The doorbell rang.

"What time is it?" I asked.

"Three o'clock."

"Shit."

"What is it?"

"I have a date coming over."

"You? Have a date?"

I frowned at him. "It's not that big a deal."

Edward was grinning like the proverbial cat. He stood up. "You're all fixed up. I'll go let him in."

"Edward, be nice."

"Me, nice?"

"Alright, just don't shoot him."

"I think I can manage that." Edward walked out of the bathroom to let Richard in.

What would Richard think being met at the door by another man? Edward certainly wasn't going to help matters. He'd probably offer him a seat without explaining who he was. I wasn't even sure I could explain that.

"This is my friend the assassin." Nope. A fellow vampire slayer, maybe.

The bedroom door was closed so I could get dressed in

privacy. I tried to put on a bra and found that my back hurt a lot. No bra. That limited what I could wear, unless I wanted to give Richard more of a look-see than I had planned on. I also wanted to keep an eye on the bite wound. So pants were out.

Most of the time I slept in oversize t-shirts, and slipping on a pair of jeans was my idea of a robe. But I did own one real robe. It was comfortable, a nice solid black, silky to the touch and absolutely not see-through.

A black silk teddy went with it, but I decided that was a little friendlier than I wanted to be; besides, the teddy wasn't comfortable. Lingerie seldom is.

I pulled the robe out of the back of my closet and slipped it on. It was smooth and wonderful next to my skin. I crossed the front so the bordered edge was high up on my chest and tied the black belt tight in place. Didn't want any slippage.

I listened at the door for a second and heard nothing. No talking, no moving around, nothing. I opened the door and walked out.

Richard was sitting on the couch with an armful of costumes hung over the back. Edward was making coffee in the kitchen like he owned the place.

Richard turned at my entrance. His eyes widened just a little. The hair still damp from the shower, and the slinky robe—what was he thinking?

"Nice robe," Edward said.

"It was a present from an overly optimistic date."

"I like it," Richard said.

"No smart remarks or you can just leave."

His eyes flicked to Edward. "Did I interrupt something?"

"He's a coworker, nothing more." I frowned at Edward, daring him to say anything. He smiled and poured coffee for all three of us.

"Let's sit at the table," I said. "I don't drink coffee on a white couch."

Edward sat the mugs on the small table. He leaned against the cabinets, leaving the two chairs for us.

Richard left his coat on the couch and sat down across from me. He was wearing a bluish-green sweater with darker blue designs worked across the chest. The color brought out the perfect brown of his eyes. His cheekbones seemed higher. A small Band-Aid marred his right cheek. His hair had gentle auburn highlights. Wondrous what the right color can do for a person.

The fact that I looked great in black had not escaped my notice. From the look on Richard's face, he was noticing, but his eyes kept slipping back to Edward.

"Edward and I were out hunting down the vampires that have been doing the killings."

His eyes widened. "Did you find out anything?"

I looked at Edward.

He shrugged. It was my call.

Richard hung around with Jean-Claude. Was he Jean-Claude's creature? I didn't think so, but then again . . . Caution is always better. If I was wrong, I'd apologize later. If I was right, I'd be disappointed in Richard but glad I hadn't told.

"Let's just say we lost today."

"You're alive," Edward said.

He had a point.

"Did you almost die today?" Richard's voice was outraged.

What could I say? "It's been a rough day."

He glanced at Edward, then back to me. "How bad was it?"

I motioned my bandaged hands at him. "Scrapes and cuts; nothing much."

Edward hid a smile in his coffee mug.

"Tell me the truth, Anita," Richard said.

"I don't owe you any explanations." My voice sounded just a tad defensive.

Richard stared down at his hands, then looked up at me. There was a look in his eyes that made my throat tight. "You're right. You don't owe me anything."

I found an explanation slipping out of my mouth. "You

might say I went caving without you."

"What do you mean?"

"I ended up going through a water-filled tunnel to escape the bad guys."

"How water-filled?"

"All the way to the top."

"You could have drowned." He touched my hand with his fingertips.

I sipped coffee and moved my hand away from his, but I could feel where he had touched me like a lingering smell. "But I didn't drown."

"That's not the point," he said.

"Yes," I said, "it is. If you're going to date me, you have to get used to the way I work."

He nodded. "You're right, you're right." His voice was soft. "It just caught me off guard. You nearly died today and you're sitting there drinking coffee like it's ordinary."

"For me, it is, Richard. If you can't deal with that, maybe we shouldn't even try." I caught Edward's expression. "What are you grinning at?"

"Your suave and debonair way with men."

"If you're not going to be helpful, then leave."

He put his mug down on the counter. "I'll leave you two lovebirds alone."

"Edward," I said.

"I'm going."

I walked him to the door. "Thanks again for being there, even if you were following me."

He pulled out a plain white business card with a phone number done in black on it. That was all, no name, no logo; but what would have been appropriate, a bloody dagger, or maybe a smoking gun? "If you need me, call this number."

Edward had never given me a number before. He was like the phantom—there when he wanted to be, or not there, as he chose. A number could be traced. He was trusting me a lot with the number. Maybe he wouldn't kill me.

"Thank you, Edward."

"One bit of advice. People in our line of work don't make good significant others."

"I know that."

"What's he do for a living?"

"He's a junior high science teacher," I said.

Edward just shook his head. "Good luck." With that parting shot, he left.

I slipped the business card into the robe pocket and went back to Richard. He was a science teacher, but he also hung out with the monsters. He'd seen it get messy, and it hadn't fazed him, much. Could he handle it? Could I? One date and I was already borrowing trouble that might never come up. We might dislike each other after only one evening together. I'd had it happen before.

I stared at the back of Richard's head and wondered if the curls could be as soft as they looked. Instant lust; embarrassing, but not that uncommon. Alright, it was uncommon for me.

A sharp pain ran up my leg. The leg that the lamia-thing had bitten. Please, no. I leaned against the counter divider. Richard was watching me, puzzled.

I swept the robe aside. The leg was swelling and turning purplish. How had I not noticed it? "Did I mention I got bitten by a lamia today?"

"You're joking," he said.

I shook my head. "I think you're going to have to take me to the hospital."

He stood up and saw my leg. "God! Sit down."

I was starting to sweat. It wasn't hot in the apartment.

Richard helped me to the couch. "Anita, lamias have been extinct for two hundred years. No one's going to have any antivenom."

I stared at him. "I guess we're not going to get that date."

"No dammit, I won't sit here and watch you die. Lycanthropes can't be poisoned."

"You mean you want to rush me to Stephen and let him bite me?"

"Something like that."

"I'd rather die."

Something flickered through his eyes, something I couldn't read; pain, maybe. "You mean that?"

"Yes." A rush of nausea flowed over me like a wave. "I'm going to be sick." I tried to get up and go for the bathroom but collapsed on the white carpet and vomited blood. Red and bright and fresh. I was bleeding to death inside.

Richard's hand was cool on my forehead, his arm around my waist. I vomited until I was empty and exhausted. Richard lifted me to the couch. There was a narrow tunnel of light edged by darkness. The darkness was eating the light, and I couldn't stop it. I could feel myself begin to float away. It didn't hurt. I wasn't even scared.

The last thing I heard was Richard's voice. "I won't let you die."

It was a nice thought.

42

The dream began. I was sitting in the middle of a huge canopied bed. The drapes were heavy blue velvet, the color of midnight skies. The velvet bedspread was soft under my hands. I was wearing a long white gown with lace at the collar and sleeves. I'd never owned anything like it. No one had in this century.

The walls were blue and gold wallpaper. A huge fireplace blazed, sending shadows dancing around the room. Jean-Claude stood in the corner of the room, bathed in orange and black shadows. He was wearing the same shirt I'd last seen him in, the one with the peekaboo front.

He walked towards me, fire-shadows shining in his hair, on his face, glittering in his eyes.

"Why don't you ever dress me in anything normal in these dreams?"

He hesitated. "You don't like the gown?"

"Hell, no."

He gave a slight smile. "You always did have a way with words, *ma petite*."

"Stop calling me that, dammit."

"As you like, Anita." There was something in the way he said my name that I didn't like at all.

"What are you up to, Jean-Claude?"

He stood beside the bed and unbuttoned the first button of his shirt.

"What are you doing?"

Another button, and another, then he was pulling the shirt out of his pants and letting it slide to the floor. His bare chest was only a little less white than my gown. His nipples were pale and hard. The strand of dark hair that started low on his belly and disappeared into his pants fascinated me.

He crawled up on the bed.

I backed away, clutching the white gown to me like some heroine in a bad Victorian novel. "I don't seduce this easy."

"I can taste your lust on the back of my tongue, Anita. You want to know what my skin feels like next to your naked body."

I scrambled off the bed. "Leave me the fuck alone. I mean it."

"It's just a dream. Can't you even let yourself lust in a dream?"

"It's never just a dream with you."

He was suddenly standing in front of me. I hadn't seen him move. His arms locked behind my back, and we were on the floor in front of the fire. Fire-shadows danced on the naked skin of his shoulders. His skin was fragile, smooth, and unblemished—so soft I wanted to touch it forever. He was on top of me, his weight pressing against me, pushing me into the floor. I could feel the line of his body molded against mine.

"One kiss and I'll let you up."

I stared into his midnight-blue eyes from inches away. I couldn't talk. I turned my face away so I wouldn't have to look into the perfection of his face. "One kiss?"

"My word," he whispered.

I turned back to him. "Your word isn't worth shit."

His face leaned over mine, lips almost touching. "One kiss."

His lips were soft, gentle. He kissed my cheek, lips brushing down the line of my cheek, touching my neck. His hair brushed my face. I thought that all curly hair was coarse, but his was baby fine, silken soft. "One kiss," he whispered against the skin of my throat, tongue tasting the pulse in my neck.

"Stop it."

"You want it."

"Stop it, now!"

He grabbed a handful of hair, forcing my neck backwards. His lips had thinned back, exposing fangs. His eyes were drowning blue without any white at all.

"NO!"

"I will have you, *ma petite*, even if it is to save your life." His head came downward, striking like a snake. I woke up staring at a ceiling I didn't recognize.

Black and white drapes were suspended from the ceiling in a soft fan. The bed was black satin with too many pillows thrown all over the place. The pillows were all black or white. I was wearing a black gown with spaghetti straps. It felt like a real silk and fit me perfectly.

The floor was ankle-deep white carpet. A black lacquer vanity and chest of drawers were placed at far corners of the room. I sat up and could see myself in the mirror. My neck was smooth, no bite marks. Just a dream, just a dream, but I knew better. The bedroom had the unmistakable touch of Jean-Claude.

I had been dying of poison. How had I gotten here? Was I underneath the Circus of the Damned, or somewhere else altogether? My right wrist hurt.

There was a white swathe of bandages around my wrist. I didn't remember hurting it in the cave.

I stared at myself in the vanity mirror. In the black negligee my skin was white, my hair long and black as the gown. I laughed. I matched the decor. I matched the damn decor.

A door opened behind a white curtain. I got a glimpse of stone walls behind the drapes. He was wearing nothing but the silky bottoms of men's pajamas. He padded towards me on bare feet. His bare chest looked like it had in my dream, except for the cross-shaped scar; it hadn't been there in the dream. It marred the marble perfection of him, made him seem more real somehow.

"Hell," I said. "Definitely Hell."

"What, *ma petite*?"

"I was wondering where I was. If you're here, it has to be Hell."

He smiled. He looked entirely too satisfied, like a snake that had been well-fed.

"How did I get here?"

"Richard brought you."

"So I really was poisoned. That wasn't part of the dream?"

He sat on the far edge of the bed, as far away from me as he could get and still sit down. There were no other places to sit. "I'm afraid the poison was very real."

"Not that I'm complaining, but why aren't I dead?"

He hugged his knees to his chest, a strangely vulnerable gesture. "I saved you."

"Explain that."

"You know."

I shook my head. "Say it."

"The third mark."

"I don't have any bite marks."

"But your wrist is cut and bandaged."

"You bastard."

"I saved your life."

"You drank my blood while I was unconscious."

He gave the slightest nod.

"You son of a bitch."

The door opened again, and it was Richard. "You bastard, how could you give me to him?"

"She doesn't seem very grateful to us, Richard."

"You said you'd rather die than be a lycanthrope."

"I'd rather die than be a vampire."

"He didn't bite you. You're not going to be a vampire."

"I'll be his slave for eternity; great choice."

"It's only the third mark, Anita. You aren't his servant yet."

"That's not the point." I stared at him. "Don't you understand? I'd rather you let me die than have done this."

"It is hardly a fate worse than death," Jean-Claude said.

"You were bleeding from your nose and eyes. You were bleeding to death in my arms." Richard took a few steps towards the bed, then stopped. "I couldn't just let you die." His hands reached outward in a helpless gesture.

I stood up in the silky gown and stared at them both. "Maybe Richard didn't know any better, but you knew how I felt, Jean-Claude. You don't have any excuses."

"Perhaps I could not stand to watch you die, either. Have you thought of that?"

I shook my head. "What does the third mark mean? What extra powers does it give you over me?"

"I can whisper in your mind outside of dreams now. And you have gained power as well, *ma petite*. You are very hard to kill now. Poison won't work at all."

I kept shaking my head. "I don't want to hear it. I won't forgive you for this, Jean-Claude."

"I did not think you would," he said. He seemed wistful.

"I need clothes and a ride home. I've got to work tonight."

"Anita, you've almost died twice today. How can you . . ."

"Can it, Richard. I need to go to work tonight. I need something that's mine and not his. You invasive bastard."

"Find her some clothes and take her home, Richard. She needs time to adjust to this new change."

I stared at Jean-Claude still cuddled on the corner of the bed. He looked adorable, and if I'd had a gun, I'd have shot him on the spot. Fear was a hard, cold lump in my gut. He meant to make me his servant, whether I liked it or not. I could scream and protest, and he'd ignore it.

"Come near me again, Jean-Claude, for any reason, and I'll kill you."

"Three marks bind us now. It would harm you, too."

I laughed, and it was bitter. "Do you really think I give a damn?"

He stared at me, face calm, unreadable, lovely. "No." He turned his back on us both and said, "Take her home,

Richard. Though I do not envy you the ride there." He glanced back with a smile. "She can be quite vocal when she's angry."

I wanted to spit at him, but that wouldn't have been enough. I couldn't kill him, not right then and there, so I let it go. Grace under pressure. I followed Richard out the door and didn't look back. I didn't want to see his perfect profile in the vanity mirror.

Vampires weren't suppose to have reflections, or souls. He had one. Did he have the other? Did it matter? No, I decided, it didn't matter at all. I was going to give Jean-Claude to Oliver. I was going to give the city to Mr. Oliver. I was going to set the Master of the City up for assassination. One more mark and I'd be his forever. No way. I'd see him dead first, even if it meant I died with him. No one forced me into anything, not even eternity.

43

I ended up wearing one of those dresses with the waist that hit you about at the hips. The fact that the dress was about three sizes too big didn't help matters. The shoes fit even if they were high heels. It was better than going barefoot. Richard turned up the heat in the car because I'd refused his coat.

We were fighting, and we hadn't even had one date. That was a record even for me.

"You're alive," he said for the seventieth time.

"But at what price?"

"I believe that all life is precious. Don't you?"

"Don't go all philosophical on me, Richard. You handed me over to the monsters, and they used me. Don't you understand that Jean-Claude has been looking for an excuse to do this to me?"

"He saved your life."

That seemed to be the extent of his argument. "But he didn't do it to save my life. He did it because he wants me as his slave."

"A human servant isn't a slave. It's almost the opposite. He'll have almost no power over you."

"But he'll be able to talk inside my head, invade my dreams." I shook my head. "Don't let him sucker you."

"You're being unreasonable," he said.

That was it. "I'm the one with my wrist slit open where the Master of the City fed. He drank my blood, Richard."

"I know."

There was something about the way he said it. "You watched, you sick son of a bitch."

"No, it wasn't like that."

"How was it?" I sat with my arms crossed over my stomach, glaring at him. So that was the hold Jean-Claude had on him. Richard was a voyeur.

"I wanted to make sure he only did enough to save your life."

"What else could he have done? He drank my blood, dammit."

Richard concentrated on the road suddenly, not looking at me. "He could have raped you."

"I was bleeding from my eyes and nose, you said. Doesn't sound very romantic to me."

"All the blood, it seemed to excite him."

I stared at him. "You're serious?"

He nodded.

I sat there feeling cold down to my toes. "What made you think he was going to rape me?"

"You woke up on a black bedspread. The first one was white. He laid you on it and started to strip down. He took your robe off. There was blood everywhere. He smeared his face in it, tasted it. Another vampire handed him a small gold knife."

"There were more vamps there?"

"It was like a ritual. The audience seemed to be important. He slit your wrist and drank at it, but his hands . . . he was touching your breasts. I told him that I had brought you so you could live, not so he could rape you."

"That must have gone over real big."

Richard was very quiet all of a sudden.

"What?"

He shook his head.

"Tell me, Richard. I mean it."

"Jean-Claude looked up with blood all over his face and said, " 'I have not waited this long to take what I want her to give freely. It is a temptation.' Then he looked down at you, and there was something in his face, Anita. It was scary as hell. He really believes you'll come around. That you'll . . . love him."

"Vampires don't love."

"Are you sure?"

I glanced at him, then away. I stared at the window at the daylight that was just now beginning to fade. "Vampires don't love. They can't."

"How do you know that?"

"Jean-Claude does not love me."

"Maybe he does, as much as he can."

I shook my head. "He bathed in my blood. He slit my wrist. That isn't my idea of love."

"Maybe it's his."

"Then it's too damn weird for me."

"Fine, but admit that he may love you, as much as he's able."

"No."

"It scares you to think that he loves you, doesn't it?"

I stared out the window as hard as I could. I didn't want to be talking about this. I wanted to undo this whole damn day.

"Or is it something else that you're afraid of?"

"I don't know what you're talking about."

"Yes, you do." He sounded so sure of himself. He didn't know me well enough to be that certain.

"Say it out loud, Anita. Say it just once and it won't seem so scary."

"I don't have anything to say."

"You're telling me that no part of you wants him. Not a piece of you might love him back."

"I don't love him; that much I'm sure of."

"But?"

"You are persistent," I said.

"Yes," he said.

"Alright, I'm attracted to him. Is that what you wanted to hear?"

"How attracted?"

"That's none of your damn business."

"Jean-Claude warned me to stay away from you. I just

want to know if I'm really interfering. If you're attracted to him, maybe I should stay out of it."

"He's a monster, Richard. You've seen him. I can't love a monster."

"If he was human?"

"He's an egotistical, controlling bastard."

"But if he was human?"

I sighed. "If he was human, we might work something out, but even alive, Jean-Claude can be such an SOB. I don't think it would work."

"But you're not even going to try because he's a monster."

"He's dead, Richard, a walking corpse. It doesn't matter how pretty he is, or how compelling, he's still dead. I don't date corpses. A girl's got to have some standards."

"So no corpses," he said.

"No corpses."

"What about lycanthropes?"

"Why? You thinking of fixing me up with your friend?"

"Just curious about where you draw the line."

"Lycanthropy is a disease. The person's already survived a vicious attack. It'd be like blaming the rape victim."

"You ever date a shapeshifter?"

"It's never come up."

"What else wouldn't you date?"

"Things that were never human to begin with, I guess. I really haven't thought about it. Why the interest?"

He shook his head. "Just curious."

"Why aren't I still pissed at you?"

"Maybe because you're glad to be alive, no matter what the cost."

He pulled into the parking lot of my apartment building. Larry's car was idling in my parking space. "Maybe I am glad to be alive, but I'll let you know about the cost when I find out what it really is."

"You don't believe Jean-Claude?"

"I wouldn't believe Jean-Claude if he told me moonlight was silver."

Richard smiled. "Sorry about the date."

"Maybe we can try again sometime."

"I'd like that," he said.

I opened the door and stood shivering in the cool air. "Whatever happens, Richard, thanks for watching out for me." I hesitated, then said, "And whatever hold Jean-Claude's got on you, break it. Get away from him. He'll get you killed."

He just nodded. "Good advice."

"Which you're not going to take," I said.

"I would if I could, Anita. Please believe that."

"What does he have on you, Richard?"

He shook his head. "He ordered me not to tell you."

"He ordered you not to date me, too."

He shrugged. "You better get going. You're going to be late for work."

I smiled. "Besides, I'm freezing my butt off."

He smiled. "You do have a way with words."

"I spend too much time hanging around with cops."

He put the car in gear. "Have a safe night at work."

"I'll do my best."

He nodded. I closed the door. Richard didn't seem to want to talk about what Jean-Claude had on him. Well, no rule said we had to play honesty on the first date. Besides, he was right. I was going to be late for work.

I tapped on Larry's window. "I've got to change, then I'll be right back down."

"Who was that dropping you off?"

"A date." I left it at that. It was a much easier explanation than the truth. Besides, it was almost true.

44

This is the only night of the year that Bert allows us to wear black to work. He thinks the color is too harsh for normal business hours. I had black jeans and a Halloween sweater with huge grinning jack o' lanterns in a stomach-high line. I topped it off with a black zipper sweatshirt and black Nikes. Even my shoulder holster and the Browning matched. I had my backup gun in an inner pants holster. I also had two extra clips in my sport bag. I had replaced the knife I'd had to leave in the cave. There was a derringer in my jacket pocket and two extra knives, one down the spine, the other in an ankle holster. Don't laugh. I left the shotgun home.

If Jean-Claude found out I'd betrayed him, he'd kill me. Would I know when he died? Would I feel it? Something told me that I would.

I took the card that Karl Inger had given me and called the number. If it had to be done, it best be done quickly.

"Hello?"

"Is this Karl Inger?"

"Yes, it is. Who is this?"

"It's Anita Blake. I need to speak with Oliver."

"Have you decided to give us the Master of the City?"

"Yes."

"If you'll hold for a moment, I'll fetch Mr. Oliver." He laid the receiver down. I heard him walking away until there was nothing but silence on the phone. Better than Muzak.

Footsteps coming back, then: "Hello, Ms. Blake, so good of you to call."

I swallowed, and it hurt. "The Master of the City is Jean-Claude."

"I had discounted him. He isn't very powerful."

"He hides his powers. Trust me, he's a lot more than he seems."

"Why the change of heart, Ms. Blake?"

"He gave me the third mark. I want free of him."

"Ms. Blake, to be bound thrice to a vampire, and then have that vampire die, can be quite a shock to the system. It could kill you."

"I want free of him, Mr. Oliver."

"Even if you die?" he said.

"Even if I die."

"I would have liked to have met you under different circumstances, Anita Blake. You are a remarkable person."

"No, I've just seen too much. I won't let him have me."

"I will not fail you, Ms. Blake. I will see him dead."

"If I didn't believe that, I wouldn't have told you."

"I appreciate your confidence."

"One other thing you should know. The lamia tried to betray you today. She's in league with another master named Alejandro."

"Really?" His voice sounded amused. "What did he offer her?"

"Her freedom."

"Yes, that would tempt Melanie. I keep her on such a short rein."

"She's been trying to breed. Did you know that?"

"What do you mean?"

I told him about the men, especially the last one that had been nearly changed.

He was quiet for a moment. "I have been most inattentive. I will deal with Melanie and Alejandro."

"Fine. I'd appreciate a call tomorrow to let me know how things went."

"To be sure he's dead," Oliver said.

"Yes," I said.

"You'll get a call from Karl or myself. But first, where can we find Jean-Claude?"

"The Circus of the Damned."

"How appropriate."

"That's all I can tell you."

"Thank you, Ms. Blake, and Happy Halloween."

I had to laugh. "It's going to be a hell of a night."

He chuckled softly. "Indeed. Good-bye, Ms. Blake." The phone went dead in my hand.

I stared at the phone. I'd had to do it. Had to. So why did my stomach feel tight? Why did I have the urge to call Jean-Claude and warn him? Was it the marks, or was Richard right? Did I love Jean-Claude in some strange, twisted way? God help me, I hoped not.

45

It was full dark on All Hallows Eve. Larry and I had made two appointments. He'd raised one, and I'd raised the other. He had one more to go, and I had three. A nice normal night.

What Larry was wearing was not normal. Bert had encouraged us to wear something fitting for the holiday. I'd chosen the sweater. Larry had chosen a costume. He was wearing blue denim overalls, a white dress shirt with the sleeves rolled up, a straw hat, and work boots. When asked, he'd said, "I'm Huck Finn. Don't I fit the part?"

With his red hair and freckles, he did fit the part. There was blood on the shirt now, but it was Halloween. There were a lot of people out with fake blood on them. We fitted right in tonight.

My beeper went off. I checked the number, and it was Dolph. Damn.

"Who is it?" Larry asked.

"The police. We've got to find a phone."

He glanced at the dashboard clock. "We're ahead of schedule. How about the McDonald's just off the highway?"

"Great." I prayed that it wasn't another murder. I needed a nice normal night. At the back of my head like a bit of remembered song, two sentences kept playing: "Jean-Claude is going to die tonight. You set him up."

It seemed wrong to kill him from a safe distance. To not look him in the eyes and pull the trigger myself, to not give him a chance to kill me first. Fair play and all that. Fuck

297

fair play; it was him or me. Wasn't it?

Larry parked in the McDonald's lot. "I'm gonna get a Coke while you call in. You want something?"

I shook my head.

"You alright?"

"Sure. I'm just hoping it's not another murder."

"Jesus, I hadn't thought of that."

We got out of the car. Larry went into the dining room. I stayed in the little entrance area with the pay phone.

Dolph picked up on the third ring. "Sergeant Storr."

"It's Anita. What's up?"

"We finally broke the paralegal that was feeding information to the vampires."

"Great; I thought it might be another murder."

"Not tonight; the vamp's got more important business."

"What's that supposed to mean?"

"He's planning on getting every vampire in the city to slaughter humans for Halloween."

"He can't. Only the Master of the City could do that, and then only if he was incredibly powerful."

"That's what I thought. Could be the vampire's crazy."

I had a thought, an awful thought. "You got a description of the vampire?"

"Vampires," he said.

"Read it to me."

I heard paper rustling, then: "Short, dark, very polite. Saw one other vampire twice with the boss vamp. He was medium height, Indian or Mexican, longish black hair."

I clutched the phone so tight my hand trembled. "Did the vampire say why he was going to slaughter humans?"

"Wanted to discredit legalized vampirism. Now isn't that a weird motive for a vampire?"

"Yeah," I said. "Dolph, this could happen."

"What are you saying?"

"If this master vampire could kill the Master of the City and take over before dawn, he might pull it off."

"What can we do?"

I hesitated, almost telling him to protect Jean-Claude, but it wasn't a matter for the police. They had to worry about laws and police brutality. There was no way to take something like Oliver alive. Whatever was going to happen tonight had to be permanent.

"Talk to me, Anita."

"I've gotta go, Dolph."

"You know something; tell me."

I hung up. I also turned off my beeper. I dialed Circus of the Damned. A pleasant-voiced woman answered, "Circus of the Damned, where all your nightmares come true."

"I need to speak to Jean-Claude. It's an emergency."

"He's busy right now. May I take a message?"

I swallowed hard, tried not to yell. "This is Anita Blake, Jean-Claude's human servant. Tell him to get his ass to the phone now."

"I . . ."

"People are going to die if I don't talk to him."

"Okay, okay." She put me on hold with a butchered version of "High Flying" by Tom Petty.

Larry came out with his Coke. "What's up?"

I shook my head. I fought the urge to jump up and down, but that wouldn't get Jean-Claude to the phone any sooner. I stood very still, hugging one arm across my stomach. What had I done? Please don't let it be too late.

"*Ma petite*?"

"Thank God."

"What has happened?"

"Just listen. There's a master vampire on his way to the Circus. I gave him your name and your resting place. His name is Mr. Oliver and he's older than anything. He's older than Alejandro. In fact, I think he's Alejandro's master. It's all been a plan to get me to betray the city to him, and I fell for it."

He was quiet so long that I asked, "Did you hear me?"

"You really meant to kill me."

"I told you I would."

"But now you warn me. Why?"

"Oliver wants control of the city so he can send all the vampires out to slaughter humans. He wants it back to the old days when vampires were hunted. He said legalized vampirism was spreading too fast. I agree, but I didn't know what he meant to do."

"So to save your precious humans you will betray Oliver now."

"It isn't like that. Dammit, Jean-Claude, concentrate on the important thing here. They're on their way. They may be there already. You've got to protect yourself."

"To keep the humans safe."

"To keep your vampires safe, too. Do you really want them under Oliver's control?"

"No. I will take steps, *ma petite*. We will at least give him a fight." He hung up.

Larry was staring at me with wide eyes. "What the hell is happening, Anita?"

"Not now, Larry." I fished Edward's card out of my bag. I didn't have another quarter. "Do you have a quarter?"

"Sure." He handed it to me without any more questions. Good man.

I dialed the number. "Please, be there. Please, be there."

He answered on the seventh ring.

"Edward, it's Anita."

"What's happened?"

"How would you like to take on two master vampires older than Nikolaos?"

I heard him swallow. "I always have so much fun when you're around. Where should we meet?"

"The Circus of the Damned. You got an extra shotgun?"

"Not with me."

"Shit. Meet me out front ASAP. The shit's going to really hit the fan tonight, Edward."

"Sounds like a great way to spend Halloween."

"See you there."

"Bye, and thanks for inviting me." He meant it. Edward had started out as a normal assassin, but humans had been too easy, so he went for vamps and shapeshifters. He hadn't met anything he couldn't kill, and what was life without a little challenge?

I looked at Larry. "I need to borrow your car."

"You're not going anywhere without me. I've heard just your side of the conversations, and I'm not getting left out."

I started to argue, but there wasn't time. "Okay, let's do it."

He grinned. He was pleased. He didn't know what was going to happen tonight, what we were up against. I did. And I wasn't happy at all.

46

I stood just inside the door of the Circus staring at the wave of costumes and glittering humanity. I'd never seen the place so crowded. Edward stood beside me in a long black cloak with a death's-head mask. Death dressed up as death; funny, huh? He also had a flamethrower strapped to his back, an Uzi pistol, and heaven knew how many other weapons secreted about his person. Larry looked pale but determined. He had my derringer in his pocket. He knew nothing about guns. The derringer was an emergency measure only, but he wouldn't stay in the car. Next week, if we were still alive, I'd take him out to the shooting range.

A woman in a bird costume passed us in a scent of feathers and perfume. I had to look twice to make sure that it was just a costume. Tonight was the night when all shapeshifters could be out and people would just say, "Neat costume."

It was Halloween night at the Circus of the Damned. Anything was possible.

A slender black woman stepped up to us wearing nothing but a bikini and an elaborate mask. She had to step close to me to be heard over the murmur of the crowd. "Jean-Claude sent me to bring you."

"Who are you?"

"Rashida."

I shook my head. "Rashida had her arm torn off two days ago." I stared at the perfect flesh of her arm. "You can't be her."

She raised her mask so I could see her face, then smiled. "We heal fast."

I had known lycanthropes healed fast, but not that fast, not that much damage. Live and learn.

We followed her swaying hips into the crowd. I grabbed hold of Larry's hand with my left hand. "Stay right with me tonight."

He nodded. I threaded through the crowd holding his hand like a child or a lover. I couldn't stand the thought of him getting hurt. No, that wasn't true. I couldn't stand the thought of him getting killed. Death was the big boogeyman tonight.

Edward followed at our heels. Silent as his namesake, trusting that he'd get to kill something soon.

Rashida led us towards the big, striped circus tent. Back to Jean-Claude's office, I supposed. A man in a straw hat and striped coat said, "Sorry, the show's sold out."

"It's me, Perry. These are the ones the Master's been waiting for." She hiked her thumb in our direction.

The man drew aside the tent flap and motioned us through. There was a line of sweat on his upper lip. It was warm, but I had the feeling it wasn't that kind of sweat. What was happening inside the tent? It couldn't be too bad if they were letting the crowd in to watch. Could it?

The lights were bright and hot. I started to sweat under the sweatshirt, but if I took it off, people would stare at my gun. I hated that.

Circular curtains had been rigged to the ceiling, creating two curtained-off areas in the large circus ring. Spotlights surrounded the two hidden areas. The curtains were like prisms. With every step we took, the colors changed and flowed over the cloth. I wasn't sure if it was the cloth or some trick of the lights. Whatever, it was a nifty effect.

Rashida stopped just short of the rail that kept the crowd back. "Jean-Claude wanted everybody to be in costume, but we're out of time." She pulled at my sweater. "Lose the jacket and it'll have to do."

I pulled my sweater out of her hand. "What are you talking about, costumes?"

"You're holding up the show. Drop the jacket and come on." She did a long, lazy leap over the railing and strode barefoot and beautiful across the white floor. She looked back at us, motioning for us to follow.

I stayed where I was. I wasn't going anywhere until somebody explained things. Larry and Edward waited with me. The audience near us was staring intently, waiting for us to do something interesting.

We stood there.

Rashida disappeared into one of the curtained circles. "Anita."

I turned, but Larry was staring at the ring. "Did you say something?"

He shook his head.

"Anita?"

I glanced at Edward, but it hadn't been his voice. I whispered, "Jean-Claude?"

"Yes, *ma petite*, it is I."

"Where are you?"

"Behind the curtain where Rashida went."

I shook my head. His voice had resonance, a slight echo, but otherwise it was as normal as his voice ever got. I could probably talk to him without moving my lips, but if so, I didn't want to know. I whispered, "What's going on?"

"Mr. Oliver and I have a gentleman's agreement."

"I don't understand."

"Who are you talking to?" Edward asked.

I shook my head. "I'll explain later."

"Come into my circle, Anita, and I will explain everything to you at the same time I explain it to our audience."

"What have you done?"

"I have done the best I could to spare lives, *ma petite*, but some will die tonight. But it will be in the circle with only the soldiers called to task. No innocents will die tonight, whoever wins. We have given our words."

"You're going to fight it out in the ring like a show?"

"It was the best I could do on such short notice. If you had warned me days ago, perhaps something else could have been arranged."

I ignored that. Besides, I was feeling guilty.

I took off the sweatshirt and laid it across the railing. There were gasps from the people near enough to see my gun.

"The fight's going to take place out in the ring."

"In front of the audience?" Edward said.

"Yep."

"I don't get it," Larry said.

"I want you to stay here, Larry."

"No way."

I took a deep breath and let it out slowly. "Larry, you don't have any weapons. You don't know how to use a gun. You're just cannon fodder until you get some training. Stay here."

He shook his head.

I touched his arm. "Please, Larry."

Maybe it was the please, or the look in my eyes—whatever, he nodded.

I could breathe a little easier. Whatever happened tonight, Larry wouldn't die because I'd brought him into it. It wouldn't be my fault.

I climbed over the railing and dropped to the ring. Edward followed me with a swish of black cape. I glanced back once. Larry stood gripping the rail. There was something forlorn about him standing there alone, but he was safe; that was what counted.

I touched the shimmering curtain, and it was the lights. The cloth was white up close. I lifted it to one side, and entered, Edward at my back.

There was a multilayered dais complete with throne in the center of the circle. Rashida stood with Stephen near the foot of the dais. I recognized Richard's hair and his naked chest before he lifted the mask off his face. It was a white mask with a blue star on one cheek. He was wearing glittering blue harem pants with a matching vest and shoes. Everyone was in costume but me.

"I was hoping you wouldn't make it in time," Richard said.

"What, and miss the Halloween blowout of all time?"

"Who's that with you?" Stephen asked.

"Death," I said.

Edward bowed.

"Trust you to bring death to the ball, *ma petite*."

I looked up the dais, to the very top. Jean-Claude stood in front of the throne. He was finally wearing what his shirts hinted at, but this was the real thing. The real French courtier. I didn't know what to call half of the costume. The coat was black with tasteful silver here and there. A short half-cloak was worn over one shoulder only. The pants were billowy and tucked into calf-high boots. Lace edged the foldover tops of the boots. A wide white collar lay at his throat. Lace spilled out of the coat sleeves. It was topped off by a wide, almost floppy hat with a curving arch of black and white feathers.

The costumed throng moved to either side, clearing the stairs up to the throne for me. I somehow didn't want to go. There were sounds outside the curtains. Heavy things being moved around. More scenery and props being moved up.

I glanced at Edward. He was staring at the crowd, eyes taking in everything. Hunting for victims, or for familiar faces?

Everyone was in costume, but very few people were actually wearing masks. Yasmeen and Marguerite stood about halfway up the stairs. Yasmeen was in a scarlet sari, all veils and sequins. Her dark face looked very natural in the red silk. Marguerite was in a long dress with puffed sleeves and a wide lace collar. The dress was of some dark blue cloth. It was simple, unadorned. Her blond hair was in complicated curls with one large mass over each ear and a small bun atop her head. Hers, like Jean-Claude's, looked less like a costume and more like antique clothing.

I walked up the stairs towards them. Yasmeen dropped her veils enough to expose the cross-shaped scar I'd given her. "Someone will pay you back for this tonight."

"Not you personally?" I asked.

"Not yet."

"You don't care who wins, do you?"

She smiled. "I am loyal to Jean-Claude, of course."

"Like hell."

"As loyal as you were, *ma petite*." She drew out each syllable, biting each sound off.

I left her to laugh at my back. I guess I wasn't the one to complain about loyalties.

There were a pair of wolves sitting at Jean-Claude's feet. They stared at me with strange pale eyes. There was nothing human in the gaze. Real wolves. Where had he gotten real wolves?

I stood two steps down from him and his pet wolves. His face was unreadable, empty and perfect.

"You look like something out of *The Three Musketeers*," I said.

"Accurate, *ma petite*."

"Is it your original century?"

He smiled a smile that could have meant anything, or nothing.

"What's going to happen tonight, Jean-Claude?"

"Come, stand beside me, where my human servant belongs." He extended a pale hand.

I ignored the hand and stepped up. He'd talked inside my head. It was getting silly to argue. Arguing didn't make it not true.

One of the wolves growled low in its chest. I hesitated.

"They will not harm you. They are my creatures."

Like me, I thought.

Jean-Claude put his hand down towards the wolf. It cringed and licked his hand. I stepped carefully around the wolf. But it ignored me, all its attention on Jean-Claude. It was sorry it had growled at me. It would do anything to make up for it. It groveled like a dog.

I stood at his right side, a little behind the wolf.

"I had picked out a lovely costume for you."

"If it was anything that would have matched yours, I wouldn't have worn it."

He laughed, soft and low. The sound tugged at something low in my gut. "Stay here by the throne with the wolves while I make my speech."

"We really are going to fight in front of the crowd."

He stood. "Of course. This is the Circus of the Damned, and tonight is Halloween. We will show them a spectacle the likes of which they have never seen."

"This is crazy."

"Probably, but it keeps Oliver from bringing the building down around us."

"Could he do that?"

"That and much more, *ma petite*, if we had not agreed to limit our use of such powers."

"Could you bring the building down?"

He smiled, and for once gave me a straight answer. "No, but Oliver does not know that."

I had to smile.

He draped himself over the throne, one leg thrown over a chair arm. He tucked his hat low until all I could see was his mouth. "I still cannot believe that you betrayed me, Anita."

"You gave me no choice."

"You would really see me dead rather than have the fourth mark."

"Yep."

He whispered, "Showtime, Anita."

The lights suddenly went off. There were screams from the audience as it sat in the sudden dark. The curtain pulled back on either side. I was suddenly on the edge of the spotlight. The light shone like a star in the dark. Jean-Claude and his wolves were bathed in a soft light. I had to agree that my pumpkin sweater didn't exactly fit the motif.

Jean-Claude stood in one boneless movement. He swept his hat off and gave a low, sweeping bow. "Ladies and gentlemen, tonight you will witness a great battle." He began to move slowly down the steps. The spotlight moved with him. He kept the hat off, using it for emphasis in his hand. "The battle for the soul of this city."

He stopped, and the light spread wider to include two blond vampires. The two women were dressed as 1920s flappers, one in blue, the other in red. The women flashed fangs, and there were gasps from the audience. "Tonight you will see vampires, werewolves, gods, devils." He filled each word with something. When he said "vampires," there was a ruffling at your neck. "Werewolves" slashed from the dark, and there were screams. "Gods" breathed along the skin. "Devils" were a hot wind that scalded your face.

Gasps and stifled screams filled the dark.

"Some of what you see tonight will be real, some illusion; which is which will be for you to decide." "Illusion" echoed in the mind like a vision through glass, repeating over and over. The last sound died away with a whisper that sounded like a different word altogether. "Real," the voice whispered.

"The monsters of this city fight for control of it this Halloween. If we win, then all goes peaceful as before. If our enemies win . . ." A second spotlight picked out the top of a second dais. There was no throne. Oliver stood at the top with the lamia in full serpent glory. Oliver was dressed in a baggy white jump suit with large polka dots on it. His face was white with a sad smile drawn on it. One heavily lined eye dropped a sparkling tear. A tiny pointed hat with a bright blue pom-pom topped his head.

A clown? He had chosen to be a clown? It wasn't what I had pictured him in. But the lamia was impressive with her striped coils curled around him, her naked breasts caressed by his gloved hand.

"If our enemies win, then tomorrow night will see a bloodbath such as no city in the world has ever seen. They will feed upon the flesh and blood of this city until it is drained dry and lifeless." He had stopped about halfway down. Now he began to come back up the stairs. "We fight for your lives, your very souls. Pray that we win, dear humans; pray very, very hard."

He sat in the throne. One of the wolves put a paw on his leg. He stroked its head absently.

"Death comes to all humans," Oliver said.

The spotlight died on Jean-Claude, leaving Oliver as the only light in the darkness. Symbolism at its best.

"You will all die someday. In some small accident, or long disease. Pain and agony await you." The audience rustled uneasily in their seats.

"Are you protecting me from his voice?" I asked.

"The marks are," Jean-Claude said.

"What is the audience feeling?"

"A sharp pain over the heart. Age slowing their bodies. The quick horror of some remembered accident."

Gasps, screams, cries filled the dark as Oliver's words sought out each person and made them feel their mortality.

It was obscene. Something that had seen a million years was reminding mere humans how very fragile life was.

"If you must die, would it not be better to die in our glorious embrace?" The lamia crawled around the dais to show herself to all the audience. "She could take you, oh, so sweetly, soft, gentle into that dark night. We make death a celebration, a joyful passing. No lingering doubts. You will want her hands upon you in the end. She will show you joys that few mortals ever dream of. Is death such a high price to pay, when you will die anyway? Wouldn't it be better to die with our lips upon your skin than by time's slowly ticking clock?"

There were a few cries of "Yes . . . Please . . ."

"Stop him," I said.

"This is his moment, *ma petite*. I cannot stop him."

"I offer you all your darkest dreams come true in our arms, my friends. Come to us now."

The darkness rustled with movement. The lights came up, and there were people coming out of the seats. People climbing over the railing. People coming to embrace death.

They all froze in the light. They stared around like sleepers waking from a dream. Some looked embarrassed, but one man close to the rail looked near tears, as if some bright vision had been ripped away. He collapsed to his knees, shoulders shaking. He was sobbing. What had he seen in Oliver's words? What had he felt in the air? God, save us from it.

With the lights I could see what they had moved in while we waited behind the curtains. It looked like a marble altar with steps leading up to it. It sat between the two daises, waiting. For what? I turned to ask Jean-Claude, but something was happening.

Rashida walked away from the dais, putting herself close to the railing, and the people. Stephen, wearing what looked like a thong bathing suit, stalked to the other side of the ring. His nearly naked body was just as smooth and flawless as Rashida's. "We heal fast," she'd said.

"Ladies and gentlemen, we will give you a few moments to recover yourselves from the first magic of the evening. Then we will show you some of our secrets."

The crowd settled back into their seats. An usher helped the crying man back to his seat. A hush fell over the people. I had never heard so large a crowd be so silent. You could have dropped a pin.

"Vampires are able to call animals to their aid. My animal is the wolf." He walked around the top of the dais displaying the wolves. I stood there in the spotlight and wasn't sure what to do. I wasn't on display. I was just visible.

"But I can also call the wolf's human cousin. The werewolf." He made a wide, sweeping gesture with his arm. Music began. Soft and low at first, then rising in a shimmering crescendo.

Stephen fell to his knees. I turned, and Rashida was on the ground as well. They were going to change right here in front of the crowd. I'd never seen a shapeshifter shift before. I had to admit a certain . . . curiosity.

Stephen was on all fours. His bare back was bowed with pain. His long yellow hair trailed on the ground. The skin on his back rippled like water, his spine standing like a ridge in the middle. He stretched out his hands as if he were bowing, face pressed to the ground. Bones broke through his hands. He groaned. Things moved under his skin like crawling animals. His spine bowed upward as if rising like a tent all on its own. Fur started to flow out of the skin on his back, spreading impossibly fast like a timelapse photo. Bones and some heavy, clear liquid poured out of his skin. Shapes strained and ripped through his skin. Muscles writhed like snakes. Heavy, wet sounds came as bone shifted in and out of flesh. It was as if the wolf's shape was punching its way out of the man's body. Fur flowed fast and faster, the color of dark honey. The fur hid some of the changes, and I was glad.

Something between a howl and a scream tore from his throat. Finally, there was that same manwolf form as the night we fought the giant cobra. The wolfman threw his muzzle skyward and howled. The sound raised the hairs on my body.

A second howl echoed from the other side. I whirled, and there was a second wolfman form, but this one was as black as pitch. Rashida?

The audience applauded wildly, stamping and shouting.

The werewolves crept back to the dais. They crouched at the bottom, one on each side.

"I have nothing so showy to offer you." The lights were back on Oliver. "The snake is my creature." The lamia twined around him, hissing loud enough to carry to the audience. She flicked a forked tongue to lick his white-coated ear.

He motioned to the foot of the dais. Two black-cloaked figures stood on either side, hoods hiding their faces. "These are my creatures, but let us keep them for a surprise." He looked across at us. "Let it begin."

The lights went out again. I fought the urge to reach for Jean-Claude in the thick dark. "What's happening?"

"The battle begins," he said.

"How?"

"We have not planned the rest of the evening, Anita. It will be like every battle, chaotic, violent, bloody."

The lights came up gradually until the tent was bathed in a dim glow, like dusk or twilight. "It begins," Jean-Claude whispered.

The lamia flowed down the steps, and each side ran for the other. It wasn't a battle. It was a free-for-all, more like a bar brawl than a war.

The cloaked things ran forward. I had a glimpse of something vaguely snakelike but not. A spatter of machine-gun fire and the thing staggered back. Edward.

I started down the steps, gun in hand. Jean-Claude never moved. "Aren't you coming down?"

"The real battle will happen up here, *ma petite*. Do what you can, but in the end it will come down to Oliver's power and mine."

"He's a million years old. You can't beat him."

"I know."

We stared at each other for a moment. "I'm sorry," I said.

"So am I, *ma petite*, Anita, so am I."

I ran down the steps to join the fight. The snake-thing had collapsed, bisected by the machine-gun fire. Edward was standing back to back with Richard, who had a revolver in his hands. He was shooting it into one of the cloaked things and wasn't even slowing it down. I sighted down my arm and fired at the cloaked head. The thing stumbled and turned towards me. The hood fell backwards, revealing a cobra's head the size of a horse's. From the neck down it was a woman, but from the neck up . . . Neither my shot nor Richard's had made a dent. The thing came up the steps towards me. I didn't know what it was, or how to stop it. Happy Halloween.

47

The thing rushed towards me. I dropped the Browning and had one of the knives halfway out when it hit me. I was on the steps with the thing on top of me. It reared back to strike. I got the knife free. It plunged its fangs into my shoulder. I screamed and shoved the knife into its body. The knife went in, but no blood, no pain. It gnawed on my shoulder, pumping poison in, and the knife did nothing.

I screamed again. Jean-Claude's voice sounded in my head, "Poison cannot harm you now."

It hurt like hell, but I wasn't going to die from it. I plunged the knife into its throat, screaming, not knowing what else to do. It gagged. Blood ran down my hand. I hit it again, and it reared back, blood on its fangs. It gave a frantic hiss and pushed itself off me. But I understood now. The weak spot was where the snake part met human flesh.

I groped for the Browning left-handed; my right shoulder was torn up. I squeezed and watched blood spurt from the thing's neck. It turned and ran, and I let it go.

I lay on the steps holding my right arm against my body. I didn't think anything was broken, but it hurt like hell. It wasn't even bleeding as badly as it should have been. I glanced up at Jean-Claude. He was standing motionless, but something moved, like a shimmer of heat. Oliver was just as motionless on his dais. That was the real battle; the dying down here didn't mean much except to the people who were going to die.

I cradled my arm against my stomach and walked down the steps towards Edward and Richard. By the time I was at the bottom of the steps, the arm felt better. Good enough to change the gun to my right hand. I stared at the bite wound, and damned if it wasn't healing. The third mark. I was healing like a shapeshifter.

"Are you alright?" Richard asked.

"I seem to be."

Edward was staring at me. "You should be dying."

"Explanations later," I said.

The cobra thing lay at the foot of the dais, its head bisected by machine-gun fire. Edward caught on quick.

There was a scream, high and piercing. Alejandro had Yasmeen twisted around in his arms, one arm behind her back, his other arm pinning her shoulders to his chest. It was Marguerite who had screamed. She was struggling in Karl Inger's arms. She was outmatched. Apparently, so was Yasmeen.

Alejandro tore into her throat. She screamed. He snapped her spine with his teeth, blood splattering his face. She sagged in his arms. Movement, and his hand came out through the other side of her chest, the heart crushed to a bloody pulp.

Marguerite shrieked over and over again. Karl let her go, but she didn't seem to notice. She scratched fingernails down her cheeks until blood ran. She collapsed to her knees, still clawing at her face.

"Jesus," I said, "stop her."

Karl stared across at me. I raised the Browning, but he ducked behind Oliver's dais. I went towards Marguerite. Alejandro stepped between us.

"Do you want to help her?"

"Yes."

"Let me lay the last two marks upon you, and I will get out of your way."

I shook my head. "The city for one crazy human servant? I don't think so."

"Anita, down!" I dropped flat to the floor, and Edward shot a jet of flame over my head. I could feel the wash of heat bubbling overhead.

Alejandro shrieked. I raised my eyes only enough to see him burning. He motioned outward with one burning hand, and I felt something wash over me back towards . . . Edward.

I rolled over, and Edward was on his back, struggling to his feet. The nozzle of the flamethrower was pointed this way again. I dropped without being told.

Alejandro motioned, and the flame peeled backwards, flowing towards Edward.

He rolled frantically to put out the flames on his cloak. He threw the burning death's-head mask onto the ground. The flamethrower's tank was on fire. Richard helped him struggle out of it, and they ran. I hugged the ground, hands over my head. The explosion shook the ground. When I looked up, tiny burning pieces were raining down, but that was all. Richard and Edward were peering around the other side of the dais.

Alejandro stood there with his clothes charred, his skin blistered. He began walking towards me.

I scrambled to my feet, pointing my gun at him. Of course, the gun hadn't done a whole lot of good before. I backed up until I bumped the steps. I started shooting. The bullets went in. He even bled, but he didn't stop. The gun clicked on empty. I turned and ran.

Something hit me in the back, slamming me to the ground. Alejandro was suddenly on my back, one hand in my hair, bending my neck backwards.

"Put down the machine gun or I'll break her neck."

"Shoot him!" I screamed.

But Edward threw the machine gun on the floor. Dammit. He got out a pistol and took careful aim. Alejandro's body jerked, then he laughed. "You can't kill me with silver bullets."

He put a knee in my back to hold me down; then a knife flashed in his hand.

"No," Richard said, "he won't kill her."

"I'll slit her throat if you interfere, but if you leave us alone, I won't harm her."

"Edward, kill him!"

A vampire jumped Edward, riding him to the ground. Richard tried to pull her off him, but a tiny vampire leaped on his back. It was the woman and the little boy from that first night.

"Now that your friends are busy, we will finish our business."

"NO!"

The knife just nicked the surface, sharp, painful, but such a little cut. He leaned over me. "It won't hurt, I promise."

I screamed.

His lips touched the cut, locked on it, sucking. He was wrong. It did hurt. Then the smell of flowers surrounded me. I was drowning in perfume. I couldn't see. The world was warm and sweet-scented.

When I could see again, think again, I was lying on my back, staring up at the tent roof. Arms drew me upward, cradled me. Alejandro held me close. He'd cut a line of blood on his chest, just above the nipple. "Drink."

I put my hands flat against him, fighting him. His hand squeezed the back of my neck, forcing me closer to the wound.

"NO!"

I drew the other knife and plunged it into his chest, searching for the heart. He grunted and grabbed my hand, squeezed until I dropped the knife. "Silver is not the way. I am past silver."

He pushed my face towards the wound, and I couldn't fight him. I just wasn't strong enough. He could have crushed my skull in one hand, but all he did was press my face to the cut on his chest.

I struggled, but he kept my mouth pressed to the wound. The blood was salty sweet, vaguely metallic. It was only blood.

"Anita!" Jean-Claude screamed my name. I wasn't sure if it was aloud or in my head.

"Blood of my blood, flesh of my flesh, the two shall be as one. One flesh, one blood, one soul." Somewhere deep inside me, something broke. I could feel it. A wave of liquid warmth rushed up and over me. My skin danced with it. My fingertips tingled. My spine spasmed, and I jerked upright. Strong arms caught me, held me, rocked me.

A hand smoothed my hair from my face. I opened my eyes to see Alejandro. I wasn't afraid of him anymore. I was calm and floating.

"Anita?" It was Edward. I turned towards the sound, slowly.

"Edward."

"What did he do to you?"

I tried to think how to explain it, but my mind wouldn't bring up the words. I sat up, pushing gently away from Alejandro.

There was a pile of dead vampires around Edward's feet. Maybe silver didn't hurt Alejandro, but it had hurt his people.

"We will make more," Alejandro said. "Can you not read this in my mind?"

And I could, now that I thought about it, but it wasn't like telepathy. Not words. I—knew he was thinking about the power I'd just given him. He felt no regret about the vampires that had died.

The crowd screamed.

Alejandro looked up. I followed his gaze. Jean-Claude was on his knees, blood pouring down his side. Alejandro envied Oliver the ability to draw blood from a distance. When I became Alejandro's servant, Jean-Claude had been weakened. Oliver had him.

That had been the plan all along.

Alejandro held me close, and I didn't try to stop him. He whispered against my cheek, "You are a necromancer, Anita. You have power over the dead. That is why Jean-Claude wanted you as his servant. Oliver thinks to control you through controlling me, but I know that you are a necromancer. Even as a servant, you have free will. You do not have to obey as the others do. As a human servant, you are yourself a weapon. You can strike one of us and draw blood."

"What are you saying?"

"They have arranged that the loser be stretched over the altar and staked by you."

"What . . ."

"Jean-Claude, as affirmation of his power. Oliver, as a gesture to show how well he controlled what once belonged to Jean-Claude."

There was a gasp from the crowd. Oliver was levitating ever so slowly. He floated to the ground. Then he raised his arms, and Jean-Claude floated upward.

"Shit," I said.

Jean-Claude hung nearly unconscious in empty, shining air. Oliver laid him gently on the ground, and fresh blood splattered the white floor.

Karl Inger came into sight. He picked Jean-Claude up under the arms.

Where was everybody? I looked around for some help. The black werewolf was torn apart, parts still twitching. I didn't think even a lycanthrope could heal the mess. The blond werewolf wasn't much better, but Stephen was dragging himself towards the altar. With one leg completely ripped away, he was trying.

Karl laid Jean-Claude on the marble altar. Blood began to seep down the side. He held him lightly at the shoulder. Jean-Claude could bench press a car. How could Karl hold him down?

"He shares Oliver's strength."

"Quit doing that," I said.

"What?"

"Answering questions I haven't asked yet."

He smiled. "It saves so much time."

Oliver picked up a white, polished stake and a padded hammer. He held them out towards me. "It's time."

Alejandro tried to help me stand, but I pushed him away. Fourth mark or no fourth mark, I could stand on my own.

Richard screamed, "No!" He ran past us towards the altar. It all seemed to happen in slow motion. He jumped at Oliver, and the little man grabbed him by the throat and tore his windpipe out.

"Richard!" I was running, but it was too late. He lay bleeding on the ground, still trying to breathe when he didn't have anything to breathe with.

I knelt by him, tried to stop the flow of blood. His eyes were wide and panic-filled. Edward was with me. "There's nothing you can do. Nothing any of us can do."

"No."

"Anita." He pulled me away from Richard. "It's too late."

I was crying and hadn't known it.

"Come, Anita; destroy your old master, as you wanted me to." Oliver was holding the hammer and stake out towards me.

I shook my head.

Alejandro helped me stand. I reached for Edward, but it was too late. Edward couldn't help. No one could help me. There was no way to take back the fourth mark, or heal Richard, or save Jean-Claude. But at least I wouldn't put the stake through Jean-Claude. That I could stop. That I would not do.

Alejandro was leading me towards the altar.

Marguerite had crawled to one side of the dais. She was kneeling, rocking gently back and fourth. Her face was a bloody mask. She'd clawed her eyes out.

Oliver held the stake and mallet out to me with his white-gloved hands, still wet with Richard's blood. I shook my head.

"You will take it. You will do as I say." His little clown face was frowning at me.

"Fuck you," I said.

"Alejandro, you control her now."

"She is my servant, master, yes."

Oliver held the stake out towards me. "Then have her finish him."

"I cannot force her, master." Alejandro smiled as he said it.

"Why not?"

"She is a necromancer. I told you she would have free will."

"I will not have my grand gesture spoiled by one stubborn woman."

He tried to roll my mind. I felt him rush over me like a wind inside my head, but it rolled off and away. I was a full human servant; vampire tricks didn't work on me, not even Oliver's.

I laughed, and he slapped me. I tasted fresh blood in my mouth. He stood beside me, and I could feel him tremble. He was so angry. I was ruining his moment.

Alejandro was pleased. I could feel his pleasure like a warm hand in my stomach.

"Finish him, or I promise you I'll beat you to a bloody pulp. You don't die easily now. I can hurt you worse than you can imagine, and you'll heal. But it will still hurt just as badly. Do you understand me?"

I stared down at Jean-Claude. He was staring at me. His dark blue eyes were as lovely as ever.

"I won't do it," I said.

"You still care about him? After all he has done to you?"

I nodded.

"Do him, now, or I will kill him slowly. I will pick pieces of flesh from his bones but never kill him. As long as his heart and head are intact, he won't die, no matter what I do to him."

I looked at Jean-Claude. I couldn't stand by and let Oliver torture him, not if I could help it. Wasn't a clean death better? Wasn't it?

I took the stake from Oliver. "I'll do it."

Oliver smiled. "You've made a wise decision. Jean-Claude would thank you if he could."

I stared down at Jean-Claude, stake in one hand. I touched his chest just over the burn scar. My hand came away smeared with blood.

"Do it, now!" Oliver said.

I turned to Oliver, reaching my left hand out for the hammer. As he handed it to me, I shoved the ash stake through his chest.

Karl screamed. Blood poured out of Oliver's mouth. He

seemed frozen, as if he couldn't move with the stake in his heart, but he wasn't dead, not yet. My fingers tore into the meat of his throat and pulled, pulled great gobbets of flesh, until I saw spine, glistening and wet. I wrapped my hand around his spine and jerked it free. His head lolled to one side, held by a few strips of meat. I jerked his head clear and tossed it across the ring.

Karl Inger was lying beside the altar. I knelt by him and tried to find a pulse, but there wasn't one. Oliver's death had killed him too.

Alejandro came to stand by me. "You've done it, Anita. I knew you could kill him. I knew you could."

I stared up at him. "Now you kill Jean-Claude, and we rule the city together."

"Yes."

I shoved upward before I could think about it, before he could read my mind. I shoved my hands into his chest. Ribs cracked and scraped my skin. I grabbed his beating heart and crushed it.

I couldn't breathe. My chest was tight, and it hurt. I pulled his heart out of the hole. He fell, eyes wide and surprised. I fell with him.

I was gasping for air. Couldn't breathe, couldn't breathe. I lay on top of my master and felt my heart beating for both of us. He wouldn't die. I laid my fingers against his throat and started to dig. I put my hands around his throat and squeezed. I felt my hands dig into flesh, but the pain was overwhelming. I was choking on blood, our blood.

My hands went numb. I couldn't tell if I was still squeezing or not. I couldn't feel anything except the pain. Then even that slipped away, and I was falling, falling into a darkness that had never known light, and never would.

48

I woke up staring into an off-white ceiling. I blinked at the ceiling for a minute. Sunlight lay in warm squares across the blanket. There were metal rails on the bed. An IV dripped into my arm.

A hospital—then I wasn't dead. Surprise, surprise.

There were flowers and a bunch of shiny balloons on a small bedside table. I lay there a moment, enjoying the fact that I wasn't dead.

The door opened, and all I could see was a huge bunch of flowers. Then the flowers lowered, and it was Richard.

I think I stopped breathing. I could feel all the blood rushing through my skin. There was a soft roaring in my head. No. I wasn't going to faint. I never fainted. I finally managed to say, "You're dead."

His smile faded. "I'm not dead."

"I saw Oliver tear out your throat." I could see it in front of me like an overlay in my mind. I saw him gasping, dying. I found I could sit up. I braced myself, and the IV needle moved under my skin, the tape pulling. It was real. Nothing else seemed real.

He raised a hand towards his throat, then stopped himself. He swallowed hard enough for me to hear it. "You saw Oliver tear out my throat, but it didn't kill me."

I stared at him. There was no bandage on his cheek. The little cut had healed. "No human being could survive that," I said softly.

"I know." He looked incredibly sad as he said it.

Panic filled my throat until I could barely breathe. "What are you?"

"I'm a lycanthrope."

I shook my head. "I know what a lycanthrope feels like, moves like. You aren't one."

"Yes, I am."

I kept shaking my head. "No."

He came to stand beside the bed. He held the flowers awkwardly, as if he didn't know what to do with them. "I'm next in line to be pack leader. I can pass for human, Anita. I'm good at it."

"You lied to me."

He shook his head. "I didn't want to."

"Then why did you?"

"Jean-Claude ordered me not to tell you."

"Why?"

He shrugged. "I think because he knew you'd hate it. You don't forgive deceit. He knows that."

Would Jean-Claude deliberately try to ruin a potential relationship between Richard and me? Yep.

"You asked what hold Jean-Claude had on me. That was it. My pack leader loaned me to Jean-Claude on the condition that no one find out what I was."

"Why are you a special case?"

"They won't let lycanthropes teach kids, or anybody else for that matter."

"You're a werewolf."

"Isn't that better than being dead?"

I stared up at him. His eyes were still the same perfect brown. His hair fell forward around his face. I wanted to ask him to sit down, to let me run my fingers through his hair, to keep it from that wonderful face.

"Yeah, it's better than being dead."

He let out a breath, as if he'd been holding it. He smiled and held the flowers out to me.

I took them because I didn't know what else to do. They were red carnations with enough baby's breath to form a white mist over the red. The carnations smelled like sweet cloves. Richard was a werewolf. Next in line for pack leader. He could pass for human. I stared up at him. I held out my hand to him. He took it, and his hand was warm and solid, and alive.

"Now that we've established why you're not dead, why aren't I dead?"

"Edward did CPR on you until the ambulances came. The doctors don't know what caused your heart to stop, but there's no permanent damage."

"What did you tell the police about all the bodies?"

"What bodies?"

"Come off it, Richard."

"By the time the ambulance got there, there were no extra bodies."

"The audience saw it all."

"But what was real and what was illusion? The police got a hundred different versions from the audience. They're suspicious, but they can't prove anything. The Circus has been shut down until the authorities can be sure it's safe."

"Safe?" I laughed.

He shrugged. "As safe as it ever was."

I slipped my hand out of Richard's grasp, using both hands to smell the flowers again. "Is Jean-Claude . . . alive?"

"Yes."

A great sense of relief washed over me. I didn't want him dead. I didn't want Jean-Claude dead. Shit. "He's still Master of the City, then. And I'm still bound to him."

"No," Richard said, "Jean-Claude told me to tell you. You're free. Alejandro's marks sort of canceled his out. You can't serve two masters, he said."

Free? I was free? I stared at Richard. "It can't be that easy."

Richard laughed. "You call this easy?"

I looked up. I had to smile. "Alright, it wasn't easy, but I didn't think anything short of death would get Jean-Claude off my back."

"Are you happy the marks are gone?"

I started to say, "Of course," then stopped myself. There was something very serious in Richard's face. He knew what it was to be offered power. To be one with the monsters. It could be horrible, and wonderful.

Finally I said "Yes."

"Really?"

I nodded.

"You don't seem too enthused," he said.

"I know I should be jumping for joy, or something, but I just feel empty."

"You've been through a lot the last few days. You're entitled to be a little numb."

Why wasn't I happier to be rid of Jean-Claude? Why wasn't I relieved to be no one's human servant? Because I'd miss him? Stupid. Ridiculous. True.

When something gets too hard to think about, think about something else. "So now everyone knows you're a werewolf."

"No."

"You were hospitalized, and you've already healed. I think they'll guess."

"Jean-Claude had me hidden away until I healed. This is my first day up and around."

"How long have I been out?"

"A week."

"You're joking."

"You were in a coma for three days. The doctors still don't know what made you start breathing on your own."

I had come that close to the great beyond. I couldn't remember any tunnel of light, or soothing voices. I felt cheated. "I don't remember."

"You were unconscious; you're not supposed to remember."

"Sit down, before I get a crick looking up at you."

He pulled up a chair and sat down by the bed, smiling at me. It was a nice smile.

"So you're a werewolf."

He nodded.

"How did it happen?"

He stared down at the floor, then up. His face looked

so solemn, I was sorry I'd asked. I was expecting some great tale of a savage attack survived. "I got a bad batch of lycanthropy serum."

"You what?"

"You heard me." He seemed embarrassed.

"You got a bad shot?"

"Yes."

My smile got wider and wider.

"It's not funny," he said.

I shook my head. "Not at all." I knew my eyes were shiny, and it was all I could do not to laugh out loud. "You've got to admit it's nicely ironic."

He sighed. "You're going to hurt yourself. Go ahead and laugh."

I did. I laughed until it hurt, and Richard joined in. Laughter is contagious, too.

49

A dozen white roses came later that day with a note from Jean-Claude. The note read, "You are free of me, if you choose. But I hope you want to see me as much as I want to see you. It is your choice. Jean-Claude."

I stared at the flowers for a long time. I finally had a nurse give them to someone else, or throw them away, or whatever the hell she wanted to do with them. I just wanted them out of my sight. So I was still attracted to Jean-Claude. I might even, in some dark corner, love him a little. It didn't matter. Loving the monsters always ends badly for the human. It's a rule.

That brought me to Richard. He was one of the monsters, but he was alive. That was an improvement over Jean-Claude. And was he any less human than I was: zombie queen, vampire slayer, necromancer? Who was I to complain?

I don't know where they put all the body parts, but no police ever came asking. Whether I'd saved the city or not, it was still murder. Legally, Oliver had done nothing to deserve death.

I got out of the hospital and went back to work. Larry stayed on. He's learning how to hunt vampires, God save him.

The lamia was truly immortal. Which I guess means lamias can't have been extinct. They just must always have been rare. Jean-Claude got the lamia a green card and gave her a job at the Circus of the Damned. I don't know if he's letting her breed, or not. I haven't been near the Circus since I got out of the hospital.

Richard and I finally had that first date. We went for something fairly traditional: dinner and a movie. We're going caving next week. He promised no underwater tunnels. His lips are the softest I've ever kissed. So he gets furry once a month. No one's perfect.

Jean-Claude hasn't given up. He keeps sending me gifts. I keep refusing them. I have to keep saying no until he gives up, or until hell freezes over, whichever comes first.

Most women complain that there are no single, straight men left. I'd just like to meet one who's human.